ONCE IN A BLACK MOON

D. LIEBER

First paperback edition March 2020

Cover Design and Layout by Bryan Donihue, Section 28 Publishing

Edited by Cover to Cover Editing

ISBN 978-1-951239-00-8

ACKNOWLEDGMENTS

To Aunt Debbie, who instilled in me an unquenchable wanderlust both in reality and in reading.

I want to give a special shout out to all my betas as well as those who helped me with the many languages, folklore, and the sensitive topics surrounding the First Nations. Thank you, John, Laura, Amy, Iuliana, Gen, Rebecca, Odessa, Julieta, Abi, Sandra, Tammy, P.E., Kerry, Vijaya, Tracy, Beth, Aria, Linda, Sharon, and C.J.

DEFINITIONS AND PRONUNCIATIONS

CHINESE

Aiya (Eye-yah) = exclamation of dismay or surprise

FIRST NATION/NATIVE AMERICAN

Čanotila (chawn-oh-tee-lah) = a forest-dwelling creature similar to fairies from Lakota folklore
Wechuge (Way-chu-gay) = Of varying descriptions. A man-eating monster of Dené or Athabaskan people folklore. In use here as a person who has been possessed or overwhelmed by the power of one of the ancient spirit animals.

FRENCH

Belle (Bell) = Beautiful
Bonjour (Bohn-zhurh) = Hello

Chambre (Shahmbr) = Bedroom

En français (Ohn frhohn-say) = In French

Madame (Mahd-ahm) = Mrs

Mademoiselle (Mad-deh-mwoh-zelh) = Miss

Merci (Merhe-si) = Thank you

Mon amie (MohN Ah-me) = My friend

Monsieur (Muss-yuh) = Mister; Sir

Non (Noh) = No

Oui (We) = Yes

Romantique (Rhoh-man-teek) = Romantic

Ton amie (TohN Ah-me) = Your friend

Tout pour toi (Tooh-poorh-twah) = All for you

Très bien (Trhey byen) = Very good

NAMES

Alejandro (Ah-lay-HAN-droh)

Alexandru (Ahl-lick-SSAHN-droo)

Amélie Roussel (Ah-may-lee Rhoo-sell)

Buvons (Boo-vohn)

Camila (Kah-ME-la)

Capreanu (Kah-pREHA-noo)

Chloé (Klow-ay)

Chuthekii (CHOOT-key)

Crina (Kree-nah)

Delaforet (Della-forh-ay)

Dumitru (Doo-mee-troo)

Dzindo (TsEEN-doe)

Grigore (Gree-gor-eh)

Ion (EE-yohn)

Jacques (Szahk)

Langundo (LANE-gun-doo)

Laurier (Loh-rhe-ay)

Likinoak (LEEK-een-oak)
Louis (Loo-ee)
Marguerite Dubois (Mar-geh-rheet Do-bwah)
Mariana (Mah-ree-ana)
Mitica (Mee-tEE-kuh)
Montmartre (Mohn-marh-trhuh)
Piyiets (PIE-ee-yets)
Pówahkai (POH-wah-Kai-ee)
Testooklah (Tess-TOO-klah)
Tsesikó (Tseh-TSEE-ko)
Yejeták (YEH-jey-tak)
Xi Lin (Shee Leen)
Xi Wei (Shee Way-ee)

ROMANIAN

Balaur (Bah-lAH-oor) = A type of Romanian dragon
Bou (bOW) = Asshole; Bull
Bucuria mea (BOO-coo-re-ah Mheh) = My joy
Bucurie (boo-COO-ree-eh) = Joy
Ce? (che) = What?
Crugul Pământului (KrOO-gool Pa-mUHN-too-loo-ee) = Where the hultan are trained
Da (dah) = Yes
După ploaie, vine soare (Doo-pUH plo-AH-ee-ey vEE-neh Ssoo-ah-ray) = After rain comes sunshine
Ești frumoasa (Yesht froo-moh-AH-suh) = You're beautiful
Făt-Frumos (FUHT froo-mohs) = A Romanian hero of folklore akin to Prince Charming
Hora (HKor-uh) = A circle dance
Hultan (whOOl-tahn) = Romanian wizard, also known as Șolomonar
Iele (Yell-eh) = Type of Romanian fae
Iti dau inima mea (its dOW ene-mah mheh) = I give you my heart

Mamă (MAH-mah)= Mother
Noapte buna (Nu-AHp-te bOO-nuh) = Goodnight
Nu (noo) = No
Pentru totdeauna (pent-rOO TOT-dyeha-una) = Forever
Sânziene (SsUHN-zee-en-nay) = A festival in honor of the fairies
Tărâmul Celălalt (TUH-ruh-muhl CHEl-lal-alt) = Otherworld
Tată (TA-tah) = Father
Te iubesc (TAY you-besk) = I love you
Zână (Zzuh-nuh) = A type of Romanian fae
Zgrimties (Zgreem-tee-es) = In folklore, another name for a hultan. In this book, the governing council of hultan
Zmeu (Zzmeh-oo) = Romanian shapeshifting dragon

SANSKRIT

Dhyana mudra (Dee-ahn Muh-drah) = A hand position used in yoga and meditation

SPANISH

Canta Hermosa (Kahn-tah Ehr-MOH-sah) = You sing beautifully
Con gusto (Kohn GOOS-toh) = With pleasure
Fantastico (fahn-TAHS-tee-koh) = Fantastic
Gracias (GRAH-syahs) = Thank you
Hola (OH-lah) = Hello
Por favor (Pohr Fah-bohr) = Please
Señora (SEH-nyoh-rah) = Ma'am; Mrs.
Sí (SEE) = Yes
Usted también (oo-sted tahm-BYEHN) = You too

WYBOKA

Amâwe (Ah-MAH-way) = Mother

Azeohkwii (Ahz-ay-OH-qwe) = Sister-in-law

Ni'aze (NEE-ahz-ay) = Older brother

Ohkwii (OH-qwe) = Wife

Seyko (SAY-koh) = Son

Seyohkwii (SAY-OH-qwe) = Daughter-in-law

Wic'aze (WEEK-ahz-ay) = Younger brother

Wyboka (Why-BOW-ka) = A First Nation created for the purpose of this story

ONE

I ground my teeth, stomping toward my editor's office. I didn't
bother with my usual courtesy knock as I pushed open the glass
door.

"What the Hell is this, Bill?" I demanded, waving tomorrow's edition
at him.

He raised his eyebrows at my question, waiting for me to explain.

"Why didn't you print my article?"

"It was unsubstantiated. Give me proof, and I'll print it." He leaned
back in his chair and laced his fingers, peering over his glasses at me.

"Unsubstantiated? Are you fucking kidding me? I have electronic
account transfers and sources in the mayor's office who swear he's embez-
zling money from the widows and orphan's fund to finance his re-election
campaign."

Bill shook his balding head at me sadly and used that infuriatingly
calm voice to try to soothe me. "Erin, I know your father was a Chicago
police officer, and I understand you're upset the department is getting
fewer funds from the city, but that's no reason to accuse the mayor."

"My father has nothing to do with this," I growled, prying my
clenched jaw apart.

"I'm not printing your article. End of story." He turned to his computer, dismissing me.

I froze, having never been shut down by Bill without a proper explanation. *My story is breaking news. My evidence is solid. Why won't he print it? Unless...* "No," I whispered.

Bill looked up at me.

"Tell me it's not true. Bill, are you...in the mayor's pocket?"

His face reddened in anger, but not before I saw his eyes flicker with guilt. "How dare—"

"How could you? My mentor, the man who taught me ethics in journalism..." My shock gave way to determination, and I steeled my gut. "This story is getting out. I'll sell it to another paper. I'll go to the Internet if I have to."

Bill stood slowly, his face pale as he removed his glasses. "Erin, listen to me. Don't do that."

"Oh, it's happening."

"You're leaving me no choice. You're fired."

My stomach rolled. "Fine! I can't work for a dirty editor anyway. And guess what, Bill? The mayor is going down, and you're going down with him."

I strode from his office, not heeding his angry protests.

The office was too quiet as my heart raged. Most of my previous coworkers had left for the night, heading home to trick-or-treat with their kids.

My limbs were tense and my movements jerky as I emptied the personal belongings from my desk. I couldn't believe the last six years of my life at *The Chicago Telegraph* fit into one empty printer paper box.

Pausing, I stared at that day's edition and the last article I would ever write for the paper. "Black Moon Day Before Halloween" the headline announced on the bottom corner of page two.

I closed my eyes when they started to burn. *No crying. Not yet.* Letting out a steadying sigh, I grabbed my belongings and went toward the elevator.

As I tried to resituate my box to press the down button, another employee beat me to it.

"Thanks," I mumbled to him.

"No problem."

The large elevator felt small as the two of us shuffled in. My box of shame, the signal that I'd been canned, made my self-consciousness take up most of the breathing room. With a bowed head, I peeked at the tall man with dark hair as he pressed the button for the first floor then looked down at his smartphone. *I don't think I know him. He must be new. Working extra to get in good with the boss? Good luck with that. They will burn your soul and dance around the ashes.*

Outside, I paused on the sidewalk, breathing in the chilly autumn night. The streets of downtown Chicago were not nearly as busy at eight at night on a Sunday as they would have been on Friday or Saturday.

With my box getting heavier by the minute, I considered hailing a taxi back to my apartment. I decided against it since I no longer had income. *Besides, I might as well take advantage of my CTA card the paper pays for while I still can.*

I readjusted the weight and hunched my shoulders against the lake wind as it whipped my short, brown hair in front of my glasses. I blew up to clear my vision. When that didn't work, I tilted my head back and shook the hair from my face.

The sky is never truly dark in the city, light pollution makes sure of that. However, if it's not cloudy, sometimes you can see the moon. Of course, that night was a new moon, so the clear sky was an empty void above the haze of city lights.

What's out there? I knew the stars and planets were there, even if I couldn't see them. I'd gone to the planetarium on a school trip once. Having lived in the city my entire life, I'd only ever truly been able to appreciate the night sky when I went to Wisconsin for sixth-grade camp.

I remembered making a wish on every star I could see. There were a lot of them, but my wish was always the same.

If I saw a star right now, what would I wish for? My job back? No. I know what I'm doing is right. The predicament I was in reminded me of the feeling from my favorite poem. I hadn't read it since college, but I still knew it by heart:

Were I away with my love fair,
Her eyes are shining emeralds rare,

Upon my breast she'd often lie,
Before we had to say goodbye.

I travel to the dragon's lair,
Cowardly and brave men, beware!
I came here for wealth, not to die,
Were I away.

As I approach with cautious care,
I find I miss my true love's hair,
I miss her laugh, I miss her sigh,
I wish I would have kept her nigh,
Were I away.

The regret and longing from the poem made my heart ache as I stared into the cave-like sky. *I can't turn back now, even if I wished to. I must move forward.*

I sighed, my resolve giving me strength, and readjusted the box again. I tried to look around it as I descended the stairs to the red line subway station, the feat making me slightly off balance.

At the bottom of the stairs, I put my box down so I could dig my CTA pass out of my jacket pocket. Through the turnstile and down the escalator, I sat on a bench on the platform, placing the box on the ground between my Converse.

A street musician played "Somewhere over the Rainbow" on his violin a few feet away. He played it in minor, giving it a sad, chilling quality I'm not sure Judy Garland would have approved of. I quite liked it. The longing that usually accompanied the tune was haunted by the feeling that over the rainbow was a place I would never see.

I reached into the pocket of my skinny jeans and pulled out the change left over from my morning's mocha frappuccino. The coins clinked together pleasantly as they fell into the velvet-lined violin case, and I smiled my appreciation at the musician.

The clacking of a train echoed in the subway tunnel. I hefted my box into my arms and stood at the tactile paved, blue edge of the platform.

As the clack, clack, clack got closer, the train's headlights appeared.

Passengers crowded the edge, preparing to board. Just as the train was about to pull into the station, I felt someone behind me.

The hand that caressed my shoulder gave me a nudge. It wasn't a hard shove, but it was full of purpose. I lost my balance, and my box and I fell onto the track.

There wasn't enough time for my short life to flash before my eyes. I only remember my heart screaming in fear, echoing the screech of the train's brakes as it crashed into me...

...I couldn't move. All I felt was pain as my foggy consciousness resurfaced. My heart pounded in my ears, but I heard a distant chanting. I couldn't understand the words the baritone sang, but I could feel the plea in his voice.

I struggled to open my eyes. Through the haze of semi-consciousness and the dim, flickering light, I could only make out a flash of red before the void pulled me under again.

TWO

*T*hwack...thwack...thwack...*What is that sound? Is Bryan doing something weird again?*

I strained my ears. Besides the repetitive sound, it was way too quiet. There were no car or train sounds. I couldn't hear Mrs. McTim's television upstairs or the college students, Chad and Mike, blaring their heavy metal next door.

All at once, I remembered being pushed in front of a train. *Am I in the hospital?*

But no beeping monitors, sterile smells, or bright lights shining through my eyelids answered my fears. Just silence and the distant thwack...thwack.

I took a tentative breath, expanding my lungs. It didn't hurt as I'd expected. I twitched my fingers and toes. They seemed to work just fine. Finally, I squinted my eyes open.

The ceiling was rustic wood and four empty coat hooks hung just above the headboard of the bed I was lying on.

Seeing light from the corner of my eye, I turned my head toward it. The small room had another bed near the window, an iron stove in one corner, and a small table with two chairs in the other. The walls were made of the same rustic wood as the ceiling. Outside, the repetitive sound stopped. A few moments later, the door opened to reveal a man carrying an armful of wood.

His scarlet coat and Stetson hat announced his profession.

"What the shit? A Mountie?" I gaped, jolting upright. My joints ached, and my skin smarted as though I was covered in bruises.

"I see you're awake. How are you feeling?" the Mountie asked.

"Who are you? Where am I? How did I get here?" My panicked voice sounded unfamiliar in my ears.

He walked over to the corner and stacked the wood near the stove. "You must have hit your head pretty hard there. I'm Constable Delaforet. You're in Farrloch. As for how you got here, I found you in the forest near the barracks, half-clothed, unconscious, and chilled to the bone. I carried you in here."

Farrloch? Alberta?

I eyed the Mountie, squinting suspiciously, as he removed his hat and placed it on the table.

His steady voice sounded as though he was trying to calm a frightened animal, and his light blue eyes were soft with pity. His brown hair was tousled from his hat, and his face was shadowed by what looked like two-day stubble. He seemed to be in his mid-twenties, around my age.

I took in his strong, broad shoulders and solid frame, and I knew I wouldn't make it past him if he tried to stop me.

I was unconscious in a forest in Canada after I got hit by a train in Chicago? I looked under the blanket at what I was wearing. *He said I was half-naked.*

I wore what seemed to me to be pajamas: white cotton capris with lace cuffs and a short-sleeved chemise. *What the...? Okay, this obviously isn't real. I must be in a coma somewhere.*

I nodded to myself before swinging my bare feet out of bed.

"You should rest, Miss," Constable Delaforet advised as I got to my feet. When the blanket fell away to reveal my pajamas, he cleared his throat and averted his eyes.

"I'm fine," I assured him. *I mean, what can happen in a coma dream anyway?* I marveled at how vivid everything was. It didn't feel at all like a dream. Then again, I'd never been in a coma before, so maybe it was normal.

I took a few steps toward the Mountie, amazed at the feeling of the cold floorboards under my feet. Delaforet instinctively reached out to steady me when I wobbled a little. His large hands were warm on my shoulders.

"Miss, I really must insist you rest until you're well. At the very least, you can't go out in your undergarments."

Undergarments? What kind of coma dream is this? "Tell me, Dudley, what year is it in this coma-created world?"

His eyebrows pulled together in concern. "Miss, this is very much the real world. We just celebrated the turn of a new century. It is 1900. Please, it's clear you're disoriented."

I allowed him to lead me back to bed. *1900, huh? My subconscious is amazing. Everything is so detailed.*

I stared at Delaforet's profile as he tucked my legs under the blankets. *Have I seen him somewhere before? I've heard that your brain never dreams faces it hasn't seen. Where would I have seen such a hot guy? I feel like I'd remember that. A movie? Well, since this is a dream, I can do whatever I want. Right?*

I grinned mischievously and grabbed the front of Delaforet's red tunic. He turned to me, eyes wide with surprise. I leaned up and kissed him full on the mouth. It had been a while since I'd kissed a man. I put all my pent-up passion into it. His lips were soft and warm. They sent a thrill through me, my body heating in an instant. He gently distanced himself from me.

I breathed hard, my eyes wide as the blood drained from my face. *There's no way. It feels too real, and I've never been rejected in a dream before... But how is it possible?*

"Miss," he said gently. "You're distressed. You should rest." If not kissing me back and pulling away hadn't made his rejection clear, his unmoved mask as he called me crazy certainly did.

How can I rest? I'm more than a century in the past in another country, and I just kissed a complete stranger. Calm down, Erin, calm down. This guy helped you, right? As he said, he brought me in here when I was in trouble. Even when I threw myself at him, he didn't respond. He's a Mountie for christsakes! He's a police officer. I'm safe with him.

I tried to swallow my panic and took a few slow, deep breaths.

After watching me calm myself, Delaforet asked, "Do you know who you are?"

I nodded, peeking over at him. "Erin Nichols," I mumbled.

"Do you know how you came to be in the woods, Miss Nichols?"

"No."

"All right. Do you know where you're from?"

"Chicago."

"An American? Chicago is a long way from here. Do you know why you might be here?"

I'd love to know that. Any ideas, Universe? I sighed. *But I can't tell him I'm from the twenty-first century.* "I don't remember," I said.

He nodded gently. "I'm sure it will all come back to you in time," he soothed. "Can you tell me anything else about yourself? You remember your name and where you're from. Do you have a family?"

"Just my mother." *Mom is going to be distraught when she can't find me.* "And I guess Bryan will notice I'm gone eventually."

"Bryan is your brother or...?" he trailed off suggestively.

Is he asking if Bryan is my boyfriend or husband? Of course, at my age in 1900, I would've been an old maid. Then again, I did just kiss him, which is definitely not proper, even by modern standards...Maybe he thinks I'm a prostitute. Oh, jeez... The confidence I'd had while I'd thought this was a dream crumbled under the reality of the situation. My face and neck flushed in the fiercest blush of my entire life. *I totally just kissed a complete stranger, likely the most attractive stranger I've ever met.*

"Bryan is my roommate," I mumbled, averting my gaze and trying to not think about the kiss. *Yeah Erin, good one. I'm sure it's not suspicious that you're living with a man.*

Delaforet nodded thoughtfully.

"It's difficult to afford housing in Chicago on a journalist's pay. Bryan is a friend from college. He's a..." *software developer.* "H-he's a writer...of sorts," I rambled.

"You're a journalist?"

I nodded.

"Perhaps you were sent by a newspaper to write a story?"

"That would explain why I'm so far from home..." I mused, grabbing hold of the explanation.

"Could you be a travel writer? Since the railroad was completed and the hotel opened, there have been quite a few newsmen who've come to town."

I nodded. *It's as good a cover story as any.* "That sounds familiar. I think you're right."

"Of course, that doesn't explain how you came to be in the forest in such a state. You could be the victim of foul play." He eyed me gently. "I think perhaps you should stay in the barracks until you're well enough to remember. Since the railroad was finished, I'm the only Mountie stationed here, so you need not fret over inconveniencing anyone."

It's not like I have anywhere else to go, and he seems safe enough. I smiled sheepishly and nodded. "Thank you very much."

After we'd agreed I would stay with Delaforet, he left to go get breakfast for us. He'd told me to stay in bed, but I ignored that directive entirely. I slipped out from under the blanket and moved toward the window. As I passed a pitcher and washbasin on a cabinet, a light flashed off a small shaving mirror.

When I saw my reflection, I cried out and rushed toward the mirror.

"What the Hell?" I demanded of the blonde-haired, blue-eyed woman in the mirror. I blinked hard a few times, hoping my green eyes would appear.

Bringing my shaking fingertips to my cheeks, I caressed my new face. My hair was long, much longer than I ever would have bothered with. It was blonde where it should have been brown. My face seemed a few years younger, and my usually warm skin seemed paler. I hadn't noticed before that I wasn't wearing any glasses, but I could see perfectly without them. I looked down at my new body. I was slightly thinner than before, having none of my city-walking leg muscles. I was also a few inches taller. I grabbed my breasts and found they were smaller.

"Jesus Christ," I cursed in a voice not my own. I'd noticed I sounded strange before, but I'd thought it was panic that had made my voice higher. "What the fuck is happening to me?"

I looked away from the mirror, my stomach flopping and my head spinning. Closing my eyes and bracing my hands against the cabinet, I took long, steadying breaths.

After the feeling had passed, I continued to the window, determinedly avoiding my reflection. I knew I was in Alberta, so I'd expected to see mountains. But nothing had prepared me for the breath-taking sight that lay before me.

The snow-topped mountains towered over a clear, frozen lake. The rounded rocks on the shore had small patches of snow between them. Evergreens flanked the sides of the lake, dwarfed by the surrounding peaks. The clear sky dyed everything blue.

"Wow" was the only exclamation my brain could come up with. I couldn't pry myself away from the view, not even when Constable Delaforet returned with a basket of food. He frowned at my complete disregard for his orders but set the basket on the table.

"I brought chicken and dumplings," he informed, unpacking a pot, bowls, and spoons.

I reluctantly left the window and went to the table.

Deliberately averting his eyes, he said, "We need to find you some clothes if you're going to be out of bed. We can go down to the church to see if they have any extra dresses they can spare, but for now..." he crossed to the foot of the bed I'd been lying in and opened a trunk. Rummaging around, he continued. "I believe Subconstable Taylor left some things behind. They will likely be too big, but, ah, here they are."

He pulled out a buckskin pair of pants, a buttoned shirt, and a coat. "I'm sorry to ask a lady to wear men's clothes, but it's far better than you freezing."

I took the clothes from him, and he went toward the door. "I'll get more wood for the stove," he said delicately.

After he'd left, I pulled on the clothes over my undergarments. I would've just removed them, but the pants wouldn't have stayed up without the extra layers and the shirt tucked in. The clothes were comfortable and would certainly keep me warm. I vowed to fight the Mountie on exchanging them for a dress. Beside the bed was a pair of impractical women's boots. *Whoever's body I'm in, she didn't seem to walk around outside much.*

I dug through the trunk for alternatives and found a pair of moccasins. They were too big, but they would have to do. *Being soft and flexible, it shouldn't be too difficult to walk in them, even if they are too big.*

By the time Delaforet returned, I was dressed and dishing the meal into our bowls. The soup was warming and pleasant, and I told him as much.

"No one makes food like Mellie," he commented.

I raised my eyebrows at his compliment. "Is Mellie your sweetheart then?"

He nearly choked, and it took him a moment to settle his coughing. "No, Mellie operates the best restaurant in town." He paused before continuing. "I don't have a sweetheart."

I smiled to myself as my stomach twanged with unwarranted satisfaction. "So what exactly does a Mountie do besides keep the peace?"

"Well, being that this is a tourist town, or aims to be since the railroad was finished, Ottawa stationed me here to make visitors feel safe. I do keep the peace, but I also patrol the area for criminals, deliver mail to settlements farther out, and work with the Indian agent when need be."

"The Indian agent? Is there a First Nation around here?"

He tilted his head at my question. *Oh, I guess they aren't called that yet.* "There's a reserve near Farrloch?" I rephrased.

He nodded. "The Wyboka Reserve is very near here."

"How long have you been stationed here?"

"Nearly half a year. I was posted in the Yukon before this."

Oh, that's right. There was a gold rush there around this time, wasn't there? I nodded to show I'd heard him and the conversation lapsed. *What am I doing here? I've no place in 1900 western Canada. I need to figure out how to get home. Well, I suppose all I can do at the moment is get my bearings.*

Before we'd even finished our food, a man burst through the door. His eyes widened when he saw me. "I'm sorry to interrupt Constable, but they found another one."

Delaforet sighed and shook his head. He grabbed his hat as he headed for the door. "Stay here," he told me before leaving.

"Pfft, yeah right," I said to the empty room.

I opened the door quietly, and a large, brown horse watched me sneak toward a nearby stable. I listened to the two men talk as Delaforet saddled a black horse.

"Who was it this time?" Delaforet asked.

"A boy around fifteen. His name was Testooklah," the other man responded.

"This is the third Wyboka found dead in as many weeks."

"And this time it was a kid. I know."

"How are the elders taking it?"

"As one would expect. Some are scared, and some are on the warpath. We need to figure out what is going on before we have an uprising on our hands."

"I intend to," Delaforet declared, his tone shifting as he climbed into the saddle.

I ran to hide behind the stable so he wouldn't discover me. As I watched the two men ride away, I wished I had the means to follow them.

"Damn." The cold wind off the lake carried my curse after them.

I knew I should probably listen to Delaforet and rest, and had his steady, blue gaze been on me at that moment, I know he could have persuaded me. But what's a journalist without an unhealthy sense of curiosity?

I left the barracks and the lake behind me as I hiked down the hill toward what I'd rightfully assumed was town. The temperature seemed to be in the upper forties, and I was grateful for my long hair, which I used to cover my chilled ears in lieu of a hat. The ground was still frozen, but there was an unmistakable promise of warmth to come. Early spring birds called to one another. My body hummed with every step, the fresh mountain air invigorating me.

As buildings started to flank the main dirt road, I read their signs. There was a blacksmith—whose hammering echoed from inside his forge —a laundry, a trading post and dry goods store, Mellie's Restaurant, a recreational outfitter, a tavern and brothel, and a bank.

There weren't many people about, but there were enough that I got the distinct impression I was being stared at. *I wonder whose body I'm in. Do any of these people recognize me? Or does this body not belong to someone else? Perhaps it was just created as I showed up. I don't know! Stupid time travel.*

At the other end of town, there was a train station. I considered asking people if they knew me but thought better of it. *If I did steal someone's body, I'm sure their loved ones will come to Delaforet to report a missing person. Where do people in 1900 get information? God, I miss the Internet.*

After walking to the train station ticket booth, I whistled at the clerk through the bars to get his attention.

"The next train isn't for a couple of days," he answered before I'd asked anything.

"All right." I nodded. "Does this town have a library or bookstore?"

He shook his head. "City records are kept at the mayor's office, the local newspaper keeps an archive, but if you're looking for books, the only library is up at the hotel. It's only open to guests and those who have Mr. Broadstone's permission."

I nodded my thanks. *A high-class hotel may have books on the occult. I mean, snobby twentieth-century toffs love that stuff, right?* I looked down at my borrowed clothes. *There's no way those types would even let me in the door. I bet Delaforet has access though. Maybe he would borrow a book for me, or better yet get me access.*

Not knowing when he would return, I thought it best to head back to the barracks. Hiking up the hill was more tiring than I'd expected. *Woman has no leg muscles.*

I ate the rest of my cold soup and took a nap.

THREE

*C*onstable Delaforet didn't return until late in the afternoon, but he brought food with him. I awoke with a start as the door creaked open when he entered. Upon seeing it was only him, I took a deep breath through my nose and stretched my stiff limbs before sitting up in bed.

"How are you feeling?" he inquired as he set down the basket and removed his hat.

"Better," I lied, making my voice light. I knew if this was going to work, he had to believe it.

He raised his eyebrows. "Did you remember something?"

"Bits and pieces," I said, sitting across from him at the table. "I do remember my editor sending me here, and it did have to do with Farrloch being a tourist town in a way."

"How so?"

"Well, I'm supposed to write about the mysterious deaths of the nearby natives."

I watched his reaction closely. He gave nothing away.

"You know how tourists love mystery," I continued.

He frowned. "People are dying, and you want to use it for entertainment?"

My stomach clenched at his disapproval. "Of course not. A journalist's job is to report the truth. I never sensationalize. I'm only pointing out that the story would probably bring curious tourists. I was explaining how my being here had to do with tourism. You suggested I might be a travel writer, remember?"

He nodded, his eyes still guarded.

"Well, people dying mysteriously is always newsworthy, but especially so in a tourist town. I was sent to find out what's going on. So, Constable, do you have anything to say on the subject?"

"No comment."

"Aw come on, Dudley," I prodded. "I'm just going to make a nuisance of myself if you don't tell me."

He slowly chewed his food, never taking his eyes off my face. I resisted the urge to squirm, hiding behind an innocent smile.

He sighed. "Three Wyboka died in as many weeks."

I nodded slightly, encouraging him to continue.

"We do not yet know the cause."

"But you're investigating?"

"At the Wyboka's request, yes. And I will discover what happened."

"Will you take me with you during your investigation?"

"Absolutely not," he said firmly, shaking his head for emphasis.

Undeterred by his expected response, I continued. "You said you found me roughed up in the forest, right?"

"Yes..."

"You suggested it could have been foul play."

He nodded slowly.

"So perhaps, while I was investigating this matter for my story, I uncovered something I wasn't meant to know."

"That's a reasonable assumption."

"Well if that's the case, then it would stand to reason that whoever hurt me before could come after me again. If that happens, then the safest place for me is with you." Despite the long lie I was weaving, my words felt accurate, their truth echoing through me like the reverberated hum from a bell strike.

He frowned, realizing I'd led him right where I wanted him.

"You would also be safe if you stayed in the barracks all the time. No one is going to harm you here."

"Perhaps. However, if I join your investigation, I might recall what happened to me and why I was a target in the first place. I can't stay here forever."

He paused, his features neutral, and I could only hope that he was considering my words.

"Besides," I added quickly before he could make a decision, "I'm a journalist. I may help with your investigation. I have my own set of detecting skills, and sometimes people are more willing to talk to the press than the police."

His distant eyes drifted back to me, locking with mine. I stilled, hoping the warmth that spread through me wasn't showing on my face.

"Any story you write will have to pass through me before you send it on to Chicago."

Normally, I wouldn't have agreed to the police editing my article. But since I knew I wasn't even writing a story, I beamed and held my hand out to shake on the deal.

His sturdy hand enveloped mine, and I shook it firmly. His eyes widened ever so slightly.

"So tell me about the case," I pressed.

Delaforet explained that the three Wyboka who had died were all found in a sacred hot spring on the reserve. He knew about the first two deaths but was not permitted to investigate the matter. With the third death, the Wyboka had asked for his help. He'd examined the most recent body and could not determine the cause of death. There didn't appear to be any signs of foul play. He'd requested to view the site but had not yet been given access. The elders were to convene the following day to discuss allowing him into their sacred space.

After I'd been caught up and we'd finished eating, I asked the question I'd been dreading since I awoke that morning. Delaforet pointed me to an outhouse about a hundred feet from the stables. It was not a pleasant experience. I swore to myself that if I ever made it back to the twenty-first century, I would never complain about gas station bathrooms or their tissue paper again.

When I'd returned, Delaforet had put on his hat and held a basket in each hand.

"Are you returning those to Mellie?" I asked.

"Yes, would you like to accompany me?"

I blinked, surprised he hadn't told me to stay put.

"If you're feeling well enough that is," he added, concerned.

"I think I will join you." I smiled. *I have to show him I'm well enough, or he won't let me go with him when he investigates tomorrow.*

"Very well. Then, shall we stop at the church and see about getting you more appropriate attire?"

"No, I won't be wearing a dress unless Subconstable Taylor comes and removes these clothes from me himself."

His mouth hung open, his eyes following me as I closed the door behind us.

"It's just an expression," I waved my hand dismissively at his shocked sensibilities.

"They seem to have many strange expressions in Chicago," he commented.

"Oh Dudley, you have no idea how differently we speak where I'm from."

"Miss Nichols, why do you keep addressing me as Dudley?"

I giggled. "He's a famous Mountie. Haven't you heard of him?"

"I have not."

"Well, I'm not fond of honorifics, and you haven't told me your first name."

"We have not yet known each other a day, Miss Nichols."

"And yet, you've carried me in your arms, saw me in my undergarments, and I kissed you. I'd say all that puts us on a first-name basis." I flushed despite my flippant demeanor.

He tilted his head, using the brim of his hat to hide his face from me. I liked to think I'd made him blush too, but I couldn't picture it.

"Very well, Miss Nichols."

"Erin."

"All right, Erin. You may call me Wynn."

I bent forward so I could look at his face below his hat. "That wasn't so hard. Was it, Wynn?"

I grinned at him, and he rewarded me with a gentle smile in return. My breath hitched as my heart skipped a beat. I averted my gaze to the trees lining the road, crinkling my brow at my reaction. *I never thought I was the swooning type.*

The walk into town was much the same as it had been earlier in the day.

Mellie's was what I imagined high tea at a Cracker Barrel would be like. The rural sturdiness of wood and iron were juxtaposed by white tablecloths and delicate tea services. It was both functional and pleasant in its contrast.

A young woman with big, brown eyes in a blue dress and a frilly apron came out from a back room when she'd heard us enter.

"Back already?" she smiled at Wynn, giving him sheep eyes.

I smiled just as brightly and stepped forward. "Hi there. Erin Nichols. It's nice to meet you."

She shook my hand with a delicate grasp. "Mellie Barker," she answered, a little hesitant at my overfriendliness.

"Mellie from the sign. Your food was excellent."

This compliment turned her hesitant smile genuine. "Well, thank you. I was wondering why Constable Delaforet had asked for double portions. How do you two know each other? Relatives?"

You wish.

"Miss Nichols is a journalist from Chicago. She's here to write about our town," Wynn informed.

"Oh? Wonderful. I do hope you will mention my little restaurant."

"Of course."

"How nice of you to welcome her, Constable Delaforet. Are you staying at the hotel then, Miss Nichols?"

I looked over at the Mountie, wondering if I should lie. He just stood there, all tall and honest.

He cleared his throat. "No, she's—"

"Made other arrangements," I interrupted. "I have a friend in the area, you see." *There's no need to potentially tarnish this man's reputation when he's helped me so much.*

None the wiser, Mellie smiled. "That's well then."

"Miss Nichols will be eating with me quite a lot as I show her around, so please keep making double portions."

"Oh." Mellie's frown made her large eyes puppylike. "All right then."

"Thanks, Mellie." Wynn handed her the baskets and touched the brim of his hat at her.

Her cheeks flushed.

"Yeah, thanks so much, Mellie," I chipped in. Her smile twitched as we turned away to leave.

"Mellie is very pretty," I commented as we walked back to the barracks. "Is she married? I didn't see a ring."

"She's a widow."

I feel a little bad for poking at her now. "That sucks. And she's so young."

He eyed me.

"I mean, how unfortunate," I amended.

He dipped his head in agreement.

"Still, she's done well for herself," I continued, hoping to get any little bit of information from him.

He didn't respond.

"Oh, come on, Wynn. You're telling me you can't see that girl wants you?" I demanded, taking the direct approach.

He sighed. "Are all journalists as nosy as you?"

"Uh yeah. They can't be very good if they aren't." I smiled at having finally gotten a reaction from him. "Hmmm?" I pushed harder when he still hadn't answered.

"I am aware of Mellie's affections, and I cannot return them."

"Why not?"

"Because I just don't feel that way."

"Have you told her that?"

"She has not verbally expressed her interest, so no. I do not wish to embarrass her."

"You think you're being kind," I murmured.

He didn't say anything.

"Well, you aren't. She'll be more hurt the longer she gets her hopes up."

He remained silent for a while. "You seem to know a lot about the subject," he said finally.

"How perceptive of you, Constable Delaforet. I've had my share of heartbreak. I mean, just this morning I was rejected when I kissed this guy.

It was so embarrassing. You should have seen it, but I'm glad you didn't. It might have tarnished your image of me." I laughed at myself, humor having always been my way of coping with uncomfortable situations.

"And this broke your heart, did it?"

I smirked as he played along. "Well, it was mortifying to be sure, but I wouldn't say I'm heartbroken about it. The whole thing sort of endeared him to me in a way."

"Is that so?"

"Yeah, I was in a vulnerable situation, and he didn't take advantage of me. He's quite admirable. Wouldn't you agree?"

He didn't say anything.

"Of course, there's always a chance he found me unappealing."

He paused so long, I thought he would again opt for silence. "I can't imagine that to be the case," he said finally.

My heart skipped a beat, and my face flushed. I looked at my moccasins, thinking I was silly for being embarrassed when I'd instigated the conversation. "That's nice of you to say, Wynn," I murmured, smiling to myself. Then, I took a deep breath. "But I'd still like to apologize for my behavior."

He nodded, acknowledging my apology. "I am curious though," he said, his eyes momentarily meeting mine in a sidelong glance before he directed them forward once more. "Why would you suddenly kiss a man you had just met?"

I laughed self-consciously. "An excellent question. To be honest, I'd thought I was dreaming. I mean, an attractive Mountie shows up in your dream. The only logical thing to do is kiss him, right? Isn't that what you would do?"

"I can't say I would."

I laughed sincerely. "Your loss."

I peeked sideways at Wynn as we walked. The shadow of a smile curved the edge of his lips. *I'll get him to laugh yet.*

As we reached the barracks, Wynn stepped on a letter that had been shoved under the door. He picked it up and read it.

"What is it?" I asked, noting his frown.

"Mr. Broadstone has requested my presence at the hotel. Why don't you stay here? You must be tired from the walk."

I hated to admit I was. "All right. Oh, I forgot to ask you. Do you have access to the hotel's library?"

He nodded.

"Do you think you could request access for me? I want to do some research for my article."

"I will inquire."

"Thanks."

Once Wynn had left, I didn't know what to do with myself. If I were home, I probably would have watched Netflix or spent a few hours on social media. As it was, I was too exhausted to do anything useful. Having slept that afternoon, I wasn't tired enough to take another nap. I decided to sit by the window and soak in the views nature had provided.

After a while, I found myself humming to fill the silence. Then I began to sing. I had been in choir in school and had performed in talent shows and competitions, though I'd never won first place. Singing had been such a big part of my everyday life for a long time, and I couldn't remember when I'd stopped. I sang the tunes I'd always enjoyed and realized this body's range was different from my own. I could hit high notes I'd never dreamed of as an alto.

Eventually, Wynn returned. At the creak of the door, I cut my song mid-note, biting my lip. My face heated at the thought he may have heard me belting out with reckless abandon, but he didn't give anything away as he removed his hat and put the basket with our dinner on the table.

As we ate, I asked him why Mr. Broadstone had wanted to see him.

"He heard about Testooklah, and he was concerned. He wanted to ensure I was looking into it."

"What does he think? I mean, you're a Mountie. How could you not?" I defended.

"He wanted me to know that I have support should I need anything."

I pursed my lips. "Rich people..." I muttered, not entirely ready to let go of my protective stand. "Did you ask him about the library?"

Wynn nodded. "He said you can have access whenever you need. Your name was left with the front desk."

"Great. Thank you."

He inclined his head in acknowledgment.

FOUR

$\mathcal{I}$ fell asleep immediately that night, though it wasn't terribly restful as I had a recurring nightmare, reliving memories I would have preferred stayed in the past.

I snuck away from the group of students singing silly songs around the campfire.

My arms and shoulders were already sore from having paddled a canoe all afternoon.

I strolled down the wooded trail to the lake and sat on the edge of the dock. It was a relief to be alone, to not have to smile and pretend everything was all right.

The grief counselor my mom and I went to kept telling me that what I felt was normal, but I knew my friends were burdened because they didn't know how to act around me. So I tried to be the same old Erin, even if she no longer existed.

I shifted my gaze from the calm lake to the night sky. The waning half-moon peeked out just above the surrounding trees. I stared up at the star-speckled sky and remembered cuddling up on the couch with my dad watching sci-fi movies.

Every Saturday night, we would watch space movies while eating popcorn and Raisinets. I'd probably seen *Star Wars* over a hundred times. We'd recite the lines along with the film, and sometimes we would have lightsaber battles with cheap extendable toys. The stars blurred as a sob rose in my throat.

I closed my eyes and took a few deep breaths.

My dad used to tell me we were all made of stardust. As I gazed up at my first view of a night sky full of stars, I hoped it was true. Because if it was true, it meant we were all connected. And if we were all connected, maybe the stars had some power to bring my dad back.

I made a wish on every star I could see. I wished things could go back to the way they were. I wished I could have stopped my dad from going to work that night. I wished we would have gotten to go to the Cubs game as he'd promised. But all of my wishes really came down to the same desire: I wished my dad was still alive.

I awoke from my dream with a lump in my throat, afraid to go back to sleep, afraid to be pulled back into that same time and place. I rolled over and whispered into the completely dark room. "Wynn, are you awake?"

His silence answered me.

I slipped out of bed and pulled on my clothes and moccasins. Feeling my way, I crept out into the night. I followed the path and stood at the edge of the frozen lake.

With a sharp intake of breath, I stared up at the sky. I'd been fooling myself into thinking I'd seen stars in Wisconsin, but nothing could have been further from the truth. The night sky I stood under by the lake seemed to belong to a different planet. It appeared to me that there were more stars than sky. They clustered together in bright smatterings as if someone had accidentally pressed the tab on a white spray paint can.

My breath came out in a long, frosted sigh as ribbons of murky light tinged with green rippled across the sliver of moon. I'd seen pictures of the aurora borealis. And though it wasn't nearly as bright as it appeared through the camera lens, it was breathtaking all the same to see it in real life. The entire spectacle was reflected in the clear, frozen water of the lake. I marveled at the mirror-like surface.

This was the sort of thing I would have shown Bryan on the Internet; I smiled at the thought. In fact, it was probably around the time of night I would have dragged him from his computer and told him it was time to sleep. *No one is there to look out for him now. He will just program all night, drinking meal replacement shakes instead of eating real food. How long will it take for him to notice I'm gone? Will he remember what day it is in time to pay the rent?*

Just as homesickness squeezed my chest, a shadow moved across the lake. My heart hammered, and I looked up. The dark form had large wings, and a shining yellow light on its forehead illuminated its reptilian face.

"D-d-dragon...Holy fuck. That's a dragon." My strangled scream came out an airy, high-pitched squeak.

The dragon landed on the shore of the lake near the edge of the forest. In the glow from its forehead, a man climbed down from its back. Then, he and the dragon disappeared amongst the trees.

I was frozen in place, not daring to move. *That can't be right. No way. Dragons aren't real. I must have misinterpreted something else.*

Then, I heard a song on the wind. The mellow baritone seemed familiar in a way I couldn't place. Following after the man and the maybe-dragon felt like the stupidest thing I'd ever done, but that was the direction the song beckoned me, and I wasn't about to quell the curiosity that crept over me.

At the edge of the tree line, I momentarily worried if there were bears. I laughed at myself, shaking my head in disbelief of my own thoughts. *Really, Erin? You're walking toward a dragon, and you're worried about bears?*

As I got closer, I realized the song was in a language I didn't understand. Eventually, I came upon two men sitting by a fire. The dragon was nowhere in sight. *I knew I wasn't seeing right.*

The man with crimson hair stopped singing and I froze; my mouth hung open when they both looked up at me. They were devastatingly gorgeous. Otherworldly. Ethereal. The kind of beauty no man had a right to. I blinked stupidly at them.

The man with raven-black hair and eyes that glinted gold in the firelight moved toward me and took my hand. I shivered as he kissed my fingers. And when he stared into my eyes, his eyes glowed the same color that the dragon's forehead had. His gaze surrounded me, penetrated me, engulfed me. As he smiled seductively, I started to lose myself in his presence. The world around me blurred, and everything but him drifted from my mind.

"Grigore, that is enough," the other man chided in an eastern European accent.

Grigore clicked his tongue and moved away from me.

"I am glad to see you well," the man with the crimson hair told me.

"Do I know you?" I whispered, my mind slowly gaining traction.

"We have met in a way. I saved you last night."

"Wynn saved me," I contradicted automatically.

He nodded. "Da, but I brought you to him."

"What do you mean?"

"Did he tell you he found you in the forest?"

I nodded slowly.

"When I found you, you were near death. Your body lay broken near the railroad tracks. I healed you and brought you here."

I didn't want to argue with someone I'd just met, especially not someone who I could just sit and look at for days on end, but I couldn't let the obvious lie go. "That can't be true. There's no way you could have healed severe injuries so fast."

He stared at me silently for a while, his eyes analyzing me. But I stood determinedly by my statement despite the blush growing hotter the longer his gaze was on me.

"Anyone ever tell you it's rude to stare?" I asked, more self-conscious than offended.

He took a step closer to me as if drawn in. I lowered my head a little but stood my ground.

"There is something different about you," he said uncertainly, squinting as if trying to figure me out.

"Okay…"

His blue eyes stared deep into mine, and I couldn't look away.

"You are...dissonant."

I frowned. "That doesn't sound like a compliment."

"You do not belong here."

You're right. I don't. Even with that thought, my stomach dropped as if I'd been scolded.

"Could it be...?" He murmured to himself. After another contemplative pause, he asked, "Do you believe in magic?"

A week prior, I would've answered I was an agnostic and all-around skeptic. But in light of the circumstances, I'd become a believer in the impossible. Well, time-travel at least.

"I suppose..." I answered hesitantly as if tasting a new dish I wasn't sure I was going to like.

"It was through magic that I was able to heal you."

"Uh-huh," I grunted sarcastically, my conditioned reaction coming through, though it wasn't like I had a better explanation for everything that had happened to me.

"You need more proof that magic is real?"

"That would be...helpful."

"Grigore, show her."

Grigore stood and walked a few feet away, grumbling under his breath the whole time. When he'd stopped, his eyes glowed bright yellow. The light engulfed his body, and he turned into the dragon with a shining yellow gem on its forehead.

"Holy fuck!" I cursed, leaping toward the crimson-haired man.

Grigore didn't look quite like the dragons from the fantasy movies I'd seen. He was more humanoid, with longer limbs and clawed hands, though he didn't stand completely upright like a person.

"There's no need to be alarmed." The man held his hands up in a soothing gesture. "Grigore is under a spell that binds him to me. I can stop him if he does anything to harm you or anyone else."

"What he means to say is: I am his slave," Grigore mourned, his accent the same as the man's.

"If you were not bound to me, you would be out there burning, raping, and causing chaos."

"I take issue with the word rape. I *seduce* women."

"It is rape if you use magic to seduce them."

I could tell this conversation could go on for a while. "Let me get this straight: you magically enslaved a dragon?"

"He is a zmeu. To keep him from harming people, yes."

"And you're a...what?"

"I am the product of a hultan and an iele."

"What's that?"

He frowned, searching for the right words. "I suppose you would call a hultan a wizard and an iele a fae."

"A fae? Like a fairy?"

"A soul born of the wild."

"Meaning?"

"Fae are magical beings whose magic comes from their souls' connections with wild nature."

I didn't say anything but stepped closer to the crimson-haired man, searching his eyes. He had a similar build to Wynn: tall with broad shoulders. "What's your name?"

"You can call me Mitica."

I nodded, eyes still locked on his. There was something in his gaze, something that said I could trust him. I made a decision. "I'm Erin Nichols, and I think I'm in trouble, Mitica."

"You are in danger?"

"I'm not sure. But if I tell you something crazy, will you believe me?"

"I will consider your words carefully."

I bit my lip. *I mean, it can't be crazier than fae and dragons, right?* "Mitica, I'm from the future."

His gaze didn't look away from me as he searched my eyes. "That is not possible."

"Hey! Consider more carefully," I said defensively. "I'm telling you: yesterday I was in 2016, and now I'm in 1900."

His eyebrows pulled together in thought. Finally, he said, "I think we need to ask someone with more knowledge of spirit travel. I know a woman who may be able to understand what has happened to you. Will you go with me to meet her?"

"Right now?"

"No, I need to talk with her first. Tomorrow night."

I nodded. "Okay, if you think she can help."

He placed his hand gently on my shoulder and smiled in a soothing manner. "Do not be afraid. I will help you."

I felt the anxiety I'd been carrying around since I awoke that morning slip from my body as the calming warmth of Mitica's hand seeped into me. I shivered in relief as my eyes unwittingly filled with tears. I smiled up into Mitica's kind face as the tears leaked down my cheeks. "Thank you for believing me, and thank you for saving my life."

He slowly lifted his hand and caught a tear with a bent finger, his blue eyes softening with compassion. My chest ached from either my impossible situation or the heartbreaking look in Mitica's eyes. I wasn't sure which. I took a deep breath to fortify myself.

"Until tomorrow," I whispered before stepping away and leaving the ring of firelight.

As I departed, I heard Grigore say, "I think I like her."

"No, Grigore," Mitica said firmly.

"You never let me have any fun."

"Because your idea of fun is destruction and mayhem."

I smirked at their exchange and snuck toward my empty bed in the barracks.

FIVE

The next morning, Wynn told me he'd arranged transportation for me while he was in town fetching breakfast. I couldn't hide my surprise when he led a tan horse from the stables.

"You expect me to ride that?" I asked doubtfully as the horse stared back at me.

Wynn stroked the horse between the eyes. "His name is Langundo, and he is quite gentle."

"That may be true, but I'm still not getting on his back."

"How are you going to get to the reserve then?"

"Wynn, I've never ridden a horse before. I wouldn't know the first thing about it."

He looked at Langundo and frowned. "You've never been on a horse at all?"

I've never even been this close to a horse before, or any animal this massive. I've only ever seen them in real life at a distance as they drive tourists around in carriages. "Never," I answered.

He rubbed the back of his neck. "Well, you're going to need a way to get around, and this is the easiest way. Are you open to learning? I can teach you."

I bit my lower lip. *If I don't learn, I'm going to get left behind.* "Will you take it slow?" I asked nervously.

He smiled at me kindly. "I won't do anything you're uncomfortable with."

I lowered my head but met his eyes, nodding my agreement.

"Come here." He beckoned me to him and Langundo with an outstretched hand.

I inched closer and put my hand in his. He grasped my fingers gently and brought them to Langundo's neck. Placing his hand over mine, he showed me how Langundo liked to be pet.

The horse's coat was soft, and Wynn's hand warmed mine. I held my breath as my heart pounded with nerves.

Langundo looked back at me, and I jumped away, gasping. My back smacked into Wynn's chest, and he caught my shoulders to steady me.

"You're making him nervous," he murmured near my ear.

As my heart hammered in my chest, I knew it wasn't only because the horse had startled me. "He's making me nervous," I corrected in a soft voice.

"Horses can feel emotions. If you're nervous, he will be nervous, too."

"How can I get used to him without starting out nervous?"

Wynn paused, his expression neutral. "Why don't we let Langundo rest in the stables for the day, and you can ride with me?" he asked, his tone soft as he soothed both me and the horse.

The thought of actually climbing onto a beast that size made me instinctively shake my head.

Wynn turned me around and stared deep into my eyes. My breath caught in my throat.

"It's all right, Erin. I won't let anything happen to you. You can trust me."

The firmness of his tone, his expression, and his hands on my shoulders convinced me to agree despite my inherent unease.

He nodded once, satisfied with my answer, and led Langundo into the stables. The black horse he returned with seemed even bigger. The horse snorted when he saw me and moved toward me. I internally recoiled but stood my ground. Once he'd reached me, he nuzzled his head on my neck and lipped my ears.

I giggled, and Wynn pulled him away.

"He seems friendly," I said, wiping horse spit from my ear.

Wynn didn't respond.

"What's his name?" The horse and I both looked at Wynn for an answer.

"Bou," Wynn responded.

Bou groaned at hearing his name, and I laughed. "I don't think he likes it."

"Probably not."

After tugging on his saddle to ensure it was secure, Wynn motioned for me to come to him. He talked me through climbing into the saddle. The ground seemed very far away from Bou's back, but I wasn't scared for long.

Once Wynn got into the saddle behind me and wrapped his arms around me to hold the reins, I couldn't concentrate on anything but his solid chest on my back and his breath in my ear. He explained how the reins worked, how I should hold them, and how to use my legs, but I wasn't really paying attention.

I shivered, my breath coming out in an uneven sigh. It had been so long since a man held me. The tingling I felt told me it had been far too long. It was funny how I hadn't noticed until now. Never had a man as sexy as Wynn paid me any attention. Touching me, holding me, whispering in my ear? The probability of any of that happening was incalculably small. The sensations, the images, that arose were wholly inappropriate considering the platonic and instructional nature of the situation.

I sat up straight and chided myself. *Come on, Erin. He's trying to teach you something. Get your mind out of the gutter. He's eventually going to expect you to get on a horse alone. Pay attention.* It wasn't easy to ignore how good it felt in his arms, but I eventually managed to wrestle my libido for control of my brain.

He instructed me very slowly, just like he'd promised. And Bou walked at a steady pace the entire way to the reserve.

The edge of the reserve was marked with a small sign. Beside it, astride his brown horse, was the man who had burst into the barracks the day before.

"Miss Nichols, I'm Albert Clark. I'm the Indian agent. I apologize for not introducing myself yesterday. Constable Delaforet informed me you are a journalist from Chicago."

I nodded.

He continued as he turned his horse to walk beside Bou. "I'm sorry we could not have met under better circumstances. I do hope you will be fair in your reporting of this matter."

"I report the facts as they are. Fair has nothing to do with it," I stated, slightly irritated at the suggestive pressure of his comment.

He acknowledged my assertion with a nod and a frown.

The trail into the reserve was surrounded by trees and was a rather steep ascent. At the summit, the land evened out a bit, though it was still insulated by trees and felt enclosed by mountains. Eventually, small, ramshackle houses started to appear among the rocky hills. At first, there weren't any people in sight. But the farther we went, the more they began to show themselves.

My stomach clenched as I looked at them. Their thin frames hunched under the tattered blankets in which they were wrapped. Their weathered faces looked haggard, but it was their eyes that truly got to me. Their eyes were lifeless, beaten, as if the world had taken their spirits.

I tried to hold back my tears, my heart aching for their pain and the injustice of it all.

As we continued, I witnessed a wider range of expressions from the Wyboka. Some ignored our presence entirely, going about their chores. Others glared at us with malice, which I couldn't really blame them for. And still, some welcomed us, nodding and raising a hand in greeting as we passed.

We finally stopped in front of an elderly woman with feathers braided into her long, gray hair.

Delaforet slipped out of the saddle to greet her. "Good morning, Likinoak," he said.

She responded in a language I didn't understand then smiled cheekily at him.

He dipped his head in response and returned to my side to help me out of the saddle.

Once safely on the ground, Likinoak approached me and grasped both of my hands in hers. I met the older woman's gaze as she did so. Her dark eyes were deep, and it felt like she was staring into my soul. I had no idea what she was looking for, so I just stared back curiously. After a while, she beamed at me and cupped my cheeks as my grandmother used to do.

"Come," she instructed.

We followed her into a giant teepee. Inside, a group of grave men and women sat around a small fire. I took a seat on the ground between Wynn and Likinoak.

"Delaforet has requested entrance to the sacred hot spring. Who here would like to speak?" Likinoak asked.

"We cannot allow an outsider into our sacred space," one man spat. "They have proven many times that they have no respect for what is sacred to us."

"Why does it even matter now, Pówahkai?" a woman with scared eyes countered. "The space is already defiled with the blood of the People. It is cursed."

"Piyiets is right. No one should be allowed until the area is cleansed," the man beside Piyiets said.

"Perhaps it is the presence of the whites that has cursed us," Pówahkai muttered.

"I agree with Dzindo. The sacred space needs to be cleansed," another woman stated, ignoring Pówahkai's comment.

"I have received no message about a curse," Likinoak mused.

"Three people are dead. Is that not message enough?" Piyiets challenged.

Likinoak sighed, shaking her head. "I hear what you all say." She turned her dark, gentle eyes on Wynn. "As tradition dictates, only Wyboka will be allowed in the sacred space." Her gaze seemed to say something her words did not.

Wynn lowered his eyes in defeat. "May I at least speak to you in more depth as to the particulars?"

Likinoak met the others' eyes then nodded.

"Each person who died was found in the hot spring?" he asked.

"In the water, yes," Likinoak confirmed.

"I know the deaths were roughly a week apart. Are there any commonalities?'

"As you know, they were of different ages. Two males and a female," Likinoak stated.

"Were they there for a particular purpose?" Wynn asked. "Or were they there just to bathe?"

"Each entered the spring to be cleansed before communing with The Great Spirit," Piyiets said worriedly.

"That's right," the other woman agreed. "Testooklah went to be cleansed before his first quest in the bush."

"And the others?"

"Tsesikó was a healer. He was there to be purified before healing one of our sick. Yejeták was seeking a vision."

Wynn nodded thoughtfully. "Has anyone else gone into the spring?"

"No one else has gotten into the water that we know of," Likinoak informed.

"Excuse me for interrupting, but is there a process for this type of ceremony?" I asked.

Everyone was quiet for a moment before Likinoak spoke. "There is a lot of preparation for these types of rituals. It begins with fasting for two days, during which the seeker meditates and chants the ancient songs. Only water is allowed during this time of fasting. The songs depend on the purpose of the ceremony. The seeker drinks the ceremonial tea then enters the sacred spring for a purification bath. After being cleansed, he or she is ready to commune with the spirits. He may enter the bush in search of a vision or a song as Testooklah was to, or he may visit the sick like Tsesikó."

I turned to Wynn. "Is it possible they just drowned? I mean fasting for two days and getting into a hot bath could make anyone pass out."

"It's hard to say as there will not be an autopsy. It's possible, but how likely is it that all three of them drowned in such close succession?"

"Good point."

Delaforet sat silently for a moment, his eyebrows crinkled in a pensive expression. "Without more information, I don't know what I can do to help solve this mystery." He frowned, clearly not happy with his conclusion.

"I told you asking for his help was useless," Pówahkai muttered.

"It seems we must handle this matter ourselves," Likinoak pronounced.

My heart was heavy with disappointment as we left the teepee, but as Wynn had said, we needed more information.

Albert was particularly distressed as he remounted his horse. "What am I supposed to tell Ottawa?" he asked Wynn.

"Let's just wait and see what happens for now," Wynn counseled. "If enough time passes without event, it very well could have been drowning."

Wynn was pensively quiet while we rode back to the barracks. I couldn't see his face because I was riding in front of him, but I could feel his frown.

"What are you going to do?" I asked.

"There is nothing I can do."

"You need more information?"

I felt him nod.

"Why don't we just break into the hot spring and check out the crime scene?"

He shook his head. "We cannot do that."

"Because you're the law?"

"No, because it is wrong. We cannot desecrate the Wyboka's sacred space. Too much of what was theirs has been violated already. We must respect their boundaries."

A government agent respecting the rights of indigenous populations? How novel. "But wouldn't you say this is an extenuating circumstance?"

He was silent for a moment before he answered. "They were able to do just fine without our help for thousands of years. I'm certain they are more than capable of taking care of their own in this matter."

Then why did they ask for help, and why are you so upset that you couldn't help?

After we'd had another delightful lunch cooked by Mellie, Wynn left to patrol and check in on some outlying settlements. I thought about disregarding his directive to stay at the barracks, but I decided to listen just this once.

To show my thanks and to pull my own weight, I gave the barracks as best a cleaning as I could with a bucket of water and a rag. It seemed my new body wasn't used to any kind of manual labor. Even with it being winter, I had to remove my extra layers to cool down from sweating.

Of course, after all that work and not having lived up to modern standards of hygiene for a few days, I was appalled by my own smell. I took advantage of the fact that Wynn was out to strip down, hand wash my clothes, and then wash myself. I hung my wet clothes over a chair near the stove and tied a blanket around myself like a toga.

I was huddled near the stove in my blanket toga when Wynn returned.

His eyes swept the space, taking stock of things in a few seconds. He crossed the room and pulled the blanket from his bed. Then, he wrapped it around my shivering body.

"I miscalculated," I explained, trying to keep my teeth from chattering.

He went outside and brought in more wood for the stove. After stuffing in a few more logs, he sat cross-legged near the stove and pulled me into his lap without a word.

His body heat soon relaxed my shivers and brought warmth back into my limbs.

Neither of us spoke as I rested my head on his chest and listened to his heartbeat. The dim light from the stove reflected off the brass buttons of his red tunic. I watched the buffalo on the button dance in light and shadow.

As my body warmed to its normal temperature, our current situation turned from comforting to enticing. The moment I thought how good it felt to be in his embrace, I stiffened and then shivered without chill.

He seemed to notice the change because he pulled back a little to meet my eyes. "Are you warmer now?" he whispered into the hushed cabin.

I nodded without looking away.

He reached out a hand slowly and felt my clothes on the chair. "Your clothes are dry. You should get dressed."

Though he'd said that, he didn't make a move to release me from his embrace. For a tense moment, we gazed at each other in silence. I sighed a shuddering breath then licked my dry lips. It was then that his arms loosened, and he looked away. Taking the hint, I climbed out of his lap and watched as he left the room for me to get dressed.

SIX

*I*t felt like it took forever before I heard Wynn's slow, steady breathing, indicating that he was asleep. When I was able to sneak out again, I made my way to the place where I'd met with Mitica and Grigore. They were nowhere in sight.

I huddled beside the cold, ashy stack of logs that had been a fire the night before.

After a few minutes of waiting, the dark and quiet of the forest hovered in close around me. A shiver of fear ran through me, and I regretted entering the woodland alone. The world seemed so much bigger since I'd learned magic was real. *How can an unremarkable human like me hope to survive?*

"Here you are," Mitica announced his arrival.

I let out a relieved sigh and turned toward him. "And how are you this evening, Mitica?"

I could hear the smile in his voice when he said, "I am with you. How could I not be well?"

My heart skipped, and I gave a self-conscious laugh. "Oho there, you charmer. What are you trying to do? Give a girl a heart condition?"

He chuckled in his rich baritone. The sound sent a thrill through me. I remembered how his eyes had softened in compassion as he'd comforted me the night before.

He reached out and gently took my hand. My heart danced at how natural it felt.

"Are you ready?" he asked.

"To meet your friend?"

"Da."

"Lead the way."

He led me back toward the lake, his large hand enveloping mine in its reassuring warmth. I felt a shameless moment of regret when he released it as we reached Grigore.

"How's it going, Grigore?" I asked the dragon.

"How well can I be, chained as I am for an eternity of servitude?"

Mitica sighed at him. "First of all, it is not for eternity. It is just until I die. And secondly, would you rather I had let Făt-Frumos kill you? You are supposed to be repenting for your past deeds. If you do not change your ways by the time you are released. They *will* slay you."

"They would have to find me first," Grigore muttered.

Mitica sighed again and shook his head.

I smirked at the pair. "You guys should just admit that you're actually fond of each other."

They both made sounds of disgust, and I laughed.

"How far is your friend from here?" I asked Mitica.

"Just a short flight."

"A short what now? You're not expecting me to *ride* Grigore. Are you?"

"I like the way you said that." Grigore grinned, his sharp teeth gleaming in the light of his forehead gem.

"Shut up, Grigore," I snapped.

Mitica took my hand again and stepped close to me. His blue eyes beckoned mine, pulling me back from the edge of my growing panic. "You have nothing to fear. I will protect you from any danger that may threaten you. You can trust me."

His vow loosened the knot in my stomach.

"Do you trust me?" he asked.

I let out a shaky breath and nodded.

His answering smile was devastating. My heart pounded as if it wanted him to hear.

Mitica led me to Grigore—who hunched down accommodatingly—and helped me onto Grigore's back, just behind his wings. Then, he climbed on behind me.

"Are you ready?" he whispered in my ear as he adjusted my body to rest against his.

A shiver of heat ran through me, my body very aware of his chest on my back, his thighs along mine. A dirty little thought surfaced in my mind as I wondered whether my backside pressed against him would produce a reaction from his manhood. I squashed the idea. *What is wrong with me today?* Taking a deep breath, I realigned my priorities.

"As I'll ever be," I answered, grabbing at Grigore's scaly back for something to hold on to.

"Do not worry," Mitica assured. "I will not let you fall." He produced a length of pliant wood from his jacket. After muttering a few words in a language I didn't understand, he flicked the stick. It elongated and threaded itself between Grigore's lips before the other end landed in Mitica's free hand.

With his magical reins in each hand, Mitica's arms encircled me. The feeling was familiar, probably because I'd been in a similar situation with Wynn earlier that day. The major difference was that Bou couldn't fly, so I was far more nervous on Grigore.

"Here we go," Mitica warned.

I squeezed my thighs tighter to hold my balance. With a click of his tongue, Mitica signaled for Grigore to go ahead. He spread his massive wings and pumped them hard. I felt us leave the ground, and my entire body tensed.

"Relax," Mitica urged, his breath hot in my ear.

I would've found that a total turn-on had I not feared for my life. Still, I forced my muscles to unclench in an attempt to follow his advice. I took a steadying breath and finally looked past Grigore's back.

The treetops were about a hundred feet below us, and we'd already left the lake behind. The cold air whipped the hair from my face and chilled my nose and throat. The mountains still towered around us, but the stars, swirling in the Milky Way, felt close enough to touch.

I tentatively removed one hand from Grigore's back and extended it toward the sky in wonder.

I could hear Mitica's smile as he said, "Catch one for me, too."

We soared above the dark forest, and my heart raced joyfully. I laughed a breathy sound of delight.

Not long after, Grigore began to slow and descend. I could see a large fire with people around it ahead of us. We flew a ways past the fire and landed behind a simple, log house.

Mitica and I slipped from Grigore's back, and Grigore retreated into the forest.

To my surprise, the back door of the house opened, and Likinoak emerged holding a lantern. She smiled warmly at us and motioned us in. Once we'd shut the door behind us, Likinoak turned to me.

"You have come a long way to be here," she commented.

I nodded.

"Do you know anything about time travel?" Mitica asked her.

She simply looked at him and smiled. "You did well to bring her to me, Seyko."

I looked at Mitica, quirking my eyebrow at her form of address.

"I will explain later," he assured.

As she had the first time we'd met, Likinoak approached me and took my hands in hers, staring deep into my eyes. "You are you but not you," she said as if that were enough of an explanation.

"Could you be more specific?" I asked.

"First, come and sit. Then, tell me your story."

She pulled three chairs close to the roaring fire, and we all sat, cupping the tea she'd handed us.

I told them what I remembered from the day I'd time traveled. She asked questions about what time of year it was, what the moon cycle was, and what I was feeling before I was pushed in front of the train.

I had been so distracted with everything that I hadn't bothered to wonder who had pushed me until that moment. *I suppose it's possible it was an accident. More likely, Bill alerted the mayor to my plans, and he'd directed someone to "take care of me."* I clenched my fists. *Crooked bastards.*

After hearing my story, Likinoak nodded and turned to Mitica. "You say you found her by the railroad tracks in Farrloch?"

He nodded. "She was in a horrible state. Her injuries certainly were consistent with being hit by a train."

"And the body you are in now doesn't look like the one you left in Chicago?" she asked me.

"That's right. I look totally different."

"I see." She pursed her lips in thought, and we waited in a silence that grew heavier with every passing moment. Finally, she presented her theory on the matter. "The desire you felt as you stared into the sky, it was like casting a spell. The black moon is a time of heightened magic, and in your time, it fell on a night when the veil was thinning. When your spirit left your body, it sought to realize that desire. The night you arrived here was also the night of a black moon. Your spirit jumped to a previous incarnation."

"But how did I cast a spell? I'm not magic."

"Everyone has a little magic because we all live on energy from the sun and earth," she informed. "But you may be right. Perhaps more is happening that we do not know."

She turned her gaze to Mitica, who appeared deep in thought.

"So you're saying that this was my body in a previous life?"

"Yes, your spirit sought a compatible vessel."

"How does that work? Does that mean I died in 1900 in a previous life and was reborn in 1989? And then what? I died in 2016 and returned to my vacated body in 1900?"

She listened carefully to my explanation then nodded her agreement.

"But why can I remember everything from 2016 but not 1900?"

Mitica answered, "You did not return to the spirit realm. That is where memories are cleansed between lifetimes. If you knew your true name, you would have access to the memories from all of your lifetimes."

"My true name?"

"Your name during your first lifetime."

"Oh." I fell silent for a while, considering everything I'd just heard. "So...I died in 2016?" The thought made me lightheaded. "Does that mean I can never go back?"

"I am uncertain," Likinoak said. "The trauma was enough that your spirit left your body. But Mitica healed your body in this time. So if your body in the future was healed, you may be able to return."

"How would I know? And if it isn't, what happens if I try to go back? And if it is, how do I get back?"

"I do not know, but I can try to find out," Likinoak answered.

"I will also look into the matter," Mitica promised.

I sighed at my predicament. "What am I supposed to do now? I mean, I can't stay with Wynn forever. How do I even start to build a life here? I don't know anything about this time. Wait. If I'm in my body from a previous life, that means I could have family and friends here. But I don't remember anything." I moaned, frustrated.

Mitica reached out and took my hand from my lap. "Do not worry. We will figure this out."

I met his eyes as they danced in the flickering light of the fire and nodded. "Thank you."

The low, steady pounding of a drum interrupted our moment, followed shortly by voices raised in song.

"It is time," Likinoak announced, rising from her chair and going outside.

"Time for what?" I asked Mitica as we followed her out the front door.

We walked along the dirt path, which led to a large clearing with a huge fire in the center. A tall scaffolding-like platform stood at one end, and men and women danced and sang around it.

"Time for a funeral," Mitica answered solemnly.

Looking closer, I saw an oblong shape wrapped in a blanket atop the platform. I assumed it must be the body of Testooklah.

We watched the funeral progress for a long while, silently bearing witness to the mourning and celebration of Testooklah's too short life.

"Why did Likinoak call you Seyko?" I asked Mitica quietly.

"Seyko is the Wyboka word for son. I am an honorary Wyboka," he replied. "I saved Likinoak's son, Chuthekii, not long ago. We performed a kinship ceremony and became brothers."

I nodded slowly and then jumped as a thought occurred to me. "Wait, does that mean you can enter their sacred space?"

"Da."

I turned to him, pleading with my eyes. "Would you do me a favor?"

"Whatever you need."

"Wynn was investigating the unusual deaths here on the reserve, but he's hit a wall. He needs to examine the crime scene, but he's not allowed in because the hot spring is sacred. The Wyboka didn't find anything wrong, which is why, I assume, they asked Wynn for help. Will you go in and take a look around then tell me what you find?"

He smiled gently at me, and his eyes, sparkling in the light of the bonfire, praised my cleverness. "Of course," he said.

"Thank you." I beamed at him.

After a while, Likinoak rejoined us, and we told her our plan. She nodded her approval and promised to stay with me as Mitica left to have a look.

"Mitica told me about your son. Where is he now?" I asked the older woman.

"Chuthekii is escorting the children back to the residential school. Two others had come home to seek a quest or a song in the bush at the same time as Testooklah. We felt it was not safe for them, so he took them back."

I knew about the abominable institution of native residential schools where children were separated from their families, languages, cultures, and religions in an attempt to beat the native out of them. My stomach turned in revulsion.

"How often do the children get to come home?" I asked.

"Not often enough. We had to lie to the school to take those three home. Some children try to run away to come home. Others want to stay. With the traditional ceremonies outlawed by the government and the children taken at younger and younger ages, I fear our ways will be lost."

I didn't know a lot about the Wyboka in the modern-day other than their environmental activism and their high rates of alcoholism and suicide. I honestly had no words of comfort to ease her fears besides that her First Nation still survived.

"So Mitica became a Wyboka after he helped your son? What happened?"

Her wrinkled face darkened as if remembering a particularly horrifying nightmare.

"My son is an animal person, a dreamer. He receives magic from animals. While communing with one of the ancient spirits, he became overwhelmed and turned into a wechuge. Mitica saved Chuthekii before he could hurt anyone."

It was at that point in the conversation Mitica returned. "There did not seem to be anything amiss," he informed us, shaking his head in apology.

After that, Mitica said it was time to get me back, and Likinoak promised again to look into my plight.

I was much less scared while riding Grigore the second time. My lack of fear allowed me to feel other sensations, like Mitica's broad chest warming my back, ensuring I felt no chill from the wind.

"Thank you for taking me to see Likinoak so we can figure out what happened to me," I said to take my mind off his proximity.

"I am sorry you are going through this, though I will not say I am sorry you are here," he murmured into my ear.

Warmth spread through me, and I took a deep breath.

Once we'd landed, Mitica slid to the ground first then held his hand up to me. He pulled gently and steadied my descent with his strong arms. Feet on the ground, I stood gazing into his eyes, still wrapped in his embrace.

"When can I see you again?" I asked in a hushed tone.

He smiled softly down at me, and my heart jumped as my cheeks heated.

"Do you think you can fool the Mountie again tomorrow?"

My chest tightened at his choice of words, and I bit my lip. *I feel bad for deceiving Wynn when he has been so kind to me. He even offered me a place to stay, and he feeds me every day. But he can't help me with all this time travel stuff.*

"Wynn is not a fool," I defended, squirming out of his arms. "He's just trusting and honest. And he's my friend, so don't speak badly about him."

He gave me an appeasing smile, which irritated me somehow. "I apologize for my phrasing. I will remember you care for him in the future."

Care for him? My heart skipped at the thought, and my gaze wandered to the starry night sky. I was quiet for a while. Then, I sighed and met Mitica's eyes once more.

"I'm sorry for snapping at you. I'm sure you didn't mean anything by it. You've helped me just as much, if not more, than Wynn. I also consider us friends."

Heat radiated through my chest as he flashed me a delighted smile.

"I have something for you," he said.

"What is it?"

He dug into his jacket pocket, pulled out a corked vial, and handed it to me. "Give this to your Mountie. It is water from the hot spring. If there is something wrong with it, maybe he can find out."

"Wow, thanks, Mitica... But he's not *my* Mountie."

"Is he not?" He grinned.

"Shut up." I pushed his chest playfully to distract myself from the growing heat in my face.

He chuckled and snatched my hand, bringing it to his lips. His kiss was warm and soft on my fingers. My breath hitched, and I trembled at the sensation as goosebumps raised on my arms.

"I have something else for you," he murmured against my hand.

Then, he placed a crimson pouch in my palm.

My face and ears aflame at where my mind had gone, I swallowed my embarrassment and took the pouch. There was a lot of money inside.

"I forgot to give this to you yesterday. It is yours. You had it on you when I found you that night."

The pouch was dark crimson, stained with blood, a lot of blood, my blood. My stomach dropped, and my head spun. I sucked in a breath.

Mitica grabbed my shoulders to steady me, concern knitting his brow. "Erin, are you well?"

I took a few slow, calming breaths and nodded. "How...if my change purse is this stained, what happened to the rest of my clothes? My undergarments weren't stained," I wondered.

"I had to rip them open to see your injuries. They were ruined. I found you the only clean clothes I could, then I washed and changed you before leaving you for the Mountie to find."

I looked at him sharply. "You washed me?"

He nodded. "But that is all," he assured.

I pursed my lips. "That was good thinking though. Thank you." *It was alarming enough for Wynn to find me dressed that way. I can't imagine how he would have reacted if I'd shown up covered in blood without a scratch on me.*

He smiled, relieved I'd understood.

"I can meet you tomorrow night?" I asked.

His eyes sparkled, and he nodded once.

"All right. I'll see you then," I said, taking a step toward the barracks.

"Sleep well," he called like he wished for nothing else.

SEVEN

$\mathcal{M}$y legs were sore when I awoke the next morning. *I guess riding is more of a workout than I'd thought.* Wynn was nowhere in sight when I stiffly rolled out of bed, groaning at the pain.

When he returned with breakfast, he found me doing yoga poses to stretch my tight muscles. He quirked an eyebrow but didn't say anything.

I laughed at his confusion. "It's called yoga," I explained.

He nodded once and asked for no clarification.

"It's a form of exercise and meditation. I was doing it to stretch."

"I imagine your legs must be sore from riding yesterday."

You're imagining my legs, are you? I wouldn't say no to a massage. Instead of voicing my inappropriate thoughts, I simply hummed my assent to his deduction and thought of us cuddling by the stove for warmth. I frowned at my breakfast when I remembered how he'd pulled away.

"Is there something wrong with your food?"

"No," I muttered.

"Then, you should eat it. You're going to need the strength."

"Why is that?"

"Because I'm going to show you how to care for Langundo."

My aching muscles throbbed in protest, but I knew it wasn't right to complain. *Wynn can't keep taking care of everything for me. If I'm going to ride the horse, then I should know how to care for him. Plus, I don't know how long I'm going to be stuck here. I need to learn as much as I can.*

"All right," I agreed.

If I'd thought I was sore before, it was nothing compared to how I felt after I'd cleaned Langundo's stall and brushed him. I was more comfortable around the animal after having ridden Bou the day before, and no horse could compare to riding Grigore.

I listened carefully to Wynn's instructions about how to approach and take care of him. He was quite the happy horse once he'd been brushed and given food and water. I rather thought he was growing fond of me, though not as fond as Bou seemed to be.

Once we'd finished, Wynn went into town and brought back lunch. After we'd eaten, he said he would return the basket on his way to patrol.

"I can take it back," I offered.

His eyebrows crinkled in concern. "I'm not sure it's a good idea for you to wander around alone. What if the people who hurt you find you?"

"I'll be fine," I assured him and myself.

"I don't like it," he declared.

"You're being overly protective," I accused.

"I don't agree."

"It's fine. I won't stay long. Besides, people saw me with you when we went into town the other day, and I'm sure Mellie has mentioned my presence. That means people will know you will ask questions if something happens to me."

He frowned and met my eyes. "You will not stay long?"

"I'll be back before you are," I vowed.

He reluctantly agreed though I would've gone even if he hadn't.

After sending him off, I took out the money pouch Mitica had given me and dumped it onto the table. The coins were crusted with dried blood, and it took a lot of scrubbing to make them spendable. *If I tried to spend them like this, people would think I murdered and robbed someone.*

I wasn't surprised when Mellie took the basket from me with a stiff smile.

"How is your article coming along? You heading home anytime soon?"

"Hard to say," I answered vaguely.

After leaving Mellie's, I went down the street to the trading post and dry goods store. The shop seemed to have two distinct sections. On one side, there was a long counter that separated customers from shelves of cans and tins. On the other side, there was another counter, behind which were a wide variety of items, anything from hatchets to animal pelts.

I approached the clerk as he straightened the dry goods side of the shop. He had a thick mustache and neatly trimmed hair, and he wore a gleaming white apron. He gave me a smart, all-business smile.

"Good afternoon, Miss. How may I help you?"

"Give me a moment to take it all in."

He nodded and went back to organizing.

I scanned the cans, tins, jars, and bottles on the shelves and was surprised and pleased to see they had toothbrushes for sale. I immediately asked for one.

"Would you also like some dental powder?" the clerk asked, holding up a small jar.

Knowing how no one really regulated products like that at this point in history, I declined his offer and asked for baking soda instead. I also requested a few bars of soap.

As the clerk was wrapping my purchases, I wandered the trading post side of the shop. Scanning the variety of tools, blankets, and cookware, a flash of blue caught my eye. *Oh God, is that what I think it is?* I requested the clerk retrieve the blue fabric from a stack. He handed a bundle to me, and I squealed, unable to contain my joy. *It is! Jeans!*

The strait-laced man smiled in the face of my enthusiasm. I knew they were undoubtedly for men and probably for outfitting miners or lumberjacks, but I didn't hesitate to find what looked like my size and buy them.

As I paid, I asked the clerk where I could find a barber, and he was kind enough to point me in the right direction.

The barbershop was practically a hole in the wall. The room had only two chairs beside a counter, which held the barber's tools. Hanging on the wall, there were shelves full of mugs.

The old barber smiled kindly at me as I entered. "Are you lost, Miss?"

I smiled back brightly. "Nope, I'm in just the right place."

He tilted his head.

"I'd like you to cut my hair."

His face fell into a troubled expression. "Pardon?"

"Don't worry," I assured him. "I'm sure you don't cut many women's hair, but I don't need anything fancy."

"Miss, I have never cut a lady's hair. I don't know anyone who has."

"Well, I can be your first then."

He frowned. "I'm sorry, Miss. But it is not proper."

"Look, I know it's an unusual request. But if you don't help me, I'm just going to do it myself. Then, it's going to be all lopsided and messed up. Please, it won't take long."

He reluctantly gave in to my pleading and bright smile.

I sat in his chair and looked at the mirror as he put a towel around my shoulders and pulled my hair out from under it. His hands shook a little, but I smiled reassuringly at him in the mirror.

"You would like me just to trim the ends?" he asked, grabbing his scissors from the counter.

"No, I'd like it cut to my chin."

"Miss," he gasped, eyes bulging. "That is not advisable."

"That's what I want."

"Are you certain?"

"Absolutely."

He pulled a little clump of long, blond hair toward him and raised his scissors to it. "Miss, are you *truly* certain?"

"Please," I begged.

He sighed deeply and snipped, going a little pale as he did so.

After he'd gotten into the groove, he seemed to do a little better. When he'd finished, I was delighted with the job he'd done.

"You did beautifully," I congratulated.

He stared mournfully at the pile of blond locks on the floor as I paid him.

"If anyone asks, I'll definitely send them your way."

"Please don't."

Poor guy, I think I traumatized him. As I gathered my packages, I asked, "Do you know if there's a place I can purchase undergarments?"

He sighed in defeat like I'd dealt him a killing blow. "Madame Buvons has a shop the next street over." He pointed in the direction I should go.

"Thank you."

I'm sure he was glad to see me leave.

On the way to the ladies' underwear store, I found something of a hobby shop. It was smaller than the hobby stores in modern-day, but it had enough. I meandered the shelves of embroidery and needlepoint supplies and finally found what I was looking for: yarn. Knitting was the only craft I was good at, and I needed a warm hat. I normally would've chosen green yarn, but with my body change, I thought blue would look better. I couldn't find any circular needles, so I just grabbed some straight needles and a yarn needle.

The clerk raised one eyebrow at my short hair but didn't comment.

Madame Buvons's was indeed a ladies' shop. I had never seen so much lace in my life. There were ribbons and bows, corsets, skirts, capris, chemises. I cringed at the delicate atmosphere, afraid of soiling all the pretties with my crude and unworthy touch.

A refined woman with a long neck gasped as she came out of the backroom and saw me in her shop. Her wide eyes blinked a few times before she donned a neutral and professional expression.

"May I help you?" she asked in a French accent.

"I'm looking for some of those," I pointed at a chemise, planning on using it as a shirt.

"Very well. Suzette," she called coldly. A young woman with dark curls appeared. "Please assist this young...lady."

"Of course, Madame," Suzette answered.

Madame retreated back through the door she'd come from.

"Do not mind Madame," Suzette whispered, no doubt taking in my stony expression as I watched the older woman leave. "She is like that with everyone."

I looked at the young woman's earnest smile and couldn't help but return it.

"You are looking for a chemise? Could I also interest you in a corset?"

I stared at the torture devices she gestured toward. "You couldn't pay me."

She giggled as I shuddered at the thought. Something about her youthful joy and musical laugh endeared this woman to me. I held out my hand to her.

"I'm Erin. I'm a journalist from Chicago. It's nice to meet you, Suzette."

She took my hand gently. "An American? No wonder you are so modern. I like your hair. It is rather daring. Very fresh."

That's it. I'm adopting her. "Thank you very much. The barber was pretty scandalized."

She giggled again. "I can imagine."

Madame returned to issue Suzette a reproachful look. Suzette sobered and led me to the chemises.

I purchased a couple. As Suzette wrapped my shirts, I asked her where I could get a warm bath.

"There is a public bathhouse one block over," she informed me.

I lowered my voice to a whisper so Madame couldn't hear. "Suzette, would you like to grab a cup of coffee with me when you're free?"

Her eyes sparkled at the suggestion. "I am available Wednesday afternoon."

"Great." I smiled and gathered my packages. "Today is...?"

"Monday," she laughed.

I nodded. "I'll come by the shop on Wednesday then."

The term public bathhouse had surfaced images in my mind of ancient Roman baths. But if I'd thought I was going to bathe in such open splendor, I was sadly mistaken. The bathhouse had two doors on the outside, one for men and one for women. I entered and was asked by the attendant whether I would like a private room. I had no idea what the not-private room would entail, and I didn't want to find out. I requested a private room and was led up a set of stairs to a plain room with a clawfoot tub, a chair, and a little cabinet.

The young woman who'd led the way asked me to sit as she went to fetch the water for the tub. It took quite a few trips for her to fill the tub up. I felt like I should be helping her, but she outright refused when I'd offered. They gave me soap and what appeared to be shampoo made with honey. I used it as shampoo anyway.

I couldn't believe how good it felt to sink into a hot bath. My tense muscles eased, and I let out a long, satisfied sigh. I was able to scrub myself far better than I had in Wynn's little washbasin. When my skin was clean and pink, I dried off and changed into my new jeans and a chemise. Then, I pulled on Subconstable Taylor's warm coat before I left the bathhouse.

I stopped by Mellie's to pick up dinner before heading back to the barracks. She sneered at my transformation as if that would give her a better chance with Wynn. *Whatever. I look this way because I like it, not to impress him.*

I hadn't known how much the money in my pouch had been worth in this time period until I looked at how much I had left. *I must've been wealthy in this lifetime, or I was a thief.*

Wynn returned to find dinner ready to eat and me knitting by the stove.

"I went to Mellie's to pick up food, but she said you'd already gotten it." He stopped and stared at my change in appearance, his mouth hanging open.

I smiled broadly at his dumbfounded expression. "I told you I'd make it back before you."

EIGHT

"It seems you did a lot more than just go to Mellie's," Delaforet commented without taking his eyes off me.

His steady gaze made my skin tingle.

"Yeah, I found a purse of money in one of my boots, so I stopped a couple more places. I even made a friend: a woman at Madame Buvons's shop."

"Did anyone suspicious approach you?"

"No, everyone seemed fine. They probably found *me* suspicious if anything. It's a nice tourist spot. I can see why you thought I was a travel journalist. Oh, and this was waiting when I returned," I lied smoothly, handing him the vial of sacred spring water.

He unwrapped the paper I'd put around it and read the note I'd sloppily written saying what it was.

"So what is it?" I asked.

"It's water from the spring," he informed.

"Oh? So we can run tests on it to see if there's something wrong with the water that would kill people." I hesitantly reached out and touched his arm, smiling up at him. "This could give you the information you need to crack the case."

He met my eyes and nodded, the shadow of a smile telling me he was pleased.

Thank you, Mitica.

Then, he gently pulled away and sat at the table.

"What are you going to do with it?" I asked, sitting across from him to eat.

"I will wire headquarters and ask them where I should send it for testing."

I nodded.

As we ate, I told him about my experiences in town that day. He didn't say much, but I could tell he was listening.

When he'd left to return Mellie's basket and send his telegram, I went outside to give the horses more food and water. Then, I continued knitting by the stove. I was able to go pretty fast since this body wasn't plagued by carpal tunnel from years of knitting and computer use. I was about a third of the way done with my hat when Wynn returned.

"What do you do when you have free time?" I asked him as he removed his hat.

"Different things. Mostly, I read."

"Oh yeah? Read any good books lately?"

"I finished *A Tale of Two Cities* a few days ago."

"That's a great book."

"You've read it?"

"Of course, I've read a lot of..." *classics.* "Dickens's work."

"Have you read this?" He crossed to the trunk at the foot of his bed and pulled out a copy of *Dracula.*

"Yes." *Read it, saw the movies, even saw the spoofs. I wonder if the vampire craze took off right after Dracula was published or if it took a while.*

"I have not yet started it," he said.

"Well, it has been a while since I've read it. Why don't we read it aloud together?" I suggested.

He agreed.

Wynn read for a while, but Jonathan Harker hadn't even reached Castle Dracula before it was time for bed. I wished I hadn't promised Mitica I would meet him that night because I was pretty tired, though I couldn't deny I wanted to see him. I had a difficult time staying awake while lying in the dark room waiting for Wynn to sleep.

Like the night prior, I was the first to arrive at our secluded meeting place. I settled in to wait for him, trying to ignore the oppressive silence around me. A prickling crept over my skin, and I turned around, expecting to see Mitica. But no one was there.

Squinting, I searched the dark forest for what could've alerted me to its presence.

That's when I heard it: the sound of an ethereal flute playing on the wind. The song put my mind at ease. It was so enchanting that I felt compelled to discover its source. I followed the tune deeper into the forest, pausing every so often to ensure I was going the right way. I lost track of how far I'd walked, but that didn't matter.

Eventually, I came to a, circular clearing where the song seemed to play all around me. I looked up into the naked limbs of the surrounding trees. Sitting on a low branch, just out of reach, was a tiny person about as tall as my hand.

The little woman had long, black hair and shiny black eyes. She sat comfortably on the branch in her tan dress with her ankles crossed, playing her tiny, wooden flute.

I would've said she was a fairy of the Tinker Bell variety, but she didn't have any wings.

Her black eyes sparkled at me as I slowly approached her.

"Hello," I whispered in a voice that told her I meant her no harm. "Are you all alone out here?"

Right when I stood beneath the branch she was sitting on, she pulled the side of the flute away from her mouth and smiled. Just as she brought the flute to her mouth again, Mitica came busting into the clearing and forcefully waved a hand toward her. A strong wind blew from his direction, and the woman tumbled out of the tree.

I gasped, reaching out to catch her, but Mitica pulled me away.

"Let's go before the others show up," he urged.

"What others?" I asked.

But it was too late. The others had already arrived. On every free branch stood a tiny person with hate in their shiny, black eyes.

"Run," Mitica said calmly. "Run now!" he yelled, pushing me ahead of him.

He didn't have to tell me again. I ran in the direction he'd pushed me, trying not to fall in the dark. He was right behind me. Unfortunately, so were our pursuers. They leapt from tree to tree, shooting blow-darts from their flutes. My heart pumped adrenaline through me as I crashed through the forest. My lungs and throat burned as I panted the freezing air. Tree branches scratched my face and hands, but I didn't dare stop.

Eventually, the chase took us back to the lake, and I skidded to a halt on the rocky bank, trapped.

The wingless fairies with beady eyes smiled gleefully as they closed in on us. Mitica stood protectively in front of me, ready to take whatever came next. Just as I cringed, bracing myself. Grigore swooped down from above, breathing fire at our tormentors.

The tiny people scattered, retreating back into the forest.

I let out a sigh of relief and all the strength seemed to leave my body. Mitica caught me as I started to sink to the ground. I leaned against his broad chest and took comfort as he stroked my hair.

"What were those?" I murmured, my face still buried in his chest.

"Čanotila," he answered. He pulled away gently to meet my eyes. Satisfied that I'd recovered, he sighed and said, "We should talk."

On the banks of the lake, Mitica made a small fire among the rocks. Before he began his story, he sat me on a large stone and knelt in front of me.

"Your face is bleeding," he told me, gently caressing my cheek with his fingertips.

My breath hitched at his feather touch and the proximity of his gorgeous face. "The branches," I murmured, staring into his blue eyes.

He began to sing softly in another language. His fingers on my face glowed, and I felt my skin warm. The scratches itched as they healed.

"Thank you," I whispered.

His answering smile made my heart skip.

But before he could say anything, Grigore chimed in, "What? Do I not get a thank you? I saved both of you after all."

Grigore, the mood killer. "Thank you, Grigore."

"I take kisses as payment."

"Grigore," Mitica scolded.

"Not enough? You are right. How about—"

"Quiet," Mitica growled, cutting him off before he could say something truly sordid.

I smirked at their exchange, though I was a little disappointed at Grigore's interruption.

We settled around the fire, and Mitica began his explanation. "There are many different types of fae. Čanotila are just one type."

"Are Čanotila evil fae?"

He shook his head. "It is not that simple. Some fae are dark by nature, but Čanotila can be either or both. The problem is that many fae are being forced to utilize their darker natures to survive."

"What do you mean?"

His eyes lost focus as he stared deep into the fire's light. "There is no magic without wild nature. A fae spirit in a fae body cannot survive without magic."

"So fae without wilderness die?"

"Da, they may be reborn into a human body. They would not die without the wilderness if in a human body, but their wild spirits would not have access to their magic without being in nature. The wild places are disappearing. Soon, there will be no magic left."

He was silent for a long while. I hesitated to interrupt his contemplations, but there was something I had to know.

"You said one of your parents was fae, right? Does that mean you'll die, too?"

"I will die eventually. I am not immortal. But it will not be because of my iele mother and a lack of magic. My father is a hultan. He has magic, but he is a human. My mixed background was why I was sent here, in fact."

"Where are you from?"

"Romania."

I knew his accent was eastern European. "Why were you sent here?"

"Many of the wild places are gone. Many fae have died and lost access to their magic. My homeland has a balance of wilderness and civilization. The people there still celebrate fae festivals. Not too long ago, some Romanians immigrated here. When they were performing a hora for Sânziene, they could feel the fae here were weakening. They sent word home, requesting help. The iele and the hultan sent me to try to help them."

"And are you able to help them?"

"All I can do is try. As you saw, the Čanotila have embraced their dark natures. Even the animal spirits are having trouble controlling their power."

"Like what happened to Chuthekii," I said.

He nodded.

I sighed. *I've worried about deforestation, climate change, endangered species, and dolphin-safe tuna my entire life. But to know that humanity's lack of respect for the natural world is killing magic, too? Well, shit.*

I felt Mitica's silent gaze on me as I stared into the fire, my melancholy overwhelming me.

"You want to go home," he whispered finally.

I shrugged. "Yes and no. I mean, it's incredible here. I never thought I would have such amazing experiences. But, as you said before, I don't belong here."

His eyes softened, and he frowned. "I will help you find a way home since that is what you wish."

"Thanks, Mitica."

"I want you to be careful when you are not with your Mountie while you are here. I do not know how you came to be in the state I found you in. It is possible you were killed by that train by accident. However, it is also possible that it was not an accident."

"I'm all over it."

His eyes flickered with conflict before he nodded to himself. "I want you to call on me if you are ever in trouble. Calling a fae's true name summons him or her. If you call out my name, I will be forced to materialize before you."

"Really? All I have to do is call out Mitica, and you'll show up wherever I am?"

"That is not my true name. A fae's true name is something that is closely protected. It gives others great power over you."

"Are you sure you want to tell me then?"

He moved closer to me, looking down at me as I sat on a rock near the fire. His eyes were clear of doubt when he said, "I trust you to protect that which is precious to me."

"I'll protect you," I promised.

His smile was pure joy. He reached his hand out to me, and I took it. I didn't resist as he pulled me into his arms. My heart pounded so loudly in my ears that I was afraid I wouldn't hear him. He brought his lips to my ear, and his voice was soft and clear when he whispered, "Dumitru."

I trembled at the sound and feel of him as if knowing his name made him belong to me somehow.

"You will call on me?"

"Yes," I breathed.

He pulled back, releasing me. Reaching up, he fondled the tips of my hair. "I did not get the chance to tell you before. I like your hair like this. It suits you."

I blushed, lowering my face. "Thank you."

"I think we have had enough excitement for the night. Perhaps you should go in to bed."

I dipped my head and turned toward the barracks, but he caught my hand to stop me. "I would like to see you again," he told me.

My heart raced.

"Will you meet me tomorrow?"

I smiled my assent. "Let's meet here rather than in the forest."

"That is likely for the best," he agreed.

"Goodnight," I murmured.

I felt his eyes follow me until I was out of sight. And a little flame, one I hadn't felt in a long time, lit inside me.

NINE

*W*ynn wasn't there again when I awoke the following morning. I practiced yoga and knitted more of my hat before he returned with breakfast.

"What are you doing today?" I asked him as we ate.

"Patrolling."

"Do you mind if I come along? I want to practice riding Langundo, unless I'll slow you down."

"I'm glad you seem more comfortable with the idea of riding a horse. You may join me if you wish. I'm in no hurry."

Wynn showed me how to saddle Langundo and went through the basic controls again before helping me into the saddle. He'd been right about Langundo being gentle. He was slow and steady, and he followed Bou with little urging.

My neck and ears were cold after my haircut, and I vowed to finish my hat as soon as I could.

We had to have ridden a few miles before we came upon a homestead. It was a simple log cabin nestled among some trees near a stream. We saw no signs of life as Wynn dismounted and helped me down.

I stretched my sore legs and followed him to the front door. A young girl with a ragdoll snuggled in the crook of her elbow answered his knock.

Wynn smiled at her gently. "Hello, Clara. Is your father or brother around?"

I'd never seen him so openly pleasant before, and a gentle warmth spread through me.

"They're out back," she informed in her cute, baby voice.

Wynn tipped his hat at the child, and she grinned, revealing a gap where her front tooth had been.

I smiled to myself, remembering the stories my parents used to tell me about the tooth fairy. *I should ask Mitica if she's real.* A pang chased my happy memories as thinking of my parents made my heart sore. *I'm either dead or in the hospital soulless somewhere. Mom had a hard enough time with Dad's death. I don't think she'd survive mine.*

We left Clara and her doll in the house, and I trailed Wynn around to the back. The door of a small barn was open.

"Hello? Frank? Charlie?" Wynn called, entering.

A man in his early thirties emerged from a stall, shovel in hand. His eyes showed recognition at seeing Wynn, and he nodded a greeting to me.

"Keep going, Charlie," Frank called into the stable behind him as he moved toward us.

"Right, Pa," Charlie answered from inside.

"How's it going, Frank? Any trouble?" Wynn asked.

"Everything's fine, Constable. Beatrice will be having her calf any day now."

Wynn nodded. "Well, we didn't come to interrupt your work. I just wanted to check in and see if you all needed anything."

"We're all right here, but I hear something's going on up at the reserve. There isn't anything we got to worry about, is there?"

"I'm looking into it, Frank. No need to worry."

"Because I don't need no injuns getting riled and taking it out on us."

I glared at Frank, going from zero to pissed in the space of a heartbeat.

"There's nothing to worry about, Frank," Wynn repeated.

"If you say so, I'll take your word for it."

"I do."

Frank nodded, appeased. "Yeah, you're probably right. They don't have any fight left in them anyhow. Heck, Charlie could probably take the drunken lot." Frank grinned like he was hilarious.

"Erin." Wynn touched my shoulder, and I realized I'd readied for a fight, my glare punctuated by tense shoulders and a clenched jaw. "Will you check on the horses? Make sure they didn't wander."

I nodded stiffly and stomped out of the barn. Reaching the horses, I remembered we'd tethered them. I sighed, glad Wynn had urged me to leave. I had little tolerance for ignorance, but my raging at Frank wouldn't have helped Wynn or the neighboring Wyboka.

"What do you guys think?" I asked the horses, pausing as though listening to their responses. "I agree, Bou. Maybe we *should* subject Frank to everything the Wyboka have been through and see how he does." I stroked Bou's face. "What's that, Langundo? You think violence won't solve violence? You're probably right. I should listen to you more often. You're very sensible." I smiled at Langundo and brushed the hair from his eyes.

Wynn returned a few minutes later.

"I'm sorry," I said to Wynn.

"I understand," he replied in a tone that said he truly did.

I managed to climb into the saddle without help, and I beamed in triumph as Wynn nodded his approval. As Langundo trailed behind Bou, I watched the snowy mountains around us. *I don't think I'll ever get used to this view.* I began to hum as we steadily moved toward the next settlement. If Wynn had heard me, he didn't let on.

The next settlement had a sign in front, declaring it a mission. I felt my lip curl in distaste. I had no tolerance for missionaries. They went against everything I believed in. I viewed them as hypocrites who tried to take away the one thing they would die to keep. *Treat others as you would want to be treated, my ass.*

Not wanting to cause Wynn any trouble, I told him I'd stay with the horses when he went to check on the missionaries. I used the time he was gone to look around at the splendor of the surrounding views. As much as I was enjoying my time travel adventure, I couldn't help but think I really didn't belong there as Mitica had said. *Perhaps my views are just too modern to survive in this time.*

It didn't take Wynn long to return, and we were soon riding back to the barracks. Once we'd arrived, I took care of the horses while he went to get lunch.

As we settled into our meal, Wynn pulled some paper from his pocket and put it on the table. "I received a response from headquarters about where to send the spring water. There is a society of chemists in Edmonton who can perform tests on the water to see if it's harmful."

"Great, so you're going to send it to Edmonton?"

"I have requested permission to take it myself rather than send it through the post. I'm just waiting for confirmation."

I frowned. "If they give you permission, how long will you be gone?"

"A few days."

I bobbed my head, looking down into my food.

"I..." He paused, seemingly looking for the right words. "I would like you to come with me. I don't feel...comfortable leaving you here alone for that long."

I met his eyes, and a thrill ran through me. "You could have just said you'd miss me," I teased, knowing he only wanted to bring me to protect me.

He stared into my eyes seriously, as if to say, "yes, I would."

My heart jumped into my throat at the look, and my face flushed. I looked back down into my food. *Jeez, Wynn, I was just joking.*

Wynn had planned on continuing to patrol after lunch, but it began to rain like the clouds had something to prove. Instead, he spent the afternoon answering correspondence while I knitted.

Because I didn't have a circular needle, and I never did figure out how to crochet, I made my hat by knitting a long rectangle then sewed up the sides. The result was a hat that looked a little like cat ears when worn. I put it on and admired it in the small shaving mirror before sitting back down to start knitting an infinity scarf.

Wynn braved the downpour to bring us dinner, and he was drenched when he returned.

"You're soaked," I needlessly pointed out, taking the basket from him and putting it on the table. "Remove your jacket so it can dry."

He stilled, staring at me.

"What? Are you naked under your red serge?"

"No."

"Then, you won't shock me. Come on, you're going to get sick." I reached for his buttons, threatening to remove his jacket myself if he wouldn't.

He stilled my hands with his, and my heart raced at his cool touch. I met his eyes and held my breath.

"I can handle it," he murmured.

I lowered my face and moved away, blushing at the awkward position I'd created. *How many times does he have to pull away before you get it through your head that he's not interested?*

As I unpacked the basket, Wynn unbuttoned his jacket and laid it near the stove. He wore a long johns-style undershirt, which was also wet.

"You should change your undershirt. I can go outside for a minute if that would make you more comfortable," I offered.

"No, uh...you can just turn your back. You'll get wet if you go outside."

I turned my back to him. There was some shuffling behind me, and I'd be lying if I said I wasn't tempted to see what Wynn looked like shirtless. But I honored his wish for me not to peek, not that that stopped me from imagining him peeling the wet shirt from his sculpted chest and abs. I shivered at the thought. Closing my eyes, I took a steadying breath. *Get a grip, Erin.*

"All right," Wynn whispered, much closer than I'd expected.

I jumped as he tapped me on the shoulder.

"Did I startle you?" he asked with the hint of a smile.

"Of course not," I muttered, burying my thoughts.

Dinner was quiet except for the insistent fall of rain on the wood of the barracks. Afterward, Wynn read more of *Dracula* while I knitted.

By the time we went to bed, the rain had finally stopped. As I snuck out to meet Mitica, I failed to sidestep the mud and puddles left in the storm's wake.

The clouds obscured the moon and stars while I stood on the shore staring into the sky. The still, chilly night settled within me. The world seemed asleep, the only sound the sporadic drip of water or the splunk of snow from trees to the soaked earth.

My heart reached out with the desire to see the open sky, and I remembered a song my mom used to sing to me at bedtime. I raised my voice as I sang it to the sleeping world.

"Pale Moon,
Do not hide your mysterious beauty,
For I have waited all the day to see it.

Mysterious Moon,
Share with me your ancient magic,
For I would know all of your secrets.

Ancient Moon,
Let me love you for my fleeting lifetime,
For I have long admired you from afar.

Fleeting Moon,
Remove the veil from your pale face,
For I would have you tarry a while longer."

As I sang my mom's lullaby, the clouds shrouding the moon broke to reveal a pale crescent. I sighed, admiring the sight.

"You sing beautifully," Mitica said from behind me.

I jumped at his sudden appearance, blushing at the compliment. "Did you just use magic to move those clouds?"

He smiled gently. "You said you wanted to see it."

"You can impact the weather?"

"Da."

"You said before your mother is a fae. What kind of magic do iele have?"

"The ability to become immaterial, the power of flight, to create madness with dance or song, and the power of seduction." He paused before continuing. "Most of my magic comes from being a hultan: healing, impacting the weather, dragon taming, though other hultan tame balaur. It was my mixed background that gave me the ability to enslave a zmeu."

"Wow, is that all?" I asked sarcastically.

He smirked. "Nu." But he didn't elaborate.

"It must be nice having magic," I commented.

He didn't respond for a while. "There are far more important things," he answered quietly.

His wistful voice made my heart sink. Before I could talk myself out of the impulse, I reached out and took his hand as he had done to comfort me. When his gaze met mine, the mood shifted. The warmth from his hand and his close proximity made me overly aware of my reaction to him. I quivered with anticipation, and the little flame inside me shone brighter.

"I wish you would not look at me like that," he whispered, not taking his eyes off mine.

"Why is that?" I breathed.

"Because it makes me not want to send you home."

I licked my lips. "I know what you mean."

He reached up and ran the back of his finger gently along my cheek. I held my breath and shivered.

"I cannot be selfish and keep you here. But I would like to know you before you leave."

"What do you want to know?" I murmured.

"Everything. What you love, what you hate, what makes you laugh, what makes you cry..." he paused. "What you feel like, what you taste like."

I trembled, my breath shallow and uneven. "Okay," I agreed in a barely audible whisper.

As he slowly leaned toward me, he gave me ample time to stop him. A fleeting sweetness caressed my lips, like the fluttering wings of a butterfly, as he gently kissed me. My heart cried when he pulled away too soon. An unmistakable ache slammed into me, but I stopped myself from reaching for him.

He stroked my cheek again, and I closed my eyes to better feel the sensation.

"You should go in to bed. I will see you tomorrow," he promised.

I nodded but my feet didn't move.

"Tomorrow," he vowed again, giving me a devastating smile that thanked me for wanting to stay.

"Tomorrow," I said, forcing myself to go inside.

In the dark barracks, I grinned up at the ceiling I knew was there but couldn't see. *When was the last time I've felt like this?* Butterflies fluttered in my stomach, carrying the desire to see Mitica again.

Rolling to the side, I sobered as I faced the direction of Wynn's bed. *What about Wynn? I can't deny I'm attracted to him as well.*

I tried to make out Wynn's form under his blankets, but the room was too dark. *Wynn told me he didn't find me unappealing. But every time we get into the sort of situation where something can happen, he pulls away. I thought maybe he was just too proper, but it's more likely he isn't interested. Like with Mellie, he doesn't want to embarrass me. Still...it feels like something more. Even when enveloped in Mitica, Wynn pulls on my mind, like a little tug on my sleeve reminding me he's still there.*

My sleep was restless that night as I tried to sort out my feelings in my dreams.

TEN

I still hadn't shaken off my pensive mood by the time I awoke the next morning. I stared at my uncertain, blue eyes in the shaving mirror. I knew thinking about it that hard wouldn't help me come up with a solution, but so much had happened to me in the days prior that everything seemed to pile up and make me anxious. I'd come to rely on Mitica and Wynn in that short time. I was in an impossible situation, and their help and support were really getting me through. I wasn't surprised that I'd become attached. But I began to wonder that if I was going home, perhaps I shouldn't get too involved with either of them.

I wasn't positive how Wynn felt, but Mitica seemed pretty clear in his desires. Still, I knew I didn't belong in 1900. And though Mitica had said he didn't want to let me go, he also had promised to help me get home.

Wynn entered with breakfast, and I put my thoughts away for later.

His eyes searched my face. "What's wrong?" he asked, concerned.

I plastered on a fake smile. "Nothing. I'm just hungry. Thanks for getting breakfast."

He nodded, but his brow was crinkled. I tried to be cheerful as we ate, to forcefully ignore his prodding, serious gaze. I got the feeling I wasn't convincing anyone.

We took care of the horses, and Wynn asked me if I'd like to join him on patrol again. I declined, saying I wanted to clean up before I went to meet Suzette that afternoon. He didn't press and told me he'd be back for lunch.

Cleaning myself in the washbasin didn't take very long. I thought about knitting more of my scarf but decided a walk would clear my mind a bit.

It hadn't been cold enough for the puddles from the previous day's rain to freeze. It was a brisk morning in the forties and rising. As I stood on the edge of the forest, I hesitated, remembering the angry Čanotila. I took a deep breath and strode into the wild.

The forest was a completely different world in the daylight. The weak morning sun sparkled off the snow-clumped trees, and an alluring mist crawled along the forest floor. The fog swirled about my lower legs as my moccasined feet made no sound.

Rough, natural steps led me above the mist to the edge of a cliff overlooking a river, which led to the lake. Breathing heavily from the climb, my heart pounded more from the scene than the exercise. The roaring river bubbled white in the sunlight, surrounded by evergreens. Silvery mist danced around the green and white trees on the hills below.

I sat on the edge of the cliff, my legs dangling, and stared at the mountains of varying shades of blue. For as many people who lived in the city, I never once felt small. But facing the vastness of the untamed Rockies, I felt rather insignificant. Still, even as small as I was, I never wanted to leave this enchanted place. It was on that cliff, breathing the fresh mountain air, that I knew I could never live in the city again, even when I returned home.

Without thinking much about it, I began to hum the tune from some fantasy movie based on a book. I'd only been half-watching it with Bryan because I'd been so tired. He always wanted to start movies late at night. I couldn't remember the words, but I recollected the melody.

Recalling Mitica complimenting my voice, I smiled to myself. Then, I thought of his comment about there being things more important than magic and that wistful look in his eyes. *I thought Mitica was more open than Wynn, but maybe he's just better at covering his feelings with a smile. I wonder what could make him so sad.* The mist that crept below seemed to hide something I desperately wanted to know.

As I walked back down toward the barracks, I still hadn't chosen a path on how to deal with Wynn and Mitica. But I found I couldn't be sad on such a nice day, surrounded by so much splendor.

When I opened the door to the barracks, Wynn rushed at me.

"Erin, are you all right?" he demanded, grabbing my shoulders and raking my body with his eyes.

My heart jumped into my throat, mirroring his alarm. "I'm fine. Why? What's going on?"

He sighed heavily and hung his head. Then, he met my gaze, his eyes flashing with anger. "You said you weren't going out until this afternoon. When I got back, you weren't here. You should have left a note."

I was so shocked by his display of emotion that I didn't even try to defend myself. "I'm sorry," I said sincerely. "I'm sorry I worried you."

My apology seemed to drain his anger away. His eyes softened. "I thought something had happened to you."

Touched by his concern, I couldn't help but smile. "I'm fine," I promised.

He froze, hands still on my shoulders. Then, he slowly caressed my cheek with the backs of his fingers.

My breath hitched at the sensation and the familiar situation.

"I'm glad you're safe," he whispered.

The sweet moment was all too fleeting, and I was soon left with regret as he pulled away from me. Shame and conflict swirled within me.

"Have you heard from headquarters about Edmonton yet?" I asked him as we sat to eat.

"No, but I'm going to check again this evening when I get dinner."

I nodded. "Is there a place to get coffee or tea in town?"

"Like a tea room?"

"Yeah."

"Well, there's a dining room at the hotel, or you can go to Mellie's."

I was afraid he'd say that.

After lunch, I promised Wynn I'd be back before dinner, and I went to meet Suzette.

Madame Buvons was her same cheerful self as she greeted me. "What can I help you with today?" she asked.

"I'm here to meet Suzette."

"Erin, you remembered what day it was," Suzette teased as she came out of the back room with her hat, cloak, and gloves on.

"I did," I responded, smiling.

We bid Madame Buvons farewell and left her lace-choked shop.

"I imagine the dining room at the hotel is quite fancy and has a dress code?" I asked her.

"Oui."

"Is Mellie's all right with you then?"

She nodded her agreement, and we strolled to Mellie's.

Mellie's wide eyes bespoke her surprise when I came in with Suzette, but she managed to be polite as she showed us to a table. Suzette wasn't fooled.

"You and Mellie do not get along, non?"

"You could say that."

There was a quiet moment where Suzette watched me with her dark eyes. She didn't ask me to clarify.

"So how long have you lived in Farrloch, Suzette?"

"A few years."

"And where are you from originally?"

"France."

"Wow, that's quite a ways." *Especially by boat.*

Suzette tilted her head at my word choice.

"I mean, that had to be a long journey."

"Oui, Madame and I came here as a way to start anew."

"Oh, you came with Madame Buvons all the way from France?"

"Oui, I owe a great deal to Madame. She is like a mother to me. You could say she saved me."

"From what? If you don't mind me asking."

She nodded but stayed silent for a moment. "Since I was a child, my only family was my older brother, Pierre. He was not much older than I, but when our parents died, he took care of me. I adored Pierre."

I frowned at her use of past tense. "I'm sorry. Is Pierre gone now?"

She nodded. "He was killed. Murdered by my lover."

Holy shit. I didn't see that coming. I waited, not wanting to push her.

"I met Renard while I was searching for a job. He was handsome and charming. He was a poet. Oh, he wrote the most beautiful poetry, as picturesque as any painting. Our love was passionate. But as time went on, Renard became obsessive, possessive. He did not even like when I began working for Madame. Of course, Pierre knew nothing of this. I was young, and I knew he would not approve. One night, both Pierre and Renard came to get me from work. Renard, thinking Pierre was my lover, hit him in the head with a brick and killed him. He urged me to run away with him, but I refused. Madame took me in, and we eventually moved here."

Oh my God! I thought I had problems. I sighed and shook my head in sympathy. "I'm sorry you had to go through all that, Suzette."

She smiled sadly. "Pierre would not want me to be sad, and I like my life here."

I returned her smile.

"So tell me, what is it like in America?" she asked, changing the subject.

"I can't speak for the whole country as I haven't seen a lot of it. But life in Chicago is busy. There's always something to do. I'm never bored."

"And you are a journalist?"

"Yes." *Well, I was anyway.*

"How exciting."

"Sometimes. Other times, I just cover fluff. I mean...other times I just write superficial stories."

She smiled mischievously and leaned toward me. "And do you have a lover in Chicago?"

I laughed. "I don't even have the time. I haven't had a boyfriend since college. I went on a few dates but nothing serious."

"This boyfriend in college, what was he like? Why are you not with him now?"

"Matt was...funny. I always had fun with him. He studied to be a journalist like me. But he decided to go off to warzones to cover what was happening there. It's not like we didn't love each other. It just...wasn't enough in the end." I shrugged to emphasize my point.

She sighed, disappointed in my lackluster love story. "It seems we both will die alone."

"Hey, don't give up. I'm sure we'll find love again."

"Oui, I hope he will be dashing."

"Well, there certainly are a few of those around town," I muttered.

"Oh? I see a man has caught your eye after all?"

"Caught my eye, yes."

"Who is he?"

"There are two actually."

"Two! You must tell me."

I sighed, still uncertain about my own thoughts on the matter. But there was no way to refuse her persistent gaze.

"Both of them are the honorable, protect-the-innocent types. One is... captivating. He's...well, he's otherworldly, like a dream. It feels real at the time, but then you wake up. He's like no one I've ever met before. He's too good to be true, like my mind just made him up. He's affectionate but sort of mysterious. He seems to be hiding sadness of some kind or loneliness perhaps? I'm not quite sure, but I want to find out."

"And the other?"

I paused for a while, thinking. *How to describe Wynn...He's like Captain America. No, better still, he's like Clark Kent. Yeah, that Kansas kind of polite. Charming in that slightly awkward sort of way, but not so awkward that he's goofy.* I smiled to myself, knowing Suzette wouldn't get the comparison.

"The other is quiet and reserved. He's polite, proper. I want to figure out what goes on in his head. He's sort of stiff. I want to help him loosen up and laugh a little."

"And you cannot choose?"

"I don't even know where to start. They both...affect me. It's like I get a whiff of their pheromones, and I become someone different entirely. It takes all my brain power not to just crumble into a grinning, giggling mess like I'm a silly teenager who has no control at all. It's actually kind of irritating now that I think about it. But..." My face flushed. "I don't think I want to stop it."

Suzette grinned and nodded as if she knew exactly the feeling I was talking about. "How do they feel about you?"

"The first guy hasn't hidden his interest. He told me yesterday that he wants to know me, and I agreed. We even kissed."

"And number two?"

I snorted. "I wish I knew. He kind of told me he was attracted to me, but every time we get into a situation that could develop that way, he pulls away. I'm not sure if he's just being honorable or if he said he found me attractive just to be nice. But he does worry about me. This morning, he practically yelled at me because he thought something had happened to me."

She shrugged. "I do not see the problem. You share a mutual attraction with the first man."

"Yes, but I feel dishonest if I don't acknowledge my attraction to the second. Also, I have to go home, and they both have to stay here. So I started to think maybe I shouldn't get close to either of them. If I get attached, it will hurt too much when I leave."

"Well, I say you do not know what the future brings. Keep getting to know them if you are unsure. Perhaps your love will end like with your Matt. But "tis better to have loved and lost' as the poem goes."

"There's no arguing with that kind of romantic logic."

"Oui." She smiled.

What a sweet person. I hope she finds someone who is worthy of her.

ELEVEN

*A*fter we'd talked about such serious topics, what kind of cake we liked and our favorite seasons seemed trivial by comparison. But those mundane bits of information about a person are important when getting to know someone. Still, I was glad that over a hundred years difference didn't change how female friends related to each other.

In the end, we promised to meet up again, but we didn't set a time. I hummed to myself as I carried the basket with dinner back to the barracks. The puddles from the previous day's rain were mostly gone, having either traveled to a body of water or evaporated in the day's sun. It was still a little early for dinner, so I didn't expect Wynn to be back from patrol yet. I entered the barracks, planning to knit while I waited for him to return.

I froze, my mouth hanging open at Wynn scrubbing in the washbasin. He was splashing water on his face, so he didn't see me enter. Droplets dripped from his chin onto his bare chest, which was everything I'd dreamt it would be. He still wore his pants, the suspenders hanging around his legs and backside. He splashed his face again then grasped for a towel. As he reached over, I noticed a scar on his upper arm. The black lines overlapped as if he'd been cut deliberately. Just as I was thinking I should probably leave, Wynn had wiped his face and glanced over at me.

There was a heavy pause where we just stared at each other before I went red and turned around.

"I'm sorry. I didn't think you were back yet. I'll knock next time." I could hardly hear myself over the pounding of my heart.

There was some shuffling behind me, and then Wynn cleared his throat.

I glanced over my shoulder and met his eyes. He averted his gaze, which just made it more awkward. *Jeez, it's not like I've never seen a breathtakingly sexy shirtless guy before...on TV. But I know he didn't want me to see, and his reaction is making me more embarrassed.*

I moved to the table. "I brought dinner if you're hungry."

"Thank you," he said in a deeper voice than usual.

"How was patrol?" I asked, desperate to fill the silence and distance my brain from dwelling on what I'd just seen. I could still feel my face radiating with heat. *Oh my god. Stop with the blushing already! You're a grown ass woman.* But as always, I had no control over my blush reflex. After talking with Suzette, I'd realized just how silly I must look to Mitica and Wynn, blushing like some virgin who has never talked to a man. Now, it was irritating me.

"Fine," he answered uncooperatively.

I bit my lip and looked down at my meal. "I had fun with Suzette today." I proceeded to babble about all the unimportant stuff Suzette and I had talked about, leaving the serious topics out.

It was a relief when he left to return Mellie's basket. The barracks had begun to feel too small, too filled up with his presence and the images and memories that swam in my mind. I gave the horses food and water and was knitting by the time he returned.

"I received a message from headquarters," he announced upon entering.

"And?"

"They gave me permission to go to Edmonton. I also stopped at the station. The next train for Calgary leaves tomorrow. I bought two tickets."

"That's exciting! Let me know how much the tickets were, and I'll pay for half."

He frowned. "That's not necessary."

Mounties can't make that much money for him to be paying for everything all the time.

"All right. Then, I will buy the return tickets."

"Really—"

"I insist," I said firmly.

He didn't respond either way, and I felt like I'd have to argue with him when the time came.

Whether it was the walk or him concentrating on our journey, Wynn seemed more comfortable than before he'd gone to town, which made me less embarrassed as well.

He let me borrow a small messenger bag to carry clothes in for our trip. After we'd packed, we had a quiet evening while he read more *Dracula*.

I didn't have to wait long for Mitica as I sat by the lakeshore that night.

"How come Grigore hasn't come with you for the last two nights?" I asked him.

"He is being punished right now."

"Why? What did he do?"

"I let him go hunting, and he tried to 'seduce' a Wyboka woman he found on the mountain."

"Oh jeez. Is she all right?"

"Da, I found them in time."

"That's good. So you grounded him?"

He tilted his head at my unfamiliar wording. "He will not be allowed to fly freely for a while."

"Sounds like he deserves that. Have you and Grigore been together for a long time?"

He nodded. "Sometimes it does seem like an eternity."

I paused in thought. "What's it like in Romania?"

"Would you like me to show you?"

"How?"

"Magic." He smiled.

"All right," I agreed.

I took his outstretched hand, and he pulled me to my feet. As I stood near him, my hand in his, all doubts I had about getting closer to him flew from my head.

"Do not let go," he whispered.

As he began singing in his sweet baritone, the landscape around us blurred. When it came back into focus, we were in a completely different place.

We stood on a mountain. The blanket of trees below dazzled me with colors in the glow of sunset. Greens, yellows, oranges, and reds all blended together in an autumn feast for the eyes. The rolling mountains in the distance faded into a thick mist the farther they were from us.

"Wow, it's beautiful," I breathed.

He smiled over at me.

"Did you just teleport us to Romania?" I asked, dumbfounded.

"Nu, this is just a memory, an illusion."

"Oh."

"Would you like to see my home?"

"Yes."

The scene shifted again, and we stood in front of a small, simple cabin with mossy stepping stones leading to the front door. It was tucked among a group of shady trees like it had grown there.

"This is where you grew up?"

He nodded. "Until I was brought to school to learn hultan magic."

"It's adorable."

"My mother and father still live here."

"Do you have any siblings?"

He frowned. "Nu."

I sensed there was more to the story but didn't push. "It's a wonderful place to live, very different than where I'm from."

"I would like to see where you are from," he said.

"Can you do that?"

"If you have a particularly strong image in your mind."

"I'm not sure it's a good idea though. A lot has changed in one hundred and sixteen years. I wouldn't want to shock you."

He nodded. "Perhaps something small then. You said you look different in your time. Will you show me what you looked like?"

I thought about it. "That should be all right. What do I do?"

"Just hold a clear image of yourself in your mind, and let me in when you feel me."

I closed my eyes and pictured my body in 2016. Mitica began to sing, and I felt a little nudge like someone was knocking on my subconscious. I didn't fight the feeling but let him in.

When he'd stopped singing and I'd opened my eyes, I wore my usual attire of Converse, skinny jeans, and a tank top. I could see the dark plastic rims of my glasses and assumed my hair and eyes were back to normal as well.

Mitica's eyes sparkled with appreciation. "You are beautiful, Erin."

I smiled awkwardly as my cheeks heated. *Stop blushing, Idiot.* "Thank you," I murmured to Mitica. "I definitely feel more comfortable like this."

He gazed into my eyes as if trying to memorize every green fleck.

After a few minutes, the illusion faded away, and we were back in Canada.

"Thank you for sharing that with me." He smiled warm and gentle.

"No, thank you. I feel like I have to go visit Romania when I get back."

His smile slipped when I mentioned leaving. "It is getting late. You should go to sleep. I will see you tomorrow."

"I can't. I'm going on a trip to Edmonton with Wynn tomorrow. We're going to get that spring water you gave us tested." I frowned at the thought of not seeing him.

He nodded once. "When you return, tie a string to that tree, and I will know to come to you that night."

"Okay," I agreed. "I will."

As I turned to go inside, Mitica called to me. "Erin," he said softly.

I stopped and met his gaze.

"Be careful," he pleaded.

I smiled at him. "I will," I promised.

"Remember to call on me if you need help."

"Your name will be the first from my lips."

His eyes widened as if surprised.

Isn't that what he wanted? Why would he be surprised? "Anyway, I'll see you in a few days. Keep Grigore out of trouble."

He agreed, and we bid each other goodnight.

As I turned from him, my heart panged, knowing I wouldn't see him for a while. Still, my sadness didn't stop sleep from overtaking me.

TWELVE

"*E*rin, wake up." A whisper pulled at me in my heavy sleep. "Erin," the voice urged. A gentle touch on my shoulder nudged at my consciousness. "Erin?" Concern accompanied the breath on my face.

I squeezed my heavy eyelids tighter.

The feather stroke of a fingertip pushed the hair from my face. Finally, I mustered the strength to peek through my lids. Wynn's blue eyes stared at me from much too close a distance.

My eyes popped wide, and he flinched at the sudden motion, straightening from leaning over me.

"You have to get ready, or we're going to miss the train," he explained, taking a step back from my bedside. "Clean up, and get dressed. I'm going to ask the blacksmith to look after Bou and Langundo while we're away."

I let go of a heavy breath as he left the barracks. The jolt of surprise at waking up to Wynn hovering over me had me fully conscious, but my body was still tired as I washed and changed. I was stifling yawns even when Wynn returned.

"Ready?" he asked.

I nodded and grabbed my bag.

He held out his hand to me, and I raised my eyebrows.

"I can carry that," he explained, pointing at my bag.

"So can I."

He frowned.

"Thanks for the offer, but I got it."

His frown didn't waver when he nodded.

On the walk to the train station, we stopped into Mellie's and ate a quick breakfast. She even wrapped up some sandwiches for us to eat for lunch on the train.

"You are going with Constable Delaforet on his journey to Edmonton?" Mellie asked as she handed him the sandwiches.

"That's right," I confirmed.

"Why is that?" she queried politely.

"Research," I answered.

The vagueness of my response made her ever-present smile falter if only a bit.

We got to the platform about ten minutes before a giant steam train screeched and hissed into the station. The brakes wailed, and my vision blurred. Images of the blue tactile edge of a subway platform and a printer paper box heavy with folders and picture frames swirled before my eyes. I shivered as the cool wind that proceeds the subway train rushed past the platform. My breath was shallow as my heart raced like the train wheels along the tracks.

Then, a heavy hand grabbed my shoulder. I gasped, a scream sticking in my throat.

"Are you unwell, Erin? You look rather wan," Wynn asked.

My eyes refocused on his concerned face. My forehead was clammy with sweat, and my teeth chattered. I took a deep breath. Then another.

"Erin? What's wrong? Should we delay the journey?"

"No," I said as firmly as I could manage. "No, it's too important to find out what happened to the Wyboka. Just get me on the train, and I'll be fine."

He reluctantly agreed and helped me onto the train. I felt better once we'd settled into our bench-style seats. I slumped down, leaning the back of my head against the bench.

"Will you talk to me, Wynn?" I murmured.

"About what?"

"It doesn't matter. I just need a distraction. Tell me about yourself.

Where are you from? What about family? Or tell me about your time in the Yukon." *Just let me hear your voice.*

"I was assigned to the Yukon because of my knack for languages," he began. "When gold was discovered, the native tribes were routed from the area that was to be Dawson City. This strained the relationship between the force and the tribes."

"Did you help the natives who were displaced?"

"As best I could." His expression and tone told me he wasn't satisfied with what he'd accomplished in the Yukon.

"What was it like there?"

"Busy. We didn't get a lot of personal time. There was always something to do. Whether it was keeping the peace, guarding the transportation of gold from the bank in town, or doing a mail run with sled dogs."

"How long was the mail run?"

"About six hundred miles one way."

"How long did that take?"

"Usually just over two weeks."

Call of the Wild *was one of my favorite stories growing up. I wonder if it has been published yet.* "The transportation of gold sounds dangerous. What was that like?"

"We transported at least five tons of ingots to Seattle each trip. We took a steamboat down the river about two thousand miles. Then, we transferred the gold to an ocean vessel and took it two thousand more miles to Seattle. We never lost an ingot."

"Impressive. So where are you from, Wynn? What about your family?"

Just as he hesitated to answer, the conductor asked to see our tickets. Wynn dug into his pocket and handed them to him.

"Your coloring is coming back," he told me after the conductor had left.

"Thanks for the help." I smiled at him weakly.

"It will take us a few hours to get to Calgary. Why don't you rest a little?"

Having not gotten enough sleep, and feeling exhausted from my little episode, I didn't need much convincing. "I think you're right," I agreed.

No sooner had I leaned my head against the window and closed my eyes, than the train began to move, and I fell asleep.

I awoke at the sound of the train's bell as we pulled into the station in Calgary. As I cracked my eyelids, I realized the material of a red tunic and the shoulder it covered supported the weight of my head.

"Sorry," I yelped, sitting up straight.

"Don't worry about it," Wynn said, the corner of his mouth quirked in a small but kind smile. "I'm glad you got some rest."

I eyed the sleeve of his jacket and was relieved to see I hadn't drooled on him.

I'd thought we would have a little bit of a layover in Calgary. I didn't know much about the city other than they have a big rodeo every year called the Calgary Stampede, so I'd looked forward to exploring a little. Unfortunately, Wynn told me we only had just enough time to get on the train to Edmonton.

We managed to find a seat just as the conductor called "all aboard" and blew his whistle. He checked our tickets, and we settled in for a twelve-hour ride.

I watched out the window for a while. The winter snow had mostly melted to reveal dry pastures of brown grass. The prairie was awe-inspiring in a completely different way than the mountains. It was bare and desolate. For as far as I could see, there was just uninterrupted horizon.

I turned away from the loneliness of the prairie and said, "I don't know a lot about you, Wynn. Why don't you tell me more about yourself?"

"Well, I don't know much about you either," he countered.

Because I have a major secret I have to keep from you. Not to mention I'm supposed to have spotty memories. "All right then. I don't mind. What do you want to know? I'll tell you if I can remember."

"You said before your only family was your mother and your friend, Bryan."

I nodded.

"May I ask what happened to your father?"

It used to sting whenever I talked about my dad. But at some point, I began to take solace in my memories. "My dad died when I was in elementary school."

He nodded silently, having known before he'd asked that it wasn't likely to be a pleasant story.

"He was a police officer, like you." I smiled. "Though he wasn't nearly as serious as you are. I didn't know what exactly had happened to him for a long time. I knew we were supposed to go to a baseball game together. But there was a break in a case he was working on, so he went to work instead. He was shot and killed on the job. Later, I found out that he had been investigating corruption in his department. The call from his partner that night was actually a setup, and he was killed by other cops."

I paused and looked over at his reaction. His head was bowed as he carefully listened to my story.

"But the people who did it paid in the end. The corruption was uncovered, and they will be spending a very long time in prison."

"Do you feel your father got justice?" he asked me quietly.

I nodded. "I used to be so angry that the men who'd taken my dad away from me were still breathing. But, after a while, I remembered who my dad was and how he would have felt. His killers can't hurt anyone else anymore. My dad was a big proponent of forgiveness and second chances. I don't think he'd want me to use my energy to hate them. So why did you decide to become a Mountie, Wynn? Was it the whole protect and serve thing?"

He was silent for a long moment. "Protect and serve is a good way to put it."

I'd hoped he would go into more detail, but I could tell by his expression that he didn't plan to. After another long silence, he asked me if I was hungry and pulled out the sandwiches Mellie had packed for us.

Wynn seemed to be in a contemplative mood during and after lunch. I felt it best to leave him alone, so I took out my knitting and concentrated on it.

After we'd stopped midway to get water for the engine and dinner for the passengers, it was still another couple of hours until we reached Edmonton. I managed to finish my infinity scarf on the train.

As we disembarked, gas streetlights dimly illuminated the streets.

"So this is Edmonton," I commented as we walked past dark storefronts on the wooden sidewalk.

"No, this is Strathcona. Edmonton is across the river."

"Oh. Well, where to now?" I asked Wynn.

"Hotel," he answered.

He took me to a small establishment by the river. We entered a room with just enough space for stairs, a door, and a front desk. The clerk was a neat man with a thin mustache and well-oiled hair.

"Good evening, how may I help you?" he asked graciously.

"We would like two rooms please," Wynn answered.

"I am terribly sorry to inform you that we have only one room available at the moment," the clerk apologized.

Just as I opened my mouth to suggest we go elsewhere, Wynn said, "That's fine."

My head snapped in his direction, my eyes wide. He didn't meet my gaze.

"Very well, Sir," the clerk answered without judgment. He handed Wynn a key from the wall behind him.

Is he planning on sleeping in the same bed as me? I mean, I've shared a bed with male friends before, but not friends I was attracted to. Boyfriends don't count. That's a mutual thing.

I took in Wynn's tall, solid form as I followed him upstairs and remembered what he looked like without a shirt on and what it'd felt like in his arms.

I'm not going to get a wink of sleep. It's fine. You'll be fine.

On the third floor, Wynn unlocked our room and stood to the side for me to enter. The room was sparse with a double bed, a dresser, and a pitcher and washbasin.

I turned back toward the threshold when I'd realized Wynn hadn't followed me in. He held the key out to me, and I took it.

"There should be a small dining room through the door on the first floor. Feel free to eat breakfast whenever you wake. I will come back for you around ten."

"You're not staying?"

He looked over at the bed and back at me. "No, I should check in at the outpost, and I will stay at the barracks."

I felt a twinge of disappointment, and then my cheeks heated.

"You will be all right by yourself?" he asked, concerned.

"Absolutely. No problem at all. I will be totally fine," I assured with an embarrassed smile.

He nodded, but his worried eyes didn't waver. "I'll see you tomorrow then."

"Yep, see you tomorrow."

I closed and locked the door when he'd left. Leaning my back and head against the solid wood, I shut my eyes and sighed.

Then, I looked around the bare room and tried to stifle my loneliness.

I removed my bag and put it in the dresser drawer. Checking for bed bugs didn't take long, and I was relieved to see the hotel was clean. After taking the pitcher downstairs and asking for hot water, I cleaned the travel grime off me and crawled into bed.

I laughed aloud at myself, staring at the ceiling. *I can't believe I thought Wynn would share a bed with me. I've clearly lost my mind... I wonder if I'll ever get back to 2016. It's obvious I don't fit in this time. I doubt I would have survived without Mitica's and Wynn's help.*

I sighed again.

But I'm going to miss them when I go. I wonder why Wynn is so private about everything. He never did tell me where he was from or if he has family. Normally, I'd be a lot more pushy, but I think I'd rather him want to share stuff with me instead of my squeezing it out of him.

Maybe Suzette is right. Maybe I should just move to the friend zone with Wynn and concentrate on Mitica.

But there's just something about Wynn that I can't leave him alone. I don't feel right about moving forward with Mitica without figuring out my feelings. Of course, that rationale never seems to be there when Mitica is near me.

I remembered the feel of his embrace as he whispered in my ear and the fleeting kiss he'd given me like a promise of better things to come. I shivered under the blankets and toyed with the idea of calling his true name just to kiss him again.

I sighed, knowing that wasn't right. *What I really should be concentrating on is finding a way home. I bet Edmonton has a library even bigger than the one at the Farrloch Hotel. If a black moon the day before Halloween and reciting a poem could magic me here, maybe I just need to wait for another black moon. But it could be years before there is a second new moon in one month. And, even if it's more common, does it have to be when the veil is thin like Likinoak said? Is Halloween the only time the veil is thin? Is the black moon the only celestial event with heightened magical energy? And, even if it does all line up, how will I know if my body is alive in 2016? If it isn't and I try to go back, then I may be sending my spirit into the afterlife.*

Man, this is complicated. I need to narrow it down. All I have are questions right now. First, I need to figure out when magic will be heightened next. Mitica and Likinoak promised to look into it too. If we work together, I could be home before too long.

I ignored the tightness in my chest at the thought of leaving Mitica and Wynn behind.

"*I would like to know you before you leave,*" Mitica whispered in my memory.

There's no harm in that, right?

I curled onto my side under the blankets.

Go to sleep, Erin. You think too much.

THIRTEEN

The next morning, I awoke determined to come to terms with my crush on Wynn. It's not like I'd never had a crush on a friend before, and I usually got over it when I realized it was one-sided. In fact, some of my best friends over the years had started as unrequited loves.

I ate breakfast in the small dining room and took a cup of coffee back to my room. I was enjoying the river view from my window when a knock sounded on my door.

I opened it to find Wynn freshly shaven and impeccably dressed in his uniform. My heart jumped, and I squashed the feeling mercilessly.

"Good morning, Wynn. Did you have a good night?" I asked cheerfully, opening the door for him to enter.

His eyebrow twitched a little, telling me he'd noticed the change in my demeanor. "My evening passed as I'd expected," he answered vaguely but didn't enter the room. "Did you sleep well?"

"Yeah, after I shut my brain up. Shall we go then?"

He nodded. I grabbed my coat and room key and locked the door behind me.

Since I was staying by the river, the walk to the ferry wasn't far. The din of Strathcona was nearly as loud as modern Chicago. But, instead of cars and trains, there were the sounds of clopping horse hooves and the crunching of carriage and wagon wheels on the dirt roads. People shouted at each other as they went about their work, and horses whinnied their complaints. After we'd crossed the river, Edmonton's midmorning bustle was almost imperceptibly less than Strathcona's. I did notice, however, that while Strathcona had the railroad station, Edmonton had electric streetlights, though they weren't on as it was daylight.

The Edmonton Society of Chemists was housed in a sturdy brick building. A stiff butler-type greeted us at the door with a raised eyebrow.

"Good morning," Wynn started. "Inspector MacEvans should have sent word that I would be calling. I am Constable Delaforet."

The butler's eyes slid to me expectantly.

"She's with me," Wynn pronounced before he could ask.

Without a word, he opened the door for us to come in. The room we entered was a large receiving hall with wooden double doors leading in three directions. We followed the mute butler through the doors on the right, which led to a library. The three men present all looked up as we entered. Their eyes widened upon seeing me behind Wynn.

"Constable Delaforet and guest," the butler announced.

A wiry man with curly black hair closed the book he held and placed it on the shelf in front of him. "Very good, Shelly. I will take it from here," he said.

Shelly turned on his heel and left the room.

"Constable Delaforet, Inspector MacEvans informed me of your query. I'm William Watts." The curly-haired man introduced himself and shook Wynn's hand. Then, he turned to me. "Forgive Shelly's behavior. Women are generally not permitted on the premises. Miss...?" His words sounded nice, but his tone was disapproving.

I bristled. "Erin Nichols." I thrust my hand at him and gave him a firm shake. "And why is that, Mr. Watts? Do you find women distract you from your scientific pursuits?"

His brow furrowed at my greeting. "Well, there is that. However, chemistry can be quite dangerous. We have several laboratories here, and we would not want the gentler sex to come to any harm, especially as they are uneducated on the subject."

I didn't hide my glare. *Uneducated? I wonder whose fault that is.*

Wynn cleared his throat. "Mr. Watts, can you test a sample of water to determine if it contains anything harmful?"

"Quite."

"And Inspector MacEvans has informed you as to the importance of this task?"

Watts nodded. "I should have results for you in a week, more or less."

"That long?"

Watts gave him a stern look. "Do you have any idea how many toxins I have to test for and how long those tests take?"

"I apologize, Mr. Watts. This is a matter of some urgency."

"I understand," Watts relented, appeased. "I will send you the results as soon as I can."

"Please wire them to Farrloch," Wynn instructed, handing him the vial.

"Very well," Watts acknowledged.

I couldn't stop myself from squinting my displeasure at Watts one more time before we left.

"I guess we can leave for Calgary on the early train tomorrow. Is there anything you'd like to do in Edmonton before we leave?" Wynn asked after Shelly had shut the door behind us.

"Yeah, is there a public library in Edmonton?"

He frowned. "I don't believe so. Most of the libraries are like the one you just saw: for specific pursuits, and you usually need to be a member. There may also be some wealthy citizens with extensive libraries, but those will be even less accessible."

I pursed my lips. "Well, is there a society for astronomers or physicists?"

"I don't know," Wynn answered.

Undeterred, I walked to the front of a carriage parked outside the building and knocked on the wood to get the driver's attention.

"Excuse me, Sir. Do you happen to know if there's a society of astronomers or physicists like this one for chemists?" I asked him.

The driver nodded. "There's a group of 'em what meets at Mr. Montmartre's. I've driven them there loads of times. Seems 'e 'as a telescope."

"Would you take us there, please?"

"Course, Miss."

I grinned as I went back to Wynn. "Pro tip: cabbies always know where to go."

He gave me a small smile. "I'll keep that in mind."

We arrived at Mr. Montmartre's residence by way of bakery. Wynn insisted we eat lunch before trying to bust into someone's private library.

The Montmartre home wasn't terribly large, but it was imposing in its gothic-style architecture. A young woman in a pristine maid's uniform answered the door.

"Hello, I'm Erin Nichols. I'm a journalist from Chicago in the area working on a story. I've been told Mr. Montmartre has the best-stocked library on astronomy and physics in the area. Would it be possible for us to have a look at it? I desperately need information on the subject, and my editor will have my head if I don't deliver my article on time."

"I'm sorry, Mademoiselle, but Monsieur Montmartre is out at the moment. I have been instructed to only admit members of the Edmonton Society of Physics when the master is away."

"Who is it, Chloé?" a female voice from behind the door asked.

"A journalist and a Mountie come to see the library, Madame," Chloé answered.

A woman in a well-tailored gray dress and dark hair pinned atop her head opened the door fully. Her light eyes took us in shrewdly. "A lady journalist, you say? And you request access to my husband's library for an article?"

"That's right, Ma'am," I lied.

"Well, I see no harm. Please, come in. Chloé, make some tea for our guests."

"Oui, Madame." Chloé disappeared down the hall.

"Thank you very much, Mrs. Montmartre. You can't know how difficult it is to find good information around here," I told her as she led us through her elegant abode.

"My René prides himself on his library. I am certain he will have whatever you are looking for."

Their library was indeed well-stocked for a private collection. The well-lit room was lined by floor-to-ceiling bookshelves, each of which was full of leather-bound books.

"The books are categorized by subject then author," Mrs. Montmartre explained. "Ring the bell should you need anything, and Chloé will answer."

"Thank you again, Mrs. Montmartre."

She smiled. "Learning should never be only for the wealthy."

"I agree."

Once Chloé had brought our tea and she and Mrs. Montmartre left, Wynn turned to me. His eyes were keen and seemed to analyze me. I squirmed under his gaze.

"What are you hoping to find here that will help our case or your story?"

My heart twinged at Wynn's trusting nature. "This is going to sound strange, but I need to research moon phases and other astrological events."

He just nodded and moved to one of the shelves to help look.

Mr. Montmartre's library contained books on a wide variety of topics. Most of them pertained to physics, astronomy, and natural philosophy. However, he didn't neglect literature, mathematics, history, or other such subjects.

It took me a while to find an almanac with a list of moon phases for the next one hundred years. Mrs. Montmartre had made it sound like the library was perfectly organized, but I found only someone familiar with all the intricacies of physics's subtopics would see it as navigable.

Eagerly flipping through the volume, I was disappointed to discover the next black moon wouldn't happen until August 1905.

Shit. I can't stay here for another five years.

I sighed and put the book back. Finding Wynn across the library, I saw he was engrossed in whatever he was reading.

"Whatcha got there, Wynn?" I asked, peering around him at the book.

"It's not really related to what you're looking for, but I found it interesting. Listen to this: 'a full solar eclipse is always during a new moon when the sun and the moon are in the same sign of the zodiac. The alignment amplifies the effects of that sign.'"

"What is that? A book on astrology?"

"Yes, it goes on to say that some cultures perform special rituals during solar and lunar eclipses as they believe it is a time of heightened magic. Isn't that curious? I wonder if the Wyboka have a ritual like that."

My skin tingled with excitement. *A time of heightened magic?*

Wynn blinked when I rushed back to the almanac. "What is it?" he asked as I scoured the pages.

"Here!" I pointed animatedly at the page. "May 28, 1900. There will be a total solar eclipse. Wynn, you're a genius."

I beamed my thanks at him. My fervor seemed to be contagious because Wynn graced me with a full smile for the first time.

My face flushed, and I looked away, my stomach flopping.

"Well, I don't know what I did, but I'm glad I could help."

I barely heard him over the sound of my own heart. After taking a deep breath, I cleared my throat and asked if I could see the astrology book he still held.

Skimming through the sun sign dates, I found that the sun would be in Gemini on May 28. The Gemini section mostly talked about personality traits of anyone born under that sign, but there was one line that caught my eye. "Gemini represents duality. It could refer to two opposing forces or aspects of one being, for instance, the spirit and the body. As such, the sun in Gemini is an excellent time to explore the astral plane or attempt past life regression."

If a solar eclipse amplifies the effects of the sign it's in, and Gemini is a time to explore your past lives, maybe I could harness that energy to send me back to 2016. I have to tell Mitica about this. Maybe he or Likinoak can figure out a way to magic me back. I hope a little less than two months is enough time.

I closed the book and handed it back to Wynn.

"Did you find what you were looking for?" he asked.

"I believe I did."

I was surprised at how much time had passed while Wynn and I had been searching Mr. Montmartre's library. Before leaving, I rang the little hand-bell Mrs. Montmartre had indicated. Chloé appeared within a minute.

"We're ready to leave now, Chloé. Would you convey our thanks to Mrs. Montmartre for her hospitality?"

"Of course, Mademoiselle," Chloé assured, showing us to the door.

Wynn tipped his hat at the maid before she shut the door behind us.

"Would you like to get supper before we go to the ferry?" he asked.

"Sure, you know any good places?"

"I do."

He started down the dirt road, and I skipped to catch up.

"You've been to the place we're going before?" I asked.

He nodded. "We stopped in on our way to the Yukon. They make the best meat pies I've ever had."

"That's quite the praise coming from you, Wynn. Don't let Mellie hear you say that." I grinned at him.

We had to walk for a while before we got back to Edmonton's main street, but I didn't mind. It was warm compared to how it had been. It had to be near sixty.

The square, wooden building had a balcony on the second floor, which provided the porch with shade. The sign nailed to the balcony proclaimed the establishment as The Winchester. I followed Wynn into the tavern.

There was a bar at one end beside a set of stairs leading to the second floor. Round tables filled with thirsty patrons sat between the door and the bar.

One of the waitresses looked toward us as we entered. She beamed at us with hands on her hips. "Wynn Delaforet, as I live and breathe. I never expected to see *you* out this way."

Wynn nodded to the voluptuous brunette. "Sparrow," he greeted. He didn't exactly smile at her, but his eyes showed a recognition that was easy to decipher.

I sucked in a breath like I'd been punched in the gut, but I plastered a tight smile on my face.

Sparrow prowled over to us. "So you came to town and just couldn't stay away, eh Wynn?"

"Well, my friend here was hungry, and The Winchester has excellent meat pies," he explained.

Sparrow looked at me and smiled. "Be careful of this one, Honey. He's a real heartbreaker."

I nodded awkwardly but didn't respond.

Her smile didn't falter. "Take a seat, and I'll grab you a couple of those pies you came all this way for."

"Thank you." Wynn nodded, and I trailed him to an empty table in the corner.

He gestured for me to sit then went to the bar and brought us each back a beer. I nodded my thanks but didn't look at him, busying myself by watching Sparrow serve the other customers.

"Hey," Wynn said low, trying to grab my attention.

I reluctantly met his blue eyes.

"I'm sorry about Sparrow. The last time I saw her, she said she was going back to Toronto. I didn't expect her to be here."

I smiled at him like he was overreacting. "What are you talking about? I still would've wanted to try the best meat pie you've ever had. I don't mind meeting your old girlfriend. In fact, I can head back to my hotel early if you want to...you know, catch up."

He frowned at my nonchalant tone. "No, I—"

"Here you are," Sparrow announced the arrival of our food.

I smiled up at her. "Thanks."

I watched her buxom figure flit about the crowded tavern, and the image of her wrapped around Wynn, her beautiful features twisted in pleasure, came all too easily to my mind.

I concentrated on eating to hamper any continuation of conversation.

"Mmm so good," I praised, forcing myself to swallow the food that turned to sawdust in my mouth.

Wynn ate but watched me carefully. I couldn't let my guard down as his eyes prodded me. Somehow, I managed to eat everything around the lump in my throat, though I wasn't sure how long I'd be able to keep it down.

After we'd paid for our meals, Sparrow caught up to Wynn as he opened the door to leave. I waved to him, telling him I was going on ahead.

"I'm free tonight if you want to—"

I closed the door behind me, cutting off their conversation. Then, I took a deep breath and let it out all at once.

This is good. I nodded to myself. *This will help me let go.* I felt the telltale burning in my nose and closed my eyes. *Nope. Not going to happen.*

I was a few buildings down when Wynn caught up to me. I didn't ask him why he hadn't stayed or if he was planning on meeting Sparrow later. It was none of my business, and I didn't want to know the answers.

After taking the ferry across the river, we stopped at the railroad station to purchase our tickets back to Farrloch. I couldn't convince Wynn to let me buy his ticket, but I managed to purchase my own.

As we said goodnight at my hotel room door, I could tell Wynn was hesitant to leave. I felt torn. I wanted to be alone. But I knew if he left now, there would be no turning back. The door would close on any potential feelings I could have for him.

I stood inside my room, my hand on the door, and met his gaze on the other side of the threshold. "So...I'll have breakfast here and meet you at the train station tomorrow morning. Okay?"

He nodded, and there was a heavy pause.

I smiled up at him as cheerfully as I could manage. "All right. Well, goodnight then."

When I started to shut the door, he stopped it with an outstretched hand. I held my breath, my heart hammering in my chest. Another tense silence dragged out as his eyes bored into mine.

He squinted softly and frowned, regret written all over his face. "Erin..."

I smiled sadly at him. "Goodnight, Wynn."

He didn't resist as I shut and locked the door.

Sinking to the floor, I wrapped my arms around my knees and finally allowed the tears to flow, mourning the premature death of our potential romance. When my aching chest had hollowed out and my throat was too raw and swollen to voice any more sobs, I washed my face with cold water and crawled into bed.

My heart was still sore, but I felt better after my outpouring of emotion.

"You'll be fine," I told myself in the dark. "You always are."

FOURTEEN

$\mathcal{M}$y heart hadn't healed by the following morning, but at least I was getting my head on straight.

This is no different than the boys I had crushes on in junior high. There's no point in chasing someone who isn't interested. Wynn will never look at me with the recognition he watched Sparrow with, that gaze that said he knew her inside and out.

A twinge in my chest chased that thought.

He's had more than a few chances to make a move.

His look of regret from the night before flashed in my mind. I knew what that look meant, that look of apologetic rejection.

All right, Erin. That's enough. You're a grown woman. Put your big girl pants on and get over it. It's not like it was that serious anyway.

I ate breakfast at my hotel and paid my bill. When I saw Wynn waiting for me on the train platform, I didn't even flinch.

"Hey, Wynn." I smiled and waved at him. "How was your night?"

I could feel him analyzing my demeanor. "I'll be glad to be back in Farrloch. I didn't sleep very well."

"Aw, I'm sorry to hear that. Well, you can sleep on the train if you want."

He nodded.

The train rides back to Farrloch passed similarly to our trip to Strathcona, except we talked even less, and I didn't have anything to knit. We both took a nap and did a lot of looking out the window.

It was late when we arrived in Farrloch, and I was grateful to stretch my legs as we walked back to the barracks. It must have rained that day because I had to dodge puddles.

I wonder if I put a string on that tree tonight if Mitica would see it. It's late, but not as late as we usually meet. Maybe I should put it there first thing in the morning. Then, he'd have all day to see it.

As we approached the barracks, I saw a candle burning through the window. I stopped short and turned to Wynn.

"What's that?" I whispered. "Is someone in the barracks?"

He brought his finger to his lips. Then, he showed me his palm in a "stay here" gesture.

After pulling a revolver from his gun belt, he crept toward the door. He silently turned the knob and thrust the door open.

"Hands where I can see them," he demanded to whoever was in the room.

I held my breath and strained my ears. A few moments passed without event. The longer the silence went on the more nervous I felt. Finally, I picked up a handful of rocks and snuck to the door.

I mean, rocks aren't much compared to Wynn's gun, but I have a pretty good throwing arm.

As I peeked around the door frame, I could only see Wynn's back. I raised my arm, ready to pelt whoever the intruder was, and called out hesitantly, "Wynn?"

He turned to look at me, revealing a young Mountie before him.

"It's all right," Wynn told me. "It's only Oliver."

The young Mountie smiled genially and nodded. He was wiry with sun-bleached hair and light brown eyes.

"Wynn was just telling me about you, Miss Nichols. I'm Subconstable Oliver Taylor." He crossed the room and held out his hand.

I dropped the rocks I'd been holding to shake it. His eyes sparkled with amusement at the sight.

"That's a nice coat you've got there," he commented.

"Oh, yeah. I didn't have one, so Wynn said I could borrow yours. I'm sorry I couldn't ask first."

He grinned. "It's no problem. I'm glad I could be of assistance."

Wynn's mask-like expression drew Oliver's attention. "What's with the face, Wynn? You should be grinning like a Cheshire Cat, getting to spend all your time with such a lovely woman."

I blushed slightly at the compliment, and Oliver laughed as Wynn's frown deepened.

"What are you doing here, Oliver?" Wynn asked.

"Well, after we caught Wallace's gang, I was sure they were going to send me to Africa. But they sent me back here instead. Something about mysterious deaths on the reserve?"

Wynn nodded. "I'll explain."

As he caught Oliver up on the particulars, I excused myself.

Just in case, I took a length of yarn from my knitting and tied it around the tree at which Mitica had pointed. Then, I went to check on the horses.

Bou seemed excited to see me. He bobbed his head and hopped on his front legs. I chuckled and stroked his face. "Did you miss me? I hope you were a good boy while I was gone."

Langundo stuck his head out at Bou's commotion. "I'm sure you didn't give the blacksmith any trouble. Did you, Langundo?"

He didn't respond but chewed his oats as I patted him.

Another curious horse poked its head out of a stall. The horse was gray and white. "Well hello there, Sweetie. You must be Oliver's horse."

I let the horse smell me before I stroked its face.

After a few minutes, I went back to the Mounties. Wynn had finished discussing the case and was telling Oliver more about my predicament.

Oliver nodded in sympathy. "That must be difficult for you, Miss Nichols. I'm sure glad Wynn found you when he did or something even worse could've happened."

I nodded. "I'm very grateful to Wynn for saving me. I hope to get myself together soon so I'm not taking advantage of his kindness for too long. And, please, call me Erin."

"It's no trouble," Wynn assured me.

Oliver nodded. "You couldn't have found a more honorable man if you'd tried, Erin. Wynn is as good as they come. Of course, you're welcome here as long as you'd like, as long as you're comfortable sharing a living space with two bachelors."

"Not a problem, but I suppose I should give you your bed back."

Before Oliver could respond, Wynn chimed in. "You can sleep in my bed, Erin."

I felt my face warm at the suggestive nature of his comment. "No, I—"

"I'll sleep on the floor," Wynn interrupted in a tone of finality.

"It's no use arguing with him when he gets like this. You may as well give in," Oliver counseled.

I pursed my lips but agreed.

It wasn't long before we decided to call it a night. As Oliver blew out the light, I stared into the dark room, trying to figure out how I would sneak out with Wynn on the floor between my and Oliver's beds and the door at the far end of the room.

It wasn't difficult to tell when Oliver was asleep. He snored like a bear in hibernation. I had a hard time hearing Wynn's slow, even breathing over the noise.

I slid quietly out of bed and felt my way to the far wall in order to avoid Wynn. I was doing well until I stubbed my toe on a chair. Clenching my teeth, I held my breath.

Oliver snuffled, and it sounded like Wynn turned over. After a few tense moments, they seemed to still be asleep. I swiftly slipped out the door.

I let out a heavy sigh and snuck around the barracks to the lake shore, our customary meeting place. The clear ice of the lake had melted a bit along the edges. *It must've been warmer here yesterday, too. Though if Farrloch is anything like Chicago, there will be a blizzard tomorrow.*

"Did you miss me?" I heard Mitica's accented whisper from behind me. I turned around and met his joyous gaze. His blue eyes sparkled as he smiled at me.

I knew my blushing grin must look foolish, but there wasn't any holding it in. "I didn't know if you'd come tonight."

He tilted his head. "But you called for me. Did you not?"

I nodded. "I guess I wasn't sure when you'd look at the tree. I only arrived a few hours ago."

He grinned at me. "You could not wait to see me."

Then, he leaned in and kissed me on each cheek. "Welcome back," he whispered.

"You seem different," I murmured, pursing my lips in an attempt to get the grin off my face.

"I have been thinking about you," he said as if that was enough of an explanation.

"Okay." I waited for him to continue.

"I did not like being away from you. I do not yet know you enough to let you go."

My heart jumped. "Doesn't that seem a little backward? I mean, won't it be harder to let me go the more you get to know me?"

He shook his head. "Nothing in this life is forever. You can never truly hold onto someone. Something will always separate you. But before we are separated, I want to know you. If I can write you on the pages of my soul, then you will always be with me."

His earnest and sweet words made me shiver.

"Why do you want to know me so badly? I would've assumed it was because I'm from the future, but you haven't asked me anything about it."

He gazed down at me seriously for a moment. "I feel as though we have met for a reason. You traveled through time and space only for me to happen upon you right when you needed me. We were meant to meet in this time and place. Why did the gods send you to me? Is everyone from your time as glorious as you are? Is everyone as brave? Do they all have an inner light that would draw me to them?"

I could feel my ears get hot, and I looked down at my feet. "I couldn't say," I murmured.

"Please," he whispered. "Before you return to where you came from, please let me learn everything there is to know about you."

"On one condition," I told him.

He waited.

"That I also get to know you."

His eyes shined as if filling with tears, but he smiled gratefully. "I would love nothing more than that."

I held out my hand to shake on the deal, but he grasped both my hands in his and kissed each of them. I shivered at the sensation of his lips on me.

Seeing the breathtaking expression he gave me as his crimson hair fell into his blue eyes while he bent down to kiss my hands, it was the first time I thought it wouldn't be so bad to stay in 1900.

Of course, that thought was followed by what I'd discovered in Edmonton.

"We don't have a lot of time before I go," I admitted to him.

His eyes held many questions.

"I went to a library while I was in Edmonton. At the end of May, there will be a solar eclipse in Gemini. Apparently, magic will be heightened then."

He nodded seriously. "Then we have almost two months to discover how to get you back to your family and friends."

"I guess so."

"Let us talk to Likinoak tomorrow night. She may have an idea."

"All right," I agreed, my shoulders hunching. *I was so excited when I discovered this information with Wynn, but now I'm...not so sure.*

"Let us worry about that later. First, tell me something about yourself. How do you spend your time in 2016?"

I sighed. "Mostly, I work, or at least I did. I told you at Likinoak's I was a journalist, and I was fired the day I time-traveled."

He nodded.

"Other than work, I just..." *How do I say I watch TV?* "I guess I like stories. Sometimes I read them, and sometimes I watch them, like a play."

"I also like to read," Mitica informed. "It fascinates me that all the beings I live with every day are now viewed as fictitious. We used to be so much more a part of the world, but I guess humans stopped believing we are real when we disappeared with the wilderness."

"Fantasy and science fiction were always my favorite genres, especially the ones written in the 1800s. It's strange to think a lot of the authors I think of as classics are almost contemporary to you."

"What is your favorite book from this time?"

"My favorite book of all time is *The Count of Monte Cristo* by Alexandre Dumas. Have you read it?"

"Of course, the French have greatly influenced education in Romania."

"Yeah? I didn't know that. Did you read it in French then?"

"Oui."

"That's cool. I was never able to wrap my head around French pronunciations."

"Would you like me to teach you a little?" he offered.

"If you think you're patient enough."

"Tout pour toi," he told me.

"What does that mean?"

"It means: all for you."

I unsuccessfully tried to fight a smile and did my best to repeat the phrase.

"Try resting the tip of your tongue against your lower teeth," he instructed.

I tried again, following his advice.

"Très bien," he praised.

"Merci." I thanked him with one of the six French words I knew. "How many languages do you know?" I asked.

"Quite a few," he answered noncommittally.

"I've heard Europeans are more likely to speak multiple languages. Is everyone in Romania like you?"

"No one is like me." Though his words were proud, there seemed to be a hint of sadness in his tone.

"I guess that makes you extra special then. I like meeting unique people. They're the most interesting, and I find you can learn the most from them." I smiled encouragingly at him and took his hand.

"Not everyone thinks so," he countered.

"Well, I do, and my opinion is more important. I mean, if the universe sent me all the way here, obviously you should listen to me."

He laughed in a rich baritone, and I couldn't help but join him.

"Da, you must be right. If you say people who are unique are the most interesting to you, then I am glad to be different."

"That's what I like to hear."

He smiled at me softly, his eyes shining with admiration. "Your light heals bruised souls."

"Well, I don't know about that, but I do like to spread a little joy every-where I go."

"Bucurie," he murmured, nodding.

"What's that?"

"Joy."

"Oh. Well then, yes. Bucurie." I grinned.

He gazed at me silently for a while, and I could feel my cheeks heat the longer he stared. Finally, he said, "You must be tired from your trip. You should go to sleep. I will see you tomorrow."

"Yeah, you're probably right."

I moved to pull my hand from his, but he tightened his grip. Grabbing both of my hands again, he kissed them each in turn. Then, he leaned down and kissed me gently on each cheek, the tip of my nose, and my forehead.

"Noapte buna, bucuria mea," he whispered before placing a feather-light kiss on my hungry lips.

"What does that mean?" I murmured, feeling his breath still on my mouth.

"Goodnight," he told me, smiling gently before pulling away.

A sweet hum pervaded my body as I reluctantly bid Mitica goodnight and returned to Wynn's bed in the barracks.

FIFTEEN

The glow Mitica had elicited remained in my heart when I awoke the next morning. I knew what the feeling meant, but I refused to label it.

Wynn was nowhere in sight when I opened my eyes, but Oliver came in with an armful of wood as I fixed my hair in the shaving mirror.

"Good morning, Erin."

"Good morning, Oliver. Do you mind if I call you Oli? I've always liked the name Oli."

He chuckled. "Not at all. Though my sister is the only one who calls me that."

"It must be nice having siblings. I've always wanted a brother."

"Well, I could use another sister if you're up for being adopted."

I laughed. "Okay. But you'll have to be patient with me because I don't know how being a sibling works."

He grinned. "I'm sorry. I can't do that. There's nothing to do but jump in."

"Why do I feel like I'm going to regret this decision?"

"Too late."

We were both laughing when Wynn returned with breakfast. He raised an eyebrow at how chummy we'd gotten.

Oli put his hand on my head and mussed my hair on his way to get an extra chair from the stables so we could all eat at the table.

"Hey!" I protested, snatching a bar of soap from beside the washbasin and throwing it at him.

He dodged and laughed all the way out the door. I sighed and rolled my eyes. Then, I turned back to the mirror to fix my hair again.

Wynn retrieved the soap and placed it back where it belonged. I thought he would move away immediately, but he lingered close to me. My heart pounded at his proximity, and I scolded myself. Steeling my nerves, I looked up at him. "What's up?"

He averted his gaze, shaking his head slightly, and stepped back.

I sighed internally, half in relief and half in regret.

We all ate breakfast, and they told me they would be going on patrol.

"I'd like to visit Suzette today," I told them.

"Who's Suzette?" Oli asked.

"A woman who works at a ladies' shop in town," I said. "How haven't you met? She's been here for a few years."

"I wasn't here very long before they pulled me to help with Wallace's gang."

I nodded. "In any case, I'll bring lunch back since I'll be in town."

"Bring it? Why don't you make it?" Oli teased.

"If I ever make you food, I'll spit in it."

I packed the empty dishes back into Mellie's basket.

Mellie wasn't pleased to see me. As I handed her the basket, I sighed.

"Look, Mellie, I know you don't like me because you like Wynn, so let me tell you something for your own good. He isn't interested in you. He isn't interested in me either. That's fine. Whatever. I have enough self-respect not to chase a man who doesn't want me. There are plenty of men out there. You're young, you're pretty, and you're an excellent cook. I'm sure someone will appreciate you." *Who are you trying to convince, Erin? How many times do I have to say it's fine before it is? Well, I'm not chasing him, so that part is true.*

Her already large eyes bulged, and her mouth hung open. When she closed it into a thin line, I couldn't tell whether she would cry or rage.

"That's just my advice. Take it, or leave it," I added.

"Thank you for sharing your unsolicited opinion. I will take it into consideration."

I felt bad for being so blunt. "I hope you find happiness, Mellie."

When I entered Madame Buvons's, Suzette looked up from the counter where she was doing something with ribbon. She smiled brightly at me.

"Bonjour, Erin."

"Hey, Suzette. Are you busy?"

"Non, you are my first customer, and Madame is out for the day."

"Great. I came to tell you about some developments."

"Oui? Tell me."

I leaned my elbows on the counter across from her. "I followed your advice."

She waited for me to continue.

"I chose the one who is already interested in me."

"And the other?"

"Just friends." I went on and told her about our trip to Edmonton, about meeting Sparrow, and about my point of no return on the threshold of my hotel room.

She squinted at me. "And you have truly let go?"

I squirmed under her knowing stare. "Well, I'm working on it. It'll be fine."

She nodded "I think you made the right decision."

"Me too. And no sooner had I returned, then the first guy came on strong. And let me tell you, it was like nothing I've ever felt before, not even with Matt. It's like he's slowly unraveling me, wanting me to bare my soul. It's unnerving. It's thrilling. I'm surprised at how much I want him to know me. He wants to see me, know me, touch me, and...I want to let him."

"You are no longer worried about what will happen when you return to Chicago then?"

I frowned. "I'm supposed to go back in about seven weeks. It already hurts to think about not seeing him anymore, but it's better than not getting closer to him at all before I go. I think I'd feel more regret if I left without knowing him at all."

"You make it sound like your love story is destined to end in heart-break. Have faith. You never know what will happen."

I nodded as though I believed her. *Those sentiments don't really apply to my situation.*

"Now, if only I could find a lover," Suzette bemoaned.

"There is a handsome young man who just arrived."

She leaned forward. "Who?"

"A Mountie: Subconstable Oliver Taylor."

"A Mountie. How romantique. And this young man, he is unmarried?"

"He said he was a bachelor."

She grinned. "I think I should welcome our new policeman to Farrloch, non?"

"I'm supposed to have lunch with them tomorrow. Would you like to join us?" *There's no need for her to know I'm staying with them.*

She smiled at the invitation. "Merci. I think I will."

I told Wynn and Oli about inviting Suzette over as we ate lunch. Wynn nodded his acknowledgment, while Oli seemed more interested.

"She said she wants to welcome our new Mountie to town."

"That's kind of her," Oli said.

"Yes, she's very sweet. I think you'll like her."

During their afternoon patrol, I cleaned the barracks and did laundry. This time I was careful not to clean the clothes I was wearing.

When they'd returned, Wynn went to fetch dinner.

"So, Little Sister, where did you and Wynn sneak off to last night?" Oli asked nonchalantly as he rolled a cigarette.

I froze. "What do you mean?"

He grinned. "Come on. You don't have to hide it from me. I know you went out to have a little tryst. I almost feel bad. It must've been easier when I wasn't here."

He must've woken up when I stubbed my toe. "I only went out last night to use the outhouse," I told him.

"Yeah, I thought so too at first. But then, Wynn snuck out after you. And you didn't come back for a while."

Fear pumped through my veins. *Wynn followed me outside? Did he see Mitica and me together?* "Well, I don't know where Wynn went, but traveling always makes my stomach upset. That's why I was gone for so long if you must know."

The tip of his cigarette glowed as he inhaled. "Whatever you say," he muttered into the exhaled cloud of smoke.

Over dinner, I tried to act normal, but I watched Wynn carefully. His calm demeanor gave nothing away. He didn't even seem to notice how I watched him, which I felt was unusual. He was normally quite perceptive, but perhaps I was just good at hiding my surveillance.

I was extra careful sneaking out of the barracks that night, and I'm positive I didn't wake the Mounties.

The temperature had dropped since the sun went down. All those promises of spring seemed to have been snatched away as I shivered by the lake.

When warm arms wrapped around me from behind, my heart leapt.

"You surprised me," I said, relieved by his warmth.

He didn't speak but nuzzled his nose between my hat and scarf. I shivered as he pressed his lips to my neck.

"You like that?" he whispered. "I can make you feel a lot better."

My heart jumped into my throat at the timbre of the voice in my ear. I squirmed from his embrace. "What the fuck, Grigore?" I yelled, wiping my neck.

His yellow eyes glowed in his human face. "I missed you."

"Where's Mitica?" I demanded.

"Oh, we do not need him. He would just get in the way." He took a step closer to me.

"Back up," I ordered, glaring at him.

"There is no need to fight. I promise I will take you to pleasure you did not know existed."

I averted my eyes when I started to feel his tug on my mind.

"You liked it when I held you, when I kissed you. I could tell."

My stomach dropped, and I balled up my fists. I didn't hold back when I punched him in the gut. He grunted and stumbled back a step.

"I said back up," I explained.

He chuckled and looked up at me with a grin. "I like that."

As I tensed for a real fight, Mitica appeared beside me. He said some words I didn't understand, and Grigore growled as he dropped to his knees.

Mitica turned to me, worry in his eyes. His hands hovered over the sides of my face as if trying to ensure I was unharmed, but he was careful not to touch me. "Are you all right? Did he harm you? What happened?"

I sighed in relief. "I'm fine. He surprised me. I thought he was you."

Mitica glared at Grigore. "She is not yours, Grigore."

"Are you sure? She seemed to like it well enough." Grigore smirked.

"You think so?" Mitica challenged. "What did he do to you?" he asked me.

I told him exactly what had happened. When I was finished, he sighed away his anger and held out his arms to me. "May I?"

I nodded.

He turned me to face Grigore and wrapped his arms around me from behind, just as Grigore had. But the feel of Mitica was so dissimilar, I was ashamed I hadn't known the difference. He didn't let me feel that way for long though. He gently loosened the scarf from my neck, exposing it to the cold night air.

He exhaled warm, humid breath on the naked, sensitive flesh of my neck. Expecting a kiss, I gasped with a shiver as he flicked it once with his tongue. I pressed my back against him, urging him to continue. His answering kiss was hot and insistent. I moaned as my eyelids fluttered closed. My entire body flushed with need as his mouth sucked gently on my neck.

As my knees gave way, he supported me by tightening his arms around my stomach. He kissed up my neck and pushed my hat up with his chilled nose.

"However it feels with anyone else, it will always be better with me," he whispered, hot in my ear.

He replaced my hat and scarf and held me as my revved need lulled into a dull ache.

Irritation buzzed in my veins at my having gotten all hot and bothered without release, but I guess that always happens at the beginning of relationships.

Grigore glared at Mitica with all the loathing a fire-breathing, shape-shifting dragon could muster. A jolt of fear ran through me, though it didn't last more than a second, still in the protection of Mitica's embrace.

Mitica grinned in triumph. "That is what she looks like when she is enjoying it, Grigore. Do not fool yourself into thinking she wants you, in case her striking you was not hint enough."

My face flushed at having had my intimate moment with Mitica watched, but I couldn't bring myself to be angry. I knew Mitica was trying to teach Grigore a lesson, and I had given him permission to touch me in Grigore's presence. I never wanted to forget what it had felt like for Mitica to touch me, and his caresses had erased all traces of Grigore from my body.

I sighed out a steadying breath. "Weren't we going to see Likinoak tonight?" I asked, changing the subject entirely.

Mitica frowned. "We were, da. But I do not think it is a good idea to ride Grigore right now. He is agitated, and it will take a lot of magic to handle him like this. I do not feel comfortable putting you at risk if something went wrong."

I nodded. "I understand. Thank you for thinking of me."

He smiled softly. "I am always thinking of you."

My heart thumped. *It's not fair that I seem to be the only one aroused.* "Hey, Mitica, I'd like to give you something."

He waved his hand. "That is not necessary."

"Please."

He paused. "Very well."

"First, can you send Grigore away?"

He tilted his head but said something to Grigore in another language. Grigore stomped off. When he was out of sight, I moved closer to Mitica.

"Can I kiss you, Mitica?" I asked, stepping into his personal space.

"Da."

He bent down, running the backs of his fingers along my cheeks as if memorizing every line of my face. I could tell from his pace that he was going to give me another fleeting kiss.

I grabbed the front of his coat and pulled him to me. His wide eyes softened and closed as I pressed my lips insistently to his. I wrapped my arms around his waist, and he urged me close with his hands on my face. I flicked his soft lower lip with my tongue, and my lips tingled as he moaned against my mouth. An electric shiver ran through me when the tip of his tongue met mine.

The need that had lulled from before returned with a vengeance. As I sagged against him, worrying my knees wouldn't hold me, he broke our kiss.

"Erin," he whispered, his breath hot on my mouth and his eyes like the blue center of a flame. He grinned down at me. "I feel as though you have marked me as your own."

I quivered at the implication and his thrill at the idea.

"We had better stop here for the night," he murmured.

I could see that I'd driven him to the edge, and I was at my limit as well. *Any further and it'll be painful for us both if we stop.* I nodded.

"Noapte buna, bucuria mea," he whispered before pecking me on the mouth.

"Goodnight. I'll see you tomorrow then?"

"Da."

I could feel his eyes on me while I walked back to the barracks.

As I lay in the dark cabin, I realized I'd forgotten to mention Wynn may have seen us together. *Wynn...* I rolled over on my side, ignoring the tightness in my chest. *I should bring that up tomorrow. Maybe we should find a new place to meet.*

SIXTEEN

I wasn't surprised by how well Oli and Suzette took to each other at lunch the next day. When they left to go for a walk, I smiled to myself and hummed cheerfully as I cleared our dishes from the table.

"You seem happy," Wynn commented. "Aren't you disappointed?"

I tilted my head at him. "Disappointed? Why would I be?"

"With the way you and Oliver have been since he arrived, I thought you might be interested in him."

"In Oli?" I laughed. "Not at all. He's easy to get along with. He reminds me of some friends I have back home. He's more like a brother." *In fact, it's quite refreshing to have someone who's so easy to be around. Oli reminds me that I haven't lost my mind despite Mitica and Wynn driving me to the edge.*

He nodded thoughtfully and was silent for a moment. "Still, you seem different since we got back from Strathcona."

I smiled softly. "That's probably true. I..." *I guess there's no harm in telling him, right? It might help me put all this behind us actually. Also, I may be able to gauge his reaction and see if he saw Mitica and me together.* "There is someone I'm interested in."

"Oh? Anyone I know?"

I shook my head. "Probably not. He's a Romanian immigrant."

He dipped his head to show he was listening but didn't give away his thoughts.

"And before you say anything, I'm sure he's safe. There's no way he's involved in whatever caused me to lose my memory. He's like you. He's honorable, and he helps people."

I watched his response carefully. If he had seen me with Mitica the other night, he gave no indication.

"And he...he makes you happy?" Wynn asked quietly as if hesitating to pry.

My heart squeezed, but I smiled and answered honestly. "Happy isn't a strong enough word. I can't say how much I'll miss him when I go home to Chicago." I paused. "But I'm going to miss you too, Wynn. You're a great friend. You're kind-hearted, and I wouldn't have survived without your help. I'll never forget you, and I'll treasure our memories together."

Wynn lowered his gaze and a slight blush of pink dusted his cheeks. "As will I," he murmured.

My face reddened at the adorable expression, and I had to look away.

When I met Mitica that evening, he smiled sweetly at me, a hint of adoration shining in his eyes.

My heart pounded. I hadn't seen that look in a man's eyes for a long time. To have someone like Mitica look at me that way, I wasn't sure my heart could take it.

He kissed each of my cheeks in greeting. "How are you tonight, bucuria mea?"

Perfect because I'm with you. I felt myself flush and scolded myself internally. "Good. And you?"

He smiled more broadly and ran the backs of his fingers over my cheek. "You are blushing. What are you thinking about?" he teased.

My face got even hotter, and I pressed my palms to my cheeks. "Jeez, you aren't supposed to point it out."

He gently pulled my hands away. "Please do not cover your face. I find the expression most becoming."

I lowered my head shyly. *It doesn't matter how old I get; a well-placed compliment always makes me blush. I wish I could see Mitica's cheeks dusted with embarrassment. I bet it's even more adorable than Wynn's. I wonder if there's anything I could say to get that reaction.* "So are we going to see Likinoak tonight?" I asked, changing the subject.

"Da, I believe Grigore has calmed down a bit."

"Good."

Grigore was his usual grumpy self, but he wasn't nearly as hostile as he'd been the night prior.

The cold wind didn't bother me as we flew over the treetops on Grigore's back. In fact, I found it rather refreshing. I was feeling overheated as Mitica's chest pressed against my back while I sat between his thighs.

When we knocked on Likinoak's door, a man with long, black hair and wide, dark eyes answered. He grinned at us.

"Welcome home, Ni'aze," he greeted Mitica.

I looked to Mitica for a translation.

"Older brother," Mitica murmured to me. "Thank you. I am glad to see you back as well," Mitica answered the man. "How were your travels?"

The Wyboka shook his head. "I bear sad news. But before we discuss it, will you introduce me to your ohkwii?"

The man's dark eyes found mine, and he smiled.

Mitica responded to him in another language, and the Wyboka's eyes danced with laughter.

"Erin, this is my brother, Chuthekii. Wic'aze, Little Brother, this is Erin Nichols."

I stuck out my hand, and Chuthekii clasped it warmly. "You have finally come," he said happily.

I tilted my head. "What do you mean 'finally'?"

Mitica chided him in a language I didn't understand.

Chuthekii smiled slyly at him, unphased. The expression clearly said, "that's what you think."

"Yes," Chuthekii answered. "My mother told me about you."

I nodded but squinted at him, knowing I'd missed something.

"Please, come inside. It is cold." Chuthekii opened the door to let us in.

He ladled hot stew into small bowls and handed them to us. We all sat around the fire.

"What sad news do you bring, Wic'aze?" Mitica asked.

"When I returned the children to the school, the headmaster informed me that another Wyboka had succumbed to consumption."

Mitica sighed heavily. "Did they let you bring the child home?"

Chuthekii shook his head. "They gave him a Christian burial on the grounds before I arrived."

"How old was the boy?"

"Six."

"His parents?"

"Amâwe is with them now, burning what few belongings he'd left behind."

"Amâwe is Mother," Mitica translated for me.

"How sad," I sympathized. "Does this happen often? Is it common for children to die at school?"

Chuthekii nodded. "Yes, it happens quite often, Azeohkwii."

I looked to Mitica for another translation, but he just pursed his lips at Chuthekii. I frowned. "Is there anything we can do?"

"We do what we can," Chuthekii responded.

I nodded solemnly.

"We came to update Amâwe on what Erin discovered. She will likely not return for a while. How much did she tell you of Erin's situation?" Mitica asked.

"She told me some. Hawk showed me more." His smile implied that Hawk had shown him much more.

"What did Hawk show you?" I couldn't stop myself from asking.

"That if my brother's hair was as long as mine, you would have braided it."

"What?"

Mitica harrumphed, telling Chuthekii not to clarify.

I squinted at Mitica. *Really?* "Whatever." I sighed. "If Likinoak already told you everything, then I'll tell you what I found. You can relay the message to her."

Chuthekii nodded.

I told him about the full solar eclipse in Gemini at the end of May.

"The most assured way to send you back is to use the same magic that brought you here," he observed meaningfully. "However, if that is not possible, which I would say is the case, we can find another way. I will ask Raven. Perhaps she has a song to send you back when the time comes."

I nodded, not quite sure what he'd meant. Still, it seemed clear he would look for a solution. "Thank you."

"There is no need to thank me, Azeohkwii. I am happy to help if this is truly what you and Ni'aze want."

I frowned at his word choice. *Is this truly what I want? I mean, it's not really about what I want. It's more about what needs to happen. I don't fit in here. I need to go home to my mom and friends. I need to go back and be unemployed in a city with no magic.*

I looked over at Mitica. I'm sure his dejected expression mirrored mine.

The ride back to the barracks was cold and quiet. The thought that I wouldn't be able to feel the warmth of Mitica's arms around me once I'd returned to 2016 swirled in my mind like the clouds Grigore's wings blew away.

Mitica's hands lingered on my hips after he'd helped me dismount the dragon. The contemplative sadness in his eyes reflected my own.

"Can I see you again tomorrow?" I asked, wanting to take advantage of every possible chance to see him.

"Da," he murmured, smiling softly.

I nodded and started to pull away, but he tightened his grip.

I met his gaze again and moved closer to him. I wrapped my arms around him, resting my cheek over his heart.

He embraced me gently as if holding something precious and breakable.

"Hold me tighter," I whispered. "I want there to be no doubt that you were real."

He crushed me to him, the air in my lungs squeezing out in a satisfactory sigh.

I tried to memorize everything about this moment. My soft form yielded to his hard body as we pressed together with one of his arms around my waist and his other hand clutching the base of my neck. His arms encased me in his warm embrace. I breathed deep his scent of campfire and pine—a woodsy smell, smoky and fresh, warm and cool.

An ache in my chest told me that we still weren't close enough. *Slowly. Savor the sweet agony. Remember this feeling later.*

"You won't forget me. Will you, Mitica?" I murmured self-consciously.

He loosened his hold on me and cupped my face in his hands. His blue eyes demanded my attention.

"Never," he declared seriously. "I would forget my own name before I forgot yours. I have known what it is to be kissed by the sun. The moonlight will never be enough again."

My heart wrenched at the sweetness of his words. "Me too," I responded, hushed. "Living in the daylight will be too harsh now that I've known the magic that is you in the gentle moonlight."

He stroked my cheeks with his thumbs and smiled as his eyes shined with unshed tears, the bittersweet expression heartbreaking.

"How appropriate, right?" I said bitterly, remembering a poem I'd once read.

"The sun and the moon, eternally separated by time and space.
One of the seasons, the other of the seas, time defined by their pace.
A boundless sky of clouds or stars, a garden where they dance.
Never be they together, but for a passing glance.
Destiny and fate are cruel to lovers, as often is the case."

Mitica still caressed my face. "Our time may be short, bucuria mea. But it will be memorable."

I nodded. "Yeah, let's make memories."

He smiled down at me and kissed me sweetly on the mouth. Then he kissed my cheeks, nose, and forehead as had become our nightly farewell.

SEVENTEEN

Since the Mounties had to patrol, I offered to return the breakfast basket to Mellie's. It was a brisk morning, but I found it refreshing.

"You're going to want your scarf," Oli commented as I opened the door to step outside.

Touched by his concern, I smiled at him. "It's not that cold though."

He smirked. "That's not why you'll want it."

"What are you getting at, Oli?" I looked to Wynn for clarification, but he pursed his lips slightly, seemingly peeved.

"Why don't you take a look in the mirror?" Oli suggested, nodding his head in that direction.

I walked over to the mirror and examined my face. There didn't seem to be anything wrong with it. Then, I tilted my chin up to look at my neck, giving a small cry. Halfway down my neck was a light red hickey.

"For fuck's sake," I cursed, grateful I'd worn my scarf the day before. I watched as my reflection's cheeks flushed at the thought of Mitica's mouth on my neck.

"Told you." Oli grinned.

He held out the scarf to me, and I wrapped it around my neck. I checked my reflection, and I couldn't see it anymore. Then, I turned to the Mounties.

"Better?" I asked them to be sure.

Oli nodded, chuckling, but Wynn approached me.

He frowned and reached up. His broad back blocking Oli from view, he pulled down the scarf. He ran his thumb over Mitica's mark, and I quivered as he caressed the sensitive skin.

Holding my breath, I searched his eyes. A fierceness I hadn't expected burned in his blue gaze. *Don't. Don't look at me like that.*

Another tense moment and he replaced my scarf, covering Mitica's love bite.

My head spun, dazed by Wynn's reaction, and a little knot of guilt toward Mitica formed in my gut because of my body's response to Wynn's touch. I vowed to be more careful around Wynn lest my body betray me.

That night, Mitica was unapologetic when we met by the lake.

"You caused me some trouble today," I told him.

"Did I?"

"I thought I would die of embarrassment when Oli and Wynn saw the hickey you gave me the other night."

He grinned, his eyes sparkling with mischief, and I fought a smile.

"Don't look so pleased with yourself," I harrumphed, not truly upset.

He stepped closer to me and wrapped his arms around my waist. "But I am pleased," he whispered.

"Because other men saw the mark you left on me?"

He nodded, still grinning.

I pursed my lips. "I feel like there's something inherently sexist about this situation like you're marking your territory."

He tilted his head at my statement. "Would it make you feel better if you left a mark on me?"

I looked up into his gorgeous face, and my eyes traced the column of his neck to the collar of his buttoned shirt. I felt my cheeks warm. *Mitica would let me claim him? He sees himself as belonging to me?*

His eyes twinkled in amusement. "I see the thought arouses you."

My ears grew hot, and I averted my gaze.

He bent down to whisper in my ear. "You want me to be yours, da?"

I shivered and nodded slightly.

I could feel the smile on his lips as he kissed my cheek.

Taking the encouragement, I laced my fingers with his and slowly led him to a large rock nearby. I nudged him, pressing my palms gently into the unyielding muscles of his chest. He followed my unspoken direction and sat. My fingers trembled only slightly as I brushed the crimson hair from his face. His blue eyes burned, following my every move.

I boldly climbed onto his lap and straddled his hips. His sturdy hands grasped my waist to keep me steady.

My hair fell into my eyes when he gently removed my hat. His torso expanded between my thighs as he breathed heavily below me, and his fingertips left trails of heat as he stroked my face and neck.

I dropped a tentative kiss to his lips and then another, slowly building our desires. His eyes never left mine, though they soon clouded with desire. He didn't press the issue. He was patient, and I was determined to make him wait.

Our kisses grew more heated, more insistent, and I pulled back. His curious eyes watched me as I caressed his face the way he always did to me. He smiled blissfully when I kissed his cheeks.

I trailed my lips along his jaw to his ear. "Why did you mark me, Mitica?" I whispered. "Who did you want to see it?"

He shivered beneath me. "I did not mean to at first," he admitted in a husky voice.

"No?" I murmured. "Then, why were you so pleased?"

"Once it was there, I wanted them to see that you had chosen me."

"Who?"

"Grigore, the Mounties, anyone who saw you."

I pulled back and searched his eyes. "You want to be claimed by me, Mitica?" The idea that he saw the mark he'd left on me as a signal to other men that I'd chosen someone else, that I'd allowed a man to touch me, that I'd given myself to him rather than having been taken, was a different approach than I was used to. I wanted to give him the same choice before I went any further.

"Whether you claim me or not, I am already yours," he said simply.

Something about his words in this situation seemed particularly intense. The certainty with which he stated he belonged to me gave me pause. I stared back into his trusting gaze and grasped at how to respond.

I like Mitica. I don't think I've met a man I like more. He's everything I've ever wanted in a lover. But that's the problem. Isn't it? If all he was asking for was sex, I'd accept him right now. But to claim him, to truly choose him as he wants, I need to make such a decision carefully. Misleading him will be worse than stopping it here.

I was comfortable giving myself to him, having him claim me, but not yet ready to take the responsibility of claiming him. The irony of the situation wasn't lost on me, though that didn't exempt me from having to make a tough decision.

"Mitica," I started, stroking his face. "I know we don't have a lot of time together, but I think we should slow down. I don't think we know each other well enough to belong to one another yet. Look, if it was only a physical thing, then I would have no problem. If you just wanted to spend the next seven weeks having fun, I wouldn't hesitate. But I get the idea you're asking for more, and I want to respect that request by taking it seriously."

My skin prickled with nerves as I awaited his reaction.

He closed his eyes and heaved a deep sigh. When he met my gaze again, he smiled softly, but he could not hide the hint of sorrow in his eyes. "I understand. Thank you for thinking of me."

I squinted at his response. "You're not angry?"

He tilted his head. "Angry? Nu, I am sad I put you in this position. I am sorry I gave you distress, bucuria mea."

My mouth fell open in what I'm sure was a ridiculous and unattractive expression. I pouted and my eyes burned. "Jeez, Mitica. Could you even be more perfect?"

He frowned at my assessment but didn't respond.

I kissed him on the tip of his nose. "Hey, don't be so serious," I said cheerfully, trying to break the tension.

My attempt to cheer him up seemed to make the situation worse. He squinted in a mournful expression. I wrapped my arms around the back of his neck and pulled his head gently to my chest. He gingerly held me back.

"Don't be sad. All right? I'm not upset with you for being honest about your feelings. It makes me so so happy that you feel that way about me. You make me feel things I've never felt before. That's why I'd like to be completely certain when I give you an answer. You're wonderful, Mitica. No matter what happens, you'll always have a special place in my heart."

He squeezed me tighter without a word. I closed my eyes and pressed a kiss into his soft hair.

We sat like that for a while, taking comfort in each other's arms. I stroked his hair as I sat in his lap by the lake. Knowing how miserable I'd be if his feelings for me weren't the same level as mine were for him, I let him decide when he was ready to break our embrace.

After I'd climbed out of his lap, Mitica looked down at me with that look of adoration. "I do not deserve you," he said. "You are far too good for me."

I smiled up at him. "Funny. I was going to say the same thing."

EIGHTEEN

After only a few days of us all together, my time with Oli and Wynn started to feel like a routine. We took care of the horses and ate together. They would go on patrol. And in the evenings, Wynn would read *Dracula* while Oli went for a stroll with Suzette.

Oli was rambunctious, and Wynn was reserved. It made me a little sad to see Wynn retreat back into his shell after we'd made such progress together. When we were alone, he'd soften a bit, but he was always serious when Oli was around. It only emphasized their contrasting personalities.

Two nights after telling Mitica we should slow down, we sat cuddling by a fire near the lake. I was wrapped in his arms as I sat between his legs, leaning my back against his chest.

"You must've seen some amazing things in your life," I commented, staring into the fire.

"I find the details of your life far more interesting."

"Oh, come on. My life is way more boring than yours. What do you say? Will you share another memory with me? I'll share one with you."

I could feel him smile against my cheek. "Very well," he agreed. "I will show you something few humans have seen and lived to speak of."

"Whoa, talk about a lead-in."

He chuckled. After a short pause, Mitica began to sing quietly as if worried someone else might overhear. As he sang, my view of the fire blurred. When the world came back into focus, we sat in the grass on the corner of a forest crossroads.

The paths were speckled with moonlight, which filtered through the thick trees.

At the center of the crossroads, a group of naked women holding candles danced facing each other in a circle. Their long hair barely covered their breasts as they executed the steps in perfect unison. The flames of their candles flickered as they danced, leaving trails of light. The fire shined through their incorporeal forms, adding to the beauty.

"Wow," I whispered as though afraid they would hear me. "It's so enchanting. What are they?"

"They are iele," he answered, arms still around me.

"Like your mother?"

He nodded.

As we watched the voluptuous women dance naked in the night, I said, "I guess I can understand why they don't want people watching them."

"Da, they have bad tempers, too. If anyone is unlucky enough to get caught observing their dance, he will surely be cursed with madness."

"You were allowed to watch because you're half iele?"

He nodded.

"But you didn't get to dance with them?"

His quiet response came after an uncomfortably long pause. "Nu."

The sense that I'd struck a nerve made my heart sink. *But I bet Mitica is a wonderful dancer.* "Would you like to see my memory now?" I asked though I was reluctant to leave the crossroads.

"Da."

"Okay. I just picture it in my mind, right?"

He nodded.

I closed my eyes and imagined the scene I'd witnessed countless times. When I felt Mitica knock on my mind, I let him in.

Opening my eyes, I held my breath at how real the illusion felt. The breeze of Lake Michigan caressed my skin and carried its unique lake-water scent. Seagulls called overhead as they soared in the golden glow of dawn. The sand was cold beneath the seat of my jeans and my bare feet, having yet to be warmed by the day's sunlight.

I let out a contented sigh. When Mitica didn't say anything, I looked over my shoulder at him. His blue eyes shined in wonder, and he smiled unhindered.

I grinned, glad he was happy with what I was showing him. "When I was in college, I used to come down here before class to watch the sunrise and get some fresh air. There's a bakery a few blocks away that makes the best chocolate croissants."

"This is something you would see often?"

I nodded. "Almost every day. It was a great way to slow down and de-stress. Everything about this place calms me: the waves, the sand, the smell, even the seagulls. I don't know why everyone hates seagulls. They're my favorite birds. Something about their call just...reminds me of home I guess."

"It seems like a very nice place to call home."

"Well, this is pretty much as chill as it gets here. It's not nearly as enchanting as your home, but I like it."

He shook his head. "You are far more enchanting than any magic I have ever encountered."

My cheeks heated, and I looked up at the horizon. I didn't know how to respond to that. Normally, if a guy said something like that to me, I'd just have a snarky remark and play it off. But it was difficult to know what to say when I knew he was sincere. "Thank you," I muttered, my usual wit falling flat, as it always seemed to when Mitica was around.

I couldn't see Mitica's face, but I felt his cheek smile against mine.

"If we'd met in 2016, we could've come down here together," I commented. "Do you think you're alive in 2016?"

"It is possible I will be reborn and living at that time."

"You would be reborn as a human?"

"Most likely."

"So you'd only have magic if you lived in a place with wilderness?"

"Da, assuming I even know I am part fae."

"What do you mean?"

"If I grew up in a city like you and I never discovered my true name, I may not know I have magic."

"Oh, right." I paused. *It wouldn't matter anyway. I could already be dead in 2016.* "We could've met and not even known it if you're a city kid like me."

"Perhaps."

I met his eyes over my shoulder. *Would I have recognized you if I've met you before? How different would you be? You'd certainly look different. How much of your personality would be the same? I always thought personality was just biology and socialization. What about your soul makes it Mitica?*

I don't know how, call it reporter's intuition, but I felt I would know Mitica if I met him again in 2016. I didn't know if we'd met before. But after making a connection with him in 1900, I knew I'd recognize him if we met again.

The illusion crumbled around us as I lost interest in the landscape and concentrated on Mitica. The summer breeze off Lake Michigan was replaced by the winter chill of the frozen mountain lake in Farrloch.

I shivered, and Mitica held me closer. Snuggling deeper into his embrace, I looked up at the nearly full moon. A contentment I couldn't remember ever feeling settled into me. I closed my eyes, enjoying Mitica's warmth and the crackling sound of the fire.

NINETEEN

J awoke the next morning and couldn't remember how I'd gotten into Wynn's bed. I recalled cuddling with Mitica, but I didn't remember saying goodnight and returning to the barracks. *Did Mitica magic me back inside, or was I just so tired that I forgot?*

"You're finally awake," Wynn said, coming into the barracks. "We already ate breakfast and cared for the horses, but we left some food for you."

As he spoke, he crossed the room to where I still lay in bed. He sat by my feet. "Are you unwell?"

"I'm fine," I assured him, sitting up.

He analyzed my face. "I was worried. I think you were walking in your sleep last night."

"What do you mean?"

"Sometime in the middle of the night, you must have gotten up. When you were going back to bed, you tripped over me on the floor."

"Oh jeez, Wynn. I'm sorry. I didn't hurt you. Did I?"

"No, did you get hurt when you fell? I couldn't tell at the time, but I helped you to bed to be certain."

"I'm all right. Thanks for looking after me." *I guess I must've walked in on my own after all.*

He smiled gently. I was happy to see how easy it had become for him to smile in front of me, and I felt my cheeks warm.

Just then, Oli entered, and Wynn jumped to his feet. I crinkled my eyebrows at his haste, but a glance at Oli explained his reaction. He grinned with a knowing look that said, "I know what you two were up to."

I sighed and rolled my eyes, but I knew I was blushing even harder. "I'm sorry if I woke you when I tripped over Wynn last night, Oli. I must've been half asleep when I went to the outhouse."

He frowned and raised an eyebrow at me. "I didn't hear anything."

"Oh. Well, good then."

"We won't be back until after supper," Wynn said, putting on his hat. "A tree fell on a barn a few nights ago, so Oliver and I are going to be gone most of the day helping to fix it."

"Oh, if that's the case, let me come help, too. If you saddle Langundo for me, I can be ready in five minutes."

"Are you certain?" Wynn asked. "You haven't even eaten, and you slept late. Perhaps you need more rest."

"No worries. I can eat some bread in the saddle. I told you I'm fine," I reassured, stuffing my feet into Oli's moccasins.

Wynn frowned, and Oli slapped him on the shoulder. "Come on. She said she's fine."

Wynn nodded once and went outside to saddle Langundo. I rushed to get ready and grabbed some bread from Mellie's basket. I held it in my mouth as I pulled on Oli's coat and ran outside.

Once we were on our way and I'd eaten my breakfast, I asked Wynn whose barn needed repairs.

"The Capreanu's," he answered.

"Will you be able to fix a barn in a day, or will you have to come back tomorrow?"

"The Romanians seem to have a pretty close-knit community. I'm sure some of their neighbors will come to help. I don't see why we wouldn't be able to finish today with everyone working together."

My heart thumped. "The Romanians?" I demanded, louder than I'd intended. Langundo's ears twitched, and I bit my lip.

Wynn looked over his shoulder at me and met my eyes. I'm sure he was thinking about how I'd told him the man I was interested in was a

Romanian immigrant. *Will Mitica be there? I mean, he's got to have a life when he's not with me, right? Maybe he sleeps during the day though and helps the fae at night.*

"Are you one of those who has something against the Sifton immigrants?" Oli asked.

"Of course not." I didn't know what that even was, but I knew I wasn't against immigration.

"I have to admit they have some pretty strange ways, but they don't seem any harm," Oli mused.

I just nodded to him, lost in my own thoughts.

When we arrived at the Capreanu farm, a group of hearty men was already at work cleaning away the broken pieces of wood. I scanned the group for Mitica's crimson head, but all I saw was brown or black.

As we dismounted, two of the men approached us. The older man smiled and shook Wynn's hand in greeting. "Constable Delaforet, thank you for coming to help with our barn."

"Mr. Capreanu, this is Subconstable Taylor and Erin Nichols."

The older man dipped his head with a smile. "And this is my son, Ion."

Ion, a man in his early twenties, greeted the Mounties then smiled at me in appreciation. My eyes widened when he checked me out so blatantly. I had to admit he was attractive, lean and strong from farm work, but he didn't really compare to Mitica or Wynn. He didn't even attempt to hide his interest in me, and his father chuckled.

"My wife and daughter are in the house cooking for everyone. Ion, show her the way."

"I'd rather help out here if that's all right," I countered. "I'm not good in the kitchen."

Mr. Capreanu's eyebrows rose at my suggestion.

Wynn stepped close to me and whispered softly. "Erin, I know you're more than capable to help us if you say you are, but your presence is going to make them uncomfortable. They aren't used to women like you."

I pursed my lips, swallowing the retort that they better *get* used to women like me.

Ion watched our interaction with interest, no doubt wondering what the nature of our relationship was.

I heaved a heavy sigh. "Fine. I'll go off to the kitchen with the rest of the women."

Wynn placed his hand on my shoulder. "Thank you."

I gave him a resigned look and nodded at Ion. "All right. Where should I go?"

Ion smiled charmingly. "This way."

As I followed Ion toward the small farmhouse, I looked back at Wynn and Oli, who were removing their hats and jackets to get to work.

"I have never seen you before, Miss Nichols. Did you just arrive?" Ion asked, demanding my attention.

"Yeah, I haven't been here very long, and you can call me Erin."

He grinned. "How do you know Constable Delaforet, Erin?"

Wow, jumping right in, eh? "Wynn and I are friends. He helped me out of a bit of trouble."

He nodded, clearly pleased by my answer. Lucky for me, we'd reached the house. He led me to the kitchen where an older woman and a teenage girl were doing kitcheny stuff.

They looked up as we entered. The older woman said something to Ion in a language I assumed was Romanian.

"This is Erin Nichols, Mamă. Erin, this is my Mamă and my sister, Mariana. Tată sent Erin to help you."

Mrs. Capreanu nodded and waved her son away. Before he left, he turned to me. "Please let me know if there is anything I can do for you, Erin," he said earnestly.

"Uh, thanks, Ion. I will."

He gave me another charming smile and strode from the room. I turned to the two women, feeling incredibly out of place. Mrs. Capreanu said something in Romanian to Mariana, who nodded and approached me.

"Mamă said you can help me," Mariana told me, smiling kindly.

"Okay, but I have to warn you: I'm really awful in the kitchen."

Her dark eyes sparkled in amusement. "That is all right. We are going to wash and chop vegetables."

"I guess I should be able to handle that."

As Mrs. Capreanu did something with dough and a rolling pin, Mariana and I stood at a table and washed vegetables in a metal tub.

"I think my brother likes you," Mariana confessed like it was some huge secret.

"You think so?"

She nodded. "I am glad. He has not been very happy since we moved here, and you are quite pretty."

"Thank you, Mariana. You're also very pretty."

"Are you married?" she asked me. "You are not wearing a ring."

"No, I'm not married. But I am kind of seeing someone. In fact, I was hoping to see him here today. He's also Romanian."

She pursed her lips. "Is it Alexandru?"

I raised my eyebrows at her dejection. "No, it's not Alexandru."

She immediately perked up, and I couldn't hold in my chuckle.

"Who is it then?"

"You would definitely know him if you saw him. He has dark red hair and blue eyes."

She gasped and dropped the potato she was washing into the water with a splash. Mrs. Capreanu looked up at her reaction. Mariana waved her hand, telling her mother she was fine. The older woman went back to work.

Mariana shifted her eyes as if to see if anyone else was near and dropped her voice. "You speak of the hultan?"

Whoa, she knows about magic? I nodded. "You know him?"

"I have heard the others speak of him, but I have never seen him."

Oh, I guess not then. "I was hoping to find out what he gets up to during the day."

Her eyes were wide with awe. "You have seen the hultan? You met with him?"

"Yeah, I said we were sort of involved."

Her brow furrowed. "But how?" She paused. "Hultan must be celibate, or they will lose their magic."

"What? Really?"

She nodded slowly. "That is how it is in all the stories."

Are you effing kidding me? What the Hell is Mitica thinking? Why would he get so involved with me if he knows he will lose his magic if things progress? When I realized I was squeezing a carrot, I took a deep breath.

Calm down. I'm sure there's an explanation. I'll just ask him when I see him tonight.

I shrugged at Mariana. "I mean, it's not like our relationship has gotten that far."

She nodded her understanding. "I would be careful if I were you."

"What do you mean?"

"Hultan are powerful, and they can help people. But they also have dark magic. It is best not to anger them."

Jeez, so dramatic. I mean, sure. I guess Mitica could use his magic to hurt someone, but I can't see him doing that. He's all about helping people.

I acknowledged her warning and attributed her fear to the fact that she didn't know him.

I would call my first attempt at cooking in 1900 a success. Okay, so my vegetables were cut all uneven and chunky compared to Mariana's but whatever. They were just vegetables.

When the time for supper came around, the barn had been fixed. The men had worked hard and deserved the hearty meal we served them.

When I handed Oli his bowl, he stared at it suspiciously. "You didn't *really* spit in this. Did you, Erin?"

I just grinned at him and gave a bowl to Wynn before sitting between them.

Ion lost no time chatting me up. He sat across from me as soon as he got his food. He was a decent guy, so I saw no reason to snub him. I was polite but careful not to be overly friendly.

At some point, I glanced over at Wynn. He seemed to be eating very deliberately as if his food was going to bite him back. It occurred to me that perhaps Wynn thought Ion was the Romanian man I was interested in.

When they were finished, I took their empty bowls. As I got up to go to the kitchen, I saw Mariana whisper something in her brother's ear. I can only guess what she'd said to him, but he was markedly less forward when I returned to my seat.

I don't know what was so amusing, but Wynn's lips held the shadow of a smile.

Everyone was on friendly terms when we said our goodbyes, and we were told we were always welcome.

TWENTY

I managed to maintain my chilly demeanor when Mitica greeted me with a cheerful smile that night. His grin slipped, and he met my accusing squint with grave dignity.

"Have you forgotten to tell me something important?" I demanded.

He waited silently to see if I'd continue. When I just stared back, he asked, "Such as?"

I clicked my tongue. "Come on, Mitica. I don't like being lied to. A lie by omission is still a lie."

He took a deep breath. "If I have not told you, it was to protect you or others."

"What about protecting yourself a little?" I said, my worry breaking the irritable defensiveness. "Is it really true you have to stay celibate or you'll lose your magic? Why wouldn't you disclose that? I would've been a lot more careful around you."

He let out a long breath. "That is not true," he told me.

My eyes widened. *For fuck's sake, Erin. This is what happens when you jump to conclusions. You call yourself a journalist? You know better.*

I hung my head in shame. "Excuse me while I go kill myself now." I turned to go back to the barracks and hide under the covers of Wynn's bed.

"It is not true for me, but it is true for other hultan," he clarified.

I stopped my retreat.

"Because I am half iele, I do not have to stay celibate to keep my magic."

"Oh. Well, that's...good then."

He gently placed his hands on my hips as he stood behind me.

"You were quite distressed by the thought," he pointed out quietly.

"Of course I was. I didn't want to make things hard for you."

He slowly embraced me, wrapping his arms around my stomach. "I am sorry you were upset," he murmured.

"God, Mitica. I should be the one to apologize. I even accused you of lying. *I'm* sorry." *It's not like I have any room to talk either. I mean, I've been lying to Wynn this whole time.*

He paused for a little longer than I'd expected, and I started to squirm to try to look back at him. He tightened his embrace and buried his face in my scarf.

"Everyone has secrets—things they need to keep to themselves," he muttered.

A shiver raised the hair on my neck. "Yeah..." Mariana's warning about Mitica's dark magic gnawed at my mind. I could feel the curiosity bubbling up, and I knew I wouldn't be able to resist. "You said we were supposed to be getting to know each other. Right?"

He didn't respond.

I bit my lip. *Given his comments about secrets and keeping them to protect me, it's obvious there are things he isn't telling me. Establishing trust is a two-way street. Give a little to get a little. At the very least, maybe I can figure it out in a round-about way.*

"Mitica, if I show you my most cherished memory, will you share the memory that's most important to you?"

He was quiet as he wrestled with his desire to know me and keep whatever he was hiding.

"Da," he finally agreed. "Show me what you cherish most."

"Okay," I said and took a steadying breath. "Ready when you are."

I closed my eyes and imagined the memory I held closest to my heart. I'd seen it so many times that it was like watching a film rather than reliving it. It was just like any other Saturday in spring.

Mitica sang his spell softly into my ear, and he didn't even have to knock on the door to my mind. It was already ajar for him.

I opened my eyes to the all-too-familiar scene. A girl in a Cubs jersey stood behind a chain-link fence. Her Converse were planted shoulder-width apart as she stared down the barrel of a pitching machine in a borrowed batter's helmet.

A man in a baseball practice shirt leaned into the fence behind her, his fingers curled around the metal links. His blue Cubs hat hid his features, but I knew he had neat brown hair and gentle brown eyes.

"Keep your elbow up," he encouraged the girl as she missed another pitch.

Mitica and I watched them. Distant, apart, as if we didn't belong to their rose-tinted afternoon.

"That's my dad," I said finally. "He was a Chicago police officer. He loved baseball, the Cubs in particular. He taught me everything he knew about the game. He uh...he was killed shortly after this day. It's the last time I ever picked up a bat. After a while, I started to watch baseball and go to games and stuff, but I never played again. I don't know. It sort of felt like playing catch by myself. But this...this memory of when we were together and happy, it reminds me of how precious innocence is. I can't say I haven't been happy since my dad died, but I haven't been as carefree. Maybe one day... I can't get my innocence back, but I hope to be free again."

I figured Mitica would have tons of questions about how my dad died or at least about how different the modern world looked. Instead, he watched silently as younger me finally hit the ball. The ting of the ball off my bat was drowned out by my dad's satisfied cheers.

"Freedom," Mitica murmured. "A full heart has wings."

"Yeah. Maybe."

The scene shifted back to Farrloch.

"Aren't you going to show me?" I asked Mitica. As I turned to look at him, he let me loose.

Nodding seriously, he said, "I will, but I must explain first."

He was hushed for a moment, staring up at the nearly full moon. He faced me with a sigh. "There is much in this world that is hidden, dark places where even the brave dare not go. They say one should not know his own fate, but I... Ever since the tale was told to me, I knew I must go.

"Deep in the Carpathian Mountains, there is a cave. It is dark and dangerous but houses a special treasure: The Obsidian Mirror. The legend says if you go before the mirror on the night of the dead, you will see your fate. A night where the dead return to the realm of the living and creatures far more wicked than the Čanotila prowl the forests for anyone not safely huddled by the warm hearth. Even magic is no match for what some of these beings can do.

"Still, I went. I left the candles flickering in the cemeteries and traveled through the cold mist to the cave. It took me years to discover its exact location, but I found it."

"And the mirror?" I whispered.

He nodded. "That is what I am going to show you: my most important memory."

My heartbeat was loud in my ears, my breath heavy, and my fingers trembled as I reached my hand out to him. "Show me."

He took my hand and began his song. When the world came back into focus, we stood before a smooth wall of black obsidian. A torch, which Mitica held in his other hand, illuminated his dark reflection.

His frosted breath fogged the mirror as he leaned closer to it. "Are you ready to see what The Obsidian Mirror showed me?"

I nodded, not sure I could answer around the lump in my throat.

He turned back to the mirror, and the scene shifted into the memory of what the mirror had shown him.

On the bare forest floor, where sunlight never reaches to nurture plants, Mitica sat leaning against a thick tree trunk.

His weary face looked up into the dark canopy. No moon or stars could be seen through the thick foliage of the towering treetops. Still, they must have been out because their light reflected off the mist that hung in dips and hollows, illuminating the forest with an eerie glow.

From one of the hollows came a steady humming buzz.

Mirror Mitica slowly turned his head toward the sound with an expression that said he wasn't truly interested. But his eyes widened when a small chirping bird flew from the fog.

I squinted at the creature, which darted from place to place in its excitement. "Oh, a hummingbird," I said to the Mitica who held my hand.

"Da, I did not know what it was when I was shown this vision, but I have learned since coming to Canada."

"I guess there aren't hummingbirds in Romania."

He shook his head.

The hummingbird chattered happily at mirror Mitica, flitting around him.

His once tired eyes glinted in fascination as he continued to watch the little bird. His fascination turned to amusement. Soon, he smiled joyfully at the creature.

When the hummingbird flew up toward the treetops, mirror Mitica rose to follow it. As he climbed to stay with the bird, we watched him scramble not to lose it. Up the tree he went, hopping from branch to branch, the bird never far ahead.

Finally, he broke through the barrier of leaves and gasped at the open sky. He reached his hand out toward the bird, and it landed delicately on his finger with a satisfied cheep.

In the east, the amber dawn painted the sky with morning. Mitica laughed at the scene, reveling in the rosy glow.

But as the sun broke the horizon, the hummingbird flew away.

"Wait!" he called to the creature with longing.

My chest swelled, and my heart broke at the sound of his pleas.

The bird got farther away, and Mitica looked at the ground far below, his eyes flickering with desperation.

Shutting his eyes, he took a deep breath. As he released it slowly, he gazed toward the direction the hummingbird had gone.

He spread his arms wide as if he would fly, and he leaned forward. I cried out as he began to fall.

Mitica clutched my hand, reminding me he was still beside me.

As mirror Mitica's feet left the tree, he transformed into a bird and flew away toward the hummingbird.

"A nightingale," Mitica informed me.

When we'd returned to the moonlit lake shore in Farrloch, I took a steadying breath, my hand on my chest.

"That was your most important memory?"

He nodded.

"Do you know what it means?"

"In part. The trouble with fortune-telling is you never seem to know what it means until after it happens"

Well, that did little to give me insight into Mitica's secrets. I met his eyes. But it must be significant to him in some way or it wouldn't be so important to him. I should think on it more carefully.

"Thank you for sharing your most important memory with me, Mitica. I don't quite know what it means, but I appreciate you opening up to me."

He brushed my cheek with his thumb. "And you, bucuria mea. Knowing what you have lost and how you still share your light with others, you are even more brave and glorious than I had thought."

My face flushed at his compliment. "Mitica, I..." *I want to know more about you. I want to know everything about you. Will you let me?* "Thank you, Mitica," I whispered, unable to give voice to my true desires.

He seemed to pick up on my hesitation. "It is late. You must rest. May I see you tomorrow, bucuria mea?"

"Of course."

Before he could kiss my cheeks and say goodnight, I wrapped my arms around him and buried my face in his chest.

He must've been surprised because it took him a second to return my embrace. I breathed in his woodsy scent and floated in the timeless moment.

Just for that moment, I allowed myself to let go. With so much uncertainty in my life and so many unanswered questions, I took a chance to indulge myself. And for the length of a single embrace, the needs I never allowed myself to acknowledge were met. I was safe. I was protected. There was nothing to fear in Mitica's arms. He was there with me. I could feel him, hear him, touch him. He was solid and real, and no one could take that away from me. As long as he was with me, I didn't have to be brave or strong. I could allow myself to feel whatever I felt without worrying about whether it would harm my determination to go on.

My thoughts quieted, and it didn't matter what secrets Mitica could possibly be keeping. All that mattered were his arms around me and his breath in my hair. Patience was never something I had been good at. But as long as Mitica's secret wouldn't separate us, I didn't really care what it was.

"Mitica," I murmured into his chest. "I don't want to be alone right now."

He pulled back, meeting my solicitation with wide eyes.

I could feel my cheeks warm slightly before I said, "Don't you have someplace we can go? You must live somewhere."

He closed his eyes, wincing. His eyebrows crinkled in regret as he gazed at me. "That is...not a good idea tonight."

My stomach plummeted at the rejection, and my ears grew hot with shame.

"The Mounties would be alarmed if they awoke and you were gone, da?"

I didn't respond even though I knew he was right.

He caressed my face and lifted my chin so I would meet his gaze. I bit my lip but complied.

"Let me find another way, bucuria mea."

I frowned and squinted into a pout. He smiled gently at me.

"I am sorry to send you back inside, especially since you want to stay with me. But I want you to know: you are not alone. I will be beside you even when I feel far away."

Pretty words, but it doesn't change the fact I'm sleeping alone.

I was a little less irritated as he kissed each of my cheeks and my forehead.

"You better figure it out soon," I whispered a moment before he placed a soft kiss on my lips.

"I will," he promised with a smile.

Just as I'd expected, the Mounties' presence did little to alleviate the vulnerable loneliness I felt in the pitch-black cabin.

TWENTY-ONE

*I*n the light of the following morning, I felt mortified by what had transpired the night before.

I can't believe I reacted that way. I was feeling vulnerable, and I took comfort in Mitica. I didn't have to suggest we spend the night together. I wanted to think carefully before going there, what with the whole claiming him thing. Am I ready to "claim" him?

I had always been a fairly balanced person, equally guided by both logic and intuition. The trouble came when my brain and my heart told me different things. Those situations usually resulted in unease followed by anxiety and agonizing over what to do.

My brain is saying I haven't known Mitica very long, and he's clearly keeping something from me. It's saying don't fully trust him until you know him better.

What's my heart saying?

I didn't even have to ask. I already knew the answer. I knew I felt it: the pull. The quickening of my pulse when I knew I would see him, the loneliness when he wasn't around. The problem was I couldn't lie to myself and pretend he was the only one I felt it toward.

I squeezed my eyes shut and gritted my teeth. *Stupid. Stupid, stupid, stupid. And don't forget wrong. I don't deserve either of them. Mitica would give himself over to me, and I don't have the courtesy to get over a crush on a man who isn't interested? What is my problem? Maybe it's because I see Wynn every day. I mean, I've never had this problem before. Maybe I should move out of the barracks. I wonder if Suzette would let me stay with her. But is leaving a good idea? I still don't know who killed me in this lifetime. Mitica brought me to Wynn to keep me safe. Why didn't Mitica just keep me with him?*

As I stewed in my own guilty juices, the devil I spoke of entered with breakfast.

"Good morning," Wynn greeted, removing his hat.

My heart thumped at the sight of him. I rolled toward the wall and curled into a ball under the covers. Unfortunately, that just meant I was surrounded by Wynn's scent as I buried myself in his bed.

He crossed the room and stood over me. "Erin, are you not feeling well?"

"I'm fine," I mumbled.

"Are you certain? Can I do anything?" He placed his hand gently on my shoulder.

I jumped at his touch. "I said I'm fine," I snapped, glaring at him.

He pulled back and nodded with a mask-like expression.

Stop being nice to me. Ignore me, be mean, just stop making it so hard to let you go.

I'm sure Wynn was confused as to why I'd responded so nastily to his concern, but he didn't ask. He returned to the table and dished breakfast into three bowls.

That day, the Mounties had business to take care of in town. They said something about buying horse feed, but I wasn't really listening. I declined their invitation to join them in favor of moping around the barracks.

After looking out the window for a while, I went to the chest at the foot of Wynn's bed. He kept *Dracula* in there, so I surmised he would have other books I could read as well.

Lifting the heavy, wooden lid, I stared into the well-organized trunk. Most of the contents were neatly-folded clothes, but on the right side, there were stationary and writing tools.

There was only one other book besides *Dracula*. I grabbed it and cracked the soft leather binding.

Opening to a random page, I had already seen too much by the time I'd realized it was Wynn's journal. His entries were short and neat.

5 April 1900

Trip to Strathcona to test spring water sample. Erin nearly fainted on train. Everything she does draws me to her. I want to protect her.

---

6 April 1900

Chemists say test could take a week. Erin found something at library. We met Sparrow at The Winchester. I couldn't close the distance. It's better this way.

---

7 April 1900

Back to Farrloch. Erin pulling away. Oliver in barracks when we arrived.

---

8 April 1900

Erin and Oliver fast friends. No word from chemists.

---

9 April 1900

I don't know how much longer I can hold out. Still haven't heard about exemption request. I am already hers.

My hands shook, and my heart pounded. My breath caught as the sound of hooves approaching came from outside. After quickly returning the journal to its proper place, I managed to shut the lid of the trunk before Wynn entered.

Wynn took in my wide eyes, open mouth, and pale face. "Erin, what's wrong?" he asked, alarmed.

I averted my gaze, not sure I could handle looking at him at the moment. "Nothing. I uh...need some fresh air."

"Would you like me to come with you?"

"No, I'll be fine. I need to be alone."

I ran past the stables and Oli putting away the horses' tack. When I reached the treeline, I didn't slow down. I ran all the way to the cliff that overlooked the river. Once I'd reached the ledge, I bent, panting and clutching my cramped side.

With nowhere to run, my mind started spinning.

What is even happening? Wynn is interested in me? How? What—?

I crouched and hugged my legs, ignoring my screaming lungs and thumping my forehead on my knees.

"What do I do?" I moaned.

Misery gnawed at me as guilt made my eyes burn. The thought of hurting Wynn or Mitica made my tears well and spill over.

"I'm lost," I told the trees, but they didn't hear over the roaring of the river below.

My mind grasped for any words of wisdom I'd ever heard. My dad telling me to "spit on it" didn't really help in this situation.

I recalled the few times in my life where I'd felt an overwhelming level of anxiety. It came up with anything from arguments with friends to worrying about which college I would get into. Whatever the reason, I always called my mom. She was busy, being a small business owner will do that, but she was never too busy to talk when I got like this.

"Mom, I need help," I told the wind.

The advice my mom gave me usually came down to three things: be patient, be honest, and don't try to take on others' emotions.

All of these phrases I'd heard her say applied to this situation. I could practically feel her stroking my hair. "Okay, take a deep breath," she would say. "So two boys like you, and you're unsure which boy you like back. You're upset because you know you can only choose one, and you don't want to hurt the boy you don't choose. Don't take on others' emotions,

Erin. I know you don't want to hurt them, Honey, but that kind of comes with the whole love territory. If you're really unsure of whom you like better, you should just be honest with them. Tell them what you're feeling, and be patient as they work out their responses. It'll all be okay. Whatever will be will be."

I took a few steadying breaths and raised my head. *All right. I'll talk to them.*

I walked slowly back to the barracks, trying to figure out what I could say. Wynn was a particular problem because I probably should tell him I read his journal, too. I still hadn't determined whom I would talk to first when I arrived.

As I turned the corner of the stables, I saw Oli and Wynn packing Oli's saddlebags.

"What's going on?" I asked them; they seemed in a hurry.

"I got a telegram from my sister. My mother is ill, so I'm going home."

"Oh, no. I'm sorry to hear that, Oli. I hope she's all right."

He nodded. "Thanks. I don't know how long I'll be gone, but I'll send word when I know more."

"Yeah, no problem. Should I let Suzette know?"

"No, I'm going to stop by the shop before I leave town."

"All right. Well, be safe."

"Will do," he assured, climbing into the saddle.

As he rode away, Wynn turned to me. "We also got word from the chemists in Edmonton. The water is safe. There's nothing in it that would kill a person at the present amounts."

"Well, shit. I guess we're back to a lack of information."

He nodded.

After a pause, he said. "You missed lunch. Are you hungry? We left some food for you."

"I'm fine, thanks. It's almost dinner time anyway."

As he gazed at me, I could feel my cheeks heat. *Can he tell I've been crying?* I averted my eyes. "I'm going to wash my face," I muttered, escaping into the barracks.

My eyes weren't nearly as red and puffy as I'd imagined, but I splashed my face with cold water anyway.

All through dinner, I tried to decide how I wanted to broach the subject with Wynn, but I couldn't get the words right in my mind. Just as I was going to jump in, he said he had some correspondence to write, so he wouldn't be able to read *Dracula* that night.

I acknowledged his plans, sighing internally. *It will be easier to talk to Mitica first anyway.*

When I heard Mitica's sweet baritone greet me that night, I flinched.

"What is wrong, bucuria mea?" he asked, tilting his head at my sorrowful expression.

"I have something I need to tell you, Mitica."

He took my hand and smiled reassuringly. "Then tell me."

I looked down at my moccasined feet. "I don't want to hurt you, but I need to be honest with you."

"Do not be distressed. You can be honest. I promise to listen."

I closed my burning eyes, willing the tears to wait. Taking a deep breath, I looked up into Mitica's patient, compassionate gaze.

"Mitica, I love you, but I'm also in love with someone else. I'm sorry. I don't know what else to say. I want to choose between you, but my heart is torn."

Mitica froze at my confession, his face giving nothing away.

Though he showed no reaction, I knew I must have caused him pain. An aching lump formed in my throat as tears rolled down my face. "I'm sorry," I choked.

His eyes softened as he watched me break. "Who is he?" he murmured.

"What? Why?"

He took a deep breath. "Who?"

"Wynn," I whispered.

He squeezed his eyes shut as if he were in pain. He was silent for a while before he said, "I am sorry."

My heart squeezed. *What does that mean? He's going to leave.* A sob escaped me, and I brought my shaking fingertips to my lips.

"I am sorry you are going through this."

"Mitica, no. Please don't apologize. I feel horrible for doing this to you. You have nothing to be sorry for. You're perfect."

He shook his head and held up a hand to shush me. "No, Erin. You feel this way because I have not been honest with you."

I furrowed my brow, trying to figure out what he meant through my own foggy misery.

He met my eyes, and his blue depths pleaded with me to understand. "I am Wynn."

His words washed over me like a bucket of freezing lake water.

"Um...what?"

"More accurately, Wynn does not exist."

My mind pulled away from the idea. "What are you saying? Of course Wynn exists." Adrenaline made my body hum with anxiety.

He sighed. "I do not know how to explain. I am Wynn, and Wynn is not real. He is a persona I created to infiltrate the North-West Mounted Police. Look. Look at me."

My eyes snapped to his face, which blurred. When it came back into focus, Wynn stood before me.

"What the holy Hell? Wynn? Mitica?"

Wynn nodded. "This is a glamour: an illusion to hide my true identity."

"What? Why?"

"That's a long story, one you deserve to hear."

Anger bubbled in my gut. "You're damn right I deserve to hear it. Jesus fucking Christ, why did you lie to me? Do you know how much I've been struggling with these feelings of guilt? And come to find out you were the same guy. Gah, I can't even tell you how pissed I am right now!"

"I understand, but please listen to my story before you get angry. Won't you?"

I ground my teeth and crossed my arms. "Fine. Go ahead."

Wynn sat on a large rock and motioned for me to join him. "This will take a while," he said when I didn't move.

"Whatever. Just go," I snapped.

He sighed. "I told you civilization is killing magic. In Canada, the North-West Mounted Police are at the forefront of this destruction. They protect settlers who tame the wilderness, they facilitate unfair treaties between the government and the natives, their main purpose is to civilize the west. When the Romanian immigrants realized the Canadian fae were in trouble, they did what they always do: asked the hultan for help.

"The hultan leaders, a council known as the Zgrimties, sent me to infiltrate the organization and discover their motives. I was to see how much of the leadership knew about the British Empire's mission to eradicate magic and to help the fae and natives when I could.

"I created this disguise and passed myself off as Canadian to join the ranks."

"But why didn't you just tell me? You had to see I was attracted to you both."

He hung his head and shifted his appearance back to Mitica. "The Zgrimties made me swear an oath to keep my purpose secret. If I was to reveal the truth, all support for my mission would be withdrawn, and I would no longer be welcome in Crugul Pământului."

I cringed. *Shit.* "What's that?"

"It is the hultan's base of operations and where they train."

I frowned. "So because you told me, you can't go home or get support while trying to save magic? Now you're an outcast?"

He stood and took my hand, squeezing it reassuringly. "This is not your fault, Erin. When you arrived and I realized who you were, I requested an exception from the Zgrimties so I could tell you."

"And what did they say?"

"I have not received an answer yet. But they have to approve it. You are too important."

"What do you mean I'm too important. Who am I?"

"You are mine, and I am yours."

I stared at him, waiting for more of an explanation.

"My parents were forbidden from being together. But they loved each other so deeply they were willing to sacrifice everything for each other. My father even gave up his magic. When I was born, it shook the magical world. A half-iele half-hultan, what an abomination," he said bitterly. "But I never knew that, not until it was time for me to be trained in magic. My parents loved me, and they fought to get me into Crugul Pământului so I could go to school.

"It was miserable. Everyone despised me, but no one could deny my gifts. When I finished school, the Zgrimties and iele both laid claim to my abilities. Neither of them truly accepted me, but I was glad to be useful. I wanted to help people and save magic. People need me. They ask for my help, and I am happy to give it. But there has never been anyone who needed my mere existence. Someone who did not need me to do anything but just be, and there has never been anyone who I needed in the same way.

"During the last dark moon, looking into the moonless sky, I knew there had to be someone out there in that void. I wanted to meet her, to know her if only for a short while. So I made a wish. That is when I found you. I was not positive until we talked with Likinoak. You are my soul mate, Erin. The gods have brought us together through time and space."

"Your magic is what pulled me through time?" I asked in wonder.

"Well, my magic coupled with your desire and the black moon."

The irresistible pull I felt around Mitica and Wynn, the sense of innate trust and safety, I'd explained those uncharacteristic feelings by the precarious situation I was in and the fact that they had helped me. *While those things still apply, is it possible there's more to the explanation?*

I searched Mitica's eyes for the answers and was again struck by the thought that I'd recognize that soul anywhere.

"You know your true name. If we're soul mates, can you remember if we've met in previous lives?" I asked him.

"We have never met before. This is my first lifetime," he whispered.

"Oh." As I gazed at him, the flame in my heart blazed. *Mitica is my soul mate.* The words echoed in my mind like ringing the bell of truth. "I guess we belong to each other after all," I told him.

He beamed, and my heart welled in my chest.

"Bucuria mea," he whispered lovingly as he leaned toward me.

"You always call me that. What does it mean?" I asked.

"My Joy," he murmured, his breath against my lips.

I smiled. "I love you, Mitica."

"Te iubesc, bucuria mea," he whispered. "I love you."

The soft sweetness of his kiss released the zmeu in my heart. I met his next kiss with a fierceness he took as a challenge. The rough fabric of his jacket rubbed harshly against my clenched fists as I pulled him down to me. His sturdy hands on my waist urged me closer. My body flushed as his tongue met mine.

"Mitica," I gasped, breaking for air.

His blue eyes, heavy with lust, answered my call.

"I'm ready to claim you now, Mitica. Will you also claim me?"

He smiled a promise, and I shivered with heat. "Da."

I yelped as he scooped me off my feet, and my face flushed. "I can walk," I protested.

"I know," he said, striding toward the barracks.

"Then put me down," I told him.

He smiled down at me. "You do not like it?"

I buried my blushing face in his chest. "Shut up," I muttered.

He chuckled as he carried me inside. Setting me gently on my feet, Mitica slowly embraced me from behind in the dark cabin, his chest solid against my back and his breath warm even through my hat.

"I always thought you were asleep when I snuck back in at night," I whispered.

"That is why I keep it so dark," he said, sliding my hat from my head.

"Well, can't I see you now?" I asked.

He pronounced a few words of magic, and the lamps illuminated the room.

"I want to know you," he whispered, his breath in my ear.

I took in a shaky breath. "Me too."

I shuddered when his cool fingertips trailed against my neck as he fiddled with the edges of my scarf. He slipped it over my head.

Goosebumps followed his every kiss down my neck to my collar as if my flesh mourned his abandonment in favor of another spot.

I shivered as he gently removed Oli's coat, eliminating one more obstacle between his flesh and mine. As it fell to the floor, I turned to face him.

While I unbuttoned his coat, I memorized the lines of his face in the flickering lamplight. The dancing light in his lustful eyes sent a thrill through me, like the feel of lighting from a gathering storm.

His coat slipped from his shoulders and joined Oli's on the floor, and I reached for his shirt buttons. With every button that popped smoothly through its buttonhole, I placed a kiss on his newly-exposed skin. The sensitive skin of my lips yielded to the firmness of his chest and abdomen.

With the last button undone, I was on my knees before him. I splayed one hand across his abs as he looked down to meet my gaze. His crimson hair fell into his fierce eyes as I ran my thumb just under the waistband of his pants.

He stilled my advance by sinking to his knees as well.

My hands pressed into his bare chest when he crushed me to him, kissing me deeply with a deep, guttural moan.

I squeaked in surprise when he shifted my weight and lay me down beneath him. His crimson hair hung in his face as he looked down at me.

My heart pounded, and I smiled up at him, brushing his hair from his eyes. His unshaven cheek scraped my hand as he turned his head and pressed a sweet, breathy kiss to my palm.

He lowered his weight on top of me and pressed a passionate kiss against my lips. I welcomed his solid heft between my legs. One of his hands slid under my chemise, and I squirmed at the sensation of his hot flesh on my bare stomach. His other hand pressed against my lower back and pulled me closer to him, drawing a whimper from me. His calloused thumb flicked over my pert nipple, and I gasped.

He smiled down at my reaction.

"You are maddening," I accused in a breathy voice.

"Am I?" he teased.

I squirmed out from under him, and he didn't resist as I climbed atop him and pinned him to his back.

"My turn," I said, straddling his hips.

A shadow of a smile that was more Wynn than Mitica played on his lips as I pulled my shirt off and freed my breasts. He cupped them with his large hands, rubbing my nipples with the pads of his thumbs.

Arching my back, his rigid manhood ground hard between my legs. He hummed low in his throat, and I flashed him a smile.

I didn't protest when he sat up to embrace me but wrapped my legs around his waist.

I removed his shirt from his broad shoulders and gave only a fleeting thought to the black scar on his upper arm.

I pressed kisses down his strong neck to where it met his shoulder and flicked the sensitive spot with my tongue.

He groaned, and I smiled before I sucked the flesh gently, marking him as my own. His breath escaped in short bursts until I bit him playfully. He hissed and refused to sit still any longer.

He rolled me onto my back again, and it didn't take him long to remove my shoes and jeans. As he settled his weight on top of my naked body, his burning skin made up for the cold floorboards beneath us.

He kissed me thoroughly as if he had nothing but time, but my core throbbed in protest. I wanted him, and I was not prepared to wait.

I trailed my hand down his abdomen and slipped my fingers into his pants and around his solid cock.

He moaned into my lips and ground his hips against me.

I broke our kiss and brought my lips to his ear. "Mitica, please," I begged.

He met my eyes with a barely restrained expression. "I am trying...to be gentle with you, bucuria mea. We do not know who you are in this time. If you are a virgin, it could be painful for you."

I knew what he was saying was sweet and kind, but I couldn't wait anymore. "Mitica, please. Just touch me. I want you now."

His concern warred with his desire as he trailed his hand down my body. When he ran his thumb over my clit, I bit my lip against my moan.

His fingers were hot and firm as he felt between my legs, and he smiled when my wetness trickled down his hand. I held my breath.

He gazed into my eyes. "Will you give yourself to me, bucuria mea?" he asked sincerely.

"I am yours," I told him. Staring at him, I slowly reached down and unfastened his pants. I wrapped my hand around his cock, letting the rigid weight slide through my fingers.

Mitica shuddered. "And I am yours," he murmured, slowly gliding his manhood into my core.

The sweet pleasure of his every inch filled my empty void. I shivered as he shook.

"Deeper," I told him. "Make sure I miss the feel of you inside me."

With every sweaty thrust, every shuddering moan, we claimed each other. And with screams of completion, I realized what Mitica had meant when he'd said a full heart has wings.

TWENTY-TWO

For the first time since we'd met, I awoke before Mitica. At some point, he must have moved us to the bed because we were crammed into his small bunk.

I was having a difficult time breathing with my face pressed against his chest and his arms around me like he was trying to smother me. I managed to wiggle loose without waking him.

I held my breath as he sighed in his sleep, my eyes drawn to his restful face. It was the first time I'd seen him by daylight. While he was still as beautiful, I noticed certain features I hadn't seen before.

I thought I'd memorized him. I reached out and traced his Roman nose.

I was concentrating so hard that I gasped when Mitica snatched my hand and kissed it.

"Good morning, bucuria mea," he murmured, smiling sleepily at me as he opened his eyes.

I shivered pleasantly. "Hey," I whispered.

"How are you feeling? Are you sore at all?"

"No, I'm fine. Thanks for asking."

I had so many unanswered questions I still wanted to ask him, but as his warm, blue eyes gazed into mine and he gently stroked my face, I suddenly didn't care about those questions.

When he softly kissed each of my cheeks, heat spread through me. It seemed once I'd had a taste, I only wanted more.

"Mitica," I breathed, not able to keep the desire from my voice.

He smiled and kissed me tenderly on the lips.

My heart skipped. And just as I thought he would give me what I wanted, my stomach growled.

He pulled back, and I frowned.

"You are hungry, bucuria mea. I will go get food."

Stupid stomach.

He chuckled at my pout. "I will return soon," he promised.

As he climbed out of bed, the relatively small space he emptied seemed a massive void. I grabbed his hand to stop him from walking away. He knelt down and gathered me in his arms before kissing me fiercely.

My mind went fuzzy, and the moan against his mouth seemed to come from someone else.

Alas, the goodbye kiss was much too short. "I will return," he repeated.

I curled onto my side grumpily, watching him dress in his red serge and change into his Wynn face.

After he'd left, I thought I might as well do something useful while I waited. Before I went to feed the horses, I washed in the washbasin. I'd never missed a shower more than when I was trying to clean our dried fluids off me.

I paused only for a moment when I opened the door to find it raining. The horses greeted me by sticking their heads out from their stalls. I fed Langundo first, talking to him as always.

When I fed Bou, a thought occurred to me. *What does Mitica do with Grigore when he's Wynn?* I eyed Bou suspiciously as he chewed his oats. Rolling my eyes at myself, I shook my head.

"No way." I laughed at the absurd notion and turned to walk away.

I halted and squinted, pursing my lips. I looked at Bou once more. "Grigore?" I asked the horse, feeling stupid.

Bou's eyes flashed yellow.

I gasped, nearly tripping as I reflexively jumped back.

"So you figured it out, did you?" the horse asked.

My mouth hung open as his human voice left the horse's lips.

"It took you long enough."

I just stared, seemingly having forgotten how to use words.

"Hmm? Or did he tell you? You look too surprised to have discovered it on your own."

"Yeah, he told me."

Grigore chuckled. "He is going to be in so much trouble."

"Is it really that bad? He said he asked for an exception."

He snorted. "The Zgrimties are an unforgiving lot. He will be an outcast for sure."

My heart raced as alarm shot through me.

"Does that scare you?" he asked.

"But how will they know? I can keep a secret."

"I can help with that if you want."

"What can you do?" I wondered.

"He will not be in as much trouble if I tell them I told you."

I bit my lip. "You would do that?"

"Of course, for a favor in return."

"What?"

"His scent is all over you." He snuffled. "Let me cover it with mine."

I stepped back, curling my upper lip.

"They already know," Mitica said from the stable entrance. "They would have known the moment I broke my oath. It's how the spell was cast."

I ran to Mitica, still in his Wynn face. "Is he right? Will you really be an outcast?"

"Don't worry," he smiled, resting a reassuring hand on my shoulder. "I'm certain they will understand."

I sighed, though my skin still prickled with unease.

Mitica took my hand and kissed it. "Let's eat."

I nodded and followed him through the rain to the barracks.

"This rain is no joke," I commented, removing my wet coat and placing it by the stove.

"I guess we will just have to stay in today," Mitica suggested.

I smirked at him. "I like that plan."

As I reached up for his brass buttons, he stilled my hands.

"But first, you eat," he urged.

I pursed my lips. "Fine."

He removed his tunic and put it by the stove. This time, I didn't hide my appreciation when he changed his soaked undershirt. My eyes clung to his every move.

As we ate, I began asking Mitica some of the questions I still had.

"You said the Mounties are killing magic, and your mission was to discover if their leadership knows about the British Empire's goal to eradicate magic."

He nodded.

"So the British Empire has been actively trying to kill magic? For how long and why?"

"Centuries. I can't say exactly why. The Zgrimties believe most of the magic in Britain was destroyed when the groves were burned. It seems after they later converted to Christianity, they convinced themselves magic was evil. And when the British started exploring the world and subjugating others, they didn't like the magic they found."

"Jeez, so what about the Mounties? Do they even know about magic?"

"I don't believe so. By now, the 'civilize the heathen' narrative is so entrenched in the culture that no one needs to know the real reason anymore."

I thought about it. "It's hard to believe someone like Oli could be that bad."

He nodded, frowning. "Good people can do bad things when they're told their entire lives that it's right. Unfortunately, there isn't a good way to educate them on what's truly happening. I can only try to help the fae and natives when I can."

I sighed. "It's like you're fighting a losing battle."

"But every bit of magic I save is worth it."

I reached out and grabbed his hand on the table. "You aren't in this alone anymore. Let me help you."

His eyes widened.

"Does it surprise you that much?"

"No, I just... I'm used to being alone."

"Well, get used to having me around because I'm not going anywhere."

He paused, searching my eyes. "You would sacrifice your life in the future to stay with me?"

I thought about my mom and how I didn't have any idea how to live in 1900. "Do you really think I could leave after the universe brought us together in such a way?"

He closed his eyes and kissed my hand, his lips trembling on the thin skin.

My heart thumped hard.

When he met my gaze again, his eyes blazed with the desire I had never dared to hope for. The answering heat in my core made a shiver run through me.

Without a word, he stood from the table, and I willingly left my half-eaten breakfast to follow him to the bed.

TWENTY-THREE

*T*he rain fell outside, and I listened to the steady, calming sound as I lay on Mitica's bare chest in the small bed. His Wynn face was content, the quiet joy a sight I'd so longed to see. My eyes found the edge of the black scar on his upper arm.

"What's this?" I asked, tracing the raised skin with my fingertips.

"That's the symbol of my kinship with the Wyboka. During the kinship ceremony, they cut the skin. Once it's cleaned, they rub ash in the wound. That's why it's black."

"Do Chuthekii and Likinoak know Mitica and Wynn are the same?"

"I suspect they do, though I didn't break my oath to tell them. They've never said anything outright, but some of their comments lead me to believe they know."

"What was Chuthekii saying last time that you were so keen to keep from me?"

"He knew you were my soul mate. He told me you would not want to return to the future, and he kept calling you 'sister-in-law.'"

"Jeez, I guess the animals really do show him stuff."

He nodded. "We should go back to the reserve soon and ask him if he has learned anything about what's happening at the sacred spring."

"I agree. Any information would be helpful at this point. We should go tonight."

He pursed his lips.

"What is it?"

"He's going to gloat when he hears you're staying."

I laughed. "That reminds me, we have to figure some stuff out."

"Such as?"

"Well, I should probably get a job, and I can't exactly stay in the barracks forever. It's not a long-term solution."

He frowned. "I don't like the idea of you leaving. You could still be in danger."

I hadn't thought of that.

"I will just have to go with you," he pronounced.

"Can you even do that?" I asked, lifting my head and meeting his gaze.

"Nothing will keep me from your side for as long as you want me," he said seriously.

My heart gave one hard thump. "I guess we'll always be together then."

He lifted his head and kissed me sweetly on the mouth. "Iti dau inima mea," he whispered.

"What does that mean?" I asked.

"I give you my heart."

I met my lover's gaze seriously, a pleasant flush on my cheeks. "I will cherish it. Don't worry. You'll never be lonely again."

The rest of that rainy day was spent proving our love for one another. The feel of him, his taste in my mouth, his breathy whispers in my ear, all were like floating in timelessness. I didn't know what energy, what force, what deity, had made that blissful day possible, but I didn't take the blessing for granted.

I ensured Mitica knew I was his and that I claimed him as mine with every beat of my heart and with every breath I took. I never thought of how it would feel to give myself fully to another person and to truly accept him. But once I'd let go, I found a peace I didn't know was possible, like floating in a calm lake looking up at the clear night sky. I was swimming with the stars. The trust I felt for him was freeing, and I knew he would never betray it. I was safe with him.

Likinoak and Chuthekii were not surprised to see us that night.

After we were all seated near the hearth with warm tea, Mitica turned to his family. "Erin will not be returning to the future. She wants to stay with me."

Chuthekii smiled without a word.

"Be quiet," Mitica muttered.

"I said nothing," Chuthekii laughed.

"You did not have to."

When Likinoak stood, we all rose from our seats. She beamed at us. Embracing Mitica, she said something to him in what I assumed was Wyboka. Then, she turned to me and took my hands.

"I knew you were special from the moment I saw you. Your light has given his heart wings."

"And he has freed mine."

She hugged me. "May the spirits bless you both."

"Thank you, Likinoak," I said.

"There is no need for thanks, Seyohkwii. We are family now."

My heart glowed in the older woman's warmth, a warmth reminiscent of my own mother's love.

"I also have bad news," Mitica told them. "The Mountie tested the spring water, and the chemists say it is fine. Have you heard anything about what may have caused these deaths, Wic'aze?"

Chuthekii frowned. "I asked Hawk again when I returned from the residential school. What he showed me seemed consistent with your conclusion that they were poisoned. But perhaps I misinterpreted the vision. I will think on it."

Mitica nodded. "Has anyone entered the spring since Testooklah?"

"No," Likinoak answered. "But we cleansed the space today. And now that we know the water is safe, those seeking the sacred spring will be permitted to enter."

"Let us hope no one else will come to any harm," Mitica said.

They all tensed in an expression of uneasy hopefulness.

"We just have to keep looking," I said confidently into the heavy silence. "If we can find cause of death or motive, we can figure out what's happening and stop it."

"Azeohkwii is right. We will not quit until we can give the dead the peace they deserve," Chuthekii added.

We all nodded grimly with renewed purpose.

Before we left, Mitica promised to visit in a few days, and Chuthekii said he would re-evaluate his visions in that time.

The following day, we received a telegram from Oli. His mother was not mortally ill, and he said he would return on Wednesday. We knew everything would be different once Oli arrived, so we tried to enjoy those few days to their fullest.

I couldn't remember the last time I'd been so happy. Every smile, every laugh, every glance from him made my heart soar. We rode our horses through the forest, staring up at the towering peaks above as Mitica visited settlers, executing his Mountie duties. We chopped wood and ate together. And every night, in the flickering light of the oil lamps, we made love, our caresses giving life to all our wordless promises.

When the day came for Oli's return, I clenched my eyes shut and snuggled deeper into Mitica's arms. "I don't want it to be Wednesday," I whined.

Mitica chuckled in his Wynn voice. "You don't want to see Oliver?"

I sighed. "It's not that. I just don't want to go back to the way things were."

"Don't fret, bucuria mea. Even if I cannot touch you every day, you will never have to suffer through not knowing whether I love you."

"That's true. Ugh, fine. I guess I should get dressed in case he returns early."

I climbed out of bed, but Mitica grabbed my wrist and pulled me back. I landed in his lap. His eyes shined with adoration as he gently stroked my cheek with his thumb.

"Te iubesc, bucuria mea," he declared.

"I love you, too."

He brushed a fleetingly sweet kiss to my lips. Then, he pressed into the kiss with more purpose.

I squealed with laughter as he rolled on top of me. "What about Oli?" I asked.

"We have time."

I wrapped my arms around the back of his neck and grinned. "We better get started if you don't want him to see."

Though we didn't have long, that didn't make Mitica any less thorough. As I screamed his name, I was grateful the barracks were so isolated from the rest of the town. I was well satiated, washed, and clothed before Oli returned.

When we heard hooves approaching, we went outside to meet him.

"Hey, Oli." I waved cheerfully. "How is your family? Is your mother feeling better?"

He smiled. "Much better. She's a hearty woman. So when she fell ill, my sister panicked. Everything is fine." He climbed out of the saddle.

"That's good to hear. They must've been glad to have you home."

He nodded. "Did I miss anything while I was gone?"

I felt my face heat and glanced at Mitica. His Wynn face gave nothing away.

"The Wyboka cleansed the spring. They'll be allowing people to use it again."

"Mmhmm," Oli acknowledged, squinting at me. "Anything else?"

I laughed. "Come on, Oli. What were you expecting? Did you think you would leave and the whole place would fall apart?"

He smiled. "Don't lie to me, Little Sister. You aren't good at it."

Pfft. If only you knew. I glanced at Mitica again, and he shrugged. "Fine. Wynn and I are...courting." The word felt strange in my mouth, but I couldn't think of another way to say it.

"Oh? What's this? You two finally admitted your feelings?"

I rolled my eyes at him. "Yeah, whatever. You were right."

He nodded once in satisfaction. "Right, so some things are going to have to change around here."

"What do you mean?" I asked.

"Well, I can't very well have Wynn sleeping so close to you. I will be taking the floor from now on, and Erin will sleep in my bed until we can think of a better solution. And you two will have a lot less time alone."

"Excuse me?" I demanded.

"Subconstable Taylor, remember to whom you are giving orders," Mitica scolded.

Oli flinched then straightened his spine. "With all due respect, Constable. Erin has no male relatives to look after her. I feel it is my responsibility to ensure her honor remains unblemished."

Is this a fucking joke?

I looked at Mitica expecting to see outrage, but he frowned as though considering Oli's words.

"Wait just a minute, Oli. You and Suzette take walks alone together almost every day. Are you saying you should be chaperoned, too?" I demanded.

"We don't live together."

"This is unreasonable. We don't have much time alone as it is with you here, and no one even knows I'm staying here. Suzette doesn't even know."

Oli pursed his lips.

"I'll agree to the sleeping arrangements, but having a chaperone is unnecessary," Mitica said.

Oli stared hard at him. "Very well. But I'll have you know, Constable Delaforet, Erin is under my protection."

I felt both touched and exasperated by Oli's display of masculinity.

Mitica nodded seriously. "Noted, Subconstable Taylor. Now, take care of your horse. She has had a long ride."

Oli led his horse into the stables to carry out Mitica's orders.

I scowled in his wake. Mitica placed a comforting hand on my shoulder. "Don't fret, bucuria mea. This won't be for long. I'll find a place where we can live together in peace. But for now, you must learn this society's rules if you're to stay."

"Whatever. They're stupid," I grumped, though I knew he was right.

He chuckled and kissed my head. "Be patient."

"Hmph."

The rest of the day was fairly normal. It was strange to see Mitica go back to playing the part of the formal Mountie. But I followed his lead and returned to how we were before Oli had left, not wanting to blow his cover.

After dinner, Oli went to visit Suzette. Before he'd left, I made him promise not to tell her about Wynn and me.

"I'll tell her the next time I see her. She'll be angry if she hears it from anyone but me," I told him.

He agreed.

I waved goodbye to him nonchalantly as he left. But as soon as he'd shut the door, I went to it and peeked out.

Watching him fade into the distance, I asked Mitica. "How long do you think he'll be gone?"

He came up behind me and pressed a hot kiss to my neck. "Long enough."

I spun around, facing the tall Mountie in full uniform.

"Do you think so?"

"Trust me," he assured, dipping his head to kiss me.

I slid my fingers into his brown hair, urging him closer.

His strong hands grabbed my bottom and easily lifted me, and I wrapped my legs around his solid torso. I hummed as he pleasantly squished me between his hard body and the door, kissing me deeply.

Never taking his burning lips from mine, he moved us to the bed and sat with me in his lap.

I pushed my palms gently on his ungiving chest, telling him to lie on his back. After climbing off him, I quickly removed my pants before mounting him again. The smooth cotton of my chemise bunched slightly at my hips as I straddled him.

His rough hands trailed heat from my knees slowly up my outer thighs. I shivered as a pleasant tickle ran through me when he brushed his thumb along the crease where my thigh met my hip. My cheeks flushed, and I couldn't look away as his lustful gaze watched me.

With unerring accuracy, he found the sweet spot between my thighs. As he expertly rubbed my clit with the rough pad of his thumb, I let my breath out in a restrained moan and ground my ass into his hard manhood.

A low rumble sounded deep in his throat, but his hand never faltered. On shaky knees, I raised myself and reached behind me to unfasten his trousers.

He didn't stop the sweet, circular motion even as I slid his solid cock deep into me.

Our mutual groans echoed off the rustic wood of the empty cabin.

I took in the sight of the still-dressed Mountie beneath me, his face twisted in the pleasure I was giving him.

It took all of my concentration to repeatedly lift myself up only to thrust him back into me. My thighs shook, and my mind fogged.

But as I heard him call my name and felt him pump into me, euphoria finally overtook me.

TWENTY-FOUR

I'd planned to visit Suzette the following day, but I awoke to find an unexpected surprise. It was snowing heavily.

"It doesn't look like it's going to stop anytime soon," Mitica commented from the window.

"We should go to town and get provisions in case it lasts," Oli added.

Mitica nodded, his Wynn face all business. "Erin, would you go outside and bring in as much wood as you can? We need to keep it dry. Oliver and I will go to town and get food for the next few days and oats for the horses."

I agreed, and we all went to work. By the time they'd returned with vegetables, bread, and cheese to last us a few days, I'd piled enough wood to keep the stove running.

I was surprised when Mitica volunteered to cook while Oli and I took care of the horses. After we'd fed and put blankets on them to keep them warm, we returned to the barracks and settled in.

It snowed all day, all night, and the following day. It wasn't exactly a blizzard, but I was glad I didn't have to drive in it. Still, it was unusual for me to see so much snow in the middle of April, though not remarkably so.

The Mounties spent most of the time writing correspondence. Mitica read some of the time, and we all played poker. Not surprisingly, Mitica won more than not.

Over that two-day period, Mitica and I only ever managed to get a few minutes alone together. It was frustrating, to say the least, but we survived.

When the snow finally stopped, we were all relieved to go outside. Mitica offered to go into town for breakfast, and Oli and I heartily agreed. He had been right about one thing: no one cooked like Mellie.

I told Mitica I'd join him as I wanted to visit Suzette. Oli stayed behind to care for the horses.

I was concerned about walking in the snow with moccasins, but they must've been treated with something because my feet didn't get wet.

Strolling at a leisurely pace, I laced my fingers with Mitica's.

"So do you have a plan in regards to what we're going to do next?" I asked him.

"I've thought about it. It depends on how the Zgrimties respond to my request. If they approve, I will likely have to stay with the Mounties. In which case, perhaps I'll purchase some land and build a house, or we could rent a room in town."

"And if they don't approve?"

"Then, we can go wherever we wish. There will be nothing to keep us here."

"So it's a waiting game."

"For now."

I was surprised to see Ion and Mariana outside the trading post and dry goods store once we'd arrived in town. Mariana sat on the wagon seat as Ion loaded goods into the back of the wagon.

"Good morning, you two," I called to them, waving the hand that wasn't holding Mitica's.

They looked up at my greeting, and their eyes widened.

"Good morning," they returned, a little shaken.

I tilted my head at their reception. From the corner of my eyes, I noticed Mellie sweeping snow from her front steps. She openly glared at me, but I didn't miss the hurt in her eyes when she turned to go inside.

"Constable Delaforet," Ion beckoned. "May I speak to you for a moment?"

Mitica nodded. "Of course."

"I'll go order breakfast," I told them, wanting to talk with Mellie alone. "It was nice seeing you again, Mariana, Ion."

Mitica released my hand, and I went on ahead.

I was glad no one else was in Mellie's when I entered. She turned at the sound of the door, and her features tensed upon seeing me.

"Mellie?"

"Yes, Miss Nichols. How may I help you?" Even in a strained voice, she kept her manners.

"Mellie, I'd like to apologize to you and explain."

"That's not necessary."

"But I want to regardless. I'm sorry if it seems like I lied to you before. At the time, I truly believed Wynn wasn't interested in me. I'm just as surprised as you are."

She sighed, defeated, and shook her head. "I'm not surprised... The truth is, I knew Constable Delaforet wasn't interested in me. And I knew... I could tell from the first time I watched him look at you that he saw you differently than he saw me."

There was a long pause.

"Still, I am sorry."

"Don't be. I'm starting to think I only fixated on Constable Delaforet because I knew he didn't want me. I'm not sure I'm even ready to move on after...after Sean..."

Her shoulders slumped, and I felt compelled to comfort her. I placed my hand gently on her shoulder.

"Hey. Take your time. Anyone who's worth it will wait."

She nodded silently while hanging her head.

"Mellie, listen to me. You're awesome. You've managed to accomplish all this at a time when women have little to no rights in society. Just do you, and you'll be fine."

"Do me?" she asked, tilting her head at me.

"Yeah, just be yourself."

She took another deep breath and let it all out at once. "You're right. I've worked hard, and I'm not going to let anything stop me."

"Right on."

She smiled shyly at me, and I couldn't help but admire her.

"Thank you," she said.

"Anytime."

"Now." She squared her shoulders. "What can I get you?"

I ordered our breakfasts, and she said it would be ready in a bit. Telling her I would return, I went out to meet Mitica.

He watched Ion and Mariana drive away, chuckling quietly to himself.

"What was that about?" I asked him.

"Ion wanted to warn me."

"What?"

Mitica turned to me, his eyes sparkling with laughter. "It seems you are beloved by a powerful and dangerous man. Ion was concerned I may get myself into trouble if I didn't leave you be."

"Are you serious?"

He nodded.

"Oh jeez, what did you say?"

"I thanked him for his concern, of course. He was worried for my well-being." He smirked. "It seems I have competition for your heart."

"Yeah, you better watch out. My boyfriend is big and scary."

He grinned. "Is he?"

"Yeah, he would totally kick your ass."

"Would he now?"

"Yep."

Mitica snatched my hand and brought it to his lips. "I'll keep that in mind."

The sensation of his soft, warm lips on my fingers brought a blush to my cheeks.

He released my hand with a smirk. "When will breakfast be ready?"

"In a few. But, hey, I'm going to run to see Suzette real quick. I'll be back in a few minutes. Okay?"

He nodded, and I hurried to Madame Buvons's.

As I approached Madame Buvons's shop, I saw a carriage parked outside. I walked around the back of the carriage and hoped Suzette wasn't too busy to talk. When I entered, Madame Buvons and a young woman in a dark blue dress and a large hat looked over at me. Madame Buvons nodded at me civilly, but the customer openly gaped.

Yeah, yeah, I get it. Oh my god, a woman wearing pants! Whatever.

"Madame," the customer gasped in a heavy French accent. "I did not know you were arriving today." She rushed to me.

I pulled back at her approach. "I'm sorry, Miss. I think you have me confused with someone else."

Her brows crinkled. "Madame, why do you look this way? I was so worried when you left without a word. Monsieur insisted you went home, but why would you not take me with you, Madame?"

My heart pounded as the young woman talked to me so familiarly. "Who exactly do you think I am?" I asked.

"Madame Celeste Broadstone," she said in a confused tone.

Broadstone. Why does that sound familiar?

"But Madame, Monsieur will be so pleased you have returned. He has been worried. I have brought the carriage. We can return immediately."

When I made no move to leave, she grabbed my hand a pulled me outside.

"Let go of me. I don't know you," I told her, my voice rising in pitch as my heart raced. I snatched my hand from hers.

"Madame," she gasped. "I do not understand. What has happened to you? Are you unwell?"

"Leave me alone. I don't know you."

"Madame, if you are unwell, let us return home. I will send for the physician."

I turned and walked away from her, but she followed. When I ran, she fell behind but kept pursuing me. I reached Mitica outside of Mellie's, and I threw myself at him.

"Whoa, what's going on?"

"There's a woman chasing me. She keeps calling me someone else. She says she knows me."

"Thank goodness," the woman sighed when she'd caught up. "Constable, you found her. I think Madame is ill. Can you please bring her home so we can call a physician?"

"Who do you think this is, Miss...?"

"Marguerite Dubois. Madame is Celeste Broadstone, wife of Monsieur Broadstone, who owns Farrloch Hotel."

Our mouths hung open as we stared at her, wide-eyed.

I turned to Mitica desperately. "But Wynn, you've been to the hotel, right? You'd recognize if I am who she says."

He turned to me, his face lined with a worry that made my stomach drop. "I've never met Mrs. Broadstone. Mr. Broadstone hasn't been married long, and she never seemed to be around when I was there."

"But what about the townspeople?" I grasped.

"Madame has never been to town except to board a train. There is no need. The hotel has everything you could ever want."

"And who are you to Mrs. Broadstone, Miss Dubois?" Mitica asked.

"I am Madame's lady's maid."

My stomach clenched into knots.

"Please, Miss Dubois. As you can see, the lady is quite shaken. Let me calm her, and we will meet you at the hotel. Then, we can straighten this entire situation out."

With the assurance of an honorable Mountie, Marguerite nodded. "Merci, Constable. I will inform Monsieur Broadstone to expect you."

"Very well," Mitica agreed.

As soon as Marguerite was out of sight, Mitica grabbed my hand and pulled me down the road toward the barracks. I couldn't see his face as he strode ahead with purpose, but I had to almost jog to keep up.

"Mitica, wait," I heaved, tugging his hand in the deserted road.

He halted. Before I could catch my breath, he wrapped me in a crushing embrace.

"Don't worry. I won't take you to a man you don't know, even if he is this incarnation's husband."

My heart ached at the desperate determination in his voice.

"We'll return to the barracks, pack quickly, and leave," he promised.

"But what about your mission? The Wyboka? The fae? You can't just leave without the Zgrimties permission. Can you?"

"It doesn't matter. Even if they tell me to stay here, you can't stay where people know your identity in this life."

My stomach dropped, and my mouth went dry. "I can't," I whispered. "I can't let you run away if there's a chance the Zgrimties will let you stay undercover. The fae need you. Magic needs you." I pulled back and looked up into his unsure eyes. "Listen, if they approve me as an exception, ask for a new assignment. I'll go with you. If they don't approve, then there's no reason for you to stay undercover, and we can find another way to help magic. But we can't just leave. That woman would know we ran away together, and they would pursue us. Besides, we don't know anything about Celeste Broadstone. We need to know more about who she was so we can avoid being recognized in the future. Also, we need to find out how she died."

Wynn's face scrunched, pain in every line. "You want me to send you to Mr. Broadstone's, your husband's, house?"

"It's not like I want to go. I just think it's the least bad option. It will only be temporary, right? I'll find out everything I can about Celeste, and you'll come up with a plan to get us both out of here safely."

"Nu, I do not like it," he proclaimed, his Romanian accent slipping through as he got more upset.

I hugged him tightly around the middle. "I don't like it either, but is there a better way?"

He was silent for a while as he grasped for alternatives. Finally, with a sigh of defeat, he murmured, "I understand."

Gazing into Wynn's broken eyes, I whispered, "I love you. We won't be apart for long."

My eyes burned as tears threatened my resolve. He kissed me tenderly as if it was the last time he would ever get to kiss me. "I will come for you as soon as I can," he vowed.

The walk to the barracks was slow, our footsteps hindered under the weight of our depression.

"What took you so long?" Oli demanded as we entered. "I'm starving." He took in our sullen demeanors and our lack of breakfast. "What happened? Did Mellie run out of food?"

"Sorry, Oli. I guess we forgot in all the commotion," I apologized. "I... have to return home immediately."

"Your editor is calling you back?"

I shrugged vaguely.

"I see." He frowned. "I guess it's time for farewells. I'm sorry you have to go, but it may be best you leave the area since we never discovered who hurt you."

Mitica cleared his throat. "I'll saddle the horse and take you to the station."

I quietly packed my few belongings into the bag I'd taken on our trip to Edmonton. It didn't take long. I removed Oli's coat and held it out to him. "Thanks for letting me borrow it while I was here."

He shook his head. "Keep it. It's a long journey back to Chicago. You might need it."

I nodded my thanks.

"Hey." He plopped his hand onto my head and smirked at me. "Don't think just because you're leaving that I'll stop being your big brother. I want letters."

I smiled sadly at him, my heart welling. "Okay," I agreed softly. "Will you do something for me, Oli?"

"Name it."

"Watch over Wynn. I have a feeling he isn't going to take this well."

He nodded. "You have my word."

"Thanks."

Bidding Oli and the barracks goodbye with a slow, lingering glance, I went to meet Mitica and Grigore.

TWENTY-FIVE

*M*itica climbed into Grigore's saddle behind me, and we began our ride to Farrloch Hotel. With his chest pressed against my back, his presence brought me both reassurance and despair. I wanted to be strong for him. I knew what needed to be done, but every step closer to our destination made me want to embrace him and never let go.

"What do you know about Celeste Broadstone?" I asked him.

He sighed but answered quietly. "A while back, Mr. Broadstone took a trip to Toronto. Everyone was surprised by how long he stayed. He returned a few months ago with a new wife. Not many people have seen her. It was winter, and she was busy learning how things ran at the hotel. I heard she was young and beautiful but not much else."

I hesitated over my next question, but I needed to know what I was getting into. "What about Mr. Broadstone? He's the one who summoned you to offer help with the Wyboka, right?"

A tinge of sadness colored his soft reply. "Yes, he's an upstanding man in his mid-forties. He made a fortune with the railroad, and then he settled here to build a hotel. I don't have cause to meet with him often, but he's cordial when I do."

I could tell it was difficult for him to praise the man in this situation, but he was honest as ever.

"Was he kind to his wife do you think?" I asked.

He paused, tightening his arms around me. "I don't believe you have to be concerned about that. He will likely take good care of you. And you can always call on me should you need anything at all."

I nodded.

"I mean anything, bucuria mea," he reiterated.

The rest of the ride, we discussed our story to explain where I'd been the past few weeks.

As we approached the imposing, castle-like hotel, Mitica distanced himself as if to appear more like a lawman escorting a lost woman home.

The structure towered above the tops of the evergreens at the summit of a large hill. I counted at least five stories, three of which had balconies on one side.

Seeing the grand prison suddenly made my situation feel all too real. I closed my eyes and took a steadying breath. *You can do this, Erin. It's the right thing to do. It would be easy to just run away with Mitica, but he's too important to keep to yourself.* I gently touched Mitica's hand, which held the reins. Squeezing my eyes shut tighter, I fought nausea and swallowed a sob. *Be strong. I need to be strong. If he sees me this upset, he won't do what's necessary.*

When Grigore stopped near the hotel entrance, I took one more deep breath and resigned to meet my fate.

Mitica helped me out of the saddle. His strong hands lingered on my waist for a moment too long. As his fingertips reluctantly pulled away, I whispered, "I love you." My voice sounded shattered in my ears.

He frowned but nodded once. "And I you, bucuria mea," he murmured.

Unable to face his gaze and keep my resolve, I patted Grigore on the neck. "Goodbye, Grigore. Be good, all right?"

He dipped his head in farewell. His brown horse-eyes seemed sad to me, but perhaps it was my own emotions reflected in his eyes.

I followed Mitica into the foyer of the hotel, a few steps behind as would be expected of a scared amnesiac.

In the lobby, a man with neat graying hair and a Clark Gable mustache directed a bellhop to carry suitcases to a guest's room. He wore a high collar with a tie, a long coat, and a vest. He was the picture of a successful hotel owner. When he turned away from the stairs, his eyes immediately found Mitica and me.

"Celeste, my darling. I have been beside myself with worry," the man exclaimed in what sounded like the accent between English and American that they used in old movies.

He approached me, reaching out to touch my face.

I flinched and took a step toward Mitica. The stranger raised his eyebrows in surprise.

"Mr. Broadstone," Mitica addressed. "Is there somewhere quiet we could speak in private?"

"Of course." Mr. Broadstone nodded and led us away from the front desk to a room off the foyer.

Sliding the doors open, he revealed a library, not as large as Mr. Montmartre's but still respectable. We entered the deserted room, and he closed the door behind us.

Mitica motioned for me to sit in an armchair, and I silently complied. Mr. Broadstone sat in a chair nearby, and Mitica stood near me.

"Mr. Broadstone, I fear I have some troubling news about your wife. I found her near the railroad tracks a few weeks ago. She must have hit her head because she doesn't remember who she is. If I had known she was Mrs. Broadstone, I certainly would have brought her home. I have been looking after her, and she has yet to recall anything prior to me finding her. Miss Dubois mentioned she was traveling to visit her home?"

Mr. Broadstone's brow crinkled in a troubled expression. "Yes, Celeste had a friend from school who was getting married. She was to travel to Toronto for the ceremony. When I didn't hear anything of her arrival, I assumed she was just busy with preparations." He turned his dark eyes on me. "Oh, my dear. What a dreadful experience. Had I only but known your plight, I would have come to you immediately. But fear not, you are safe at home now, and I will have the best physician examine you." He stood and reached out a hand to Mitica. "Thank you, Constable Delaforet. Thank you for protecting my precious wife and returning her home safely.

I am relieved to have such a man in Farrloch. I will be writing to your superiors to express my admiration and gratitude at the job you've done."

Mitica nodded and shook his hand formally. "I will visit again to see how Mrs. Broadstone's recovery progresses."

"That is very kind of you, Constable. You are welcome as always. But I assure you, she will be well cared for."

Mitica nodded again and touched the brim of his hat to me. "Mrs. Broadstone, I do hope everything will be better for you soon."

"Thank you, Constable. I have faith that it will."

Mr. Broadstone held out a hand to me, but I didn't take it. "Come, my dear. Why don't you rest in our room while I send for Dr. Hollander?"

I froze, my eyes wide. "Our room?" I asked.

"Perhaps Mrs. Broadstone would feel more comfortable in a separate room until she regains her memories," Mitica suggested.

Mr. Broadstone frowned. "Of course. I apologize, my dear. It was careless of me. I will have Frederick assign you a separate room. Marguerite can move your things there later."

I gave him a small smile and nodded. "Thank you...Mr. Broadstone."

His eyes saddened at my formal address. "William," he corrected.

"Yeah, sorry. William. I mean, yes, I apologize."

I trailed William past Mitica.

"Thank you again, Constable," William dismissed as he headed for the front desk.

I paused near Mitica, meeting his eyes without knowing when I would see him again. I wanted to tell him how much I loved him, how I would miss him every moment we were apart, and how he was taking my heart with him. But as I opened my mouth, his eyes flashed with a warning.

"Be well, Mrs. Broadstone," he said, bowing to me slightly.

"And you, Constable."

A gentle hand on my elbow pried my attention from Mitica as William returned.

"Come, my dear. Let us get you settled," William directed, leading me away from the man I loved and toward the unknown.

I tried not to squirm as William led me to a room on the second floor. His hand was foreign on my arm, but I thought pulling away wouldn't be worth the potential consequences.

The plush rugs on the second floor were lit by the gentle glow of electric hall lights.

William stopped before a corner room and unlocked the door. I stepped in before him as he motioned me forward.

"I am sorry about the assumption that you would be returning to our chambers. I do not know what I was thinking. I suppose I was relieved to have you home safe," William apologized again as I took in the luxurious suite.

The hotel room was nearly as big as my two-bedroom apartment in Chicago. It had a large living room with a fancy couch and two chairs, the kind antique lovers keep in their houses that no one is allowed to sit in. A small dining table and two chairs were set before a heavily-curtained window.

Through a set of paned French doors, there was a bedroom with a large, neatly-made bed. An ornate fireplace sat opposite another set of doors, which opened onto a balcony.

But it was the bathroom that made me gape in wonder. It had a sink with a mirror, a flush toilet, and a bathtub with running water.

I turned to William, having forgotten what he'd just said.

He smiled gently at me. "I see the room pleases you. I am delighted, my dear. Would you like to freshen up before the doctor arrives?"

I couldn't deny that I eyed the bathtub with desire. "Would that be all right?" I asked.

"Of course, I will instruct Marguerite to bring you more suitable garments."

"Oh, don't worry about it. I have a clean shirt in my bag."

William glowered. "I do not wish to offend you, dear one, but your current attire is not appropriate for your station. I would not wish our guests to see you thus."

I bit my lip. *Eck, what a pain. Whatever. I guess I'll play along for now.* "Oh, I'm sorry," I muttered. "I hadn't thought of that."

He nodded in satisfaction. "I will leave you to it then." He bowed his head at me and exited the suite.

As the tub filled with hot water, Marguerite knocked and entered.

"Madame," she greeted. "Monsieur informed me of your memory loss. How horrible! I am certain I must have frightened you when we met at

Madame Buvons's. I apologize. But I am glad I found you. Had I not gone to purchase some unmentionables, we may never have brought you home."

Yeah, thanks ever so much, Marguerite. What would I have done if I had to stay with the man I love forever? I nodded silently at her.

"Would Madame like me to wash her hair? It looks like it has been a while."

"I think I can handle bathing myself. Thank you."

"Very well. Then, I will go to Madame and Monsieur's chambre and retrieve some essentials, oui?"

"That's fine. Thanks." *Whatever will get you to leave me in peace.*

As I sank into the steamy bliss of a bath, I tried not to blame Marguerite. *It's not really her fault. I mean, it's her job. I wonder if we were any sort of friends in this lifetime.*

The only thing more heavenly at that moment than a bath would have been to be in Mitica's arms. I closed my eyes and swallowed around the lump in my throat. *It's fine. You're fine. You're an adult, and this is the responsible thing to do right now. You'll be together again. We have time. We have the rest of our lives. One day, this will all be a distant memory.* I took a deep breath and let it out all at once.

Knowing the doctor was on his way, I didn't take as long of a bath as I would have liked. Still, I scrubbed hard and felt refreshed when I was finished.

Marguerite was waiting for me as I exited the bathroom in a towel, and we began the epic journey of dressing in appropriate attire. I put on the undergarments she handed me, a chemise and shorts, drawers as she called them. With a suppressed sigh, I pulled on the thigh-high stockings she offered and the garters. But when she held up a corset, I started dubiously at her.

"Um no," I said with finality.

She tilted her head in confusion. "But Madame, how can you—"

I held up my hand to stop her. "There is nothing you can say to get me into that thing. I've agreed to wear a dress, but I'm not going to torture myself."

She frowned but didn't force the issue. "I had no idea Madame was so progressive."

"Call it whatever you like."

Next, she tied a little pillow around my waist.

"What's this?" I asked.

"Your bum pad, Madame," she informed me.

"Of course it is."

I chose the simplest skirt and blouse from the options Marguerite had presented, and I picked the pair of boots with the shortest available heel. The thought that this wasn't so bad after all lived only a moment in my mind before Marguerite destroyed it with three layers of petticoats under my skirt, another undershirt, a blouse, and a belt.

As she approached me with a comb, I thought about doing it myself, but I just gave in.

"What happened to Madame's hair? Do you remember?"

"I had a barber in town cut it. It was far too long to maintain."

She gasped at my answer. "Well...perhaps with pins in the right places and a hat, no one will notice." She stared at me seriously, considering how to make me presentable.

I sighed, allowing her to have her way. "Marguerite, I'm sorry I don't remember you. How long have we known each other?"

"Monsieur hired me shortly after you were married before you left Toronto."

"And when was I married?"

Her face fell as if the thought of me forgetting my husband broke her heart. "Madame has been married less than half a year. Madame and Monsieur are still newlyweds."

Her sadness at someone else's broken love reminded me of Suzette. "Marguerite, could you do me a favor?"

"Of course, Madame."

"Please call me by my given name."

"Madame, I couldn't," she said, aghast.

"I have a feeling I don't have many friends here, just William and his employees. It would make me feel more comfortable if you called me by my first name."

She paused for a while, frowning as she thought. "Very well. If that is your request, then I will address you as Celeste."

My heart sank at the name. I'd almost forgotten she would know me by a name that was no longer mine. *Oh well, better get used to it after all. I need to be able to recognize it.* On the other hand, it was good she didn't call me Erin. Addressing me as Celeste was a reminder that this wasn't who I truly was, not in my soul's current lifetime anyway. It would remind me that this was temporary and that I would return to the one who knew me one day soon.

TWENTY-SIX

*D*r. Hollander was an older gentleman with a wrinkled face and a steady hand. He sat beside me on the couch as William and Marguerite stood nearby.

After checking my pulse, he asked, "You say the furthest you can remember is Constable Delaforet finding you?"

"No, I remember waking up in the barracks. The constable told me he found me and brought me to safety."

"Why didn't he contact me?" the doctor asked.

Oh, shit. "Well, my only injury was a bump on my head. I couldn't remember anything, but he said someone would report to him if I were missed. Also, we thought I would remember if just given time."

Dr. Hollander pursed his wrinkled lips but nodded. "Well, he is quite right, of course. There is not much to be done in cases of amnesia. Still, it will be much easier for you to remember surrounded by a place and people you know. Are you feeling weak at all? Fatigued?"

"Oh, no. I'm fine physically. My bump is gone and everything."

He checked the spot I'd randomly chosen on my head. "Very well, Mrs. Broadstone. I suggest resuming your routine. Read letters from your family and friends and speak to your husband about the past. In short, be exposed to anything that may trigger your memory."

I nodded like I took everything he said seriously. "I understand, Doctor."

He smiled gently and patted my hand. "Worry not, Mrs. Broadstone. I'm certain your memories will return in time. For now, rely on those around you, and let me know if you experience any headaches or dizziness."

"I will. Thank you."

"I will return next week to see how you are faring. Mr. Broadstone, would you mind showing me out?"

"Of course, Doctor," William agreed and left with the doctor to discuss my treatment amongst men no doubt.

I stared after them wondering exactly what was being said.

"It is a relief to hear your memories will return, non, Celeste?" Marguerite encouraged. "I am certain they will come back soon, now that you are home and with Monsieur."

I nodded as if comforted. *At least I have an alibi for not knowing anything. Dr. Hollander didn't seem too suspicious of Mitica. I wonder how long it will take to figure out what happened to Celeste or if I ever will. I hope Mitica hears from the Zgrimties soon. In the meantime, I should gather as much information as I can on Celeste Broadstone. It will be easier to avoid being recognized as her once I leave the more I know about her.*

"Marguerite, the doctor said I should get back to my daily routine. What exactly do I usually do all day?"

As Marguerite opened her mouth to answer, William returned and interrupted her. "That can wait until tomorrow. Today, I think you should rest. Are you hungry?"

"I am. I didn't have a chance to eat breakfast." *Because Marguerite uprooted my life.*

William frowned as if displeased at Mitica's treatment of me. "Marguerite, go to the kitchens and order a repast for Madame."

"Right away, Monsieur." Marguerite nodded and left to complete her mission.

"I don't need to rest, William. As I told the doctor, I'm feeling strong."

He sat beside me, took my hand, and kissed it lightly.

I gritted my teeth and resisted the urge to snatch it back as my stomach clenched.

"I know, my dear. However, before you concern yourself with your daily duties here at the hotel, I would like to speak to you in private at more length."

Eck. "In private" sounds too intimate.

"I'm certain you have more personal questions than how the hotel functions. Perhaps you would like to know about your family or how we met?"

That is much more valuable information than what Celeste did at the hotel. "Yeah, I would like to hear about that," I agreed. "I mean, yes, you're right."

"As I thought. Well, I have some things to attend to this afternoon, but shall we talk about it over dinner?"

I nodded. "That's fine. In the interim, would you happen to know if I kept a journal? Reading it could help a lot."

William stilled for a moment then quirked his mouth. "I don't believe you did."

"That's a shame."

"Indeed," he answered without hesitation. Then, he excused himself, promising to return that evening for supper.

Left alone, I heaved a sigh of relief. *It's going to be tough with everyone watching me so closely.* I scanned the comfortable suite again. *This place is beyond nice.* My heart sank. *But I'd rather be in the cramped barracks with Mitica and Oli, even if I can't bathe every day.* My chest tightened, and my body flushed, anxiety making me uncomfortably warm. I went onto the balcony for some fresh air.

The empty second-floor balcony had a white, wooden railing like a picket fence marking the boundary of my captivity. The balcony was big enough to hold the table and chairs in the sitting room of the suite, but it was far too cold to eat outside. I brushed the accumulated snow from the railing and leaned my elbows on it.

"Well, at least the tourists are getting their money's worth," I muttered to the gorgeous scenery.

The small valley before me was covered in snow, which sparkled in the afternoon sun. In the distance, wooded mountains climbed to picturesque peaks. Though the snow obscured it, I knew the winding trail that led through the valley and into the mountains. I had traveled it once before when I'd first visited the Wyboka Reserve. The reserve was likely a few miles away, but I would never forget that first horse ride. The scenery, the company, the thrill—I couldn't believe how much had changed in just a few weeks.

"Celeste?" Marguerite called from inside.

She frowned as I came in from the balcony. "You should not go outside in such weather without a coat. You could catch a chill."

"I wasn't out there very long," I assured her. *Besides, why would I need a coat with so many layers?*

I sat at the table, the meal she brought in front of me. It was simple, a ham and cheese sandwich more or less, but it satisfied my hunger.

"So what do you say we go exploring after I eat?" I asked Marguerite as I reached for my cup of warm tea.

She raised her eyebrows. "Monsieur said you should rest today."

I took a sip of tea and squinched my nose at the taste. "What kind of tea is this?"

"Earl Gray, your favorite."

"Oh. Well, could I have English breakfast tea with milk and sugar in the future, please?"

A line formed between her eyebrows. "Breakfast tea? Very well."

I returned the cup to its saucer. "I know he said I should rest, but I really am fine. I can't stay still in this room all afternoon. Come on. If we're careful, he'll never know the difference." I smiled encouragingly at her.

Her expression became stern. "I do not think you should go against Monsieur's wishes. If he is telling you to rest, then it is for the best."

Tch, I see where your loyalties lie, Marguerite. Fine, then. I sighed, seemingly defeated. "You're probably right, Marguerite. I'm sure William knows what's best. Instead of exploring, how about I get acquainted with my everyday things. You only moved a few essentials from our room, right? Why don't you go get the rest of my things? I bet everyday items are great for triggering memories."

She nodded in satisfaction. "Oui, that is a good idea. You rest here, and I will return."

I smiled at her. "Okay."

As soon as she'd left the door, I rushed to it and peeked outside. She went down the hall and entered another room. Smirking to myself, I slipped out of the room and quickly descended the stairs before she could see me.

When I was far enough down the stairs to see the lobby, I peeked down to determine if there was anyone there. The man William had called Frederick was the lone resident, but his back was turned to me.

The wooden stairs had a rug down the middle, but most of the lobby's floor was uncovered wood. I removed my shoes. Holding them in one hand and lifting my skirts with the other, I crept down the stairs, across the lobby, and out the front door.

Outside, I quickly put my shoes on. It was chilly out, but I wasn't cold.

I scanned the scenery before me and weighed my options. *Right is the direction Mitica and I came from. I saw a stone wall with an iron gate beside the hotel when we approached. Left it is then.*

Not far down the cobbled road, I came upon a few wooden buildings adjacent to a corral. There didn't appear to be anyone around, so I entered the wide, open door to the stable.

The unmistakable scent of horses and straw was unexpectedly comforting for a city dweller like myself. Long rows of stalls flanked the center aisle. There must've been at least ten on each side.

I peeked into stalls as I strolled through the stable. The first few were empty. When I did meet a resident, she was a dark brown pony with a white spot between her gentle eyes.

I smiled as she stuck her head out to greet me. "Hey there, sweetheart," I cooed. "What's your name?"

I found the name Saundra etched neatly into a wooden nameplate when I scanned the frame of her stall door.

"Saundra?" I asked.

Her ears flicked in recognition.

"That's a pretty name for a pretty girl." I held my hand to her nose so she could sniff me before petting her neck.

"She's sweet, isn't she?" a deep voice beside me asked.

I jumped, and Saundra snuffled.

"Jesus, you scared me," I laughed, turning to the owner of the voice.

A tall, black man with high cheekbones and a square jaw smiled down at me from under his cowboy hat. "I'm sorry. I didn't mean to startle you, Miss."

"It's all right. I should've been paying attention."

He nodded his acknowledgment. "Are you a guest?" he asked. "We don't have any trail rides scheduled today because of the snow. But you can put in a request at the front desk if you want to get a group together for after it melts. It shouldn't be more than a few days."

He must have never met Celeste. "A guest? No, I guess you could say I work here." *Maybe? I'm not really sure what I do yet.* "And what about you? Do you work here, Mr....?"

"Oh, I beg your pardon, Miss. You aren't wearing a uniform, so I just assumed. You can just call me Butch. I run the stables for the hotel."

I waved my hand. "Don't worry about it, and you can call me Erin." *Damn. I meant Celeste. Oh, well.*

He smiled kindly at me. "You like horses, Erin?"

I shrugged. "Sure. I like them a lot better when I'm not riding them though."

"An animal lover then?"

I nodded. "That's probably more accurate. So Butch, how long have you worked here? I haven't seen you before." *At least I assume I haven't since you don't recognize me.*

"Not long. Just a few months. I don't go up to the house much, and Campbell and I generally eat in the hand quarters with the lads."

"Who's Campbell?"

"Campbell drives the carriage for the hotel."

I vaguely remember there being a carriage in front of Madame Buvons's when Marguerite accosted me. Was Campbell driving it?

"I hope you guys are being taken care of out here."

"We have no complaints. A solid roof and warm food? It's better than most of us are used to."

"I'm glad to hear it."

"So you work up at the hotel?"

I nodded, not even sure how to elaborate, but Butch was nice enough not to push.

"Well, feel free to come visit the horses anytime you like."

"That's nice of you, Butch. I think I will come down when I get the chance."

He nodded. "If you'll excuse me. I've got some work to do yet."

"Go for it," I said, apologizing for distracting him.

"You have a nice day, Erin."

"Thanks, Butch. See you later."

As Butch headed out of the stables, a slender, pale man met him at the door. Whatever he'd planned to say was forgotten when he saw me.

"Losh!" the man exclaimed with a Scottish accent. "I didn't know the lady was coming to visit. You should have had the lads clean more thoroughly."

"The lady?" Butch looked over his shoulder at me, and I pretended not to overhear their conversation.

"Aye, the lady: Mrs. Broadstone."

Butch grunted. "Well, I had no idea who she is, Campbell. In any case, she seems comfortable with the way things are. She didn't complain to me, so I think it's fine."

Campbell snorted. "You best be careful, Butch, being alone with the lady. I don't know if Mr. Broadstone is a jealous man, but I would be if she were my wife."

"If anyone needs to be careful, it's you, making comments like that," Butch chided.

Campbell didn't respond.

"All right, we have work to do. Stop staring, and get to it," Butch ordered, dragging Campbell away from the stable entrance.

I sighed heavily. "Butch seems nice," I told Saundra. "I could use a friend in a place like this. Anyway, at least I can come visit you whenever I want. Next time, I'll bring you something delicious. Maybe an apple or a carrot, eh? Or how about a sugar cube? Would you like that?"

Saundra bobbed her head as if she recognized the words, and I laughed. "All right, it's a promise then."

I petted her velvety coat absently and wondered how long I'd been gone. *Marguerite is probably freaking out right now. Should I feel bad for tricking her? Maybe, but I don't. She's a little too eager to please William for being Celeste's maid. Not that I care, but that means I can't trust her. I better head back though. I don't want her to find me here. I'd rather this be a place where I can go to get away.*

"Well, have a good night, Saundra. Sleep well. I'll see you again soon." I gave her one last stroke and left the stables.

As I approached the hotel's front entrance, Marguerite exited the iron gate in the stone wall beside the building. She heaved a sigh, pressing a hand to her chest.

"Celeste, I was worried when I returned and you were gone. Monsieur told you to rest today. I thought you had gone to the garden as usual, but you were not there. Where did you go?"

I shrugged. "Nowhere special. I just took a walk. I needed fresh air." *Wait. Why am I explaining myself to her anyway?*

"And you did not even wear a coat." She tsked.

I didn't respond.

"Well, come inside before Monsieur realizes you have disobeyed him." She waved me toward the door.

I curled my lip. *Disobeyed? Really? She's got to be fucking kidding me.* I clenched my jaw instead of saying something churlish.

Frederick nodded a good afternoon to us as we passed by on the way back to my room.

"Which room is William's?" I asked Marguerite when we reached the second floor.

"Monsieur and you share this room," she corrected, pointing at the door nearest the stairs.

It appeared that Marguerite had left in a rush after having found me missing from my room. A large trunk lay near the entrance in the middle of the walkway, and an armful of garments was folded over the back of the couch.

She rushed forward to move the trunk and organize the strewn clothes. "I will take care of this presently," she assured.

Normally, I would've offered her assistance, but I wasn't feeling generous.

As I sat at the small table, I rested my head in my hand and stared out the window. *It's boring here. Lonely.* I ignored the pang in my chest as I thought about Mitica. Having always expressed myself through the written word, I wished I had a journal to ease my anxiety. *It's probably not a good idea though. Anything written could be easily found.*

My eyes slid to Marguerite, who was organizing in the bedroom. *She wouldn't think twice about handing stuff I wrote over to William. She didn't turn me in for leaving when he'd told me to stay, but that was probably to save herself.*

The world outside the paned window was snowy and perfect. My eyes lost focus the harder I stared at the freedom that beckoned me.

TWENTY-SEVEN

*T*he rest of the afternoon was dull and uneventful in my confinement. I was almost grateful when William arrived in the evening for dinner, though I would've preferred he was a dashing brunet in a red serge or a crimson-haired Romanian with a magic all his own.

"Good evening, my dear," he greeted. "I hope you are feeling rested."

"I wasn't tired to begin with," I couldn't help but retort.

He nodded, squinting ever so slightly. "Forgive me. It is a husband's prerogative to worry about his wife."

Casually referring to me as his wife made my stomach curdle, but I tried for a neutral expression. "You said you would tell me about my past?" I asked after a pause.

"Indeed. Let us discuss it as we dine."

It wasn't five minutes before room service arrived with dinner. The smell of steak and potatoes made my mouth water as the waiter set it on the small table.

"Shall we?" William asked, pulling a chair out for me.

I know it's the manners of the time, but ugh it's a little creepy.

I sat, and he pushed my chair in. As I lay my napkin in my lap, he took the seat across.

He smiled sweetly as he said, "This almost reminds me of when we were courting."

Eck. "Yeah? How did that happen exactly? How did we meet?"

His smile softened. "We met at an art exhibition. You love art and music. You've often used your family's wealth and position to patronize artists and musicians."

"I did, huh?" *Celeste was wealthy then?* "So I was sponsoring an artist's show?"

He nodded. "Indeed, a talented young painter from Toronto."

"Is that where I'm from?"

"Yes."

"But why were you in Toronto if your hotel is all the way out here?"

"I was in town for business, looking to entice the people of Toronto to travel west."

"You were advertising the hotel?"

He nodded. "The art show had many people who enjoy travel and can afford to do so."

"I see. So that's how we met. Then what happened?"

"You were quite taken with the idea of the west, the Rockies, the Indians, the adventure. You invited me to tea so you could hear all about it."

"And we began courting after that? How did my family feel about me marrying someone who lives so far away?" *Not to mention who is twice my age.*

"I cannot say they were pleased to have you moving away, but you would hear no objections. Your father and brother were particularly sad to see you go. On the other hand, your family's logging company has a claim in British Columbia, and your father often travels there for business. It is not as if they would never see you."

That's good to know. "I have a brother? Do I have any other siblings?"

He frowned. "Jacques would be distraught if he knew you'd forgotten him. No, you have just one younger brother and your parents."

Celeste and her brother must've been close. "How much younger is Jacques?"

"Two or three years," he answered.

I nodded, internalizing the information. Before I could pull away, William reached across the table and covered my hand with his. "You're not wearing your wedding ring. Did you lose it somewhere, I wonder? The vows we made to each other still hold true, my dear."

Mitica would've noticed if I'd been wearing a ring when he found me. Did I lose it when I was killed? Was it stolen? No, if Celeste had been mugged, they would have taken her money, too. I gently pulled my hand away, using it to grab the glass of wine before me. "Which vows are those?" I asked, watching him closely.

His eyes bored into mine, and I tried not to flinch as the hair on my neck and arms stood up.

"I vowed to bring you out here and give you partial dominion over the hotel. I went to Toronto to invite guests, and you were determined to help me make the hotel attractive to polite society. You wanted a grand project in the west, and I have given you just that."

"And what did you get out of it?"

"Well, your assistance, of course. Not to mention the love and duty of a beautiful, young wife."

I cringed at the thought of this man touching me intimately. It's not that he was unattractive or that the age gap particularly bothered me. It was more about who he wasn't than who he was. *Did Celeste love him? He seems to think she did. I guess he is mature and gentlemanly. But her soul mate wasn't three miles away. I sort of feel sorry for William. I suppose she should be grateful she and Wynn never met. Then again, she is me, and we did meet. In this body, am I not Celeste?* That philosophical spiral of thought was interrupted when I noticed William staring at me intensely.

"Do you truly remember nothing? Not our courtship, our home, our wedding, not even your family?" His tone made it sound like it was all some elaborate ruse.

Why would he think Celeste would do that? "I'm sorry. I don't remember anything. I don't remember meeting you. I don't remember loving or marrying you. I didn't recognize my own name when Marguerite found me."

His stony expression gave nothing of his emotions away.

Is he upset? Angry? Shocked? Heartbroken?

"Worry not, my dear. We have time. You fell in love with me not long ago. I am positive you will again."

Not likely. I didn't respond.

"In the meantime, I will just have to be patient. As Dr. Hollander recommended, you will return to your daily routine in the hopes you will recover your memories. Tomorrow, I will show you around the hotel and explain your duties."

"Okay."

"As for tonight, I suggest you go to sleep early. I will send Marguerite in to assist you."

"I can handle changing into pajamas by myself. I'll see you tomorrow."

"Very well. Goodnight, my dear."

He reached out to me as if by habit. When I shrunk back, he froze and lowered his arm.

"Of course. Forgive me," he muttered. He bowed to me then left the room.

After locking the door behind him, I took a steadying breath. *What am I even supposed to do in this situation?*

I numbly got ready for bed, though it was still early. Marguerite had neatly organized the clothes in a dresser, and it took only seconds to locate a nightgown. Having washed my face, I stood uncertainly in the center of the bedroom.

Mitica wouldn't risk riding Grigore this close to the hotel, and he wouldn't know which room I'm in anyway. Should I call for him? But it's still early. What if he disappeared when Oli was right beside him? I miss him, but it's not really an emergency. I feel like this isn't a reason to call his true name.

My chest ached as I came to terms with the idea I wouldn't be seeing Mitica that night. I squeezed my eyes shut against the burning in my nose, and I took a slow, deep breath.

The safety and comfort I'd allowed myself to feel with Mitica were far-gone. When I'd let him in, I'd felt nothing could take him or that security away. The hollow ache inside me at that moment told me I'd been very wrong. Even though I'd been the one to leave, I was abandoned, alone on a raft in a stormy sea. Forlorn. Vulnerable.

Still, I couldn't bring myself to regret letting him in. The brief moments when he'd given my heart wings, when he'd showed me I was brave and beautiful, it was worth the pain.

I will be with him again soon. Nothing to worry about. And I can call on him if I really need him. My mind assured me, but my heart didn't believe.

The pain in my chest told me I needed him. I refused to concede. *You're being silly. Come on. Adult time.* The agony and despair didn't subside, but my resolve didn't waver.

After opening the balcony door, I stepped into the cold night. The waning half-moon lit up the blanket of snow, creating more light than usual.

I thought about the night Mitica had overheard me singing my mother's moon lullaby, the night he'd told me he wanted to know me. So much had happened since then. Everything had changed.

In a tone too broken by longing, I began to sing the song again, hoping the light of the moon would carry my love to him when it lit upon his face. My voice nearly broke as I sang, the words soft, thick with emotion. I knew Mitica would be feeling the same as I, and I had to believe my message would reach him.

It took me a while to fall asleep that first night alone. The bed was far too big and too comfortable.

When I was finally able to sleep, I awoke in the middle of the night, overheated and sick to my stomach. Had I not experienced this feeling many times before, I would've thought I was going to vomit. But I knew. My stress always manifested physically. Of course, my stomach hadn't acted this nervous since the night before I'd started my job at *The Chicago Telegraph*.

I threw off my blankets and rushed to the balcony door before pressing my forehead to the cold glass. It cooled my clammy face, but it only gave me mild relief.

I cracked the door and lay on the floor with my face near the opening. Frozen night air wafted over my skin. I sighed in relief as the nausea subsided. After a few minutes, I started to shiver, which was exactly what I wanted. I wouldn't feel sick if I was cold. I curled into a ball on my side and drifted into a fitful sleep.

Sometime in the night, I must've gotten too cold because the balcony door was closed when I awoke. I cracked my eyelids and stared out at the predawn light through the window.

I stretched out onto my back, groaning at the soreness left from shivering for most of the night on the floor. The shoulder I'd been lying on was particularly stiff.

Closing my eyes, I took long, deep breaths and systematically willed my body to relax. My head throbbed against the hard floor, but at least I wasn't nauseated.

I hate when stress gets the better of me. I feel so weak. Maybe I should try meditating. It may help me deal. In any case, the first day is always the worst.

I didn't know when William or Marguerite would come for me, but I knew I was in no condition to receive them. I hoped more sleep would help my headache, and I crawled into bed and dozed for a few more hours.

TWENTY-EIGHT

*G*olden rays of sunlight filtered into the room, tickling my face. I cracked my eyelids cautiously then took a deep breath. I felt much more rested. My limbs were still sore, but my headache was gone.

As I lay in bed, the room I'd thought was so nice the day before felt uncomfortably large and empty in the sparkling morning light. The silence smothered my ears, and my own sighs sounded too loud.

"I miss you," I whispered. "Hurry up, will you? I don't want to need to be strong."

A soft knock at my door announced a visitor. I sighed again and threw off my blankets. *I would've liked to loosen up with some yoga before anyone came around.* The floor was pleasantly cool beneath my bare feet. Before I was halfway to opening the door, Marguerite unlocked it and entered.

"Whoa there, lady," I said, taken aback. "Don't just enter someone's room without her answering. How did you even get a key?"

Marguerite stopped and bowed her head in apology. "I am sorry. Monsieur gave me the other key so I may help you more easily."

"Did you used to enter my room unbidden before?"

"Non, you usually called for me. Monsieur was concerned you would need more assistance in your delicate state."

I held out my hand, and she passed me the key. "Let's just keep it the way it was. I can call if I need your help."

She dipped her head again. "Very well."

I sighed. "When am I supposed to meet William?"

"Monsieur requested you meet him in the dining room shortly."

"All right, I'll get ready then."

It took almost an hour for me to bathe and dress, and another fifteen for Marguerite to pin my short hair under a simple hat. *Will I ever get used to having a personal maid? I don't like it, but I should probably play along.*

On the ground floor, Marguerite led me to a cozy dining room with small tables covered in pristine white tablecloths and east-facing windows alight with morning sunshine. The cheerfulness of the scene tasted bitter. I spotted William at a table near a swinging kitchen door and went to meet him. He noticed my approach over his newspaper and stood from his chair.

"Good morning, my dear. I hope you slept well."

I took a seat without answering, and he sat again.

"So what does my normal day look like, William?"

His eyebrows rose slightly. "Right to business I see."

When a young waiter in a smart butler-type uniform brought me a cup of tea and asked what I'd like for breakfast, I told him buttered toast. He nodded without judgment and left to fill my order. After he'd gone, I drank some water, leaving the tea untouched.

"You are not hungry this morning?" William asked.

More like my stomach can't handle anything else right now. "No, I'm not very hungry."

He frowned, analyzing me.

"So what do I do here?" I repeated.

He paused for a moment before answering. "In the morning, you check on the kitchen staff to ensure everything is ready before they start breakfast. Then, you eat."

"Okay. Then what?"

"Then, you meet with Harrison, our activities coordinator."

"What do I do with him?"

"You plan and schedule activities for the guests."

"Like what?"

"Skiing, horseback riding, cards, hunting, the sort of pastimes our guests would enjoy."

At this point, the waiter returned with my toast. I thanked him before he left.

"What do I do after I meet Harrison?"

William nodded toward my food. "Why don't you eat? I promise I will explain everything as we go along."

I nibbled at my toast, not wanting to upset my stomach.

The scene before me was so surreal. I was eating breakfast in a glowing dining room with my husband, not a day after leaving the arms of my soul mate. *If Mitica was sitting across from me now, it would be romantic.* As it was, a stranger I was supposed to know and love sat in his place. The juxtaposition turned my stomach, but I stuffed the last bite of toast into my mouth and forced it down with water. I stared out into the shining valley, knowing he was out there somewhere.

When we'd both finished breakfast, William took me to the kitchen. Two immaculate chefs went about cooking. They looked up at our presence and acknowledged us shortly with a nod.

"This is Louis and Gabriel, my dear. Gentleman, the lady is in delicate health at the moment. I expect you to be understanding."

They dipped their heads in reply without stopping their work.

William gave them no further explanation, and I made a mental note to clarify to them that I didn't remember anything.

"Every evening after supper, you come to the kitchen and set the menu for the following day," William told me.

"Okay."

On the way out of the kitchen, I officially met our waiter, Oscar.

Next, William took me to the front desk where Frederick, a pale man with light hair and piercing eyes, stood guard.

"Welcome back, Madam," he said formally.

"Uh, thank you," I muttered.

"Sometimes, you tend the front desk so Frederick may complete other tasks," William informed. "Frederick can show you how to check guests in and out later."

"All right." *Jeez, it feels like my first day at a new job. I should have brought a notebook. I wonder if Celeste knew what she was signing up for when she got married.*

Behind the front desk, there was an office with two additional desks. One was empty, and a young man with broad shoulders and wavy, golden hair poured over a pile of papers at the other.

"This is Harrison," William told me.

Harrison looked up from his work and smiled at me. "Celeste, you're back," he proclaimed happily in an Australian accent.

William frowned and cleared his throat, but Harrison appeared unapologetic.

"My wife has had an accident. She does not recall anything from her time here."

Harrison gaped at William's declaration. "Is that true? That's dreadful. You don't remember anything at all?"

I shook my head, wondering why William had chosen to tell Harrison about my memory loss but made it sound like it was only my time at the hotel I didn't remember.

Harrison's expression told me the news hurt him. *We must've been friends for him to call me by my first name and for him to be that upset that I've forgotten him.*

"I'm sorry this happened to you," Harrison said sincerely. "But don't worry. We'll help you adjust. You let me know if you need anything."

Touched by his earnest concern, I was glad to know Celeste had a friend like him.

"And you will inform me immediately if my wife is in need of assistance, Harrison," William ordered.

I blinked at William, startled by his territorial tone.

Harrison paused for a moment too long. "Of course, Mr. Broadstone."

"Through there," William pointed to a door at the other side of the office, "is my office. If you need anything, you can often find me there."

I nodded.

"Come, my dear. Let us continue the tour," William instructed, grabbing my elbow and leading me out the way we'd come.

I met Harrison's eyes and smiled gently, trying to thank him without words.

Near the library, I followed William down a hall. Through a set of double doors was a large, empty room with tall, arched windows on either side. At the far end, paned French doors led to what looked like a patio and garden.

"This is our ballroom."

Rain pelted the glass windows, and I could see it melting the snow in the garden. *The weather changes fast here.*

William pursed his lips. "I will show you the garden another day."

"Okay. Is there anything else I need to know?"

"Not particularly. You generally attend most meals with the guests and host tea every afternoon. You also have time to yourself to do with as you wish."

Host tea? I hope that's not as intimidating as it sounds. "So you've shown me the entire hotel then?"

He nodded. "Everything except the laundry and employee quarters."

And the stables, but I guess that's not necessarily part of the hotel. "I'd like to see those as well."

He raised his eyebrows as if that was an unusual request. "Very well. This way."

I followed him down a hallway near the front desk. It was clean but simple, clearly a place guests were not supposed to see.

"All employees may be housed here should they wish, though some choose to stay elsewhere," William said, gesturing down the hall of doors. "Most of the maids are local and live nearby, and the stables' staff stays nearer to the horses."

I'd like to see one of the rooms, but I don't want to invade someone's privacy. "And the laundry?"

He nodded, and I trailed him through a door and down a flight of stairs.

In the dimly-lit basement, a group of at least five Asian men labored over washtubs, hand-washing bed sheets and towels.

They chatted at each other in a language I could only just recognize as Chinese. When the man nearest us noticed our presence, he said something to the others. They all went silent and paused in their work. The men bowed far too low and for too long.

Ducking my head at their uncomfortable show of fealty, I was relieved when they started working again. I looked around the basement. There was hardly any light, the heat from the washtubs was like a sauna, and there was little ventilation. I frowned. *It would suck working in this environment. I can't believe William allows such working conditions. Maybe I can figure out a way to help them.*

The young man who had announced our presence approached and bowed again.

"My dear, this is Xi Wei. He manages the laundry and these men."

I bowed to Xi Wei to the same extent he had to me. "It's nice to meet you, Xi Wei. Thank you for your hard work."

I looked up into Xi Wei's dark eyes, wide with shock. When I got a closer look at him, I saw that he was quite pretty. I smiled, thinking he looked like a guy who would be an international pop idol back home.

"Mrs. Broadstone," he started in a thick accent. "It is an honor to finally meet you. I have known your husband for many years. My father worked for him on the railroad. He was generous enough to give us work."

"I hope you'll let me know if you or your men need anything," I told him.

He dipped his head. "We are all very well here."

I frowned at the working conditions again.

"That concludes our tour, my dear," William announced, looking at his pocket watch. "It is nearly time for the next meal. Why don't you go to the kitchen to see if Louis and Gabriel have everything they need? I have paperwork to attend to."

I nodded. "All right." I turned to Xi Wei. "It was nice to meet you," I said again in farewell.

He bowed. "May you have peace wherever you go."

I smiled and bowed back. "You too."

TWENTY-NINE

*B*ack in the foyer, I split from William and went toward the kitchen. The dining room was empty except for Oscar, the waiter, who was folding napkins in preparation for the next meal. He didn't look up when I passed through to the kitchen.

Louis and Gabriel were busy cutting meat and chopping vegetables. They spared me a glance as I entered through the swinging door. I smiled into their uninterested faces.

"Hey, guys, I just want to make sure you have everything you need."

They didn't respond.

I watched them expectantly.

Louis, the older of the two, had long, gray hair, which was pulled back at the nape of his neck. His stiff expression seemed to say he was less than pleased as he expertly cut beef into even slices.

Gabriel's younger face was more indifferent. He was taller than Louis, and his chin-length, golden brown hair was tucked neatly behind his ears.

"So...do you have everything you need then?"

"Oui," Louis answered shortly.

"Okay. Well, that's good." I tried not to let their coldness affect my tone. *Did Celeste not get along with them?* "So listen, guys. I don't want to distract you while you're working, but William didn't exactly tell you the whole story earlier. The truth is: I was in an accident. I don't really remember anything about my life here. I don't want to be a burden, and I'm going to work really hard to support you guys in whatever you need. Please be patient with me, and feel free to correct me if I'm doing anything wrong. Okay?"

They stopped what they were doing and looked up at me.

Gabriel's brow crinkled as if he'd only partially understood what I'd been saying, and Louis clicked his tongue in irritation. Louis muttered in French.

"We do not understand," Gabriel said slowly with a thick, French accent. "Please repeat en français."

I frowned, thinking how my Mom had forced me to take Spanish in high school, saying it would be more useful. *Mitica never did teach me very many words.* "But I don't speak French."

Just then, the door swung open as Oscar entered the kitchen.

"Oscar, do you speak French?"

He blinked. "Oui, Madame."

I sighed in relief. "Would you mind translating for me?"

He tilted his head. "Of course, but Madame speaks French very well."

"It's a long story. Please tell Louis and Gabriel what I'm saying."

After Oscar had translated, they all seemed to understand my situation.

Louis spat something unpleasantly, and Gabriel answered in a soothing tone. Then, Gabriel turned and asked Oscar something.

"They would like to know how involved you will be in the kitchen if you can't remember anything," Oscar told me.

I frowned, thinking. "I'm going to be honest with you guys. I don't know anything about cooking. The only things I care about is that the food is good and prepared in a clean and safe way. If you have ideas for the menus, I'll gladly rely on your expertise. You guys just let me know what you need."

Oscar translated. Gabriel's eyebrows rose in response, and Louis's stern expression gave way to a satisfied hint of a smile.

I get the feeling William and Celeste micromanage them. "So does that work for everyone?" I asked, giving them two thumbs up.

They blinked at me. Oscar translated, and they nodded their approval. Gabriel even hesitantly raised his thumbs in a sympathetic gesture.

"Great. I'll let you get to it then," I said before leaving.

I heaved a deep sigh once I was in the dining room. Oscar soon returned with silverware. I insisted on helping him set the tables, not really knowing what else to do with myself.

After we'd finished, I sat by the window and watched the rain streak lazily down the glass. The snow that had blanketed the landscape that morning had melted into inconsistent patches.

It's so strange here, like a completely different world than when I was with the Mounties and Mitica. It's so...mundane. How long will it be before I can leave with Mitica? Will all the snow be melted? Will spring be in full bloom? I hope he's staying out of the rain.

I thought of his soaked undershirt clinging to his broad chest and felt my face heat. Then, sadness squeezed my heart.

Oscar approached the table at which I sat with a warm plate. "Would you like to try the dish before the guests arrive?" he asked me, setting the plate before me.

"Sure," I answered, picking up my fork and spearing a cream-covered, sliced potato. I blew on it softly before I took a bite. It's soft texture and delicate sauce melted on my tongue. "Mmm," I complimented. "It's very good."

Looking over at the kitchen, I saw Gabriel's golden-brown head peeking out around the door. I smiled and gave him a thumbs up from across the room. He returned my smile with a nod of satisfaction.

As I continued to slowly eat the meal, I wondered how Celeste had stayed so skinny with such deliciously rich food to eat. By the time I was finishing, guests began to filter into the dining room. I watched Oscar seat them and take their orders before I approached to introduce myself.

I went to the table nearest me first, where a pair of older gentlemen sat. "Good afternoon, how are you both today?"

Their dulled eyes lit up. They both had thick muttonchops that led to prestigious mustaches.

"We are quite well, lady. Quite well indeed," the shorter, ruddier man declared.

I smiled. "I'm glad to hear it. I'm Er... Celeste Broadstone. I hope you'll let me know if there's anything you need while you stay with us."

"We are quite comfortable, dear lady," the grayer of the two said. "Your father, Mr. Broadstone, is an excellent host."

I ducked my head and cleared my throat. "Actually...Mr. Broadstone is...my husband." Sickness bubbled in my stomach, and I silently apologized to Mitica.

The older man blinked in surprise, but his counterpart was quick to cover for him. "We had heard Mrs. Broadstone was young and beautiful, but you are much lovelier than described. Forgive Higgins for his misstep."

I waved my hand dismissively. "It's not a problem. Don't worry about it Mr....?"

"Oh, pardon me, lady. I am Reginald Sheffield, and this is Colonel George Higgins."

I smiled and nodded at them. "Well, it's nice to meet you, Mr. Sheffield, Colonel Higgins. Please let me know if you need anything during your stay."

"Of course," Reginald promised.

Not far away, a young couple gazed lovingly at each other. I didn't want to intrude, but it was my job to mingle.

"Good afternoon, are you both doing well today?"

The young lady with big, blue eyes blushed an attractive shade of pink. Her companion, a well-dressed young man, answered. "Very well. Thank you."

"I don't mean to interrupt your meal. I just wanted to introduce myself. I'm Celeste Broadstone. Please let me know if there's anything you need while you're here."

"It's a pleasure to meet you, Miss Broadstone. I'm Alfred Durant, and this is my wife Jane."

Jane blushed deeper and smiled at me.

"Are you on your honeymoon?" I asked.

"Why, yes, we are," Alfred responded.

"Congratulations. Thank you for staying with us on such an important occasion. I hope you make many happy memories while you're here."

"Thank you, Miss Broadstone," Jane said softly.

"And you'll let me know if there's anything I can do?"

"Of course." Alfred nodded.

A trio of giggles drew my attention, and I stopped at the next table as a matronly woman sat with three young women. They stifled their laughter as she censured them with a look.

I smiled at them. "Good afternoon, ladies. How are you?"

"We are well, thank you," the matron answered formally.

"I'm glad to hear it. Well, I just stopped to introduce myself. I'm Celeste Broadstone. Please let me know if there's anything you need during your stay."

"I will, thank you. I'm Elizabeth Pickens. This is my daughter, Mary, and her friends, Sarah Grant and Juniper Willis." The elder woman indicated each girl in turn.

They smiled and nodded at me.

"It's nice to meet you all. I hope you enjoy your stay."

"Miss Broadstone," Mary began. "Is there anything planned for tonight after supper?"

"I'm not sure. Let me check with our activities coordinator, and I'll get back to you."

"Thank you."

"No problem."

As there was only one more occupied table, I decided to introduce myself to the two young men before going to see Harrison. Having been slyly watching the three young ladies, the men were not surprised by my approach. Their dark eyes locked on me with polite appreciation.

"Won't you join us, Miss?" the more attractive of the two offered. He was long and lean with a confidence that said he knew of his charms.

"Oh, I've already eaten," I told him.

"Well, that's all right. Sit down and have a cup of tea and a chat," the broader man insisted, adding to his friend's invitation.

I hesitated. *Well, I guess William did tell me to be a good hostess.*

"All right. I could use a cup of tea." I sat in the free chair between them.

They smiled congenially. "What's your name, Miss?" the first man asked.

"I'm Celeste Broadstone. And you?"

They didn't seem to recognize the last name. "I'm Stewart Thomas, and this is my friend, Cole Linton."

"It's nice to meet you both. Are you here on vacation?"

"Yes," Cole answered.

"That's nice. Thank you for choosing to stay with us."

"Of course." Stewart was silent a moment then added as if by afterthought. "Had I known such a lovely woman worked here, I would have come sooner."

I paused, uncomfortable with his compliment. "That's...kind of you," I forced out.

"What is it you do here, Miss Broadstone?" Cole asked.

I thought about all the duties William had described to me. "I guess you could call it guest relations. I ensure you have everything you need and assist in other ways."

Stewart smirked like I'd said something unintentionally humorous. "Indeed? There is something I need."

"Yeah? Well, let me know if it's something I can help with."

"Oh, I'm positive you're just the woman for the job."

I frowned at his suggestive tone. "What is it?" I asked suspiciously.

His answering smile was meant to be inviting. "I'm in room 403. Come there after supper, and I'll let you know all about it."

Eck. I stood, flaring my nostrils. *He seems like the type I need to be clear with.* "I'm not available tonight. In fact, I'm never available after hours. Incidentally, I'm spoken for." I thought about how Mitica would respond to someone making such an overt pass at me.

Before I could walk away, Stewart grabbed my wrist to stop me. "There's no need for such a response. I apologize for upsetting you. I just wanted to express my interest. There's no harm in that, is there?"

Oscar approached the table with the pair's meals. He took stock of the situation without effort. "Is there anything you require, Mrs. Broadstone?"

Cole's eyes widened, and Stewart released my wrist.

I sighed internally. "No, thank you, Oscar. I was just leaving."

"What about your tea?" Stewart asked, not quite giving up.

"I forgot that I'm busy at the moment."

As Oscar and I left, I heard Cole and Stewart whispering.

"You need to be more careful," Cole said.

"I didn't know she was married. She isn't even wearing a ring."

"Would it have mattered if she were?"

"It never has before."

They laughed.

THIRTY

*H*arrison wasn't in his office when I went to see about the schedule. I asked Frederick if he knew where he was.

"He left for the stables not long ago," Frederick informed.

I sighed. *I wanted to talk with him after his reaction this morning.* "Do you happen to know if there are any activities planned after dinner tonight?"

He reached behind the front desk and consulted a sheet of paper. "There appears to be a card game scheduled in the library," he said.

"Yeah? Okay, thanks." I turned to walk away then turned back. "Hey, do you have time to show me how to work the front desk in a bit?"

He nodded stiffly.

"Great. I'll be right back after I tell a guest the schedule."

Mary, Sarah, and Juniper were delighted to hear there was something to entertain them after dinner. I promised to see them at tea and returned to the stoic Frederick.

"Sorry about that," I apologized for making him wait.

He didn't respond but reached behind the counter and pulled out his guest book.

"Hey, Frederick, did William tell you why you have to show me this stuff again?"

He stilled for a moment. "Mr. Broadstone informed me of your memory loss."

"Good." After a heavy pause, I asked, "How long have you worked here, Frederick?"

"I have been here since the hotel opened."

"That long, huh? So you would've met me when I first arrived."

He gave me a slight nod.

"Will you tell me something?"

He waited for my question.

"Was I happy here? With William and everything?"

Frederick was silent for so long I thought he wasn't going to answer. But after a while, his sharp eyes softened ever so slightly. "I try not to pry into others' personal affairs...but yes. I believe you were quite happy, especially at first."

"And later on?" I pushed softly.

He paused again. "I have some duties to attend to presently. I shall show you how to man the desk now."

I frowned at his evasive maneuver. "Right. So what does it entail?"

Frederick turned out to be an excellent trainer. He was concise and easily answered all of my questions. He showed me how to check guests in and out, where the room keys and mail was kept, and gave me all manner of points of interest information should the guests ask for it.

I felt confident I could handle the job for a short time, and I told Frederick I would watch his post.

Not long after I'd taken up residence at the front desk, Marguerite entered the lobby from the library. I waved her over.

"How can I help?" Marguerite asked once she'd reached me.

"How much of my stuff have you moved to my room?"

"I moved your clothes and some of your jewelry. But you will be returning to Monsieur's bed as soon as you regain your memories, so I did not move everything."

I froze, internalizing my cringe. "I think it's best if you move everything. I was hoping to read some letters from home. I hear I was close to my family. Surely, we wrote to each other."

"Oui, that is an excellent idea. I will move the rest of your things today."

"Great, thanks. Oh! Do you happen to know where I could get a candle?"

She tilted her head. "But the hotel has electric lights."

"I know, but I still need one."

She nodded. "Very well, I will find one for you."

"Thanks."

I had hoped Harrison would return before Frederick, but Frederick soon relieved me.

Maybe I should go down to the stables and look for him. No, I'd be interrupting his work. I'm supposed to meet with him every day after breakfast. So if I can't catch him today, I'll see him tomorrow.

As I stood in the lobby thinking, William appeared in a flurry. "My dear, what are you still doing here? Are you not to host tea at this hour?"

"Uh, what time is tea?"

"Why, three in the afternoon, of course."

Of course, I mean, obviously. "And that's starting now?"

"Indeed. Hurry along. You mustn't keep the guests waiting."

I sighed internally and headed for the dining room.

When I arrived, I noticed some of the guests were missing. Colonel Higgins and his friend Reginald, as well as Stewart and Cole, were not in attendance.

As the newlyweds were basking in each other's presence, I opted to sit with Mrs. Pickens and her three charges.

"Good afternoon, ladies. May I join you for tea?"

"Of course," Mrs. Pickens granted me permission while the young women all smiled.

I'd never hosted tea before, but I placed my napkin in my lap and hoped standard table manners were good enough. I had assumed I would be pouring and serving the tea and little sandwiches, but Oscar didn't leave much for me to do.

"So where are you guys from?"

The women blinked at my modern word choice.

"I mean, where are you ladies from?"

"Québec City," Mrs. Pickens answered after a pause.

"Oh yeah? What brings you all the way out here? Just a vacation?"

"My daughter is to be married."

"You are, Mary? Congratulations."

"Thank you. Yes, John and I are to be married in a few months. And since he wishes to return to England, this was my last chance to see the great west." She sounded a little regretful but not so much that I was concerned about whether she wanted to marry John the Englishman.

"So you and your friends came out here for one last adventure, eh?"

The trio smiled a little sadly and nodded. "Just so," Mary agreed.

"Well, it's an excellent place to come for adventure. What sort of things have you done so far?"

That was all the encouragement they needed. The girls told me all about their long train ride, how Juniper's trunk was lost along the way, how the heel of Sarah's boot broke, how they'd gone shopping in Farrloch, strolled the gardens of the hotel, and played cards in the evening. They were still trying to convince Mrs. Pickens to allow them to join Harrison on a trail ride, but she seemed unwilling to budge on the matter.

"We noticed your hotel has a ballroom," Sarah said.

"Yes, we do."

"Do you ever have balls or dances?"

"I'm not sure. Why? Do you guys want to have one?"

The girls nodded with enthusiasm.

"There don't seem to be many guests here at the moment, but I'll talk with Harrison and see. Maybe we could have a small dance."

They practically hummed with excitement.

"Did you hear that, girls? How wonderful. Perhaps you two will find some handsome strangers," Mary gushed.

"Those two gentlemen staying here are awfully handsome," Juniper whispered as Sarah nodded with a giggle.

Mrs. Pickens cleared her throat.

I looked around the room and saw that the four men had still not arrived.

"Oh, you won't find them at tea, Miss Broadstone," Sarah informed. "They go hunting after lunch with the two older gentlemen."

I pursed my lips. *Of course they do.*

"Indeed, they brought down a bear a few days ago," Mary said.

What do people staying at a hotel do with the carcasses?

"Oh, how do you know, Mary? We only just arrived the day before yesterday," Sarah said.

Mary flushed. "Well, I overheard them talking while we were all in the library last night."

"You did? I didn't hear that," Juniper added excitedly.

"Perhaps we should ask them tonight after supper," Sarah suggested.

My frown mirrored Mrs. Pickens's. *I'll have to keep an eye on these girls. Stewart and Cole will waste no time taking advantage of them.*

After Oscar cleared away our dishes, I was given my first bit of free time. I went to see if Harrison had returned to his desk.

As I entered the office, Harrison met my eyes as William stood over him, censuring him for being gone all morning.

Harrison winked at me then tilted his head toward the door to tell me to make my escape. I bit my lip and nodded. William never even realized I was there as I snuck out the way I'd come.

With no work to do, I went to my room. I found Marguerite still putting things away.

"How's it coming, Marguerite?"

"Everything is moved. I am just putting things in order."

"Awesome. Did you find the letters?"

She tilted her head at my choice of words but picked up a decorative wooden box from the coffee table and held it out to me. I was finding it difficult to change my speech patterns, and all the strange looks just reminded me how understanding Mitica had been. *It helps that he knew I was from the future.*

"Oui," Marguerite said as I took the box from her. "But I am sorry. I could not find your journal anywhere. I will get you a new one when I go into town."

I sucked on my teeth. "Do I keep a journal?"

"Oui, of course. You love to write and sketch. You wrote in your journal every day."

I hummed, pursing my lips. "Well, keep an eye out for it, will you? It could be a big help in regaining my memories."

"Oui, I will."

Marguerite went back to organizing, and I took the letterbox into the bedroom. After shutting the French doors, I crawled onto the bed and sat cross-legged, resting the box in my lap.

The dark wooden lid was etched with an intricate leaf pattern, and the initials "CL." The lid was thick and heavy but did not stick or creak when I lifted it. Neatly-folded letters were packed into the box like cards in an old library catalog. I slid out a random letter near the front and began to read.

> *To my daughter,*
>
> *I hope all is well with you out there in the west. Everything is just fine here, so you need not worry.*
>
> *Are you taking care of yourself and your husband? Make sure you both get enough to eat. And wear your shawl. It is cold in the mountains, and you are forever leaving your shawl.*
>
> *I am certain William is treating you well, and I wait every day for news of a grandchild.*
>
> *Don't go wandering the forests, and be kind to the staff.*
>
> *I love you.*
>
> *Mother*

I smiled to myself at the fretful nature of mothers everywhere and pulled another letter from the box.

> *My darling girl,*
>
> *Your favorite ballet is playing at the theater on Saturday. I looked up from the paper at breakfast to tell you about it, forgetting you weren't there. I believe I've finally turned into an old man.*
>
> *I can hear your laugh as you tell me my gray hair is distinguished, but I cannot see it that way anymore.*
>
> *Was it mere months since we danced so gayly at your wedding? It feels like years. However, I am "looking to the bright future" as you always encourage me to do.*
>
> *I know you are living your dream among the snowy peaks of the Rockies, but I do hope you spare a thought for your Papa.*
>
> *Stay bright, my darling girl.*
>
> *Papa*

I gently refolded the letter and placed it beside me on the bed. Then, I reached for another one and unfolded it.

My sweet Cellie,

I could not have predicted how quiet our house would become when you married and went to live with your husband.

Father sits in his study, reading, all day with no one to interrupt him. And Mother, well let's just say she has started to turn that calculating eye toward me. I cannot tell if she is planning to find me a bride as soon as she can or if she is to confine me indoors so as to keep her other child near. In any case, I fear for my future, dear sister.

I know you were so happy to finally have your grand adventure, but did you have to move so very far away? That was rather unkind of you.

I've complained to my heart's content. Now, I shall tell you some good news. Father and I are coming to Vancouver on business in early April.

I know William is ever-busy, but perhaps you could visit us while we are there? It would mean so much to Father and me.

I will expect your reply as early as is possible.

Your loving brother,

Jacques

I closed my eyes against the unexpected burning. *Celeste's family really loved her. And when I'm gone, they'll never see her again. No, I can't think of it that way. It's not because I'm leaving. It's because Celeste died, possibly by murder. I need to figure out what happened to her.*

Jacques said they were going to be in British Columbia in April. Was she on her way to see them when she met her fate? But William said she was on her way to Toronto for a friend's wedding. Why would he lie? Either way, she never arrived. Wouldn't they have inquired as to why she never showed up?

I sighed at all the questions for which I did not yet have answers. My gaze drifted back toward the box of unread letters, and I reached for another.

In the quiet bedroom, only the soft crinkle of paper could be heard as I spent the day reading all of Celeste's letters. I read about how her family missed her, how her friends wished her well, and how the artists she'd patronized still wanted support. There was no mention of a friend getting married, but it was possible that such a letter would have contained specifics of time and place and might have been in Celeste's things when she died.

She seemed universally loved. If she'd gotten letters from her enemies, she had not kept them, at least not with the letters from her loved ones.

While her correspondents bemoaned her absence, no one seemed surprised by her marriage and subsequent move, and no one questioned her love for William. On the contrary, other than a few "heartbroken" artists, her friends commended her choice and wished such an affection for themselves.

While I couldn't comprehend her attraction, it was clear Celeste had adored her husband, or at least it appeared that way to everyone around her.

I frowned at the papers scattered around me on the bed. *If she had truly loved him, I should assume the feeling was mutual. Poor William. He's going to be devastated when his loving wife disappears. What will we have to do to make him let her go? Will I have to crush his attachment? I don't know if I could destroy someone like that. Maybe I could come up with a reason to leave, and Mitica could help me fake my death. I need to talk to Mitica.*

My stomach dropped at the thought. *When will I even see him again?*

I let myself fall to one side and curled into a ball. *Man, 1900 sucks. If we were in my time, I could call him or video chat.* I squeezed my eyes shut. "What a messed-up situation," I murmured. "Nothing I've ever learned has prepared me for this."

Not for the first time in my life, I wished I could allow myself to be childish. *It would be so much easier if we just said "screw it" and ran away.*

I knew Mitica would. Without any question, he would abandon everything just to be with me. And that only made it worse because I wasn't only fighting myself. I wasn't only struggling with my own desire in order to be an adult, to be responsible. Because he would do it, I knew I was the only thing keeping us apart.

THIRTY-ONE

*W*illiam knocked on my door to escort me to dinner that evening. Taking in his change of attire, I understood why Marguerite had insisted I dress for dinner.

He smiled gently at me when I entered the hall. "You look wonderful, my dear."

I nodded once in acknowledgment and hesitated to take the arm he held out to me. I resigned myself and placed my fingertips on his elbow. An uncomfortable feeling made me want to squirm, like the sensation of dancing closely with a person I'd just met.

All the guests were in attendance in the dining room, and I dutifully smiled my greeting to everyone in turn, even Stewart and Cole.

Apparently, it was customary for William and Celeste to eat dinner together. The guests kept to their own parties and did not interrupt us, though I wish they had because it felt pretty awkward. William asked about my day, but I didn't have much to say. I'd completed my duties as was expected.

In all honesty, I was likely the one making it awkward. After reading all those letters, it felt weird being around William in Celeste's body. They had this entire relationship, and he was expecting her to wake up one day and remember her love for him.

I was relieved when dinner was over. I popped into the kitchen, and Oscar, Louis, Gabriel, and I went over the following day's menu. I really wasn't of much use, but they seemed pleased when I just agreed with their recommendations.

I was beyond ready for the evening to be over; I was done interacting with people. Unfortunately, I had to attend the night's entertainment in the library. Along with the guests, William, Harrison, and Marguerite were also there.

Harrison informed the crowd we would be playing whist, a game I'd heard of but had never played. We were instructed to separate into groups of four. As there were fourteen of us, two had to sit out. I opted to sit out since I didn't know how to play, and Harrison sat out to manage the groups.

The three groups varied in intensity as they played through a few rounds. Colonel Higgins, Reginald, William, and Mrs. Pickens seemed to take the game very seriously. The Durants, Marguerite, and Sarah looked as though they played for fun. But the most enthusiasm came from Mary, Juniper, Stewart, and Cole's table, where they were far more interested in flirting than playing cards.

I watched for a while then decided to make myself useful. I poured after-dinner drinks for the men and went to the kitchen and retrieved coffee and tea for the women.

When everyone had played their fill of whist, they split up around the library. William, Mrs. Pickens, Colonel Higgins, and Reginald relocated to armchairs and a couch near the fire. The men smoked cigars, and Mrs. Pickens tried to hide the liquor she slipped into her tea.

Marguerite and Sarah chatted about something in French, and the newly-weds read a book together.

Once Harrison had cleaned up the cards, he excused himself for the evening. I watched him go, wishing I could escape so easily.

Mary, Juniper, Cole, and Stewart were gathered around a piano in the corner. After some pleading, Mary and Stewart sat beside one another on the bench and began to play an upbeat duet.

They laughed and smiled as if they were the only two in the room.

"That's marvelous!" Juniper praised when they'd finished. "Can I make a request?"

"Of course." Stewart smiled charmingly. "What would you like us to play next?"

"My favorite is 'Silent Woods' by Dvorák. Do you know it? Mary knows the one."

"Indeed, I do," he said, turning to Mary. "Miss Pickens, would you be so kind as to be my partner once more?"

Mary's eyes sparkled at his attention. "It would be my pleasure, Mr. Thomas."

As their melody filled the room, the other guests went silent to better appreciate the performance. Each piano hammer struck a chord in my heart, and I wished I was cuddled up by the fire in Mitica's warm embrace. I had to admit they were both very good. When the last note died out, Stewart smiled over at the blushing Mary as everyone else clapped for their performance.

The look the two young people shared unsettled me, and I moved toward them to make some space. But as I approached the piano, Juniper halted me by asking if I wanted to play next.

With everyone's eyes on me, I froze. "Um, no, I don't play the piano."

"What are you saying, my dear? You are a wonderfully talented pianist," William informed.

At his praise, the others began to insist I play something for them.

But I really don't know how to play the piano. Desperate for an out, I grasped at the only musical talent I had. "I'm not really feeling up to the piano right now, but how about I sing you a song, instead?"

Marguerite and William's eyes widened, but everyone else nodded with eager smiles.

I took a deep breath to steady my nerves then began to sing the first song that came to my mind. The longing notes and words of "Moon River" echoed through the quiet library. I probably should've chosen a song that was written before 1900, but the chances of them living to see *Breakfast at Tiffany's* were slim. At the very least, I hoped they wouldn't remember the song if they did see it.

Unfortunately, the fact that no one had heard it before meant everyone was paying rapt attention to me. My heart pounded too hard twice at the silence that greeted the conclusion of my impromptu performance, but I was able to breathe again once their enthusiastic applause filled the still void.

Marguerite rushed to me. "Celeste, I did not know you had such a beautiful voice. You always said you sang like a crow."

Oops. "I was just embarrassed to sing in front of people," I hedged. *Probably.*

As the guests returned to their previous activities, I looked around to see if I could busy myself with something else. Panic squeezed my throat for a second when I met Stewart's fleeting gaze of lust.

I squared my shoulders and glared at him. He just smiled and turned his attention toward Mary, who hadn't noticed he hadn't been paying attention to her chatting.

This spells disaster. Something needs to be done about him.

Before I could think of how to extract Mary from a potentially dangerous situation, William interrupted my thoughts.

"You sang as beautifully as a nightingale, my dear," he praised, raising my hand to his lips.

I resisted the urge to snatch my hand away but couldn't suppress my shudder.

"Thank you," I muttered, taking my hand back as soon as I could without giving rise to suspicion. *I understand William loves Celeste, but I feel like I've been clear about taking it easy on the touching. He's kind of an ass for forcing the issue in a place I can't refuse without making a scene.*

"I'm certain you are exhausted after the day you have had. Why don't we head upstairs for the night?"

Had I not known better, I would've thought he was suggesting we sleep together.

"Yeah, you're right. I'm pretty tired," I agreed, still grateful for the out.

He smiled and nodded like he knew me so well.

We said goodnight to the assembly, and I was glad to see Mary safely back in her mother's protective bubble of propriety when we left the library.

William and I were both silent as he escorted me to my room, the awkwardness returning the moment we were alone.

"Well, goodnight then," I said, turning to enter my door.

William snatched my hand to stop me from leaving. My head snapped back to his direction, and I pulled my hand from his grasp.

"I apologize," William said.

Yeah, you say that a lot, but you just keep doing it. "What is it, William?"

His eyes searched my face with an expression that bordered on intense. "You went about your daily routine all day. Did anything trigger your memory at all?" His eagerness struck me as more dubious than solicitous.

"No...nothing has come to me yet."

As he silently gazed at me, I could not decipher his reaction. "Very well," he finally pronounced. Then, he gave me an encouraging smile and asked, "Perhaps we should dine alone again tomorrow night? After all, most of your memories here are tied to me."

Is this him trying to make me fall in love with him or what? I don't really want to be alone with him. "I'd prefer being with the group actually. It was fun with everyone there."

His smile stiffened. "Very well, if that is what you wish. Go in and rest, my dear. I will see you tomorrow at breakfast."

"Right...see you tomorrow."

He didn't attempt to stop me again when I closed and locked the door behind me.

As I readied for bed, the weight of the day settled in my stomach. I knew in times such as these, it was best to stay busy. It was in the moments of stillness that Mitica's absence was felt most keenly.

While I hated the queasy sickness in my gut and the anxiety that fatigued my limbs, I wouldn't have traded them. Sure, it was easier to keep my mind off Mitica when it was occupied, but it was in these moments of longing I felt closest to him.

As I crawled into bed, I noticed a long taper in a silver candlestick on my bedside table. *Marguerite fulfilled my request after all.*

I moved the pillow from the head of the bed and sat cross-legged in its place. After lighting the candle, I settled my hands in the dhyana mudra position. Focusing my gaze on the steady flame, I took a deep, cleansing breath and let it all out. With a shiver, my body readjusted, and I began concentrating on regulating my breathing.

I don't know how long I meditated for. But when I blew out the candle, I was confident I wouldn't wake up anxious in the middle of the night.

THIRTY-TWO

I awoke early the next morning. Though I'd slept through the night, I felt far from rested. Predawn light announced the sun's approach on the eastern horizon.

As I stared out of the balcony door, a strong compulsion to be outside drove me to bathe, dress, and go for an early morning walk. The act of fully dressing without Marguerite's help made me understand why women of the time had ladies' maids. Still, it wasn't too difficult as I fastened the buttons on the back of the shirt before I pulled it on.

The hotel still slumbered; even the front desk was vacant of its stoic resident.

I took that first step outside, and the chilly mountain air stung my nostrils. But I sighed in relief as if I'd been holding my breath. Though my feet wanted to wander down the road into town, I knew I would never reach my desired destination before I was missed.

Sighing, this time in resignation, I strolled toward the stables. The walk was shorter than I remembered, and I cursed to myself for forgetting the treat I'd promised Saundra.

Unlike the last time I'd visited, the stable was bustling. Young men went about cleaning the stalls and feeding the horses. *I guess the stables' staff gets up early.* A couple of them looked over at me curiously, but no one challenged my presence.

I gazed down the row of stalls, but I didn't see Butch anywhere. I took a few steps forward and stood on my toes, trying to see if Saundra was in her stall. Pursing my lips, I decided not to get in the stable hands' ways by visiting her at the moment.

I turned to leave but stopped when I heard the deep timbre I recognized as Butch's voice coming from the tack room to my right. I couldn't hear what he was saying, but I popped in to say hello.

My head tilted in surprise when I saw the person Butch was speaking to was Harrison. As Butch rubbed oil into some leather straps, Harrison leaned his back and one foot against the wall.

I smiled to myself. *I knew Harrison and Celeste were just friends.* There was no doubt in my mind that William's jealousy was completely unfounded as I watched the Australian appreciate the sight of Butch at work.

"Good morning, guys," I called to them.

The two men stopped what they'd been doing and looked over at me.

"Good morning, Erin," Butch called with a smile at the same time Harrison said, "Celeste, what are you doing down here?"

"Wait, who's Erin?" Harrison asked.

Well, shit.

Butch's eyebrows rose, but he stayed quiet, allowing me time to explain.

"Uh...so you know I can't remember anything from before a few weeks ago... Well, they had to call me something, so I went by Erin."

"Ah," Harrison uttered in understanding.

Well, of course he believes me. I mean, it's a way more plausible explanation than: "Oh, that's my name in a future life. Yeah, sorry. I'm sort of a time-traveler."

"So you two have met then?" Harrison asked.

"Yeah, when I first came back to the hotel. I wandered down here and met Butch."

Harrison's eyes flicked to Butch, who nodded once at my recount.

"Well, in any case, I was just out for a little fresh air and stopped to say hello, so I'll let you guys get back to what you were doing."

"Are you headed back up to the hotel now?" Harrison asked.

"Yeah, probably."

"I'll walk with you then."

"Are you sure? I don't want to interrupt."

"It's fine," he assured me, looking at Butch again.

And with a locked gaze and another silent nod from the stable master, I could tell Butch and Harrison's feelings for each other were mutual.

That's nice. I'm so glad Harrison isn't mooning over someone who isn't interested. I tried to suppress my smile at their fleeting but silent exchange of affection.

We both promised to see Butch again later and left the stables together.

"I'm glad you decided to walk with me, Harrison. I wanted to talk to you."

"You did?"

"Yeah, it's clear to me we must've been friends before the accident." I watched his reaction.

He nodded slowly, frowning. "I thought we were..."

"Why do you say it like that? Did we have a fight or something?"

"I wouldn't say that."

"Then, what would you say?" I pushed when he wasn't forthcoming.

"I would say we were close, and then we weren't. I could tell something had upset you. But every time I asked, you told me it was nothing. And then you left. You didn't mention to me you were leaving. You were just gone. Mr. Broadstone told everyone you went to Toronto for a friend's wedding."

"That's...strange," I admitted.

He nodded his agreement.

"Well, I don't know what happened before, but I'm sorry I left without telling you."

"It's all right now. I'm glad you're home safe. Don't worry about that. Just try to get better."

"Right," I absently agreed. *Whatever happened to Celeste, it doesn't seem like Harrison knows about it. Why didn't she tell him if they were friends? Could she not trust him? Was it to protect him? Or was she just the shoulder-everything-yourself type? Now that I think about it, Marguerite also mentioned she left without a word when we first met.*

I filed my thoughts away for later. "So why was William scolding you yesterday?"

He smiled cockily as if whatever he'd done wrong had been worth it. "He wants me at my desk when I'm not leading activities even if I have no work to do."

"And you weren't at your desk when he wanted you there?"

"Well, the trail ride was canceled due to the rain."

"So what did you do instead?"

He hesitated then smirked. "Helped Butch in the stables."

"Oh yeah? What were you helping him with?" I teased, the tone in his voice already telling me what those guys had been doing. *He must have shared his preferences with Celeste if he's so open about it with me. That can't have been easy for him knowing how society sees gays in this time period. He trusted her. At least I wasn't a homophobe in my past life.*

As he grinned like a Cheshire Cat, I couldn't help but mirror his expression.

"Oh, just some heavy lifting."

I laughed. "I'll bet."

When we entered the hotel's front door, Frederick greeted us with all the seriousness of a Buckingham guard.

I told Harrison I'd see him after breakfast and went to the kitchen.

I entered as Louis let out an angry string of exclamations, one of which I recognized as the French word for shit. Gabriel stood against the wall with his arms crossed and a pensive crinkle between his eyebrows.

"What's going on?" I asked Oscar as he chewed his lip.

"The delivery from Farrloch said the dry goods store ran out of yeast," Oscar explained.

"We don't have enough?"

"We do not."

"All right. It's okay. What did we need the yeast for?"

"Croissants," Oscar answered.

Louis spat at the word.

Ew, Dude. This is a kitchen. My mind grasped for any cooking knowledge my grandmother had tried to teach me. I'd never had the knack for it, and she'd eventually relegated me to taster and dishwasher. But one bit rose to the surface. "What about baking powder? Do we have that?" I asked.

Oscar translated, and Gabriel dashed to the pantry to see.

"Oui." He returned with the tin.

"Great. Then let's make biscuits instead of croissants."

They stared at me like they didn't quite understand.

"You know? A biscuit: flour, baking powder, salt, butter, and milk. They're stiff on the outside and soft on the inside."

Oscar translated, Gabriel smiled, and Louis clapped once and nodded. As the cooks scrambled around the kitchen, Oscar and I moved to get out of the way.

"Madame," Louis called as I pushed open the swinging door.

I paused and looked over my shoulder.

"Merci," he said, giving me two thumbs up.

I smiled and stifled a chuckle. "You're welcome."

William turned out to be too busy to sit down for breakfast. Marguerite came in, all a flurry.

"Celeste, there you are! You never called for me this morning, and you did not answer when I knocked."

Oops. "Sorry, Marguerite."

She pursed her lips. "Please call for me tomorrow."

I made no promises. "Did you ever find my journal yesterday?" I asked, changing the subject.

"Non, I am sorry. I will go into town today and get you a new one."

"Why don't we go together?" I suggested, jumping at the chance, even if it was too risky for me to actually use a journal.

She shook her head. "Monsieur has instructed me to ensure you stay close to home for the time being. You must rest properly if you want to get better."

I gritted my teeth. *An actual prisoner then.*

"But Monsieur told me you did not get to see the garden yesterday because of the rain. Would you like to walk after you meet Monsieur Harrison?" she asked brightly.

"Yeah, that's fine," I answered, not cheered.

After breakfast, I shook Marguerite off to meet Harrison.

"So what do we have planned for the guests today?" I asked him, leaning against his desk.

"The trail ride that was scheduled for yesterday is what we have in the afternoon."

"And tonight?"

"More cards."

"Okay, and tomorrow?"

"Nothing planned as of yet."

"Hmm. How about a hike? People come out here to see the mountains, right?"

He nodded. "I could guide them up the nearest peak. It's not particularly high, but it has a nice view."

"That sounds great. What about tomorrow night?"

"The ladies could get together to do needlepoint, and the men could have drinks and cigars."

"How about something really different? Have you ever hosted a bonfire?"

"No, our guests are genteel."

"Well, let's try mixing it up. We can have a fire outside. We can even sing songs. Do you know anyone who plays the guitar?"

"One of the stable lads."

"Well, invite him to come along and play if he's up for it. And if the guests don't like the change of pace, we can just go back to needlepoint and cards."

Harrison nodded. "I'll mention it to him."

"Awesome. I mean, great. Oh! Before I forget, a few of the guests mentioned wanting to have a dance. Do we do that? I know we have a ballroom."

He thought for a moment. "Sometimes we do but not often. The ballroom is usually for grand parties when we host special guests and the like."

"But it doesn't have to be a big deal, right? I mean, all we need is music and space."

"I'll look into it."

I smiled. "Thanks."

We threw around more activity ideas, but we didn't commit to anything, wanting to see how our plans went over with the guests first.

When I'd left the back office, Frederick informed me that Marguerite awaited me in the library. Upon seeing me enter, she marked her page and shelved the book she'd been reading.

"I am excited to show you the garden, Celeste. You spent so much time there. It was your favorite place at the hotel," Marguerite said as we walked through the ballroom and out the doors to the garden.

The garden was probably breathtaking when it was in full bloom. But at that time of year, it only had the gloomy death appeal found in Poe stories, not that I was opposed to that aesthetic. The even, brick paths cut the bare hedges in half, and trellises with shriveled ivy separated the paths from bony, naked trees.

All routes seemed to lead to a fountain at the center of the garden, which was empty and stagnant. At the center of the fountain was a statue of Apollo and Daphne, their marble faces twisted in despair. I frowned at the beautiful piece of art. Theirs was a story that had always saddened me. To love someone so much and have them spurn you so completely, it just made my heart ache for them.

"Monsieur had this fountain made especially for you," Marguerite told me.

I stared at Daphne, her legs and arms the roots and branches of the laurel tree. The agony expressed on Apollo's face as he reached for her was almost too real. *What an unusual gift for your new wife.*

"Why?" I couldn't stop myself from asking.

"Laurier, the laurel," she explained. "Your maiden name."

"Ah." *Well, it is a wonderfully done sculpture anyway.*

As we continued to stroll the bleak garden, the only indication that life would soon return to the sleeping plants was the birds chattering overhead. Too busy building their nests in the barren trees, they spared no attention to those below them. As I watched their labors, I hadn't noticed Marguerite had stopped to tie her boot.

I walked on without her, only halting when an older Asian man stooped on the path before me. He dug in the dirt, preparing the garden for spring.

"Oh! Excuse me. I didn't see you there," I gasped, almost tripping over him.

Looking up at me, his eyes widened, the shock clear in his face. He shot to his feet. "You...you are not supposed to be here," he hissed in a thick accent. "I thought you had left."

I pulled my head back, surprised by his reception. "Well, now I'm back?" I said, unsure.

"Aiya! You must not be here."

"What—"

"There you are," Marguerite interrupted. "I am sorry. My boot came unlaced."

The Chinese man clamped his mouth shut at her appearance.

"Oh, I see you have met Monsieur Xi, the gardener."

I dipped my head to Mr. Xi. "Yes, Mr. Xi was just telling me how surprised he was to see me."

"Oh, Monsieur. I was also surprised when I saw her in town the other day. And then I heard about the accident! I have never heard anything so sad."

"Accident?" Mr. Xi asked.

"Oui, Celeste was in an accident, and she cannot remember anything of her time with us. It is horrible, non?"

Mr. Xi's eyes softened, and his eyebrows pulled together. "I see."

"Marguerite tells me I spent a lot of time in your garden, Mr. Xi."

He nodded. "We saw each other quite often," he answered, still flustered.

"Mr. Xi, are you related to Xi Wei, who works in the laundry?" I asked.

"I am Xi Lin, father of Xi Wei."

"Oh! Xi Wei told me you worked for William on the railroad."

He bowed his head in acknowledgment.

I could tell Marguerite's presence was making Xi Lin uncomfortable. *He has something he needs to say to me alone. He said I shouldn't be here. What did he mean? What does he know? I need to come back when we can't be interrupted.*

"Well, I'm sure I'll be back very soon, Mr. Xi. I'll probably see you then. For now, let's stop interrupting his work, Marguerite."

Xi Lin bowed again and watched me walk away with his brow still furrowed.

Marguerite and I left the garden by the iron gate in the brick wall near the front entrance of the hotel. As she'd expected, Campbell waited for

Marguerite with a carriage to drive her into town. I waved to them as they pulled away and turned to go inside.

A black horse was tethered to a pole near the front door. My heart skipped a beat.

Not entirely certain what I would find, I flew into the hotel as fast as my feet could take me.

THIRTY-THREE

My heart pounded as I scanned the foyer. A flash of red between the slightly ajar library doors caught my eye, and I rushed in that direction.

Throwing the door wide, my chest ached, and I trembled at the sight of Mitica before me. I held my breath as his blue eyes found mine, his Wynn visage blurring with unbidden tears.

I'd almost started to believe I'd imagined him. I took a step toward him but stopped short when he warned me with a glance.

He's so close. My body hummed with the compulsion to touch him, and it took all my willpower to stop myself.

His usual unreadable mask gave nothing away. But I knew it was just as difficult for him as it was for me. I could feel his tension simmering below the surface.

"Constable," I started, my voice quivering. I cleared my throat. "What are you doing here?"

He held up the copy of *Dracula* we'd been reading together.

"You finished it?"

He shook his head no. "Yes, and I wanted to get a different book."

His sweet baritone was like soft kisses against naked skin. I stepped closer to him, taking the book from his grasp.

"And I wanted to check in to see how you were adjusting," he said at a normal volume. "And I miss you," he added in a barely audible whisper.

"I'm doing fine. I've been busy learning my duties here at the hotel," I answered. "I miss you, too," I added, hushed.

"You haven't called for me," he murmured.

I made a small, sad noise. "I didn't know if I should."

He closed his eyes and breathed a sigh of relief as though he'd been worried about it.

"Can I? I wanted to."

"Of course, you can. I said you could."

"But when? How will I know when Oli isn't around?"

"10 o'clock. He's usually asleep by then."

"Tonight?" I whispered, anticipation welling inside me.

"No, not tonight."

My stomach dropped in disappointment.

"I'm going to Chuthekii to see about his vision tonight."

"Oh," I breathed.

"Tomorrow," he promised

I swallowed around a lump in my throat. "Tomorrow," I agreed.

Hesitantly, I reached for his hand. But just before we touched, William burst into the library. My heart screamed.

"My dear, I hear we have a visitor."

"Thank you for the suggestion, Mrs. Broadstone. I think I will read this one next." Wynn grabbed the book nearest where my outstretched hand had frozen.

"Wonderful. I think it will be just what you're looking for."

The book he'd picked up turned out to be a collection of Greek tragedies. *Oh jeez.*

"I'm glad to hear you are settling in here, Mrs. Broadstone. I'm certain I will see you again."

"Thank you for checking on me, Constable. I do hope you enjoy the book."

"I'm sure I will. Have a good day."

"Goodbye." I waved to Mitica cheerfully as everything within me protested. *Follow him you fool. Being apart is not worth it.*

Still, I stood unmoving as William approached me. "Constable Delaforet came to see how you are faring?" he asked.

"His primary purpose was to return a book he borrowed. But, yes, he asked me how I was."

"He's a very dutiful young man."

"I suppose he is."

Too shaken by Mitica's surprise visit to withstand William's gaze, I excused myself to check on the kitchen staff. I paused in the deserted dining room and took a steadying breath.

This whole situation is so messed up.

I felt my resolve start to fray at the edges. It wasn't as if I needed to be with Mitica every moment of every day. It was more the uncertainty. At times like this, if there ever had been times like this in the history of humanity, my instinct was to keep my loved ones close. My heart said clinging to one another was the only way to survive the storm raging around us, but my heart wasn't in control. My head was. And my head thought this reaction was downright foolish.

You're both fine. Separation sucks, but it's nothing so dramatic. You've got good leads so far into cracking the mystery of Celeste. Concentrate on that, and see Mitica when you can.

Not feeling any better, I went to check on Louis, Gabriel, and Oscar. As the cooks had everything under control, I helped Oscar set up for lunch.

This time around, I dined with Colonel Higgins and Reginald. They seemed honored by my request to sit with them.

After Oscar had placed our plates before us, I asked, "So how long have you two known each other?"

"It has been nearly five and twenty years. Wouldn't you say, Higgins?"

"Good God, that long?" Colonel Higgins responded. "Yes, I suppose it has."

"How did you meet?"

"I was stationed in Africa at the time," Colonel Higgins started as if settling in for a long story. "I joined the British army at just seventeen, you know. For Queen and country, and all that. Of course, I couldn't foresee that I would be sent straight to Grey in Waikato. What a business that was—"

"Higgins, she asked how we met not for your life story," Reginald interrupted.

Colonel Higgins blinked at us as if he'd lost his train of thought.

Reginald continued. "I was a spice trader, you see. Cloves and what have you. I was in Zanzibar. This was before the war, mind you. The crown was still trying to curb the slave trade there. Terrible business that."

"Terrible business, indeed," Colonel Higgins agreed.

"In any case, I came upon a slave auction and saw a trader beating a young negro boy. Well, I couldn't stomach the sight, so I stepped in."

"Wait a moment, Reginald. I was the one who stepped in," Colonel Higgins argued.

"No, no, old boy. I stopped the boy from being beaten to death. And when the traders detained me, you knocked one fellow on the head."

Colonel Higgins stilled, thinking, then chuckled. "Quite right. Quite right. You were in a predicament when I came upon those men dragging you off to do God knows what."

"Indeed, I was. Quite the predicament."

"So Colonel Higgins hit one of them on the head. Then what?" I asked, urging them back on topic.

"Well, we ran like mad, that's what." Reginald laughed.

"Outnumbered us they did. We were lucky to make it out alive," Colonel Higgins added

"Indeed. Well, we have been together ever since."

"And what about the slaves? Institutionalized slavery isn't still happening in Zanzibar is it?"

"Indeed not, her majesty would never allow such a barbaric institution to continue in her empire," Colonel Higgins answered.

"Here here! Long live the Queen," Reginald cheered.

"Long live the Queen!" the rest of the room answered.

I didn't quite know how to respond to their outburst, especially since I knew Queen Victoria wasn't going to be alive much longer. While I was certainly glad slavery had been outlawed, I also knew all the horrors British imperialism had inflicted on the world. *I mean, India hasn't even gotten their independence yet though I suppose Gandhi is still alive at the moment.*

The magnitude of the thought hit me

Holy crap! Gandhi is alive right now.

A man whose teachings I had so admired, the words and actions he embodied helped me cope with my father's murder. To think I was drawing breath at the same time as he was surreal. I knew the man wasn't perfect, far from it in fact. But that imperfection, that struggle to be better, to free his people, to bring peace—it was inspirational.

As I ate lunch with the two old Brits, reminiscing about their adventures, I remembered a quote from Bapu: "Live as if you were to die tomorrow. Learn as if you were to live forever."

Carpe diem, a concept with which I'd always struggled. The balance between planning for the future and living in the present is not easily achieved.

After lunch, I wanted to talk to Xi Lin. It seemed like he knew something about why Celeste had left. Unfortunately, I had to work the front desk.

Not long after I stood at Frederick's post, three men descended the stairs, leaving for their daily hunt. Colonel Higgins and Reginald tipped their hats to me as they passed on the way out the front door. I smiled at them, though a little sick to my stomach at what they were going out to do.

Stewart stopped by the front desk, seemingly waiting for Cole to arrive.

"How are you this afternoon, Celeste?" Stewart asked, leaning on my counter.

"I'm fine. Thank you, Mr. Thomas," I replied coldly.

He smiled seductively as if I'd given him some encouragement.

"I must say I was rather surprised to discover you're married to Mr. Broadstone."

I didn't respond.

"Tell me, Celeste," he started, lowering his voice to little more than a whisper. "You aren't satisfied by that old fossil, are you? He's likely as old as your father. Surely, a man with more stamina would meet your youthful needs much more adequately."

Eck. I don't want to think about either of them in bed. I met Stewart's eyes seriously. "I assure you, Mr. Thomas. My needs are adequately met."

He smirked. "Perhaps, you'd like them surpassed then?"

I guess history has no shortage of men who don't understand refusal. As

I opened my mouth to snub him again, Cole descended the stairs to join him.

Stewart smiled lazily at me again and whispered, "We aren't leaving for quite a while. Consider my offer until then."

Great. Just how long am I going to be stuck with him?

Needless to say, I was relieved when Stewart and Cole left me in peace.

After hosting tea, it was early evening before I was able to get any free time.

I scoured the garden for any sign of Xi Lin, but it was deserted. Just as I turned around to go back inside, Xi Wei pushed a wheelbarrow of fertilizer down the path toward me.

"Xi Wei," I called to him, and his head snapped up at my voice.

His eyes widened, and he gently set down the wheelbarrow. Then, he bowed to me, and I bowed back.

Approaching him, I told him I was looking for his father and asked if he knew where he was.

He lowered his dark eyes apologetically. "My father is resting now. Something has upset him."

"Oh, no. I'm sorry to hear that. Is that why you're helping him?"

He nodded. "I sometimes help my father when my work is complete."

I smiled. "That's nice of you. Do you think he'll feel better tomorrow? I'd like to speak to him when he's free."

"I am certain he will insist upon working if the weather permits. It is an important time for the plants."

"Right. Well, hey, I wanted to talk to you about something too when you have time."

"With me?"

"Yes, you're in charge of running the laundry, right?"

He nodded. "How can I help you?"

"Well, I noticed that the working conditions in the laundry are pretty awful. It's so hot down there. I want to try and help make it better for you guys, but I need you to explain your process before I can do anything."

He gave me that pop idol smile. "I will take this first, and then I will show you."

"No problem. That's fine."

He pushed the wheelbarrow out of the path to where it wouldn't be in anyone's way, and then we walked back to the hotel. On the way, he told me how they wash linens in the tubs I'd seen in the basement.

"Okay, and then what? How do you dry them?"

"We take them to the attic."

"What? Why would you do that?"

A doorway in one corner of the basement led to a back staircase. The plain white walls and creaky, wooden stairs looked like they belonged to an entirely different hotel. By the time we'd reached the attic, I was winded. Xi Wei seemed used to the climb.

The long attic had clotheslines strung from end-to-end with sheets and towels hung on them. Three fans in the roof spun overhead, propelled by the heat from the drying linens.

"Why don't you just hang them outside?" I asked.

"Mr. Broadstone does not want the guests to see them."

God forbid.

"And they would freeze in winter."

Yeah, I probably should've thought of that. "Hmm," I acknowledged. "I see the predicament. Let me see what I can do, okay?"

He bowed in appreciation.

I brought up the matter with William over dinner.

"Isn't there something we could do for the men in the laundry? I mean, it's awful down there, and then they have to walk up all those stairs."

William looked unconcerned. "What would you suggest, my dear?"

"There has to be a way to ventilate the basement better. What if we added an outside cellar door? Then, they could leave it open while they are down there. At least they'd have some fresh air."

He crinkled his brow in consideration but didn't say anything.

"And I think we should have an area outside where they can hang the linens. Maybe the cellar door could lead to a patio. If you're worried about the guests seeing, just add a cover and maybe lattices on the sides. Then, air could get in. I know we don't want the linens to freeze in the winter. Why not install an elevator so they don't have to climb all those stairs with arms full of wet sheets?"

"That all sounds rather expensive, my dear," he explained as if to a child.

I bit my lip. "Well, at the very least, digging a cellar door shouldn't be that difficult, right? And the patio is even easier."

He watched me from across the table. Finally, he said, "You are quite adamant about this."

"Well, as employers, it's our responsibility to take care of those who work for us."

"Those men would never even think to ask for this. They are happy just to be employed. There aren't many opportunities for the Chinese."

"Whether they're Chinese or not makes no difference," I declared. "They're people."

His eyebrows rose a little, his expression somewhere between curiosity and amusement. "Very well, my dear. I will make inquiries and consider it if it pleases you."

You should do it because it's right not because it pleases me, but I'll take it. I smiled in triumph. "Awesome. Thanks, William."

As curious as he'd looked by my pushing, he seemed even more so by my happy gratitude.

Perhaps Celeste would've handled things differently.

The after-dinner entertainment was much the same as it had been the night before, except I made sure to play this time. As expected, Mary and Juniper wanted to group with Stewart and Cole.

As I watched the young women heading toward the two men, I impulsively stepped in before them.

"Mr. Thomas, Mr. Linton, could I join you this time?"

The men were delighted, Stewart especially. I ignored the knot in my stomach for Mary's sake.

That night, we were playing conquinn, which I was glad to discover was similar to rummy.

"I hope you guys will help me," I said, sitting between Stewart and Cole with a shiver of unease. "I've never played this game before."

Keeping their attention on me was exhausting. Mary was not pleased. But it's not as if having Stewart's eyes on me was fun for me either. Unfortunately, the younger woman could not appreciate I was trying to keep her off the predator's radar. She did all she could to get Stewart's attention back to her.

I was just glad I didn't have to do anything overt. A smile and a little praise, and the man's slimy gaze always returned to me.

It seemed Stewart preferred experience to innocence, or perhaps it was because I'd rejected him before. *Maybe he likes a challenge. Ugh. Why am I even doing this? She's a grown woman. She can make decisions for herself.*

But as I glanced over at Mary's pouting face, I knew she was too naive. *She doesn't know. Maybe she thinks the attention he's giving her is special. She can't tell that he would seduce her, destroy her prospects with John the Englishman, and leave her flat to pursue someone else.*

He doesn't care if a woman has someone already. In fact, he seems to enjoy it more when that's the case. Maybe I should talk to her. If I can make her understand, then I don't need to call attention to myself.

THIRTY-FOUR

$\mathcal{W}$hile I was relieved to retire to my room for the night, I was having a difficult time sitting still. I stood at the balcony door and stared out into the cold night, watching the skies for a hultan riding a zmeu.

My vigilance was not rewarded, and I eventually lit my candle to try to calm my mind. The bright, steady flame burned away my restlessness over Mitica's meeting with Chuthekii.

As my vision unfocused, my eyelids became heavy. "Tomorrow," I whispered to the flame before blowing it out and going to bed.

The following day was as busy as the days prior. I pretended to guide Louis and Gabriel with breakfast and lunch, met with Harrison to plan the evening's bonfire, worked the front desk, and hosted tea.

The guests seemed intrigued by the idea of sitting around a fire outside.

I finally got my chance to talk to Mary after trying to find an opening all morning as the dining room emptied after tea. The women were going hiking with Harrison and wanted to change into more appropriate clothes. Mary told her mother and friends she would catch up after finishing her cup of tea.

I stayed behind and waited for everyone else to be out of hearing range. "Mary," I started.

She looked up politely.

"Mary, I wonder if I could talk to you as one woman to another."

"Of course, Mrs. Broadstone. But whatever could this be about?"

"Mary...why do you suppose your mother is so protective of you?"

Her eyebrows scrunched together. "To protect me from things she feels might harm me, I'd say."

"Right. So I'm sure she's talked with you about being careful around men. Hasn't she?"

Her tone turned guarded. "She has. Though I suppose most mothers are overly concerned with their daughters' virtue and virginity."

Eh, not necessarily. "This isn't really about virtue or virginity. I couldn't care less about that."

Her eyebrows rose at my assertion.

"Look, I can't really put this delicately. There are men out there like your fiancé John, who want committed relationships. I mean, he wants to share a lifetime with you, or he wouldn't have asked you to marry him. He loves you, right?"

"Yes..." she answered cautiously.

"Yeah so, then there are men like Stewart Thomas. They aren't really interested in committed relationships, which is fine if you know what you're getting into. All I'm saying is: I know the type of person Stewart is. He'll say and do anything to get a woman in his bed. He doesn't care if she's about to marry someone else or if she's already married for that matter. He'll take from her what he wants and leave her when he's done."

As I told her how it was, her face grew more and more red, and her pretty blue eyes squinted at me.

"Mrs. Broadstone, I don't know why you feel it's necessary to slander Mr. Thomas, but I don't want to hear any more. Mr. Thomas has been nothing but kind and gentlemanly toward me since the moment we met."

"It's not slander if it's true, Mary. Look, he—"

"No, I don't want to listen to any more." She cut me off and stood from the table. "My relationship with John, or any other man, is none of your concern, Mrs. Broadstone. I will not mention this to Mr. Thomas as I'm certain it would humiliate him to know you think so low of him, but I trust you will avoid such topics of discussion in the future. Good day."

My mouth hung open as she strode furiously from the room. *Well, that could've gone better.* I sighed at my failed attempt to guide the younger woman. *If that's the way she wants it, then fine. I have so many other things to worry about. I can only hope she heeds my warning before she fucks up her life.*

I thought I'd have time to talk with Xi Lin after tea, but Harrison needed help since he was leading the afternoon hike. First, I had to choose a place for the fire. I decided behind the hotel would be fine. Some stable hands helped me collect wood and build a small fire ring with stones. A few of the cleaning staff brought wooden chairs from inside for everyone to sit on.

As I helped arrange the chairs around the fire ring, Harrison returned and drew my attention to a young man, no older than seventeen, with black, wavy hair; big, dark eyes; and rich, brown skin.

"Celeste, this is Diego. He's the fellow I spoke of who plays the guitar."

I smiled at Diego, who dipped his head self-consciously. "Señora," he greeted.

"Hola, Diego. You must be pretty good if Harrison says you can play." *I have no idea if that's true, but I'd like to believe Harrison wouldn't set him up to embarrass himself.*

Diego smiled at the compliment but seemed too shy to meet my eyes.

"We're going to have a bonfire tonight. Would you play for us, Diego, por favor?"

"Sí, Señora, con gusto."

"Fantastico! Gracias." *I guess those Spanish classes Mom forced on me came in handy after all. I'm glad I continued into college and kept practicing.*

Harrison dismissed the youth to go about his business.

At dinner, I instructed the guests to dress warmly and comfortably for the evening's activities. As Marguerite helped me change for the event, I stared longingly at my jeans, knowing it would be considered inappropriate. I sighed and allowed Marguerite to choose for me. *At least she didn't get rid of them and only had them cleaned.*

As I stepped into the cool, April night, I instinctively looked up at the waning crescent moon, hanging among an expanse of stars. I strolled through the darkness toward the bright glow of the fire. The heat warmed me as I took a seat between Marguerite and Diego.

Surrounded by mountains and watched over by the distant stars, the only sound was the soft crackling of the fire. I closed my eyes, half believing Mitica would be sitting near me when I opened them. But the mist of memory dissipated when Diego started to play a soft melody on his guitar.

A few bars in, his tender voice sang a song of sorrow as if he couldn't help but call out once he'd started playing. I smiled as I recognized the poem from a college assignment, where we had to translate a poem while trying to keep its rhythm and rhyme. I didn't know if anyone else spoke Spanish. When he finished, I asked him to play it again so I could translate. Nodding, he started over. With every line, he played the melody twice. He'd sing it first in Spanish, and then I'd sing it in English.

> *"The moon hung orange and low, hardly in the sky.*
> *The candles burned in the square and where the dead do lie.*
> *The wind, so warm in the day, held October's chill,*
> *But Camila still came singing—*
> *Singing—singing—*
> *Camila still came singing, to the headstone on the hill.*
>
> *"Her hair was the feathers of a raven, black as the darkest jet.*
> *Her eyes were deep and brown, the brightest he'd ever met.*
> *Her skirt was blood-red satin. It scarcely touched the ground.*
> *And as she walked it fluttered—*
> *Fluttered—fluttered—*
> *As she walked it fluttered, but never made a sound.*
>
> *"Up the hill, she climbed to visit her family there.*
> *Her grandparents, long gone, for her, they showed such care.*
> *His parents rest beside them upon the cliff so steep.*
> *He watched her approach, staring—*
> *Staring—staring—*

He watched her approach, staring, Camila of beauty deep.

"She met his gaze with a smile. She'd seen him once before.
At the market in town, how he'd made her heart soar.
He had not seen her looking at him that summer day.
But he watched her now, dazzled—
Dazzled—dazzled.
He watched her now, dazzled. He could not turn away.

"'Alejandro is my name,' he said with a little bow.
'I know,' she told him truly. He did not ask her how.
She held her hand out to him. He took it in his own.
And kissing her palm gently—
Gently—gently—
Kissing her palm gently, his passion for her shone.

"That night they made a promise to meet again and soon,
At the bustling market by the fountain at noon.
Parting ways for the moment, they waited for the time,
And spent their long nights dreaming—
Dreaming—dreaming—
They spent their long nights dreaming for the clock bell to chime.

"They met throughout the autumn. They met in winter's cold.
They met with spring flowers in their hair and when the corn
    turned gold.
Then one fine day in August, under a willow tree,
Alejandro asked her to marry—
Marry—marry—
Alejandro asked her to marry. Camila did agree.

"The young man went to her father and told him how they felt.
He begged him for his daughter, upon his knees he knelt.
But Camila's father refused. She'd been promised to his friend.
He spurned Alejandro, beating—
Beating—beating—

He spurned Alejandro, beating. Camila's heart did rend.

"She would not marry another. She would not forsake her love.
She sent word to Alejandro, swearing by the stars above.
She'd meet him on the clifftop, where their families did rest,
And they'd run away together—
Together—together—
They'd run away together, run away to the west.

"Under the new moon sky, the stars the only light,
Alejandro waited for his love on the appointed night.
He held his breath to listen, but who should come instead?
Her father he came, yelling—
Yelling—yelling—
Her father he came, yelling. Camila, she was dead.

"He scarce could hear the tale over his pounding heart.
How Camila killed herself when her father kept them apart.
He tore at his chest in agony, hoping to stop the pain.
Then leapt from the clifftop, falling—
Falling—falling—
He leapt from the clifftop, falling, and as his love was slain.

"Every autumn night, when the moon hangs low in the sky,
When the candles burn in the square and where the dead do lie,
When the wind, so warm in the day, holds October's chill,
Camila still comes singing—
Singing—singing—
Camila still comes singing to her love's headstone on the hill."

The juxtaposition of language and pitch lightened my heart in a way only music could, but it also ached for the lovers' tragic fate.

Diego and I smiled at each other as those gathered clapped for us.

"Canta hermosa, Señora."

"Usted también, Diego."

The rest of the event would have been rather pleasant if I hadn't been anxious to go to my room.

Diego played more songs, Colonel Higgins and Reginald told stories, and the time until I could leave felt eons away. But eventually, the fire burned low. And though a few decided to stay and build it up again, it was safe for me to excuse myself.

I kept my footsteps slow and steady as I climbed the stairs, but my heart raced ahead.

After closing and locking the door behind me, I strode to the bedroom with purpose. My hands shook, and my uneven breathing was loud in my ears. I wasn't quite sure how this was supposed to work.

I planted my feet and thought of Mitica: his crimson hair, his blue eyes, his baritone song, his woodsy scent, the warmth of his skin on mine, his taste... "Dumitru," I whispered, my hushed, trembling voice expressing all of my heart's longing.

The empty room blurred as my eyes lost focus. I blinked to clear my vision, and Mitica stood before me. Smiling softly, his eyes shone with love and adoration.

I rushed to him and buried my face in his chest, breathing deep his scent as he pressed me to him.

"I am here, bucuria mea," he reassured. I looked up into his eyes. "We have much to discuss," he said.

"Later," I promised, pulling his lips down to mine.

His warmth spread through me as though he was breathing life into me. He needed little urging, sliding his hands up my back and kissing me deeply.

"Stay with me tonight," I gasped, breaking our kiss to plead with him.

His gaze, heavy with lust, answered before he purred, "Da," in a low, husky voice.

"I'm yours, Mitica. Love me so thoroughly that it hurts when I'm not with you," I begged, trailing my trembling fingertips along his cheek.

"Da," he murmured again, turning his head to kiss my palm.

He lifted me off my feet, folding me over one shoulder.

I yelped, surprised by his forcefulness. I didn't really mind the blood rushing to my head as I smiled at his backside. I prepared to be flung onto the bed. Instead, Mitica set me down with care.

He kissed me deeply; his hot tongue teased mine, causing heat to pool in my core. As he pulled back, a sweet fog disoriented all thought. I trembled as I panted.

His shadowy blue eyes met mine as he hovered over me. "This is not a night you will forget."

I shivered, knowing he would deliver. "Good."

I spent the next few hours covering my mouth to stifle my moans so no one would hear. His lovemaking was slow and thorough, savoring each caress, each stroke, each quiver, each kiss.

He seemed more desperate than before as if every heavy breath would be our last. He was intense and imposing; he demanded all of my attention. There were no problems, no worries, just Mitica and me and his hot breath in my ear, proving to me he was solid and real.

Completely undone, I nestled in Mitica's arms, my eyes growing heavy with satisfaction.

"Bucuria mea," he whispered, caressing my face as we lay on our sides.

"Hmm?" I asked.

"You cannot fall asleep yet."

"But it feels so warm and comfortable," I mumbled.

"I know, but I need to talk to you," he urged, kissing my eyelids.

"Okay. Tell me," I said, my eyes still closed.

"It's about Chuthekii's vision."

I sniffed hard, my eyes flying open. I sat up and smacked my cheeks, ensuring I was fully awake. Then, I looked over at him. "Okay. What did he say? Did he figure it out?"

He nodded. "He thinks it was the ceremonial tea that was poisoned. Remember when Likinoak mentioned that a special tea was part of the ceremony?"

I thought back to my first meeting with the Wyboka elder. "Vaguely. So what do we do next?"

"I have sent Oliver to Edmonton with a sample of the tea for the chemists."

I nodded. "It may take them a few weeks to test it."

"Da."

"And until then?"

"We try to discover who had the opportunity and motive to poison the tea. We don't have the evidence to prove the tea was poisoned yet. But Chuthekii is confident, and he has rarely been wrong before."

"What can I do to help?"

He frowned severely. "Just think about everything you have observed so far, and try to stay out of trouble. I cannot protect you as easily as when you were staying with me."

"Are you telling me to be quiet and keep my head down right now?" I asked, lifting one eyebrow.

He smirked at my tone. "Would you listen if I were?"

I pursed my lips. "Being quiet isn't something I'm terribly good at."

He pulled me on top of him. "Then, we shall have to keep that busy mouth of yours occupied."

I smiled against his lips as he kissed me.

"Still sleepy?" he inquired as I readjusted my weight to a more comfortable position atop him.

"What do you think?" I asked, trailing my hand down his body and slipping it between us to wrap my fingers around his stiff manhood. He shuddered beneath me, and I grinned.

"What do you say, Mitica? Do you still have it in you?" I let him slip through my fingers with a flick of my wrist.

He hissed with pleasure. "Do you doubt me, bucuria mea?"

The hot flesh of his ready cock slid in my hand as I continued to stroke him. He panted, his solid chest rising and lowering beneath me.

"Then show me what you're made of," I challenged.

Rolling me to my back, Mitica released himself from my grasp. "I do not think you are ready for what I am truly capable of," he taunted.

"Try me."

He smirked, amusement dancing in his eyes. "If you insist."

He pulled me to my feet until we were both standing naked in the center of the bedroom. "Close your eyes," he instructed.

I did as I was bid, and he began to sing so softly I could barely hear. I felt him knock in my mind, and I let him in.

"All right. Open them," he whispered, his breath a warm summer breeze on my face.

I gasped at the sight before me. We stood in a moonlit corridor.

Pointed archways on one side led to an open courtyard. A fountain tinkled, its water sparkling in the moonlight.

I glanced down, running my fingertips lightly over the long, white chemise I was wearing. Mitica wore tight, black pants and a tunic-like jacket with a Mandarin collar and embroidered sleeves over his bare back. Neither of us had shoes on.

"Will you dance with me, bucuria mea?" he asked, his blue eyes dark in the dim light.

"I'm not that great without practice," I admitted.

"Just follow me," he suggested, clasping my hand and wrapping one arm around me.

I gave myself over to his care, and he started a slow but simple waltz. We twirled down the corridor, moonbeams illuminating our path. Our gentle motion ruffled our hair and the edges of my nightgown. Mitica held me firmly in his grasp, and his hand on my back burned me through the thin fabric.

When we'd reached the end, we stood before a full-length mirror. Mitica had remembered every detail of my modern-day appearance and had magically rendered me thus in the illusion. He grasped my hips and pressed his chest to my back as our eyes met in the silvery surface of the mirror.

With eyes still locked, he turned his head and pressed a fleeting kiss to my cheek. Then, he trailed kisses down my neck, each more insistent than the last. Watching his progress and my own expression in the mirror made heat rise to my face.

"Eşti frumoasa, bucuria mea," he told my blushing reflection. "You are beautiful," he translated, though I hadn't asked.

His gentle fingers slowly pushed the chemise's neck from one of my shoulders. My own gasp sounded loud in my ears as his mouth replaced the fabric, bit-by-bit. He repeated the gesture on the other shoulder. The smooth fabric sliding from my skin felt so realistic; I wondered how he was accomplishing it. He tugged the chemise, and it fell to the ground. I shivered more from his fervent gaze than the air on my skin.

As I stood naked before the mirror, he trailed one hand up my side to my breast. His palm was hot as he cupped it, and the pads of his fingers were rough on the sensitive skin of my nipple. I trembled, an electric tingle racing through me. Enthralled by the eroticism created by touch and sight, watching him touch me in the mirror, seeing my lips part with that glazed look in my eyes, I couldn't have looked away if I wanted to.

I leaned against him, his arms supporting me as his chest burned my back and his manhood dug into me.

Mitica grinned, a mischievous twinkle in his eyes, as he pressed a soft kiss to where my neck met my shoulder. I quivered as he hit the sensitive spot and the hair on my neck and arms stood up. His teeth bit into the soft flesh, and my moan echoed off the stone walls of the corridor. I squirmed against him.

"Mitica," I whimpered, my voice a breathy sigh as I begged for him.

He moved us forward, pressing my naked skin against the cool glass of the mirror. I watched his reflection, his features slack with lust, and a cry, low and guttural, like the grunt of a feral animal, ripped through my throat when his hard cock slid deep into my ready core from behind.

My fingerprints smeared the silvery glass of the moonlit mirror as I held myself steady so he could enter me again and again.

We didn't take long. The moon, the mirror, our screams of satisfaction echoing off the stone walls of the corridor—and him and me, our faces clouded with desire, we never looked away from each other. I was captivated by our reflections, sleek with sweat, while Mitica thrust into me. Just as my limbs shook and shuddered with climax, I felt him pump inside me.

When Mitica's illusion had dissolved, I found myself leaning against the glass of the balcony door.

"How did you do that? I even felt the chemise against my skin," I asked as I turned around to face him.

He smiled, his eyes laughing. "Magic," he answered.

I clicked my tongue in pretend exasperation and rolled my eyes. "You don't say."

After we'd climbed back into bed, we snuggled closer and finally went to sleep.

THIRTY-FIVE

I awoke with a start the following morning to a loud knock on my suite door. Gasping, I sat up and looked over at Mitica, my heart racing in panic.

He watched me with an amused smirk.

"That's probably Marguerite. We slept too late," I whispered urgently.

"I think we earned our rest," he countered in an easy tone.

The knock sounded again, even louder, and I was relieved when I remembered I'd taken the spare key from her.

"Be right there," I called to the other room. "What are we going to do?" I asked Mitica.

He sat up in bed and kissed me sweetly on the mouth.

"Stop that. I'm serious. How are you going to get out of here?"

"You will call for me tonight, da?" he asked.

"I'm more worried about right now."

He forced his gaze on mine and stroked my cheek with his fingertips. "When will I see you next?" he murmured, more to himself than me.

"Yes, yes, I'll call for you. Now, what do we do?"

He smiled. "You summoned me, bucuria mea. Only you can send me away."

My heart jumped as the knocking pounded again. "I said hold on!" I snapped. "What do I have to do?" I asked him.

"You must say my true name and tell me to be gone."

I sighed, not really wanting him to leave. "You should probably put your clothes on first."

Mitica and I both dressed then I hugged him tightly. I looked up into his eyes and murmured, "I love you."

"Te iubesc, bucuria mea."

I did not look away from him but took a deep breath. "Dumitru, be gone."

As my vision blurred, his solid weight in my arms evaporated. When the room came back into focus, he was no longer there.

I sighed again and fought the burning in my nose as I walked to the door.

Marguerite waited impatiently in the hall. "Celeste, are you unwell? What took you so long to answer?"

"I'm fine. I just didn't get a lot of sleep is all."

She examined my face and nodded. "It appears not."

Great. I must look awful... Eh, worth it.

I rushed to get ready for the day, and I couldn't escape Marguerite's fussing since she was there before I was dressed. I did manage to take a bath in private though, which was good because there were dried fluids all over me. *At least Mitica's bite didn't leave a mark.*

I was disappointed to see it was raining again when I entered the dining room. I hoped it would be short-lived enough that I could meet Xi Lin later. The kitchen staff had everything in order, and William found time to eat breakfast with me, though I wished he hadn't. He suggested we dine alone together again that night, but I managed to fend him off.

After breakfast, we walked to the office behind the front desk. I was to meet Harrison as per usual, and William had work to do in his office.

I stopped short when I saw a man I didn't recognize sitting at the desk next to Harrison's. He was an average-sized man in a worn suit, the top-two buttons of his shirt undone as if he wore the outfit out of some contemptible requirement. He had dark, hat-mussed hair and black eyes. When I met his cold stare, I froze, my stomach dropping as I shuddered.

"Hickory, you're back," William said to the man.

The stranger nodded, the tip of his cigarette glowing, but his gaze never left mine.

"Come into my office. We have matters to discuss," William ordered, leading the way.

I held my breath until they were gone.

The angry timbre of William's voice sounded through the door, though I couldn't hear what he was saying.

"Harrison, who is that?" I asked, hushed, as I leaned over Harrison's desk.

He glanced over his shoulder at the door to William's office. "That's Winston Hickory, Mr. Broadstone's man," he whispered.

"His man? What is that? Like his personal assistant?"

He nodded. "Like Marguerite is to you."

I snorted. *Maybe if she actually worked for me and not William.* "So what? He just does odd jobs for William then?"

"More or less."

"Tell me, did this guy and I get along before?"

Harrison shrugged. "You never paid him much mind until recently."

I scrunched my eyebrows. "Around the same time you said I started to act distant?"

He thought for a moment. "I suppose it was around that same time, yes."

I pursed my lips in thought.

A loud thud from William's office, like the sound of a chair falling over, made me jump. A few moments later, Hickory exited. I averted my gaze when his hate-filled glare met mine, but not before I saw his tongue, darkened with blood, suck his teeth.

I didn't unclench until he'd left the room.

During our meeting, Harrison told me the guests enjoyed the bonfire, and we decided to continue to have one every week.

We chose to have the craft circle and drinks and cigars for that evening's entertainment since we didn't know how long it would rain.

It ended up raining for the rest of the day. I was frustrated about not getting a chance to talk with Xi Lin. I even thought about asking Xi Wei to show me where they lived but decided against it. The rain wouldn't last forever.

I'd never felt so uncomfortable working the front desk. I could hear Mary, Sarah, and Juniper giggling in the library from the other side of the foyer, but their youthful joy didn't warm me. A shiver shook my shoulders, and I peeked behind me. Hickory's black eyes glared at my back from his and Harrison's office. Facing forward, I tried to control the anxious humming of my limbs as I counted the moments until Frederick's return.

After Hickory's meeting with William, I saw him quite a bit throughout the day. I wouldn't say he watched me so much as he hovered. He just seemed to pass me a lot on his way to do whatever William had instructed him to do. He never talked to me, but I could always feel when his cold gaze was on me.

I sagged in relief once I went to my room for my afternoon break. I'd decided I should write to Suzette. I hadn't talked to her in way too long, and I had never even gotten a chance to tell her about Mitica and me. *Oli has probably told her I've left town though.*

I sighed and sat down at the small table near the window to write the letter. I took a sheet of paper and a fountain pen from the stationary box in front of me.

Dear Suzette,

 I can't tell you how sorry I am I didn't say goodbye to you before I left. I was even more surprised than you when I was called away so suddenly. I hope you can forgive me.

 I miss you and the life I had in Farrloch.

 Did Oli tell you? I did end up choosing from the men I told you about. My choice was none other than Constable Wynn Delaforet. Surprise! Don't be angry with Oli if he didn't say anything. I asked him not to because I wanted to tell you myself.

 Of course, our romance was rather short-lived since I had to leave. But, as you said, who knows what the future will bring?

 You and Oli will watch over him for me while I'm away. Won't you?

 I promise to write to you again, and I hope we will see each other as well.

 I'm sending this letter through Wynn. Should you want to reply, he will know where to send it.

 I wish you all the happiness in the world.

Your true friend,
Erin

I searched the stationary box for a stick of wax and a seal. I found what I wanted and pulled the little, wooden drawer out. Reaching for the seal, my fingers closed around something unexpected. I squinted at a pair of rings, examining them closely. One had a sizable sapphire encircled with diamonds and the other was a plain silver band.

I froze. *Wedding rings? Are these Celeste's wedding rings? But why would they be in here? I mean, they should be in her jewelry box. Or better yet, they should have been on her when she died.*

When I called on Mitica that night, I told him about all the strange things that had happened since I'd come to the hotel. He listened attentively.

"I really think Xi Lin might be the key. He seems to know something."

Mitica nodded, deep in thought. Finally, he met my eyes. "I want you to be cautious about all this. There may be more going on than we previously thought. Your safety is more important than solving this mystery."

I pursed my lips but didn't answer.

"Do you hear me, bucuria mea? It should not be long now until I hear from the Zgrimties. Find out what you can, but do not put yourself at risk."

"I hear you," I told him.

It rained for the next two days. I went about my indoor duties and was unhappy to find Hickory around every corner. His presence in the hotel was like walking through an unseen spider web. It was unexpected, distressing, and made me want to wash my entire body just to make sure it was gone.

After Saturday morning breakfast, Dr. Hollander came to visit me as promised.

"How are you feeling, Mrs. Broadstone?" he asked after checking my pulse.

"I feel fine, Doctor."

"Still haven't remembered anything?" His voice was tinged with concern, but his brow was unfurrowed.

I shook my head. "Nothing. I've been going about my regular duties every day. I even read letters from my family and friends in Toronto. But I still don't remember anything."

He nodded slowly. "Well, I wouldn't worry just yet. We mustn't live too much in the past anyway. It's important for you to concentrate on living your life. Your memories could return at any time, in pieces or in a rush."

"Thank you, Doctor."

That afternoon, I finally got the chance to look for Xi Lin. He was taking advantage of the sunshine by spreading fertilizer in what I assumed would be flowerbeds.

Though I'd made sure Marguerite and Hickory hadn't followed me, I called to Xi Lin softly. "Xi Lin, I've been wanting to talk with you. Do you have time?"

He looked around nervously then nodded. "My son told me you were looking for me the other day."

I nodded. "It's about what you said to me that day. You stopped before you were finished. Didn't you?'

He gazed into my eyes as if looking for something, but he didn't seem to find it. "You truly do not remember?"

"I really don't.

He paused for a while, and I held my breath in anticipation.

"You left this place because you felt you were in great danger," he whispered.

"What sort of danger?"

He shook his head. "That, I do not know. One night, I came to the garden, looking for a glove I had misplaced. You were here, alone and crying. I asked you if I could help. You told me Mr. Broadstone was not the man you had thought he was and that you were afraid."

"Did I tell you why I said that about William?"

He shook his head again. "You told me it was too dangerous for me to know. I said I wanted to help, and we made a plan. I purchased a railroad ticket for you to travel west. On the night you left, I went to the stables and brought you a horse."

"And then what?" I breathed.

"I do not know. You left. You said you would not return, but here you are."

Holy shit, Celeste. What was going on with you?"

"Mrs. Broadstone, you must not be here. You are in danger," Xi Lin urged.

I reached out to the old man and placed a hand on his shoulder. "It's okay, Xi Lin. I won't be here for long, I promise. Thank you for telling me this. I know to be more careful now."

He sighed in relief.

"And thank you for helping me before as well. You sound like a great friend."

He bowed at my compliment.

When I told Mitica what Xi Lin had said, he wanted me to leave immediately. Though I was scared, I couldn't show him that.

"I can't leave yet. What about the Zgrimties?"

"You know I will leave without their permission."

"But you can't. What about the Wyboka? We still haven't found out about the poisoned tea."

He frowned.

"These people, you're supposed to help them. Likinoak and Chuthekii? They're your family."

"You are my family. I will do anything to keep you safe."

"Well, I won't be kept safe at the cost of someone else. If someone poisoned that tea, then he or she could do it again."

His frustration twisted his beautiful features.

"Listen," I soothed, placing my hands on either side of his face. "I will be okay. They all think I have amnesia, and I don't really know anything. For all we know, Celeste was upset because she found out William was sleeping with Marguerite."

"Is he?"

I shrugged. "I doubt it, but that's not the point. That would've been a betrayal that would've made her want to leave."

"How would that have put her in danger though?"

"I don't know. Maybe she was upset and exaggerated to Xi Lin, or maybe she had a prenup."

His worry didn't diminish.

"The point is: we don't know what really happened. And until we do, we should follow the plan. You said you would be hearing from the

Zgrimties any day, right? What are a few more days? No one has hurt me so far. And besides being a little touchy, William has been fine."

His expression crumbled into helplessness. "You will stop looking into what happened to Celeste? If she was in danger, this could be the reason she died."

"Absolutely," I lied. *I'm sure poking around a little more won't make that big of a difference. And if William is behind Celeste's death, he needs to be brought to justice.*

He pulled me into his lap and buried his face in my neck. I hugged his head, stroking his hair in a comforting gesture.

"I do not know what I would do if something happened to you," he murmured into my neck.

"You won't have to find out," I assured. *I hope.*

I started my investigation the following day. I'd already looked through Celeste's things and found little of consequence, so I decided to search their room. It turned out to be fairly easy to get the key.

"Marguerite?" I called to her as I watched the front desk for Frederick.

"Oui, Celeste?" She stopped before it.

"William mentioned something to me about not wearing my wedding rings when I first arrived. You wouldn't happen to know where they are?"

"I did not see them when I moved your things."

"I thought so. Could you get my key to William's and my room so I can look for them when I have time?"

"Of course. I will help you search as well."

"No, it's fine. I'm sure William doesn't want you looking through his personal things."

She nodded at my seeming sensitivity. "Very well, I will fetch the key and put it on your table."

"Great. Thanks so much."

I got my chance during my afternoon break. William had called Hickory into a meeting in his office, so I knew they were both occupied for the time being. How long they would be busy, I didn't know. But I also didn't know when I'd get another opportunity.

I went to my room and grabbed the key Marguerite had left. Then, I hurried down the hall to William's room.

His suite was set up the same as mine but felt as though it was missing something. Half of the dresser was empty, half of the medicine cabinet as well. *If William cares for Celeste as much as I assume, I'm sure it's difficult for him to see the space she once inhabited so vacant.*

I looked through everything: every drawer, every corner, every chest, even under the bed. Nothing of interest was there. In fact, it was as if he had only the basics: clothes and toiletries. There weren't papers of any kind.

Standing in the middle of the living room, I scanned to see if there was any place I hadn't checked. *He must keep everything of importance in his office. That's going to be far more difficult to get into.*

Just as I was turning to leave, the doorknob clicked, and William entered the room. I froze, my shock mirroring his.

"What are you doing in here, my dear?" he asked after a tense pause.

"Oh, you mentioned before that I wasn't wearing my wedding rings, remember? I've already looked through my things and couldn't find them, so I thought maybe Marguerite had left them here."

"Not to my knowledge," he said guardedly.

"Oh, okay. Well, look for them when you get the chance. Won't you? I'd hate to think I've lost them. I'm sure they're expensive."

"Certainly. I will look for them."

"Thanks." I made my escape as fast as I could.

In my room, I locked the door and took slow, deep breaths, trying to calm my racing heart.

THIRTY-SIX

I didn't mention that I was investigating to Mitica when I called
for him that night. It was easy to hide because Oli had returned
from Edmonton, so he couldn't stay the entire night. That meant we were
too busy loving each other to talk much.

The following afternoon, I decided to go to the stables, thinking
perhaps Butch might know something about Xi Lin taking a horse to help
Celeste escape.

I remembered to grab a few sugar cubes for Saundra before I left the
hotel. I knew William was busy in his office, but I didn't know where
Hickory was. I hoped he was occupied by some enthralling task.

The stable hands must have finished most of their work because there
was no one in the stable. Saundra greeted me as I stood outside her stall.

"Hey, pretty girl. I brought you something." I offered her the sugar
cubes. Her velvety nose tickled my palm as she ate them greedily. I giggled
at the sensation.

After a few minutes of petting her neck, I heard a shuffling sound from
farther down the row of stalls. *Maybe it's Butch.* I walked toward the noise
at an easy pace, greeting the horses with a pat as I passed by. At the end of
the row, there was a room where they kept the hay and oats.

On the threshold, I saw Stewart and Mary kissing in earnest. A small sound of surprise escaped me. He had pinned her back to the wall of hay bales, and she urged him closer.

Oh Mary, you fool.

They stopped suddenly when they heard me. Mary's eyes went wide, and her face flushed.

A flash of irritation crossed Stewart's expression before he smiled easily. "Good afternoon, Celeste," he said cheerfully.

"Mr. Thomas, Mary," I responded, not attempting to hide my tone of disapproval.

"It's lovely weather we're having. Wouldn't you say?" Stewart asked.

I ignored him. "Mary, I believe your mother is looking for you." Of course, I had no way of knowing what excuse Mary had given her mother to get out of her sight, but I'm sure it had been a lie.

Mary cleared her throat and walked quickly for the exit. She had straw in her hair, but I wasn't going to tell her.

Once she'd gone, I glared at Stewart. "She's to be married soon. We both know you aren't going to offer her a life. So why don't you just leave her be?'

He gave me a charming smile. "Why Celeste, I had no idea you cared for me so much that you would feel jealousy."

I clicked my tongue and turned to leave, knowing there was nothing I could say to convince him.

"My offer stands when you're ready," he called after me as I left.

I strode down the row of stalls and out of the stable. Just as I turned the corner, I ran into Butch.

"Whoa there," he said, steadying my shoulders so I wouldn't fall.

"I'm sorry. I wasn't paying attention. Thanks."

"What has you so out of sorts?" he asked, tilting his head with a puckered brow.

"It's nothing. I'm just irritated by something one of the guests did."

He nodded as if he understood completely.

"Hey, do you have a minute? I overheard something I wanted to ask you about."

He bobbed his head in assent.

"So a while ago, probably late March, did one of your horses go missing?"

He nodded. "More like was stolen."

"Why do you make that distinction?"

"Because the mare's tack was missing, too. Horses get out, but they don't saddle themselves."

"Does that happen often?"

He shook his head.

"Do you know who could've stolen the horse?"

He shook his head again.

"Did you ever find it?"

"In a manner of speaking. We found her but not alive. She looked all the world like she'd been hit by a train."

"You found her by the railroad tracks?"

He nodded. "In pieces."

"Holy shit," I murmured.

Butch didn't seem to mind my lack of delicacy. "It wasn't a pretty sight to be sure. Mr. Broadstone was particularly upset about it. He even sent his man to find the culprit. I hear he never found the thief. Came back only a few days ago, empty-handed."

Mitica said he found me by the tracks, too. Was Celeste riding the horse when it got hit by a train? Does William know Celeste tried to run away? Did he send Hickory to find her then call him back when I came here? If they found the horse all mutilated, they may have thought Celeste was injured. But why not report her missing to the Mounties? And why lie to everyone and say she'd gone to visit a friend? Did he not want people to know she'd left him? Or maybe he just didn't want people to know about his marital problems and sent Hickory to find her and bring her home so they could work it out. Maybe he doesn't think the horse is related at all, though that may be a stretch with her and the horse going missing on the same night. But this isn't enough to prove anything. It's all still speculation. I need more information. I need to get into William's office.

I thanked Butch for answering my questions and promised to visit again.

I wasn't sure how I was going to sneak into William's office, but I knew I needed help. After much consideration, I decided to ask Harrison. It was clear Celeste hadn't told him anything before, but I thought that had more to do with keeping him safe rather than not trusting him as she'd said to Xi Lin.

That evening, when we were finishing our card games, I kept a few of my cards in my lap. Harrison cleaned up as usual then said goodnight. Right after he'd left, I pulled the cards out.

"Oh, it looks like a few cards are missing from the deck. I'll go give these to Harrison before he puts them away." It was a silly excuse, but no one seemed particularly suspicious.

After closing the library door behind me and rushing to the other side of the lobby, I caught Harrison as he was putting the cards in his desk.

"You forgot these," I said, holding the pair of sevens out to him.

He quirked an eyebrow. "Did I? Huh, I wonder how that happened. I'll go through the decks tomorrow."

"Harrison," I started, hushed. "Can I talk to you in private?"

He looked around. "We're already alone."

"No," I urged. "Anyone could walk in. Please, it's important."

With scrunched eyebrows and a frown, he rubbed his chin. "It's not proper, but you could come to my room."

"That's fine."

Harrison led me quietly to the workers' hallway and unlocked one of the doors on the left. His room was clean but simple. It was more like a college dorm than the suite I stayed in upstairs.

"Have a seat." He gestured to the only chair as he closed the door behind us.

I waited until he'd sat on the bed and was looking at me before I began. "I need your help. I still don't remember anything from before, but I've discovered a few things since I've been here. Something happened between William and me before I left. I don't know what it was, but it was awful enough that I wanted out. He lied to everyone when he said I was going to a friend's wedding. I actually stole a horse from the stables and was leaving."

Harrison kept his composure, but he pressed his thumb to his lips as he listened intently.

"I can only assume I didn't tell you before because I was trying to protect you, Harrison."

"This is terrible, but it explains a lot. What do you need my help with? Are you going to try to leave again?"

"Not yet. Right now, I'm trying to figure out whatever it was that made me leave before. I've already looked through William's room, but there weren't any clues. I need help distracting William and Hickory so I can search William's office."

He didn't respond. He just silently thought, his thumb still on his lips.

"Will you help me?" I asked, hoping I'd put my trust in the right person.

His eyebrows crinkled. "What? Of course I'll help you. I'm coming up with a plan."

I sighed in relief, and we started plotting our break-in.

I wanted to tell Mitica about the plan Harrison and I made as well as what Butch had told me about the horse. But I didn't want him to worry before I had any idea what to worry about. Even though he didn't know it, his arms around me, his kisses, his smile, his sweet whispers, he was giving me the strength and comfort to face my fears.

The following afternoon as I watched the front desk for Frederick, I heard Harrison knock on William's door in the office behind me.

"Excuse me, Mr. Broadstone. I'm sorry to interrupt, but there's a matter that needs your attention."

"What is it, Harrison?" I heard William's muffled reply.

"The mercantile in Farrloch, Sir. I went to pay the bill this morning as you asked, but the manager refused to settle with me. He will only talk to you, Mr. Broadstone. I have a feeling he wants to increase his rates, too."

"Very well, I will deal with him later."

"I beg your pardon, Sir. But this problem needs immediate attention. Because he wouldn't deal with me, I was unable to get items, which are needed today."

"Fine. Hickory, we are going into town. Fetch my coat."

A few moments later, William and Hickory left the hotel.

"All right," Harrison whispered from directly behind me. "I'll watch the desk and the door. Get moving."

"Thanks," I told him, quickly making my way to William's office and slipping in.

It's a good thing Harrison was told to settle that bill yesterday. I don't envy that manager's meeting with William, but I'm sure it won't be too terrible.

William's office didn't have much furniture, but the number of papers on and likely in his desk as well as on the shelves behind it was overwhelming.

I hope he's organized.

After pulling one of the many thin, unlabeled books from the shelf, I opened it to find an accounting ledger. Sighing as I scanned the black-inked records of every purchase William had ever made, I knew I'd never have time to go through them all.

The supple brown leather of William's chair cracked as I sat in it. I gently picked up the paper nearest me on the desk and quickly read William's correspondence to Mr. McMasters in Ottawa. It was full of nonspecific assurances that some new project was going well. I carefully replaced the high-quality paper where I'd found it.

It would help if I knew what I was looking for.

The drawer above my knees slid out easily, and I looked down at a collection of stationery supplies. The strewn blank papers were smooth under my fingertips as I pushed them aside. The irregular lines of something drawn rather than written caught my eye. I carefully extracted the large composition from under the stationary, trying not to rip the slightly yellowed map.

Not for the first time since I'd been in 1900, I wished for my cell phone. *Pictures would be a lot quicker.* The map wasn't very detailed, and I wondered what William could possibly use it for. It mostly depicted the wilderness surrounding Farrloch and the hotel. The mountains and trees were imprecisely inked, and Farrloch was just a word in elegant letters. The hotel was artistically drawn but not overburdened with detail. On the other hand, the lake and river were brilliantly done in a gorgeous blue. And through the reserve wasn't labeled, the location of the hot springs was also done in blue.

I wonder what color artists call that? It's more art than map.

I tucked it back into the bottom of the shallow drawer and reached for a deeper drawer beside me.

I bit my lip when the drawer showed resistance. *Is it locked?* But with a little more effort, I realized it was just too full. With some wiggling and one hard pull, I managed to get it open.

Not so organized after all. My eyebrows crinkled at the conglomeration of seemingly random junk. The wooden legs of the chair groaned as I slid it farther back to kneel beside the drawer. I hissed, clenching my teeth, and moved more carefully so as not to make so much noise. As I dug through the chaos, I pulled William's collection out and put it on the floor beside me.

A rusted railroad tie, a broken quill pen, a framed picture of Queen Victoria, really? The absurdity of the apparently bottomless drawer never ceased to surprise me.

Just as I was giving up to look somewhere else, I pulled out a heavy wooden box. My heart thumped hard, and I held my breath.

Slowly, I unlatched the clasp and lifted the smooth lid. My gasp stuck in my throat, and I nearly dropped the box when a large, smooth handgun stared back at me, nestled lovingly in its velvet-lined case.

Jesus. I sighed, willing my heartbeat to slow. *It's fine. This is the west, right? I mean, everyone probably has a gun. But, jeez, that surprised me.* I swallowed the nervous giggles that rose in my throat, gently closed the lid, and placed the gun box on the floor.

I saw only one item remaining in the drawer. *Finally.*

The small, black book was wrapped in a thin strip of leather. I unwound the tie, and a bundle of papers slipped from between the pages and fell to the floor. I retrieved the twine-tied bundle and read the address on the front of the top envelope.

These are...letters to Celeste? Then...

Hurriedly and with shaking hands, I flipped to the front page of the book.

Her journal. William had it all along. My heart raced, the sound of it beating loud in my ears, and I wanted to read it right then. *No time.* I reluctantly let go of the smooth leather book, setting it in the chair beside me, and began putting William's random junk back.

As I forced the overfilled drawer closed, I hoped I'd put everything in the right order. And I tried to be as quiet as I could when I pushed his chair back into place.

I wonder how much time I have left. Probably not much. That drawer took a while. I should cut my losses while I still can.

Just as I silently closed the door to William's office, I heard Harrison from the other room.

"Mr. Broadstone, how did it go? Did you settle everything?" His voice boomed in the foyer.

"Yes, and the manager seemed surprised by my presence. He claimed he'd never said he would only deal with me."

"Really? Well, that was certainly the impression he gave me, Sir. I apologize if I've inconvenienced you."

"It did give me a chance to renegotiate some of our contracts, but I suggest you be certain before calling me away over something so simple as paying a bill again."

"Of course, Mr. Broadstone."

There was a pause. "Where is my wife? Why are you at the front desk?"

Exiting their office, I said. "Thank you so much for watching the front desk for me, Harrison. I'm feeling better now. Oh, William, you're back. I wasn't feeling well earlier, and Harrison was nice enough to let me rest at his desk for a bit while he covered front desk duty."

William frowned. "You were not feeling well? Would you like to rest in your room?"

Do you even care? "No, I'm all right now. I'll rest after tea. Thank you for your concern." I smiled and nodded at Harrison, hoping he would understand that everything was okay. Then, I left for the dining room.

THIRTY-SEVEN

The creamy, sweet aftertaste of tea was still in my mouth when I retrieved Celeste's journal and letters and smuggled them to my room.

I sat cross-legged on the bed, my breathing loud in my own ears as I unwrapped the dead woman's journal.

I scanned the pages, my eyes struggling to absorb the details of her inner thoughts. She was sad to leave home but excited for her new adventure. She liked but paid Marguerite little mind. She'd overheard Louis and Gabriel gossiping about how William was much too old for her before they'd known she spoke French. She became fast friends with Harrison, finding the Australian funny and kind. And she loved William. Oh, how she loved him.

She poured her heart into the ink on the page, her hopes, her dreams, her love, her adoration for this man twice her age. She thought him so wise, so cultured, so mysterious and exciting.

I blushed and shied away from reading her intimate inner thoughts about her husband, but I trudged on.

As I neared the blank pages toward the end, her entries became sparser. She went days without writing a word. And when she did write, she didn't go into nearly as much detail.

18 March 1900

I cannot perceive the light of the world as I did only days ago. Everything is dark and dismal. Has life always been thus, and I was too naïve, too blessedly ignorant, to know the truth?

The agony, the betrayal, my chest aches as though my heart has been run through.

How could a man who has never shown me anything but kindness be so callous toward others, so evil?

Was it all a lie? Can a man capable of such atrocities also be capable of love?

I am a fool, a silly, love-blinded fool.

Am I party to this sin? But, even if I know, I cannot stop it. I am lost.

---

19 March 1900

A plan has been hatched. Not a good plan, but a plan nonetheless.

I see now how unforgivably trusting I have been. And though I cannot undo the past, my conscience will not allow me to stay here any longer.

Regret makes for a restless bedfellow.

I'm certain I will be condemned in the minds of those who truly care for me, but I must keep this endeavor hidden.

I'm sorry, friends. This is for the best.

---

21 March 1900

Has Hickory always lurked so near me, a shadow unnoticed until the bright sun of truth revealed his presence?

Does the devil know my plot, or has my forced awakening led me to paranoia?

---

29 March 1900

Tomorrow. Everything is set. I hope to soon be in the safety of my dear Papa's bosom.

Has fate finally shown me a ray of sympathy that my father and brother should be so near when I need them most?

My heart races like that of the smallest bird. May hope give me the rapid wings of one as well.

I held my breath and eagerly turned the page. The next was blank. I sighed, closing my eyes.

What was it that William did to so change her opinion of him? She didn't tell me anything I didn't already know or couldn't have guessed. Though, I suppose confirmation is valuable. Now I know she was going to meet her father and brother in BC.

The rough twine on the small bundle of letters pricked the pads of my fingertips as I pulled the neat bow loose. There were five of them in total, all from Jacques.

24 March 1900

My sweet Cellie,

I cannot tell you how pleased I am you've decided to meet us in Vancouver. Father has not stopped smiling since I told him.

We leave in a few days, so send any further correspondence to the enclosed address.

Your brother,

Jacques

---

7 April 1900

My sweet Cellie,

We have safely arrived in Vancouver.

I had thought you were to arrive before us. Did something delay your departure? Are you still coming?

Please write at your earliest convenience.

Your brother,

Jacques

---

14 April 1900

My sweet Cellie,

Father and I are beginning to feel concerned at your silence. Please respond as soon as you receive this letter.

Your brother,

Jacques

---

21 April 1900

Celeste,

Father is beside himself with worry, and I can hardly calm him with my own rising panic.

We had planned to stay in Vancouver for another month, but your silence has spurred action.

If we do not receive a letter by the week's end, we are coming to Farrloch.

Please, dear sister, let us know you are well.

Your concerned brother,

Jacques

---

28 April 1900

Dearest Celeste,

I apologize for alarming you before. I had no idea you had fallen ill.

We were all packed to leave when we received William's telegram.

It is a shame we will not get the chance to see you on this visit west, but I hope you are saving all of your energy to get well soon.

You are in good hands, Sister. I am confident you will be better in no time under William's loving care.

Your brother,

Jacques

My hand holding the letter fell into my lap. *Wow, William really does have everyone fooled. To open her letters and write a telegram so they wouldn't come to check on her? Truly diabolical. It seems Celeste must've only written that she was coming to visit and didn't tell her family anything about the crisis she faced. And based on Jacques's latest letter, there's no way William told them about my "amnesia." Whatever was going on, it's clear Celeste thought she was in danger. I really should tell Mitica what I've discovered.*

I paced the length of my hotel suite, worrying my lower lip. Finally, I paused and spoke Mitica's true name to summon him to me. I was so nervous about telling him how I'd been investigating behind his back that I didn't notice his sorrowful mood, so close to my own.

"Listen, Mitica," I started, gathering the courage to look up at him. He crushed me in an unexpected embrace. I paused a moment, taking strength from the love I knew he felt for me. "I know you're going to be angry," I whispered. "But I have to tell you anyway."

"I also have something important to tell you," he said.

"Okay, but let me go first. I want to get this off my chest."

His silence was his consent.

"For the last few days, I've been investigating what happened to Celeste. Before you blow up, I want you to know that I was really careful. And now, I agree with you. I'm ready to let it go. Whatever happened to her is too dangerous for me to mess with. I think we should just wait to hear from the Zgrimties and make an escape plan."

I cringed, fully expecting his well-deserved outburst.

But his voice was even and void when he said, "I heard from the Zgrimties today."

Dread froze my stomach. His reaction was not one that foretold good news.

"Did they...did they cut you off?" I murmured.

"Nu."

I shivered, somehow knowing his next words would be worse than I imagined.

"I am permitted to continue my work for them under the condition that I never see you again."

My head spun with the dizziness his words produced. "What?" I murmured.

"They said I must never see you again if I want to continue helping the fae with their support."

"What would be their purpose in separating us?"

"Punishment. I broke my vow. Now, I must choose." His voice sounded far away over my ragged, shuddering breath.

"If you stay with me, it will be at the price of all of those people? I can't. I can't do that. Mitica, they need your help. I—"

He cupped my face, forcing me to look at him as my eyes rolled around in panic.

"Nu, Erin. Nu."

I flinched as he called my name.

"This is their doing. Not yours. They could have let it go, but they would rather see people suffer than have someone disobey them and go unpunished."

"But the fae...magic..."

"We can still help the fae and magic without them. I will no longer serve such masters. You, you are far more important. And I know you and I will help a great many fae together."

"Are you...are you sure?" I asked weakly.

"Da, there is nothing anyone can do that would stop me from being with you."

I couldn't quell the hot tears as they streamed down my face. Mitica gently kissed each one away until all I felt was the glowing warmth of his love.

"I am very upset with you, bucuria mea," he assured gently.

I nodded.

"You lied to me."

"I know," I said miserably.

"But I know you do not give up. It is one of the things I love about you. What is upsetting is that you felt you could not tell me you wanted to investigate."

"I knew you didn't want me to because you thought it was dangerous, and I didn't want you to worry."

"It was dangerous, and it is only my fear of losing you that makes me worry."

"You're right. I won't do it again. I swear."

He kissed me lightly on the mouth to show his forgiveness and seal my promise. "Now, what did you discover?"

I recounted what Butch had told me about the horse and what I'd read in Celeste's journal and letters. "I don't know what William did that so shook her faith in him, but it must've been severe."

He nodded. "It seems likely he noticed her change in behavior and sent this man Hickory to watch her."

"You think so? I mean, he must've realized she tried to run away when he found the horse. But do you think he knew she figured whatever it was out before she tried to leave?"

"Unlikely. He would have attempted to stop her before she left if he had."

"That's true," I agreed. "But he definitely knows now that he's read her journal and letters. You don't think he killed her. Do you?"

He frowned darkly then met my eyes. "I do not know. But if he did not know she knew, then he would have had no reason to."

"Right, and if he did, he probably would've made such an attempt on me."

"Not necessarily. He thinks you have amnesia. It could be he is waiting to see if you remember something."

"So we still don't really know anything. William could be a murderer, or he could just be a guy whose wife left him and then died."

"Well, we know one thing. We have to get you out of here immediately."

I sighed. "Mitica, you're not going to want to hear this, but I'm staying."

"Nu."

"Yes. We need to pretend everything is normal until we find out what's going on with the Wyboka. In the meantime, we can make a plan to escape. If we plan carefully, we can disappear in a way that no one will ever come after us. Celeste Broadstone and Wynn Delaforet will be gone, and we can just be Erin and Mitica."

He ground his teeth. "I do not like it."

"I don't like it either, but is there a better option?"

As he glared out the window, I reached up to touch his cheek.

"Mitica, look at me."

He sighed and turned his troubled blue eyes on me.

"Everything is going to be fine. I'll lay low. I swear. I'll act totally normal, the good little amnesiac. I won't investigate anymore. We should hear from Edmonton soon. Then, we will have evidence, and we can help the Wyboka."

"I have a bad feeling."

"Of course you do. All of this is potentially incredibly dangerous. You just concentrate on solving this case, okay?"

"And what will you be doing?"

"Me? I'll be planning a party."

He tilted his head in confusion. "Ce?"

"I just had an idea. One of the guests mentioned something to me about having a dance. What if I made it this big thing, invited tons of people? If there was a crowd, it would be easy for us to just slip out. Right?"

He considered the idea then nodded slowly. "But they would still come looking for us when everyone left."

"That's true."

"I could make a false report of your death. If I claimed you threw yourself off a cliff into the river, they'd never think they could find your body."

"Right. But wouldn't that mean you'd have to stay behind?"

"Only for a little while. It is not uncommon for lawmen to retire early after facing the tragedy of not being able to save someone."

"Okay. And if you haven't solved the Wyboka case by then, that will give you extra time."

He nodded. "When should we plan for this to happen?"

"Why not the 28th, the day of the eclipse? It's the perfect excuse to have a celebration, it gives us just under a month to make sure there will be tons of people, and it gives you time to help the Wyboka."

He frowned at the timeline but agreed. "How do you plan on getting away? You are not going to steal another horse, are you?"

"No, I'll go with Grigore."

He squinted his displeasure. "I do not think that is a good idea."

"Yes, it is. Just think about it. He can get me far away much faster than a train could, and then I'd have a dragon protecting me while you're away."

"Da, and you would have a dragon trying to seduce you, too. You are not immune to his magic."

"I know not to make eye contact with him. Besides, there has to be a charm or spell or something to repel his influence. Isn't there?"

He sighed. "There is a charm, but it does not repel so much as dampen."

"That's fine then."

He didn't look happy about it, but he didn't argue either.

"How long do you think it will be before the Zgrimties realize you're choosing me?" I asked softly.

"They requested my response before the next full moon."

"So they can take weeks and weeks to answer you, but you have to answer them in a week and a half? Eck, if that's not just typical of a governing body. But then there will be two weeks between when you send word and the party. Do you think they'll sabotage us at all?"

"I do not know. However, they are not likely expecting me to choose you, and they will convene a council meeting and debate what to do with me. They are not going to like losing me as an asset."

"But they won't rat you out to the Mounties, right?"

"Nu, they will not involve the humans. They will devise a much more insidious punishment."

"Well, that's...foreboding."

He nodded. "We must disappear before they settle on a punishment."

"Right."

THIRTY-EIGHT

"William," I called over breakfast the next day.

"Yes, my dear," he asked from behind his newspaper.

"Did you know there's a full solar eclipse later this month?"

"Indeed? I did not."

"I was thinking, wouldn't it be the perfect reason to have a big party?"

He met my eyes over the top of his paper, and I steeled my nerves so as not to look away.

"One of the guests mentioned wanting to have a dance, and you said part of my job is to make the hotel attractive to easterners, right? We could invite tons of people to come to watch the eclipse and then have a celestial masquerade. I don't think it would be hard to fill up the entire hotel."

He seemed to consider my proposal as he folded the paper. "I think it is an excellent idea, my dear. When is the eclipse?"

"Yeah? May 28."

"That doesn't give us much time for a grand affair, but if we work very hard, I believe it's possible."

"Thank you, William." I beamed at him, trying to maintain the façade.

"Though if we are having a ball, I will have to ensure the digging of that cellar door and patio you requested for the men in the laundry are finished." He smiled so gently I almost believed he was a good guy.

I can see why Celeste trusted him. "You're going to go through with it after all?"

"Of course. My beautiful and compassionate wife pointed out that I must care for my employees."

What is it you want from me? Are you just trying to win me over as you said you would? Or are you trying to make me reveal what I know by keeping me off guard? "That's so nice of you, William. I really appreciate it, and I know the guys downstairs will, too."

I'd never been great at acting. I was always just in the chorus in drama club. Perhaps it was my fear that gave me the added motivation to carry out my performance. Whatever the case, I felt confident my excited expressions were flawless.

William promised he would start writing letters immediately to all the people he knew out east, inviting them to our celebration.

Thankfully, Harrison picked up that my enthusiasm for this new venture was a signal something was afoot. He jumped right into event planning with me, trusting I would inform him when we were alone.

We outlined everything we would need for the ball: food, decorations, musicians, and, of course, guests. I recalled Celeste was known pretty well in the Toronto art community. I decided to use her connections to secure an orchestra and artists to make decorations.

As for food, I had full confidence Louis and Gabriel would know what to do. The chefs ran with the task, eyes shining with the thrill of a challenge.

Harrison wrote to the press and members of the event planning community, asking them to advertise. He would also handle the logistics of travel for guests coming to the event. All-in-all, we were going to have a lot to keep us busy over the next month.

When we announced our plans to the guests that evening in the library, the young women squealed with delight. I was disappointed to hear Colonel Higgins and Reginald would be checking out before the event, as were the newlyweds. Unfortunately, Stewart and Cole planned to stay.

As Harrison said goodnight and prepared to leave the room, he asked if I could give him a hand with a detail he was struggling with. I obliged, and we went to the garden for privacy.

"So what's going on?" he asked as soon as we were outside.

"I found my journal and some letters from my brother in William's desk yesterday."

"Did they give you any idea as to why you left before?"

I shook my head. "Not really. I only know I found out something terrible, and William didn't want me to know since he kept the journal and letters from me."

"We need to do more investigating?"

"No, I'm done trying to figure it out. It feels too dangerous to dig any more."

"Then you're going to just forget about the entire matter?"

"No, I plan to leave. This time for good."

"When? How?"

I shook my head again. "I can't tell you. But I want you to know: I value our friendship, and I wish there could be another way."

He frowned at my choice of words coupled with my solemn tone. "You will be all right?"

I smiled sadly. "I will be free."

We strolled quietly in the garden for a short while before Harrison excused himself. Apparently, he had a rendezvous with Butch. I wished him goodnight but stayed.

Wandering through the garden on that cool, spring night refreshed my ragged nerves. It had been difficult to pretend all day. The gentle moonlight from the waxing crescent, peeking just over the garden wall, and the twinkling of countless starts reminded me how small I was in the universe.

"Long before you and me, the sun and moon shined down on those who breathed the fresh air of a spring night," I told Mitica as though he was right beside me.

"You and me, I like the sound of that," a voice cooed from the other side of the lattice wall I stood before.

I gasped, nearly jumping out of my skin. Stewart stepped out from behind it.

"How long have you been there?" I asked around the lump in my throat.

"Oh, I came out as Harrison went in."

I sighed internally. *He didn't overhear us then.* "What do you want?" I demanded.

"I'm a guest at this hotel, you know. Can't I enjoy the garden at night like everyone else?"

He stepped up beside me, and I edged away.

"Sure, you can. Away from me."

He gave me a charming smile, my harsh words not offending him in the least. "Is that what you truly want, Celeste?"

"Yes, Mr. Thomas. That is what I truly want."

"I don't think it is. I think you burn with passion. I can see it within you. It calls to me, drawing me to it."

My face heated. "Okay. I burn with passion, but not for you."

"You can't expect me to believe it's for your husband. I see how you look at him. He's a stranger to you. But me? You show me your inner fire."

"Are you purposely thick or were you just born that way?"

I turned to walk away, but he grabbed my wrist and pulled hard, slamming my back against the lattice wall.

My head throbbed and my wrist screamed where he still squeezed it.

"You know, Celeste," he continued in an easy tone. "You are the first woman to ever resist me. Why is that?"

"Because you're an asshole," I hissed through my teeth, which were clenched in pain.

"No, that can't be it. Women adore aggressive men. Don't you? You all just want someone to dominate you."

"You're delusional. Now, let me go," I demanded, attempting to twist my wrist from his grasp only for him to box me in by grabbing the lattice behind me with his free hand.

"How could I let you go now that your sweet scent is in my mind? I haven't shown you how charming I can be yet."

I struggled in earnest; he was too strong for me to escape. Fear instinctively pumped in my veins, but my mind couldn't seem to grasp what was happening. I froze and couldn't stop myself from shaking.

As he grabbed a fistful of hair at the base of my neck, I could feel the treacherous tears run down my cheeks, betraying my weakness. He forced my head to look up at him.

I'd always thought the eyes of a perpetrator would be cold and unfeeling, but not Stewart. His eyes burned, reveling in the power he had over me.

My mind raced, and I couldn't grab hold of a coherent thought to get me out of this nightmare. His face was too close, his breath too near, his hand too tight, too cold, too real.

Bile rose in my throat when he smiled triumphantly and crushed my lips with his. As his slimy tongue licked at me, the horrible reality of the situation cracked the ice that had frozen my protests.

He yelped as I stomped hard on his foot, giving me just enough time to cry out, "Dumitru!"

I sucked air through my teeth as Stewart yanked my hair and forced me to turn around. The crisscrossed pattern of the lattice pressed painful creases into my skin as he pushed me into it.

"That wasn't nice, Celeste. But I'm prepared to forgive you," he growled into my ear.

"Let go of me." My voice sounded weak, even to me.

I could hear his frown. "This is all wrong," he murmured almost to himself. "I want to feel that passion I see burning inside you." He nodded against my cheek. "It's all right," he reassured. "I must have to coax it out of you."

Why isn't he here yet? I must've done something wrong. He isn't coming. My mind began to pull away as if stung by the horror. "Dumitru," I whispered, not even sure I'd called him aloud.

The cool night air raised the hair on my legs as Stewart lifted the back of my skirts. Then, the fabric returned to its proper place in a rush of wind as Stewart's weight on my back disappeared.

I sank to the ground, Stewart's strength, and not my knees, having been the only thing holding me up. *Run! Run!* My mind screamed, still not completely focused. My head craned to see over my shoulder as I forced myself to my feet.

And there he was: Mitica, his face flushed in fury as crimson as his hair.

Stewart's eyes popped wide as Mitica held him by the throat. He wheezed, clawing at Mitica's hand.

"Know this before you die," Mitica hissed. "You have forced yourself on the wrong woman."

"I'm sorry," Stewart choked out.

Mitica smirked. "It is too late for that."

"Mitica, don't," I murmured.

His murderous rage didn't allow him to hear.

I approached him and gently touched his shoulder. "Stop it. I don't want you to become a murderer."

His fiery eyes met mine and softened in recognition. "Killing scum like this hardly counts as murder." But his hand on Stewart's throat loosened a little.

Stewart sucked in air, coughing.

"Just let him go," I urged.

"Oh, I will. As soon as I am finished with him." Glaring at Stewart, he pulled him closer. "You have caused many harm. Haven't you? Well, now you will feel their pain." Mitica chanted something in Romanian; it sounded much like a dirge.

Then, he flung Stewart away from him; he landed in a heap on the brick path of the garden.

"I suggest you leave. Now," Mitica demanded.

Stewart fled toward the hotel and didn't look back.

Before I could even blink, Mitica's arms enveloped me. I trembled, relief and residual fear mixing as my body tried to make sense of it all. A sob stuck in my throat.

"Mitica..." I whimpered.

"I know, bucuria mea. I am here," he hushed.

It took a while for my shivers to succumb to Mitica's warmth. I can't say how long I sagged against him in the moonlit garden, heaving unsteady breaths, his embrace the only source of heat in that cold, unforgiving night. Eventually, the all-encompassing strength of his presence soothed my nerves, and my heartbeat and breathing returned to normal. "Thank you," I whispered into his chest, my shame at my own weakness not allowing me to look up at him.

"Nu, bucuria mea. Thank you for stopping me. I would have killed him." Mitica sounded as ashamed as I felt. "You kept a clear head in the worst sort of situation."

"Don't make me sound so great. I should've never been in that type of situation to begin with. I should've known better."

He gently lifted my chin so I would meet his eyes. "This is not your fault. His sins are his own."

I knew his words were true, but I couldn't stop that nagging feeling that I could've prevented it somehow. "What did you do to him?" I asked.

"Instant karma. When he inflicts pain and suffering, so too will he have pain and suffering inflicted upon him."

"That's...kind of genius."

He grinned. "Much better than death."

"Mitica..." My face heated, and I felt silly as if I were a frightened child who was asking for her parents to leave the hall light on. "Would you stay with me tonight? I know Oli is still at the barracks, but I don't want to be alone." I couldn't meet his eyes as I asked something so vulnerable and embarrassing.

"Da, bucuria mea. I will think of something to tell Oliver tomorrow. I will not leave you tonight."

The knot in my chest loosened a little.

Mitica waited in the garden as I snuck to my room. I couldn't help but feel jittery walking the halls alone, worrying I'd run into Stewart, jumping at every shadow and the creak of every step and floorboard. But the stress turned out to be unnecessary once I was securely behind my locked door.

When I called Mitica's true name again, he completely obliged my need for the safety of his embrace. I was able to sleep soundly that night, snuggled deep in the protection of his arms.

Stewart and Cole's midnight checkout was all the talk the next morning at breakfast.

Apparently, they'd been in some sort of rush, but no one knew why their departure had been so hasty. No one except me that is. Frederick, being the discreet and professional clerk he was, would never think to question his guests about their personal decisions.

Reginald expressed his surprise to Colonel Higgins, insisting the lads had planned to stay through the ball. Colonel Higgins couldn't recall.

Mary quietly pushed her breakfast around her plate, her eyes red from recent tears, as her two friends speculated as to the gentlemen's motives.

I felt light as if I hadn't a care in the world. The jackass was gone, away from Mary and me. And neither of us would ever see him again.

I hope Mitica's spell taught him how to treat others with respect.

Karma, after all, can also bring good things into your life, as long as you give good things that is.

Dr. Hollander came for his third visit after breakfast.

After he'd asked his mandatory doctor questions, we engaged in a little small talk.

"I do love this time of year," he commented. "The mountain air is so fresh, and I love the feel of spring about to bloom."

I nodded. "Are you from here?"

He shook his head. "Montreal. My wife, my brother, and I came out here to start anew. My brother is a barber, you know, in Farrloch. He enjoys his work, takes pride in it, too. Though he has been rather stressed of late. Apparently, a woman came into his shop a while back and asked him to cut her hair rather short." Dr. Hollander chuckled. "Boy, that certainly shook him."

I bit my lip, grateful Marguerite had again pinned my hair under a hat. *Aww, I knew I traumatized him.*

Later that afternoon, I went back over Celeste's letters from her friends. I recalled one of the musicians she'd patronized had referred to the manager of the Toronto Symphony Orchestra.

Finding the name, I wrote Walter Baker a letter, naming our mutual acquaintance and asking if he would consider bringing some of his musicians to perform at our celestial masquerade.

I also wrote to a sculptor and a painter with whom Celeste corresponded, inviting them to the hotel and asking if they would make decorations.

It may be a little strange to meet Celeste's friends without remembering them, but I'm sure I can use the chaos of party planning as an excuse if I act in a way she wouldn't.

After I'd given the letters to Frederick to post, I thought all I had to do was wait for responses. Harrison and William were taking care of guest invites, and Louis and Gabriel had the food situation in hand. I'd thought I was done for the moment until I saw Marguerite's barely controlled excitement.

"Now, let us plan your costume!" she squealed.

Crap. I forgot about that.

THIRTY-NINE

Over the next few days, Marguerite pestered me about my costume for the masquerade. I had so many things I was worried about that I told her to just take care of it. My only condition was that the dress be easy to move in. When she told me she was going to hire Madame Buvons to make the gown, I was glad William had discouraged me going into town.

How would I explain that to Suzette? I thought as Marguerite took my measurements for the dressmaker.

I was relieved when Mitica brought me a response from Suzette. I'd been certain she was angry with me. But her words assured me she understood.

Dear Erin,

I was happy to receive your letter from your Constable Delaforet. I must say I was worried from not seeing you for so long.

Oliver did indeed keep your secret, but he was glad when I told him I knew. I laugh when I think of his expression. I thought he would burst. He claims to have known how you two felt about each other before you did. Is this true, or is he just boasting?

You need not worry about your Mountie. Oliver and I will look after

*him. He seems to be coping. Oliver says he was quite depressed the first
few days after you left. But now, he seems almost determined. Perhaps he
is planning to visit you?*

*I hope you get to come to Farrloch again soon. I miss you, mon amie.
Would you make the journey for a wedding, for instance? I hesitate to
even write this, but Oliver seems serious about me of late. I think I would
like to be a Mountie's bride.*

*He is so kind and considerate. Speaking of which, you should write to
him. He was upset when I received a letter and he did not.*

*That is all for now, mon amie. I am off to help Madame make a dress
for Madame Broadstone. The hotel is to have a masquerade at the end of
the month. It is wonderful, non? I wonder if they will send invitations to
people in town. Probably non, but it would have been fun.*

Ton amie,

Suzette

I made a mental note to consider inviting the townspeople to the party.
I wonder if anyone would recognize me in my mask. I hope not.

As Suzette had suggested, I wrote a quick note to Oli. It was vague,
asking him how he was and telling him to stay out of trouble.

While I waited for responses to my letters from Toronto, William and
Harrison began to get telegrams from guests excited for our party. There
was only a handful so far, but people had started to book rooms.

I couldn't wait to tell Mitica how our plan was working when I called
for him. My body hummed with the thrill of moving toward our goal,
finding purpose and balance in the activity. But when he materialized
with a solemn expression, I immediately tensed.

"What is it?" I asked, reaching for him.

"We just heard from Edmonton," he told me. "The ceremonial tea was
poisoned: hemlock."

There was a heavy silence. When I started to speak, it was in a slow,
uncertain cadence. "But that's good. Isn't it? Now, we can find who
did it."

"Is it?" he asked. "Da, we can find the culprit, but this means there is a
murderer loose. It was not just an accident."

I nodded seriously. "What do we do next?"

"I will open an official investigation tomorrow. We now have evidence of foul play."

"Won't that give the murderer warning?"

"Perhaps, but what else can I do?"

"Let's talk to Likinoak and Chuthekii. Maybe they can tell us something."

"But I cannot let them know I am Wynn. I told them I left the tea on the barracks' threshold with a note last time. How would I know the results of the tests?"

"Through me, of course. I know both Wynn and Mitica. Remember? And before you argue, I'm coming with you. As long as I'm back before dawn, no one should notice."

"But will I have the strength to bring you back?" he muttered just loud enough for me to hear.

"Yes, you will. Because you want to be with me forever, not just as long as it takes for them to find us."

"Pentru totdeauna," he whispered.

"What's that?" I asked.

"Forever," he answered, sliding his arms around my waist.

I smiled as he kissed me on the side of my head. "Te iubesc," I told him.

"I love you, too," he murmured.

After releasing Mitica from the summoning call, I dressed in my jeans and chemise under Oli's jacket, reveling in the feel of the comfortable fabric hugging my legs.

Then, I snuck cautiously downstairs and out into the garden. Pursing my lips at the rather narrow paths flanked by trees and bushes, I slipped out of the iron gate. It creaked as I shut it, and I flinched at the sound, so loud in the hush of night. Once it was closed, I crept along the garden wall and started walking down the street, knowing they would intercept me along the way.

I squinted into the darkness, searching for my ride. Waves of wind blew the hair from my face as Grigore and Mitica landed before me.

"Erin," the zmeu purred, grinning in the light of his forehead gem. "I have missed you."

"I hope you've been behaving yourself, Grigore," I told him.

"As if I have had a choice," he muttered.

His response reminded me of Stewart a little, and I frowned. "I wish you would change your ways, Grigore."

He blinked, surprise showing on his reptilian face.

"Mitica obviously thinks you can be saved, or he wouldn't have stopped Făt-Frumos from killing you, right? Wouldn't you rather a woman choose you because she wants you and not because you used magic on her?"

"Do you think I, too, do not crave true love?" he asked softly after a long pause. "I was not born a zmeu, you know. I was once a zână."

"Another type of Romanian fae," Mitica explained.

"Yes, a *fae*," Grigore spat in disgust. "I bestowed gifts and protected children. I had powerful magic, even for a zână. I lived among my people in Tărâmul Celălalt."

"What happened?" I whispered.

"Crina." He went silent for a long time. The name hung in the air like a spring fragrance with no breeze to blow it away. "She was a zână, and I loved her. But all of her promises were false. She destroyed me, and in my despair, I vowed to bring that same destruction upon the world."

"What did you do?"

He smiled in diabolical glee. "I stole the sun and the moon."

"Wait... What?" I looked at Mitica for confirmation.

"In a manner of speaking," Mitica clarified.

"I conjured the darkest of clouds. For an entire season, the sky was the blackest night. Nothing grew, and no rain fell. And everyone suffered as much as I."

"Jesus," I murmured.

"The other fae and the hultan could not dispel my bane, so they cursed me instead. They united for the sole purpose of defeating me. This was my punishment. They made me into a monster. But they failed in many ways. They tried to turn me into a balaur. But their magic could not entirely contain mine, so I became a zmeu instead."

"You wrought much fear and horror after that," Mitica added.

"They deserved it," Grigore growled.

"You must've truly loved her," I murmured to Grigore. "Crina. You must have loved her so much to be in that much pain when she betrayed you."

He was quiet for a while before he answered. "I did... I do."

I solemnly nodded my understanding. "It's not that you want the love of a woman. It's that you want the love of *that* woman."

He averted his eyes and didn't answer.

"Grigore, listen. I don't know how it feels to go through that kind of rejection. But do you really want to be this way? I can't believe someone so full of love wants to cause such pain."

"If she will not love me, then have her hate me."

"But it's not just her you're hurting. I'm sure you had other people you cared about. Friends or family?"

"They all left, the same as she."

"But Mitica didn't."

"Neither fae nor hultan is trustworthy."

"What about humans? I'm going to be honest here, Grigore. You're kind of an ass. And you and Mitica can say you dislike each other all you want, but I don't buy it. He's stuck with you this long, and I trust his judgment. If he says you can be redeemed, then I'm with him. I hope in time you can open your heart and find love again. But for now, you're stuck with us as friends."

He stared at me, and I didn't look away, though I knew I should so his magic wouldn't affect me. After a few moments, I still didn't feel his golden pull.

"You are both fools," he muttered, sliding his eyes away from mine.

The flight to the reserve was much too short. I was free, with nothing but the wind in my face and Mitica's arms around me. And then I was on the ground, knocking on Likinoak's door in search of a murderer.

"So it was the tea?" Likinoak asked as we stood in her kitchen.

Mitica and I nodded.

"Who has access to the tea, Amâwe?" Chuthekii questioned.

"Only the elders and Tsesikó," Likinoak answered.

"Well, it clearly was not Tsesikó," Mitica reasoned. "Since he was one of the victims."

Likinoak nodded seriously. "All of the elders must be searched, including me."

The old woman looked at Mitica then at me. "Tell Constable Delaforet this information, Seyohkwii. I will expect him tomorrow."

I nodded, pretending like he wasn't beside me.

"You must not tell the other elders about this, Amâwe. They may get rid of evidence if they know we suspect them," Mitica advised.

"I will do as you suggest," Likinoak said wearily as if the entire situation broke her heart.

With tensions high, we prepared to leave. But right after Chuthekii and Mitica went outside, Likinoak stopped me with a hand on my elbow.

"Seyohkwii," she urged.

"What is it, Amâwe?"

"I have a feeling in my breast."

I frowned at her ominous tone. "What's wrong? Is it the investigation?"

She shook her head. "I do not think so." Searching my eyes, she said, "I will not see you again."

I smiled gently at her and wrapped my arms around her. "I know everything seems overwhelming right now, but I'm sure we will see each other again. We're family, remember?"

She clung to me as if she truly believed her fears, and I returned her embrace for a while.

With a heavy heart, I was back by the garden wall well before dawn.

"Good luck tomorrow," I told Mitica, staring into his sorrowful eyes.

"I hope this will all be over soon. The Wyboka will be safe, and we will have a new life."

I nodded. "Three weeks from now, Grigore and I will be far away, just waiting for you to join us."

"Speak for yourself," Grigore muttered.

"Oh, hush, you," I told the snarky dragon. "I believe in you, Mitica. I know you can figure this out." I stood on my toes and pecked him on the lips.

He wrapped his arms around my waist and lifted me into a sincere kiss.

Grigore grunted from over Mitica's shoulder.

"Goodnight," I whispered sweetly. "And goodnight to you too, Grigore," I added. "Get lots of rest. You have a big day as a Mountie's noble steed tomorrow."

Grigore blew air through his lips, making a vaguely horse-like sound.

I giggled.

"Goodnight, bucuria mea," Mitica told me.

FORTY

*T*he next day, I couldn't help but worry about how the investigation was going. Even William noticed my concern.

"What is the matter, my dear? Are you unwell? Shall I send for Dr. Hollander?" he asked as I stared out the window at breakfast.

"I'm fine, William. I'm just thinking."

"What could be worrying you so thoroughly, I wonder?"

My gaze slid from the window to his face. He still held his knife and fork, but his eyebrows were raised in curiosity.

"This ball," I lied. "It's a lot more work than I'd imagined. I still haven't heard from anyone in Toronto."

"Oh. Well, I wouldn't worry about that. You are so well-loved in Toronto. I have no doubt they will accept your invitations. I should think you will hear from them next week. But if you are concerned about how much time we will have, feel free to send telegrams once you receive responses."

"Thanks."

"Might it be nice to have dinner just the two of us this evening, my dear? We can also excuse ourselves from the festivities if you are tired."

I grimaced internally at the thought of being alone with William. *But*

I've refused him a lot thus far. Will he start to get suspicious? I plastered a smile on my face. "A quiet evening is just what I need," I agreed.

"Excellent. I will inform the kitchen staff."

Marguerite was all smiles as she set my small table for dinner that night.

"What are you so pleased about?" I asked her as she hummed happily.

"You and Monsieur are dining alone tonight. *Romantique, non?*"

"No," I corrected her. "We are having dinner alone because William thought it would help with my stress level." *Though it's far more stressful to be alone with him.*

She smirked at me as though I wasn't being honest with myself. "Celeste, you have forgotten much of your past, so I know you do not recall your moments of intimacy with Monsieur. You are so rigid now. You must be frightened. You should let Monsieur in a little. He is your husband after all, and he has always been quite gentle with you."

Ew. My expression must've given away some of my feelings because Marguerite giggled like I was some untouched virgin who didn't know what I was missing.

After Oscar had brought our meal and Marguerite had left us alone, my giant hotel suite seemed to shrink into a coat closet. I concentrated on keeping my breathing even and my expression polite.

William started talking about how receptive the guests he'd invited to our party had been so far. Though I didn't really care to talk about the party, I soon wished he had stayed on the topic.

"Marguerite tells me she purchased you a journal in town a while back. Have you been writing about your day and thoughts and the like? Perhaps bits of memories? Doing so might help you recover."

"No, I haven't used it. I honestly haven't remembered a thing from before Constable Delaforet took me in. Maybe the habit of journaling just isn't for me, you know? I mean, you said I didn't do it before either, so I'm sure it's fine."

His eyes sharpened for a moment. But when I blinked, the look was gone.

"Quite right," he agreed. "I have to say, your change in other habits has been rather interesting."

"Really?" I tried for unconcerned. "That's fascinating. Perhaps memory is a big part of our personalities."

"Indeed."

"What's changed about me?" I asked, curiously.

"Quite a bit, in fact. I would almost believe you were an entirely different woman if I hadn't known better. Even the way you walk and talk is different."

I flinched.

"And other things, too. For instance, you always loved music, but you would never sing. You hated your own voice, and you could only be caught humming when you didn't realize it yourself. To think you would sing before a room full of strangers is incredible."

He watched my reaction intently.

"That is strange," I admitted.

"And Hickory tells me you've become quite fond of horses. He's seen you visit the stables on multiple occasions."

Shit. "Yes, I like horses as long as I'm not riding them. There's one horse in the stables, Saundra, who is very sweet. I bring her sugar cubes from time to time. I didn't like them before?"

"You never paid them much mind one way or the other."

This attack was feeling very one-sided. Before I could think better of it, I said, "I notice Hickory around a lot since he's been back. It feels like he's around more than Marguerite. It's almost as if he's watching me."

"That's very astute of you, my dear. Indeed, I have told Hickory to watch you."

My heart pounded in my ears, but I had a steady voice when I asked, "Why is that?"

"You are my wife, and I am worried for you at present. This all must seem strange to you, not remembering anything from before. I've asked Hickory to keep an eye on you because I cannot as much as I would like. You should feel free to ask him for help with whatever you need as well."

I eyed William's congenial smile. *Man, you are good. What are you playing at?* Picturing Hickory's icy glare, I thought about William's suggestion. *Yeah fucking, right.*

I could hardly wait to call for Mitica that evening. I had to know how the first day of investigations went. I stared at the clock, watching the seconds tick closer to ten. As soon as the second hand hovered over the twelve, I called for him.

He cursed in frustration. "Send me back," he urged. "He's on the run. Oliver and I are giving chase, and I don't want to lose him. Don't summon me until I give you a sign. Hurry!"

"B-be gone, Dumitru." I stumbled in my rush.

He vanished.

My heart raced as I stood, small and alone, in my dark room. I bit my lip. *Shit. I hope I didn't just screw this up.*

It rained for the next two days. The dark gray clouds hung low and oppressive, mirroring the squeezed feeling in my chest. Every night, I watched out the window for some sign that it was safe to call for Mitica, that Mitica was safe. And every night, I went to bed anxious.

When news did come, it was in the most unusual form of Dr. Hollander.

After he'd checked my vitals and asked me questions about whether I'd recovered any memories, we started to chat as we had been doing.

"How is your family, Dr. Hollander?"

"Oh, my wife's back has been sore with all this rain."

I nodded. "And your brother?"

"He's doing quite well. Much recovered from that earlier incident."

"That's good to hear."

He bobbed his head. "Did you hear the big news from town?"

"Not unless it was in the paper."

"It wouldn't have been. It just happened as I was on my way here."

"Ah, so what happened?"

"The Mounties captured a murderer."

I froze. "They did? Who was it?"

"I haven't the slightest. Some Wyboka fellow I believe. He gave those two hardy lads a difficult time, I hear. They chased him all over the mountains before they caught him."

I had to wait for the morning edition to find out the full details.

I rushed downstairs, nearly tripping over the hem of my many skirts and asked Frederick for a copy before I'd even had breakfast. The paper crackled under my hurried hands as I unfolded it to the front page.

MOUNTIES APPREHEND WYBOKA MURDERER

FARRLOCH—Constable Wynn Delaforet and Subconstable
Oliver Taylor apprehended and detained a Wyboka man
suspected of murdering three of his tribe.

The suspect, Talking Raven, also known as Pówahkai, declined to
comment. Talking Raven managed to avoid capture for nearly
three days until the Mounties brought him in 12 May.

"The higher authorities have been notified, and he will stand
trial," Constable Delaforet said.

When asked to speculate as to the suspect's motive, the Mounties
did not yet have an answer.

I pictured Pówahkai's dark eyes and curled lip as he'd accused the
presence of white people as the cause of the curse that took three Wyboka
lives. He'd certainly been the most hostile of the elders I'd met in the
teepee that day. *But why would he kill his own people? He seemed like he
wanted to preserve them rather than kill them.*

Later that day, I finally received word from Toronto. It seemed Celeste
was as well-loved as William had said. The manager of the orchestra was
more than happy to send a quartet to our ball. He was thorough in his
requests for compensation and travel expenses. After talking with William
about it, I dispatched a telegram via Harrison, agreeing to the manager's
terms.

That evening, I stood at my balcony window, still waiting for Mitica's
sign. Yet again, I waited in vain.

As William read his paper over breakfast the next morning, I ate only
my toast. The stress from recent days had tied my stomach in knots.

"Are you still concerned about the ball, my dear?" William asked, his
paper sagging in the middle as he looked over it. "I thought you'd heard
from the orchestra manager."

I glanced up at him. "Yeah, but I haven't heard from the artists yet.
Wait. What is that?" I pointed to the front page. "Can I see that for a
minute?"

"Of course." He folded the paper and handed it to me, his eyes squinched in curiosity.

WYBOKA MURDERER FOUND DEAD

FARRLOCH—Talking Raven, also known as Pówahkai, was found dead in the locked horse stall in which the Mounties were detaining him.

Talking Raven was being held under suspicion of murdering three of his own tribe. The suspect was found early this morning, his death apparently suicide by ingesting hemlock, the remnants of the poisonous plant still in his mouth.

Constable Wynn Delaforet and Subconstable Oliver Taylor, only yesterday lauded as heroes, are baffled by the turn of events.

Constable Delaforet assured the public he and his counterpart are looking into the matter but declined to comment on whether Talking Raven had revealed anything about his own guilt.

I pushed the paper away from me and got up from the table. *Holy Hell. What the fuck is going on out there? I need to see Mitica.*

"Where are you going, my dear?" William asked.

"To check the mail," I lied. "I'm sure you're right about the artists. Perhaps I received a response this morning."

Instead of stopping at the front desk to check the mail, I walked right out the door.

"Oh, have you come to see us off? That's very kind of you, Mrs. Broadstone," Reginald said, slowing my steps and pulling me from my thoughts.

The two men stood on the front stoop of the hotel as Campbell loaded their luggage onto his carriage. How he'd managed to mount an entire stuffed moose up there I had no idea.

"Yeah, I couldn't let you two leave without saying goodbye," I answered, having completely forgotten they were leaving that day.

"Very kind of you, lady. Very kind indeed," Colonel Higgins agreed with his friend.

"You two have a safe trip back. I hope you'll come visit us again."

"We certainly will. The hunt was fruitful, the food delicious, and the company excellent," Reginald praised.

"I'm glad to hear it." I smiled at them as they climbed into the carriage.

I waved goodbye with a sigh, thinking better of my hasty decision to head into town. *Wait for his sign, he said.* I clicked my tongue. *I hate waiting.*

It turned out I did have another letter from Toronto. The painter Gilbert Martin was distraught he could not accept my invitation. He did, however, give me the name of an excellent replacement, who was, at the moment, expecting word from me.

"Would you like me to send a response, Madam?" Frederick asked as I finished reading the letter.

Not really. I'd rather go into town and send it myself.

But as Hickory's cold eyes locked with mine over Frederick's shoulder, I sighed.

"Yes, thank you, Frederick." I sent another telegram to Toronto, this time to Amélie Roussel.

FORTY-ONE

As I stood watch at my window for the fourth night in a row, my heart was nowhere close to as calm as the nearly full moon drifting above the mountains.

I gazed up at it, hoping its gentle glow might give me some of its peace. Curiously, a part of the moonlight broke off and floated toward me. As I squinted at the moondust, it faded in and out like a firefly.

It's way too cold for fireflies.

Mesmerized, I opened my glass door and stepped onto the balcony. It floated closer and closer then hovered before my eyes. I hesitantly lifted my hand and caressed it.

At my touch, it faded like a sparkler that had run out of fuel.

I frowned. *I killed it. Wait. Could that have been Mitica's sign? It must be.* I closed my eyes and called for my lover and soul mate.

To my relief, he didn't yell at me when he appeared. However, he was downcast, his face full of failure and shame. Wrapping my arms around him, I waited for him to be ready to speak.

"I do not know what happened, Erin. I thought I checked him for weapons before we locked him in the stall."

"So it's true then? Pówahkai killed himself by eating hemlock?"

"It seems to be the case."

"Did he say anything after you caught him? Did he really kill those Wyboka?"

He nodded. "The moment he discovered we were searching the elders' homes, he ran. It took us days to catch him. And when we did, all he would say is that his people were blind. He said white men had taken their spirits, their fight. He thought by poisoning the tea and blaming the curse on the white presence, his people would go to war and drive the invaders out."

My heart was heavy with sadness. "I can see his pain, and I even understand his logic. But nothing at this point could've driven the whites out. He was only harming his own people. The tragedy is that his actions may result in even stricter rules imposed on the Wyboka and the rest of the First Nations."

Mitica sighed and shook his head in grief.

"Hey," I murmured, reaching up and stroking his cheek. "I know this isn't the way you wanted this to end, but at least it's over. The Wyboka are safe. You caught the guy."

He gazed down at me and said, "I have to give my answer to the Zgrimties tomorrow."

"Right... The full moon."

We looked over at the silent moon hanging above the mountains, its glow much more haunting than before.

I slipped my hand into his and led him into my bedroom. "Come here. Tonight, it's just you and me. Tomorrow is tomorrow."

Though we were weary, afraid, and downhearted, we found solace in each other's embrace.

I did not see Mitica the following night while he performed some magic to give the Zgrimties his answer. I couldn't help but feel a little selfish that he was choosing me over working for them to help the fae and magic, but I kept repeating his assurances. *We can help the fae together.*

I heard from the sculptor I'd contacted the following day. Apparently, he'd left the moment he'd received my letter. He assured me he would arrive shortly after his letter.

After William had outright told me he'd asked Hickory to watch me, I thought I'd at least feel more at ease knowing I wasn't being paranoid. But the knowledge had the opposite effect. As I went about my regular duties and helped Harrison plan for the ball, every unexpected sound made me jump. When Hickory was in the room, his presence loomed over me. And when he wasn't, I still seemed to feel his icy gaze. He still never talked to me, which seemed to make everything worse. He was just this silent menacing shadow, watching. I spent as much time in my room as I could, which was increasingly more difficult as the party drew nearer.

Only a few days after receiving his letter, the sculptor arrived with a flourish shortly after breakfast.

"Celeste, my glorious patroness, how different you look!" he called from across the lobby.

Out of a process of elimination, I guessed he was the sculptor. "Andrew Shaw, is that you? I can't believe it. I'm so glad you've come."

He approached me and kissed each of my cheeks. I smiled to hide my surprise.

"Well when you wrote, I told Michael here. I said, Michael, my Celeste needs me. We must go to Farrloch immediately."

I looked over his shoulder at the handsome young man he'd indicated. Michael smiled and dipped his head to me.

"I don't believe we've met," I guessed.

"Oh, of course. I was so excited to see you that I've forgotten my manners entirely. Michael, this is my magnificent patroness you've heard so much about. Celeste, this is my assistant, Michael Hamilton."

The youth took my hand and kissed it. "Miss," Michael greeted.

"Oh, she's married now, you flirt."

"I refuse to call such a beauty Madam," Michael defended.

"You best watch out around him, Celeste. I believe he's stolen half the hearts in Toronto," Andrew teased.

Michael smiled prettily at this compliment.

"Well, why don't you two get settled, and we can talk about the ball and what we need after lunch?"

"Always the excellent hostess, Celeste. Marvelous suggestion. Come, Michael. Let's wash up and have a rest."

Lucky for me, Andrew was the talkative type. There was no way he would notice I wasn't Celeste, chattering on as he did. He had plenty of ideas for decorations. He spared no details, and I only understood half of what he said. I told him a painter would be arriving as well, and he should consider that while he planned.

He nodded and said all he needed was space to work, supplies, and access to an oven.

I let them work in the ballroom and introduced them to Harrison for supplies.

Louis was less than pleased when we asked if we could use one of his ovens. But with many assurances that the artists would not destroy his kitchen, he grudgingly agreed.

As Andrew and Michael talked with Harrison, I went to the laundry to fetch old sheets to cover the floor of the ballroom. It was gratifying to see how the digging of the cellar door progressed. The laundrymen were permitted to wash everything outside during construction to avoid getting the linens dirty. *It won't be long now.*

Within a few days, the ballroom also seemed a construction zone.

When Amélie Roussel arrived a few days after Andrew and Michael, I didn't have to pretend to know the quiet woman since she'd never met Celeste. In light of everything going on, it was a small relief to not have to remain so vigilant in conversation.

"Gilbert has told me many things about you, Madame," the young painter said. "I will endeavor to live up to your expectations."

"I'm sure you'll be wonderful, Amélie. And please call me Celeste."

When we entered the ballroom, Andrew and Michael looked up from their work. Michael gave Amélie a brilliant smile and stepped toward her.

"Michael," Andrew warned. "Now is not the time."

Michael winked at Amélie, and she averted her gaze, hiding a small smile.

After examining the space and talking with Andrew, Amélie seemed to have a better idea of what she wanted to do. I introduced her to Harrison, telling her he could get her whatever she needed.

With less than a week away until the party, the hotel was in frenzy. Guests flooded through the doors every day, and I didn't even attempt to keep them straight after a certain point.

As promised, Harrison took care of all the logistics. I don't know how much William was paying him, but it wasn't enough. He dealt with every lost trunk, late coach, and fatigued traveler with ease.

I couldn't wait for the day I would start my new life with Mitica, and my stress and anxiety was getting the better of me. As soon as Mitica left and I fell asleep, I would awake, overheated and sick to my stomach. I didn't ask Mitica to stay or tell him about my troubles. He had enough to worry about.

The Zgrimties had yet to dole out their punishment, and he'd received word his superiors in the Mounties were coming to investigate whether he and Oli had been negligent when it came to Pówahkai's suicide.

At least everyone was too busy to notice my lack of sleep or appetite. Everyone except Hickory, that is. I had no idea how he found the time to carry out his duties and still be lurking in the shadows, but he did. I was beginning to question whether he was magic or had a twin or something.

Two days before the masquerade, the musicians arrived. I heaved a sigh of relief as they lugged their instruments upstairs.

The artists were scrambling to get everything ready, but they assured me it would be fine. I was only just beginning to see their visions come to life. *They're going to have to work day and night to finish in time. At least the cellar door in the laundry room is done.*

The day before the solar eclipse, we were packed to capacity. Every seat was taken at meals, and I had no time to myself.

After lunch, Marguerite found me, her eyes lit up with delight. "Celeste, I just returned from Farrloch, and I have your dress. You must try it on to see if it fits. If non, alterations need to be made immediately."

"All right, I'm coming."

I followed Marguerite's bouncing form upstairs. *She's pretty excited about a dress she isn't even going to wear. She may answer to William, but perhaps Marguerite really is fond of Celeste.*

She beamed with pride as she opened the box and revealed the gown I was to wear the following night.

It was a deep purple with simple lines and a scoop neckline. A moss-green strip of satin ran from one shoulder across the torso to the waist, like a sash. The hem was the same moss green. The sleeves were wide and sheer, fluttering like the wings of a bird.

Madame Buvons and Suzette really do excellent work, I thought as I admired my reflection in the full-length mirror.

"It fits perfectly," Marguerite marveled. "Would you like to see the mask?"

I nodded, Marguerite's excitement infecting me as I stared at the gorgeous gown. She handed the mask to me, and I held it up to my face. It had a long, green beak with green feathers around the eyes and purple feathers around the edges.

"Belle," Marguerite complimented.

"Merci, Marguerite."

Her reflection smiled over my shoulder.

After a little while, I sighed. "Well, I better take this off and get back down there."

"Oui." Marguerite stepped forward to help me out of the gown.

When I called for Mitica that evening, he looked as nervous as I felt.

"I heard from the Zgrimties."

I held my breath, waiting for him to continue.

"They sent this message:

A full heart has wings, or so they say.
But wings are supported by the threads of fate.
When the Moon embraces the Sun, darkness envelops the day,
Heart's blood wells, and obsidian shadows await."

"Well, that's creepy. What do you think it means?"

He shook his head. "We may not know until after it happens, but the moon embracing the sun could be a reference to the eclipse."

I nodded. "We need to be extra careful tomorrow then." I sighed deeply. "We had enough to worry about already." I wrapped my arms around him, desperately taking comfort and giving it in return. "It'll work out. Everything is all set," I said, trying to reassure us both.

"Not everything," he argued.

I looked up at him. "Are we forgetting something?"

He nodded and pulled a small pouch from his pocket. The buckskin was warm and smooth in my palm when he handed it to me.

"What is it?" I asked, loosening the drawstring.

I tipped what looked like a necklace into my hand. Red and white threads twisted together to form the chain, and a trio of dried, white buds hung from the bottom like a pendant.

"The charm to help you handle Grigore, should he turn his magic on you."

"What flower is this?" I gently caressed the petals, careful not to break them.

"A snowdrop. Some of the Romanians brought a few with them from home. They dried them when they bloomed earlier this year."

Remembering how Ion and Mariana had reacted to the hultan, I raised my eyebrows at him. "You didn't terrify anyone to get these did you?"

He pursed his lips. "Not on purpose."

I stifled a laugh. *It really shouldn't be funny. Those poor people.*

"It is a relief to see you smile," Mitica murmured, stroking my cheek.

"I guess I've been a little stressed of late. "

"După ploaie, vine soare,"

"What does that mean?"

"After rain, comes sunshine."

I smiled up at him. "When did you get so optimistic?"

"When you said I was yours and you are mine."

"I vaguely remember that night," I teased.

"Vaguely, you say?"

I smirked and nodded at him.

"This, I cannot have, bucuria mea. You must always remember."

I shrugged. "I guess we'll just have to do it again."

His answering smile was slow and full of heat. "Will you give yourself to me, bucuria mea?" he asked, repeating the words from what seemed like ages ago.

"I am yours." My answer was the same.

That night, as Mitica and I claimed each other anew, our worries felt far away. There were no Zgrimties, no party, no charade to maintain, no William or Hickory. There was only Mitica. There was the heat his kisses left in their wake. There was the sound of his voice whispering my name in my ear. There was the feel of him deep inside me. There was Mitica, only Mitica.

FORTY-TWO

*B*reakfast was served early the next morning so everyone could eat before the eclipse. I forced eggs and toast around the lump in my throat, knowing I'd need the energy for the long day ahead.

When Harrison announced the eclipse was beginning, everyone filed outside. Excitement hummed through the crowd like the static electricity before a summer thunderstorm as we stared at the eastern sky.

We'd told the guests not to look directly at the eclipse so as not to damage their eyes, but the urge to do so anyway was difficult to resist.

Gasps and exclamations escaped the gathering as the world dimmed. An unexpected, primal fear gripped my heart. The hush that followed was eerie and profound. Not only were the guests silent, but the birds stopped singing. Even the wind stilled.

I let out the breath I was holding as the moon released the sun from its cosmic embrace, and the sun shone brightly once more. Stifling self-conscious laughter, I shook my head at my own silliness.

I barely had a moment's peace all day. Guests were needy, and everyone wanted to talk to the lady of the house.

After tea, I had just enough time to check in on the artists. As the heel of my boots echoed in the dark ballroom, I squinted to see if I was alone.

"Hello?" I called. "Amélie? Andrew? Michael?"

All at once, an overhead light illuminated their work. Gazing up at its source, my mouth hung open at the crescent moon and stars that hung from the ceiling.

"Papier-mâché," Andrew boasted from behind me.

"Wow, you guys. They're beautiful."

The sculptor and his assistant smiled and bowed in appreciation of my praise.

The peaked windows were covered with thick, velvet curtains of dark purple and silver trim.

On either side of the room, the walls were painted to look like archways. The rich texture of stone, the sparkle of lanterns off the Venetian waterways, gondoliers steering their gondolas in the night, and revelers in the distance, celebrating Carnevale, I couldn't tear my gaze away.

"Oh my goodness, Amélie. These are incredible," I murmured, overwhelmed.

"Merci, Celeste," Amélie thanked with pride.

"You guys have done amazing work. I love it so much, and I know the guests will, too. I'm sure you're tired, but I hope you'll come to the ball tonight."

They bowed as if I'd done them some great honor and not the other way around.

"Wonderful. Why don't you go rest for a little while before it starts?"

With only a few moments to spare before I had to get ready, I went to my room and stuffed my jeans, a few chemises, Oli's coat, and the pouch with the snowdrop charm into the bag Mitica had given me for our trip to Edmonton.

Knowing I wouldn't come back to my room once the ball started, I took my bag and smuggled it downstairs. I greeted the guests who called out to me as if I wasn't doing anything suspicious whatsoever.

Since it was such a nice day, the garden was full of strolling couples, who waved and tipped their hats at me. I stood by the iron gate for a long time, chatting and smiling at people before the coast was clear. Finally, there was a break in the line. My eyes scanned the paths for onlookers, and then I stuffed my bag behind the bush near the gate.

My heart hammered as I swiftly returned to my room to bathe. The water was hot but did not release the tension in my body. The scent of rose did not soothe me as I breathed deep and released it slowly. But after a few more breaths, my pulse was forced to even.

You got this, Erin. Just keep your eye on the ball and swing. Think of Mitica. It's all for him. Mitica...Mitica.

"Celeste?" Marguerite called from the other side of the bathroom door. "Are you finished? You need to dress so I can do your hair."

"I'm coming," I answered, climbing out of the tub. I shivered in the sudden rush of cold air as water dripped off me onto the floor. The towel was rough against my skin, but the friction warmed me. I dressed in my underclothes and paused by the door.

I took one more steadying breath and repeated his name again. *Mitica.*

As nice as the gown had looked the day before, it paled in comparison to when Marguerite was finished with me. Her reflection beamed at her masterpiece as she secured the mask's ribbon over my curled and pinned hair.

When she'd finished and left, I rose from my chair and glided toward the door, the ball, William, Mitica, and my fate.

"How beautiful you are this evening, my dear," William's voice greeted from behind a white mask that was very *The Phantom of the Opera.*

I closed and locked the suite door behind me, reminding myself to leave the key somewhere Frederick could find it.

"Thank you," I said out of obligation.

He held out his arm to me, and I took it gently, ignoring my clenched stomach. *Mitica.*

"It was kind of you to invite the townspeople to our gathering," he commented as he led me downstairs.

"It's prudent to have a working relationship with them. Don't you think?" *And I could tell Suzette really wanted to come.*

He nodded. "I am fortunate to have such a clever wife."

I didn't respond and kept my expression smooth and neutral.

Just before we entered the ballroom, William stopped, forcing me to halt as well. "You will, of course, save the first dance for me?"

I got the feeling I didn't have much of a choice. "Of course, William. Who else would I dance with if not my husband?" I nearly gagged on the word as I tried to sell my performance.

"Indeed."

"Aren't we going in?" I asked after he'd forced the unnecessary pause.

"Can't I gaze upon the glorious beauty of my wife for a moment longer?"

Is this a trick question?

His eyes behind his mask crawled over me like a spider with sticky, spindly legs. I couldn't hide my shudder.

"Can we go inside? It's a bit chilly out here," I lied, covering my reaction to him.

"Of course, my dear," he obliged coolly.

Finally, he led me inside the ballroom.

The velvet curtains, which had blocked out the sunlight earlier that afternoon, were drawn back, bathing the room in starlight.

Couples twirled and laughed in their elaborate costumes as the string quartet played a waltz.

I scanned the crowd, my heart jumping when I found Mitica. He stood, tall and dashing in his red serge, with his handsome Wynn face unmasked.

He must've felt my gaze upon him because he met my eyes and nodded with a reserved smile. My heart fluttered like the wings of a bird learning to fly, and my face heated beneath my mask.

Beside him, Oli talked with a dark-haired beauty in a gilded dress and mask, whom I could only assume was Suzette.

"Constable Delaforet is here. Aren't you going to greet him, my dear?" William asked.

"I'm sure I'll get the chance later," I hedged, not wanting to approach when he was with Oli and Suzette from fear they'd recognize me.

"Indeed."

From there, William and I greeted our guests, complimenting and receiving compliments in turn. The purpose of a masquerade, of course, is so everyone can be someone else, if only for a short while. As we weren't more than passing acquaintances with most of the people there, it wasn't difficult to wonder who some of them were.

I suspected seeing Michael and Amélie on the dance floor, and I could've sworn I heard Mellie ask Ion for something to drink.

While I was listening to one lady talk about her wayward daughter, William approached me with an outstretched hand.

"May I have this dance, my dear?" he asked formally.

I smoothed my features and nodded, excusing myself from the woman's problems.

When William slipped his arm around my waist, I went rigid. My palms began to sweat, and I couldn't seem to find my feet. My eyes looked everywhere but his. Still, I could feel his gaze, insistent, as he held me in his arms.

"I'm sorry, William," I said after the third time I'd messed up our steps. "I don't think I really remember how to dance."

"I understand, my dear." He didn't sound like he understood though.

"Perhaps Mrs. Broadstone just needs a little more practice," Mitica suggested, appearing beside us. "May I? I'm a patient tutor."

"Of course, Constable. Who could say no to Canada's finest?" William passed me over to Mitica, his mask covering his reaction.

I thought about the last time I'd danced with Mitica, and my body flushed. He pulled me into his arms, and I relaxed, knowing I belonged there. Dancing with Mitica was easy, like waves advancing and retreating on a beach. The movements were natural, and the world around us blurred as if submerged below the surface.

"I couldn't stand to watch any longer," Mitica murmured.

"Because I'm so bad at dancing?"

"No, bucuria mea. Because I had to suffer another man to hold you in his arms," he whispered, letting his Canadian accent slip for his term of endearment. "You're too beautiful for this world," he added.

My face heated as his blue eyes caressed me. It had been a while since I'd seen his Wynn face, and I was surprised by how much I'd missed it.

"Wynn..." I breathed.

"I know. You don't have to say it. I see it in your eyes, so full of longing, your cheeks, that perfect blush of pink. I know." His words kissed my ears, and I warmed at the sensation.

So lost was I in the sea of his gaze, drifting on the wind of his words, that I'd hardly noticed when we'd stopped dancing.

He bowed his head to me, thanking me for the dance. "Later," he promised. "You know where to go."

I dipped my head. "I'll be waiting," I told him.

"There is nothing anyone can do that would stop me from being with you."

As Mitica tore himself away, the sounds of the party crashed into my ears. Dazed, I took a deep breath and looked around.

William was at the far end of the room, talking to some men. He didn't seem to notice me. *Now is a good time to make my way outside.*

I turned toward the garden and forced myself not to rush. I even watched my feet as I went, to ensure they didn't betray me.

"Oop, sorry," I gasped when I bumped into someone. I glanced up, and my heart stopped. *I'd recognize that icy glare anywhere, even behind a mask.* "S-sorry about that, Hickory. I wasn't paying attention to where I was going."

"And where would that be?" he drawled accusatorily.

My heart sped as if making up for the beat it missed. "Oh, I'm just a little overheated from dancing, so I'm going to get some fresh air in the garden."

He didn't stop me, but I could feel his eyes follow me as I went.

The cold, night air scraped my throat as I heaved deep breaths in the garden. I placed a hand over my racing heart. *It's fine. There's no need for alarm. It's perfectly normal for me to go to the garden. Right? Right. It's Celeste's favorite place, and there are plenty of people out here already getting fresh air. For all I know, Hickory was coming in from the garden when I bumped into him. That's right.*

I took a few more steadying breaths, the night breeze cooling my face and arms. I smiled at the people coming in and out of the garden, and my heart eventually slowed.

I took the center path to the fountain as if that were my destination, trying to keep my pace stroll-like.

Apollo and Daphne still played out their tragic fates, forever stuck in the moment of eternal loss. *Some love was just not meant to be, but ours is. Mitica, I'm coming.*

I removed my mask and tied the ribbon around the key to my suite. I left it on the wide edge of the fountain. I took a deep breath, squaring my shoulders, and cast aside my fear. Then, I strode toward the iron gate, snatched my bag from behind the bush, and slipped into the night.

FORTY-THREE

he road crunched beneath my lonely footsteps. With no moon to light the night sky, I could barely see my own frosty breath. Still, I knew if I just stayed on the road, I would eventually reach town. Beyond that, the Mounties' barracks.

Of course, Mitica would tell everyone I climbed the steep, nearby cliff and jumped to my death. But by then, I would be far away, flying with the clouds on Grigore.

The lights from the hotel glowed in the distance, and with every step, I was leaving Celeste Broadstone behind. I may not have been able to see the way forward, but I could feel it. I felt the sturdy earth of the road beneath my feet, and I felt the certainty that comes with following your heart.

The cold, mountain air stung my throat, but I could breathe again. I was free again.

I didn't worry if anyone in town saw me pass through. They could help corroborate Mitica's story later.

My feet were sore by the time I saw the welcoming visage of the Mounties' barracks. The hike had been long, and I was looking forward to riding for a while.

In the flickering light of a small fire, Grigore waited by the lake. His eyes glinted gold in his human face, and his raven-black hair lifted gently in the breeze. He gave me the same charming smile he had as when we'd first met. Then, he frowned.

"I thought we were friends now?" he asked.

The snowdrop charm Mitica gave me must've worked. I looked down at the dried flowers around my neck on their red and white string. "We are friends, Grigore. But I'm not an idiot."

He pursed his lips. "Where are we going anyway?"

"Wherever the wind takes us."

He smiled contentedly. "I like the sound of that."

"Don't get too comfortable," Mitica commented, stepping into the fire-light, still in his Wynn visage.

I jumped, my heart yelping, then sighed in relief. "Jeez, Grigore. You could've told me he was coming."

He smirked. "You could have told me about the snowdrop."

"You know, we really need to work on our communica—"

"Shhh," Grigore hushed, cutting me off and rising to his feet.

"What is it?" I whispered.

"Someone is coming," he hissed.

"Who? Oli?"

He shook his head. "Nu, I do not know the scent."

I strained my ears but couldn't hear anything over the pounding of my heart. The seconds dragged on, and Mitica took a step toward me. He froze before he reached me. I followed his wide gaze. My blood ran cold, and my stomach dropped at the sight of a gun pointed in my direction.

"You must think me an old fool," William stated, stepping into full view. "Did you truly believe I thought you couldn't remember?"

"William—"

"Quiet, my dear, I am speaking."

I clamped my mouth shut, unwilling to argue with the man with a gun.

"I didn't believe you for a moment. I don't care how different you acted. I knew you knew. I must say, it surprised me when Marguerite found you in Farrloch. I was rather frantic when your body wasn't discovered with the horse's. Hickory had assured me he'd done the job right, but then where were you?"

My eyes flicked to Mitica, still frozen and clenching his jaw.

"But I saw through your charade immediately. The only reason this upstanding Mountie would allow you to return to such a dangerous situation is if he needed evidence to build a case against me. My suspicions were confirmed as you snuck around, digging through my room and my desk."

My mouth went dry.

"Oh, yes, my dear. I noticed you took the journal and letters, and so I waited. I waited to see what you knew and when you would make a move. And here we are. You've come to report me to the Mountie, to betray me."

Dude, I can't believe how off-base you are. But what am I going to say? No, William, I really can't remember you and your henchman trying to murder me. Actually, I'm just leaving because I'm having sex with this guy.

"You think you'll get away with this? Do you think I haven't reported this to my superiors?" Mitica took the smarter route and played along, trying to get us out of this situation.

William smirked. "I know you haven't. Hickory silenced that Indian dolt before he could implicate me. You have your word and no evidence, but for what is in my wife's pretty head."

"Hickory killed Pówahkai," I murmured at the realization.

William frowned. "I thought you were more clever than that, my dear. Yes, Hickory dispatched the rat with his own poison. He'd had his own reasons for betraying his people, of course. But I didn't really care what they were so long as the Wyboka abandoned the hot springs. A little money, a fool to do the work, and the superstitious imbeciles would be happy to be rid of the land. Unfortunately, I need to go a different route now."

"Are you fucking serious? You did all this for hot spring real estate?" I couldn't help but shout.

William snorted. "Enough with the ignorant act, Celeste. You overheard the Indian and I arguing about it that night and ran before you thought I saw you. Stupid girl. You even wrote about it in your journal."

"What exactly do you get from telling us all this?" I demanded. "Even if you shoot me, Wynn and Grigore will still make sure you're brought to justice."

"Celeste, you know me better than that. I am nothing if not practical."

At his words, Hickory stepped from the shadows.

William turned the gun on Mitica. "Hickory, you handle the other one. My darling wife will be no trouble on her own."

My stomach dropped, and my chest tightened.

"No!" I cried, my body moving toward Mitica without a thought.

Wynn's eyes widened in horror as I flew toward him. He reached his hand out toward me, and I was forcefully blown in the opposite direction.

The crack from William's gun echoed off the calm lake and the ancient mountains.

I sat up and met Wynn's blue eyes as he gasped and clutched his stomach. His fingers shined with blood, black as obsidian in the firelight.

My mind slowed and came to a halt, not able to comprehend what was happening.

As Mitica sank to his knees, his glamour flickered. I ran to him, my hands fluttering around him, not sure what exactly to do.

Bright flames flashed in my peripheral vision as Grigore breathed fire in his dragon form. The back of my mind was only vaguely aware that William and Hickory presented no further danger.

I heard their shouts drift into the distance, and Grigore moved to chase them.

"Grigore, no. I need you. Mitica needs you. Do you know healing magic?" I didn't take my eyes off Mitica's as his bloody fingers reached up to caress my cheek.

"I cannot use such magic as a zmeu," Grigore murmured, his voice tinged with sorrow.

"Bucuria mea," Mitica whispered.

"Don't talk," I hushed, looking down at his wound to see how bad it was.

The front of his red serge glistened in the flickering light.

My eyes filled with tears, and I swallowed a cry. "We're going to get you help. Okay? Dr. Hollander doesn't live far away. Grigore, go get him."

My hands pressed into Mitica's, attempting to keep any more life from escaping him.

"There's no time," Mitica murmured. "Listen...you aren't safe here... you...have to leave."

"No fucking way I'm leaving you!"

He gave me a sad smile. "Bucuria mea...Come closer."

I leaned in, my face not an inch from his.

"Kiss me," he demanded.

Tears rolled down my cheeks as I pressed my shivering lips to his.

"Te iubesc," he breathed.

I sobbed. "I...I love you, too."

His blue eyes, which had begun to fade, sharpened for a moment. In a strong voice, he ordered the universe to obey. His song was sweet and full of longing. As the foreign words washed over me, my eyes lost focus.

FORTY-FOUR

The rhythmic clacking of a train echoed off the hollow tunnel as a gust of foul, metallic wind rushed across my skin. Through the cacophony of screeching brakes and the murmuring crowd, loud in their multitude, someone was singing, low and soft.

"Erin," the unfamiliar voice whispered, cracking under the weight of his emotion. "Erin, wake up," he pleaded.

I took a deep breath, and my chest screamed in protest. "Ah," I groaned with a hiss, squeezing my eyelids tighter.

The voice, so close to me, gasped. "Erin? Don't try to move," he urged. "They've called for help. You're going to be okay."

I cracked my eyelids with effort, the sounds around me so loud and overwhelming as to be painful like an insistent poking on a bruise.

A pair of deep blue eyes met mine from beneath a dark fringe of swept bangs. The man's face was very close to mine as he knelt on the platform of the red line, cradling me in his arms. I searched his features. He looked familiar somehow, like someone who had stood behind me in line at a coffee shop. My gaze landed on the White Sox beanie he wore, and I scrunched my nose.

"Your hat is ugly," I croaked.

His eyes filled with tears. He closed them and shook his head, a low, nervous laugh coming unevenly from his throat. His chuckle shook his body and mine in return.

I hissed as the motion brought a wave of pain over me.

"I'm sorry. I know it hurts. I wish I could have done more. The ambulance is on its way. Just hang tight, okay?" he assured, his brow crinkled.

"What happened?" I murmured.

The man glanced around at the crowd of onlookers and dropped his voice even lower. "Someone pushed you in front of the train. Luckily, you weren't hit head-on, or I might have not been able to save you."

The image of Mitica dying in my arms flashed in my mind. *So was it all just a dream? Wynn? Mitica? Even Grigore the shape-shifting dragon?* My chest ached with a sense of loss that had nothing to do with my injuries.

"So I didn't die like we thought," I muttered.

"Only for a moment," the man answered with a relieved smile.

I met his eyes sharply. "Who are you?" I asked.

"Don't you recognize me, bucuria mea?"

My eyes widened, and I froze. "You...how did you...? I saw you die," I stammered.

He smiled softly, stroking my cheek just the way Mitica used to. "I was reborn. It took me a long time to explain the magic I have in this life. But once I discovered my true name, I remembered everything: the Mounties, the hultan, the Zgrimties, and most importantly, you. I remembered where you were from and your name. And since you're a journalist, you weren't hard to find, especially not with the Internet. I'm sorry I couldn't heal all of your injuries like last time. I don't have a lot of magic in the city."

"When did you find me?"

"About six months ago," he admitted.

"Why didn't you tell me?"

He snorted and tilted his head. "How would that conversation have gone? Hi, I'm Greyson. You don't know me, but I'm your soul mate. We met in a past life when you traveled through time."

I pursed my lips. "Okay, you have a point. But you still could've talked to me."

He smirked. "I did. Tons of times. I even work in the same office as you."

"Shut up. You do not."

He nodded with a laugh. "I'm a photographer."

I squinted at him. The memory of a coworker with dark hair, staring at his smartphone in the elevator flashed in my mind. "Holy shit."

He grinned.

"You dirty stalker," I teased.

His smile dropped. "I tried to stop it. I swear I did. I knew you'd be fired from the paper and pushed in front of the train on the black moon. I just wasn't fast enough."

I reached up hesitantly and caressed his cheek with my fingertips. "If I hadn't been hit by the train, I never would've gone back."

"I know, but we still could've had a different life together in this lifetime."

I smiled at him. "You know what? I'm actually kind of pissed at you. I mean, what the fuck was that in 1900? I try to save you from being shot and you use magic to push me out of the way? You totally ruined my big heroic moment."

He ducked his head sheepishly.

"You're just going to have to make it up to me," I pronounced.

He smirked. "I can do that."

I snorted. "You think it will be that easy?"

"I have my ways." He hovered lower and kissed me. His lips were warm and familiar on mine. I giggled as he kissed my cheeks, my nose, and my forehead. Then, I winced as my laughter upset my injuries. Still, it was worth the warmth that spread through me.

"That life you mentioned, can I take that as a promise?" I murmured.

"Da, bucuria mea, and all the lifetimes to come."

EPILOGUE

"*H*urry up," I called over my shoulder to Greyson as we hiked up the hill.

"What's the rush? You should be taking it slower anyway. You haven't been out of physical therapy for that long," he complained.

"It has been more than six months, and we have to get there before the sun rises. Carl wants that sunrise shot."

"You know what? Carl can kiss my ass. I don't care if he's our editor. What kind of sadist interrupts a man's honeymoon to ask for a stupid shot of a sunrise over a lake and mountains?"

I paused to let him catch up and kissed him on the cheek. "The sooner you get the shot, the sooner we can go back to the hotel and commence with the honeymooning."

He smiled slyly. "Or we could just make some memories out here."

Grabbing my hips, he pulled me toward him. I squeaked in surprised delight. My core heated as he pressed his lips and body to mine.

"Okay," I breathed. "After you get the shot."

As we raced up the rest of the way to the top of the cliff overlooking the lake we'd seen over a century before, my mind was full of Greyson. I didn't think about the mayor's office lackey who'd pushed me in front of the train. I didn't think about my previous editor feeling guilty and writing an exposé about his involvement in city hall corruption. I didn't think about how the mayor had quietly retired without any sort of real retribution. I didn't think about the clerk at the Farrloch Hotel telling us about how the founder had gone mad. I didn't think about how all of Farrloch was dragon-crazy. Or about the Loch Ness-level legend of the dragon with the yellow gem on its forehead who they swear could still be seen flying over the lake at night. I didn't think about the museum in the Mounties' barracks. And I didn't think about the two small gravestones nearby, where secret lovers rested quietly beside one another.

I only thought of Greyson, the talented photographer with a sharp sense of humor and a strong moral compass, the White Sox fan who never admitted defeat even when the Cubs broke their curse and finally won the World Series, the man who would use his magic to find me no matter how many years and miles separated us.

Once we'd reached the summit, Greyson pulled me into another demanding kiss, ignoring the golden sunrise sparkling off the clear, blue water of the lake.

"Hurry," I urged as he kissed down my neck.

"It's not fun if you rush," he teased.

"Take the shot," I barked.

"Fine." After uncapping his lens, he snapped a round of pictures.

Impatiently, I stepped in front of his camera, blocking his view. "Good enough," I declared.

"You think this will be enough for Carl?" he asked.

"I'm not worried about Carl."

"Oh?" He smirked as I moved in close to him.

"I'm worried about claiming and being claimed by my husband."

"You don't need to worry about that, bucuria mea. I will claim you over and over, as many times as you need."

"Forever?"

His smile was all the answer I needed. Still, he whispered, his deep blue eyes warm and true, "Forever."

If you enjoyed *Once in a Black Moon*, please leave a review to help other readers decide on this book!

If you'd like to be notified when D. Lieber releases new books, sign up for the newsletter at www.dlieber.com

ALSO BY D. LIEBER

Conjuring Zephyr

The Exiled Otherkin

Intended Bondmates

In Search of a Witch's Soul, Council of Covens Noir, #1

Dancing with Shades, Council of Covens Noir, #0

The Fanciful Travels of D. Lieber

ABOUT THE AUTHOR

D. writes stories she wants to read. Her love of the worlds of fiction led her to earn a Bachelor's in English from Wright State University.

When she isn't reading or writing, she's probably hiking, crafting, watching anime, Korean television, Bollywood, or old movies. She may also be getting her geek on while planning her next steampunk cosplay with friends.

She lives in Wisconsin with her husband (John) and cats (Yin and Nox).

Links
    Website: www.dlieber.com
    Facebook: www.facebook.com/dlieberwriting
    Twitter: www.twitter.com/AuthorDLieber
    Instagram: www.instagram.com/dlieberwriting
    Pinterest: www.pinterest.com/dlieberwriting/
    Goodreads: www.goodreads.com/dlieberwriting
    Bookbub: www.bookbub.com/profile/d-lieber